"And the Winner Is . . ."

Other books by Randolph H. Deer:

The Shield of Atlantis, September 1988
The Avalanche List, February 1992
The Marionette Master, June 1994

"And the Winner Is . . ."

Randolph H. Deer

VANTAGE PRESS

New York

This novel is a work of fiction. Names, characters, places, and incidents are either the product of the author's imagination or, if fact, are used fictionally. Any resemblance to actual people, living or dead, events, or locales, is entirely coincidental.

Published by Vantage Press, Inc.
516 West 34th Street, New York, New York 10001

Manufactured in the United States of America
ISBN: 0-533-12974-5

Library of Congress Catalog Card No.: 98-90899

0 9 8 7 6 5 4 3 2 1

Dedicated to the energy and joy, love and humor of
Wayne P. Zink

Acknowledgments

My sincere thanks and acknowledgments to Jared Burden, Albert Groenke, David Patterson, Gerald Rush, Wayne Storch, Gene Wilkins, and Bradley Williams for all of their professional and technical help and information.

A very special thanks to Wayne Zink for all of his time, guidance, and input. And a very special recognition to Pat Golbitz for the direction, care, energy, advice, and teaching she so willingly shared with me.

"And the Winner Is . . ."

One

Monday Night, Bel Air, California

Craig Carlson pushed himself up from his leather chair to stretch out the stress cramping his back. He was tense and impatient. Another fruitless battle with the IRS was raging, it was Oscar time, and Roz's behavior was beyond his endurance. Craig had received the Oscar four times, three for acting and one for directing. After thirty years of attending the ceremonies, he had decided to sit this one out. His wife could stroll down the red carpet without him and push her way through the gauntlet of television crews and starstruck fans with her practiced smile and witty answers. Her compulsion for notoriety had driven him nuts and her damn near to dementia. Roz Marlowe loved it, and he didn't need it anymore. He would watch The Awards this year from the comfort of his suite in his Bel Air home.

Craig felt the Oscar ceremony was anything but glamorous. He found it was exhausting to stay alert so when confronted by the media or some movie honcho you looked good and said the right thing. He felt it was torture to sit in the cold, crowded auditorium for hours, afraid to go to the bathroom at just the wrong time. He found it was jolting to be confronted by a pushy photographer when you least expected it, the kind who would take the most unflattering picture and sell it to an unscrupulous editor who would hard-line it the next day.

"Hollywood bullshit," Craig muttered.

He stopped his stretching and ran his fingers through his thick salt-and-pepper hair.

It was just days ago during a turbulent scene with Roz at a Universal Studios promotion that Craig made up his mind to skip The Oscars. Roz's constant demand for the limelight clashed with his burning need for privacy. Her egomaniacal behavior that night, which Craig normally ignored, was no longer bearable.

1

He knew why. He just finished directing the film *An Honest Lie* and it was close to autobiographical.

When the major studios told him it would never make it to the screen, Craig formed his own production company and made it himself. The lead character recognizes and accepts the fact that much of his life he was incapable of recognizing the truth. He had lived a lie.

Writing the original screenplay and directing the movie gave Craig new insight into his relationship with Roz. He no longer cared to protect her or help her, no longer wanted the burden of explaining her rude behavior, and no longer wanted to be the target of her vile temper.

Down deep, Craig knew that his relationship with Roz had always been a sham. He had married her to live publicly as a heterosexual in order to protect himself from Hollywood's homophobia, and knew that Roz had married him only to further her budding career. Both knew from the beginning, that love had very little to do with their interests in each other.

Two weeks before the Universal Studios party, Craig had returned with Alan Gavin from a relaxing cruise around the Northwest's San Juan Islands and Straits of Georgia. It had been so peaceful, so quiet, and so private. When Craig contrasted that week to the self-centered pretentiousness of the Universal party, further accented with Roz's disturbing performance, he made his gutsy decision not to attend the Oscar ceremony.

*   *   *   *

Wearily, Craig softly massaged his eyelids and thought again about that ugly night.

The minute they had arrived at the party, Roz's mood soured. She started complaining loudly about the antique carousel Universal Studios featured in the banquet room. The studio was promoting its box office smash, *The Broken Carousel,* starring Marilyn Wilde, the young new actress who was one of the contenders with Roz for Best Actress. Craig tried early to head off Roz before she had one of her infamous scenes, but halfway through the evening, he quit trying.

During the hospitality hour Roz had loudly exclaimed, "Shit! Any dumbass broad can outperform a wooden horse on his brass pole. It's stupid to nominate a nobody for having a monologue with an amusement park dork."

That remark was overheard by many. But it was Roz's later scene that pushed Craig over the edge.

After dinner the dormant carousel came to life with lights and music and Universal invited their guests to enjoy a ride before they departed. Roz rose to the occasion. She pushed past Marilyn Wilde, who Universal had positioned near the carousel, and forced her way in front of the others waiting to ride. Quite drunk, Roz sat provocatively astride a painted stallion with her dress hiked up around her thighs. Clutching her champagne glass with one hand, she caressed the brass rod with the other and in sultry tones invited those watching, "Come on, boys. Take a picture of a real star. Join old Sadie Thompson on this mount."

Craig knew he had to do something. He moved to the front of the crowd, and ordered Roz to get down.

She retorted, "Ha! You've played the stupid part of a butch jock too often. Make me!"

Disgust overcame Craig. Disgust for Roz—disgust for Hollywood—disgust for his constant control in public because of his celebrity life. He wanted out. He found the carousel's main switch, turned it off, picked up the nearest ice bucket and pitched its cold slushy contents on the taunting Roz.

"You son-of-a-bitch," she screamed.

In an uncontrolled rage, Craig walked out of the Universal party. He knew he would never have another thing to do with Roz Marlowe. Nothing! A divorce was next on his agenda, and she could find her way to the Oscars and through the rest of her life without him.

Roz tried to make him pay the minute she got home, but Craig took the initiative. He told Roz she could use any excuse she wanted; he could have the flu, a migraine headache, stomach cramps, or whatever she liked, but he wasn't going to the Academy Awards. She would have to play the grateful recipient without him.

At first, Roz threw her daily temper tantrums, but suddenly became strangely calm. Craig told himself her rantings and ravings weren't over, and he was prepared for the worst to come. But for some unknown reason, Roz had remained subdued.

*   *   *   *

Craig walked to the mantle where his Oscars were lined up like toy soldiers. He was proud of them. If he had released *An Honest Lie* last year with Roz's film, and it had received any nominations tonight, he would have driven through a California mudslide to get there. But he had made that timing mistake once before and he wasn't going to repeat it again

Early in 1992, he released *The Corsican*, a film about the life of Napoleon, in which he both starred and directed. That same year, from a later release, Roz Marlowe won the Golden Globe Award for her portrayal of an indigent mother in *Salinas*, and then was nominated by the Academy for Best Actress for that performance. She lost, and he won two Oscars.

Those two awards crowned Craig's long career, but Roz's wild charges at Spagos that evening had embarrassed him beyond amends, and he tried again tonight to forget Roz's extraordinary scene. The party was a celebration for the success of Craig's three years of demanding and difficult work. But before the evening was over, Roz was screaming at him in front of the entire party. "No godamned Academy members will vote to give major awards to a husband and wife the same year. It's your fucking fault I lost!"

Now in complete contrast, last Saturday, Roz had calmly told him that, "Since you won't go, I'm taking Simia. She's speechless enough to be your replacement."

"Good. I'm glad for Simia," he had said. But he thought, *Why is she taking Simia? It doesn't make any sense. She's never done a kind thing in her life for the mute Polynesian woman.*

"Then it's settled. You're really not going. Am I right?"

"Roz, how many damn times do I have to tell you? No! I'm not! You'll win your award and can party all night without me telling you to shut up. So go and win your deserved honor."

As she left Roz had said over her shoulder, "You just made a big mistake, Mr. Carlson."

That was the last Craig heard from Roz about his non-support and defection.

* * * *

Craig settled back in his chair, ignoring the television dialogue, and thought about his good friend, Simia.

Simia had been a part of Roz Marlowe's life when Craig married Roz. Simia was simply added to the Marlowe family by Roz's second husband, the famous rock star, Mikey Marlowe, when he returned with her after his successful world tour. Mikey brazenly moved Simia into the house with Roz, using the excuse that she was the new nanny for their year-old son, Jebb.

But even after Roz had dislodged the younger Simia out of Mikey's bed and reestablished herself as queen of the castle, Mikey refused to discharge her. So Simia took care of Jebb, whom she loved, and became the surrogate mother to Juliette Savannah Marlowe, Mikey's rebellious thirteen-year-old daughter from his first marriage who lived with them and hated her stepmother.

After Mikey's unexpected death from a drug overdose, if Mikey hadn't stipulated in his will that the mute woman be taken care of the rest of her life, Roz would have tossed her out onto the street. But since she couldn't, she made Simia her personal serf as well as baby Jebb's caregiver. Roz openly enjoyed saying nasty things directly to Simia knowing she could never defend herself by talking back.

Craig knew from Simia that as time had passed she accepted her fate and worked in her lonely world. Simia not only found it difficult to communicate her true feelings about anything, but felt she could never change her employment because of her disability and her loyalty to Mikey's children.

Simia's story had always astonished Craig.

Simia was only nineteen and celebrating her graduation from high school when the truck she was riding in was hit broadside by a bus. Part of the bus's chrome grill pierced her vocal box and rendered her speechless while other injuries left her infertile. Papayete wasn't the place where a mute native could easily survive, and when an exclusive resort opened up on Bora Bora, Simia simply became an overly educated housekeeper. The fact that she had graduated first in her class and could speak French and English fluently was no longer of value.

During his exhausting world trip, Mikey Marlowe spent a week resting up on Bora Bora before plunging on to the Far East. Simia was just another beautiful young woman he took to his bed, but Simia fell in love. Mikey quickly recognized the values of the lovely Simia beyond her sex skills, and typical of the impulsive singing star, he simply packed her up with the rest of his rock group when he headed for his next concert in Australia. By the time the tour was over, he was in love. He never worried about what Roz would do when he brought Simia home, for Mikey knew how to control her. Mikey was the one who had introduced Roz into his heavy drug culture.

*   *   *   *

Fidgety and bored, Craig walked over to the mantle and picked up one of the Oscars he won for *The Corsican*. He had ended up in a hospital in Paris for ten days suffering from exhaustion after he finished filming the epic. Now, under constant scrutiny because of his star status, the IRS was still tenaciously examining his endless expenses in making that film.

Craig knew many in the industry who shoveled the green stuff off to the Caymans, British Tortola, and Switzerland, and often wondered if he shouldn't do the same. His financial and administrative assistant, Alan Gavin, even suggested Craig look into Alan's home country of Monaco as a vehicle for avoiding taxes. But, he never had.

Tonight, Craig was very sure about several things. He no longer wanted to be a celebrity; he hated the constant invasion of his privacy. He no longer wanted any part of the Hollywood scene; he was finished with its insanity. He no longer wanted to fight the IRS; he was tired of its unfounded insinuations. Most of all, he no longer wanted a life with Roz Marlowe; he was sick of her endless enmity.

What he wanted was to live in peace with Alan Gavin.

In the past, Craig had always allowed somebody else to constantly dissuade him from divorce. Craig had thought of himself as direct and determined, yet he let his agents, attorneys and studio heads influence him too many times to stay the course, all because of the homophobic public and homophobic industry.

Directors were gay. Producers were gay. Cameramen, costume designers, hair stylists, set designers, gaffers, screenwriters, songwriters and all of the above could be screamingly gay. But not an actor or a actress. Were there other actors like him? Of course. Were they well known? Top box office! But could he risk being seen often with Alan in public? Not on his life.

Even Victor Packard, his own attorney, led the parade of those who advocated, "Don't divorce Roz, or you'll never make another dime." Now Craig wasn't sure he even wanted to make money if he had to hand it all back to the government.

Craig had instructed Packard to attack his problems on three fronts: draft a new will, prepare divorce papers, and look into the legality of same-sex marriages anywhere in the world. Craig was determined to strike a settlement that would cut the money-grubbing, wild-spending Roz out of his life and live in peace and quiet with Alan. He knew that Roz would attack their prenuptial like a Siberian tigress after a spring lamb, and he needed to be the aggressor in his approach.

Craig had craftily allowed Packard to think he would have an opportunity to once again dissuade him from all of it when they met the coming Wednesday. But last Saturday, when the final draft of a proposed new will came in by overnight FedEx, he took the initiative, drove to the bank, and executed it. At least that part of his program was finished, and all the notary and the two teller-witnesses knew was that he had signed his name to his will. They didn't know there was dynamite in the document. With that single action Craig had preempted Packard from giving him another long lecture and attempt to prevent him from transferring important assets to Alan Gavin at his death.

Craig toasted his Oscars. "Damn marital law! Damn the IRS! Damn attitudes about same-sex marriage! I'm finally reversing my own honest lie."

*   *   *   *

Pleased with himself, Craig returned to his chair to listen to the announcer's voice-over. "Let's examine the history behind the venerable movie *Rain* that provided Roz Marlowe with the role of Miss Sadie Thompson. A role she portrayed so passionately it garnered her an Oscar nomination for Best Actress.

"*Rain* was first made as a silent movie in 1928. Then in 1932, United Artists remade W. Somerset Maugham's story, one of their earlier talking pictures. Joan Crawford played the part of Sadie Thompson and Walter Houston the bitter missionary. Lewis Milestone, the director, had also made the famous *All's Quiet on the Western Front* and *Of Mice and Men.* In 1946, a film version of *Rain* was called *Dirty Girty from Harlem.* In 1953, Beckworth Corporation decided to make it a musical. Beckworth produced and Columbia Studios distributed the film, *Miss Sadie Thompson.* Rita Hayworth and José Ferrer expertly enacted the story of the manipulative Polynesian prostitute who brought the embittered missionary down to his disastrous defeat. The song "Blue Pacific Blues" was nominated for an Oscar but . . . "

Craig hit the mute button, luxuriously wiggled his toes in his stocking feet, then headed for the bathroom. As he passed a mirror he checked his appearance, a trait he could never break.

Even before he had become a star, he had been taught by his parents to groom carefully, be polite, always set an example, never be abusive and never correct anyone in public. All of his life their admonishments had molded his behavior—until now.

Craig was born in Rome as Constantine Traver Papagos. It

was the studio that changed his name to Craig Traver Carlson, but Craig had always refused to legally relinquish Papagos.

His father, George Papagos, had been the Greek ambassador to Italy. His mother, Ellen Traver, was a well-to-do British subject whom George met while she was studying art in Italy. Their love was so strong that Ellen had painfully changed her religion to Greek Orthodox in order to satisfy his family and marry in his church. With their public position reinforced by their strong family traditions, it had been most necessary for their only son to be courteous and well-mannered. Even as a child, because of his parents' notoriety, Craig was exposed to the meddling media. But he was taught that privacy for a public figure was a privilege they could rarely afford.

Craig remembered at the age of six his father saying it was time for them to move West. When he had asked "Why?" His father told him that the Pact of Steel signed by Italy and Germany and was the beginning of a bad time for Greece. George Papagos had thought it would only be a matter of a few months before Greece and Italy would be at war, and his mentor in Greece, General John Metaxas, had confirmed that belief. But his father's insight was too late. They didn't move out of Rome, they had to flee before Mussolini's fascist's burned the Embassy. In England, his father took an advisory position with the Greek embassy, but after the Germans invaded France, George Papagos sent his family to live with Ellen's wealthy parents in Palm Beach.

When Craig was eleven, George rejoined his family in the United States and after an intense evaluation of the Greek communities in America, George chose Chicago for their new home. As a result, Ellen insisted that Craig attend private school. At the exclusive boy's school in Connecticut, his name, Constantine Papagos, stood out even more than in Palm Beach. But thanks to the fact that his father had been an ambassador, and his own decidedly British accent, Craig was soon accepted.

It was here that Craig first learned that some of the boys and some of the staff preferred to be with men. Craig continued to skirmish with his homosexuality during his junior college years, but later at Northwestern University and in Chicago's active gay community Craig faced the reality of its existence.

*   *   *   *

On the way back to his sitting room, Craig glanced at the clock and realized it wouldn't be too long before they would get to the Best Actress category. He set the volume on low, picked up the phone, and dialed Alan. No answer. His mind wandered.

He missed Simia. On the rare occasions when Craig stayed in his suite in the Bel Air mansion that he owned, but where Roz lived, he would ask Simia to play cards or chess with him. She normally gave him a tough go of winning anything. Craig knew Simia was probably smarter than all of Roz's staff put together.

Craig could relate to Simia. Sometimes he wished more of the world were mute. He thought, *Maybe if I could become invisible I could turn both people and noise off and on at my pleasure. I wouldn't have to watch Roz's nasty antics anymore or listen to her shouting any longer. In fact, when anyone showed up to ruin my moment, poof! I could disappear.*

Craig smiled at the ridiculous possibility.

But how could I? He shoved the ridiculous thought to the back of his mind, but it was not a new thought. Craig had fantasized of just running away before. Particularly when with Roz.

Simia was but one of Roz's servants. She lived surrounded by a driver, a housemaid, a cook, a gardener, a personal secretary, and Simia. Craig was happy without all that. He had an excellent agent in Beverly Hills who managed his film affairs; an expert tax firm in Los Angeles that fought off the IRS; his attorney in Chicago, Victor Packard, who managed his legal matters; and his administrative assistant, Alan Gavin, who handled everything else personal and financial.

Craig chuckled. He and Alan had something that no one else had: Chin Lee. The Chinese houseboy they had stolen from the Warner Brothers yacht during the Cannes film festival. Chin Lee lived with them in their home in Encinitas and was family. He was their caretaker, marketer, cleaner, cook, jack-of-all-trades.

You needed flowers because company was coming: Chin Lee. You needed a lunch because you had some drop-ins: Chin Lee. You needed your beds refreshed because of too much heavy breathing: Chin Lee.

Craig headed for the bar to fix his second scotch. There he noted the snapshots from his vacation with Alan in the San Juan Islands. He couldn't help now but laugh at the incident with a paparazzo he hated so passionately.

On the private yacht they had chartered, they had pulled into Roche Harbor to reprovision. He and Alan were reading on the same couch with their heads at separate ends and their feet propped up on each other's chests. They had fallen asleep and someone had kindly covered them with an old serape. On shore no one knew who was on the yacht or why. It was that "boat escape" Craig loved. You could be any place and no one knew you were there. Pull in —pull out—privacy guaranteed.

Craig had awakened to the flashes of a camera and was amazed to see a photographer standing four feet from him taking pictures of him and Alan sleeping.

Alan shot off the couch yelling.

The photographer was off the boat and running up the dock.

In excellent physical condition for forty-two, Alan closed the distance between them, shouting, "Stop him! My camera! He's stolen my camera!"

Four college boys with Yale sweatshirts took heed of his request and the photographer was slammed to the dock by the willing assailants. Alan caught up with the photographer and jerked the camera out of his hand.

"Get the camera bag," Alan ordered.

Yale sweatshirt number one happily obliged.

"You son-of-a-bitch," yelled Craig from the boat. He recognized the photographer as the same man who had entered the Greek Orthodox Church to take a picture of him and his mother as they left following the funeral service for his father. He had pestered Craig for years.

The photographer struggled, but was no match for his varsity opposition.

Alan held up the camera. "Who can throw this the farthest?"

Yale sweatshirt number two eagerly took it from his grasp.

"Don't you dare. You'll regret this!" choked the photographer.

"See if you can hit that breakwater over there. You know, a long hard pass."

Yale sweatshirt two obliged. The camera flew through the air and smashed into many pieces.

While Yale three and four kept the photographer pinned to the dock, Alan removed all the film from the camera bag and unrolled it.

That is an invasion of my rights! That's my film! You are destroying my property," raged the photographer.

"My God! An invasion of your privacy?" snorted Alan.

"Wasn't that your camera?" asked one of the Yalies.

"No, it was his," Alan smiled.

Captain Jolly and Craig joined the group and a larger band of onlookers had collected here and there in the otherwise quiet harbor. Craig tapped Alan on the shoulder with his fist then turned to the captain. "Can we leave?"

"Of course."

"Then, let's go. Thanks, boys. Tell the harbormaster to charge him for trespassing and littering. Don't let him go until you feel like it. He's been bugging me for years."

"Say. Aren't you the actor, Craig Carlson?" asked one of the Yalies.

"I guess I am. Sometimes I wish it weren't always so obvious."

Grinning, Alan fumbled in his pocket and found a hundred dollar bill. "This is for beer," he said and turned with Craig and Captain Jolly for the yacht.

The last thing Craig recalled was the photographer thrashing around in the freezing water as the varsity sweat shirts headed back for the verandah of the El Haro Hotel.

*   *   *   *

Craig filled the crystal tumbler half-full, added four ice cubes, and looked out the window. The estate didn't have much to look at other than a well-kept lawn, well-kept landscaping, and a well-kept carriage house that served as both a garage and as living quarters for the cook, the driver and the housemaid. The others lived off the premises. Only Simia lived in the house, on the third floor above Roz.

A long, rock wall meandered through the greenness somewhat hidden by clumps of flowers and hedges well trimmed by a Japanese gardener. The carriage house was dark; it was Monday, the staff's night off.

As he turned away from the darkening view, he admired the warm interior of his sitting room. It was the heart of his small Bel Air world that included a master bedroom, a large bath, and a small safe-room off the sitting room. His sitting room, with its book-lined shelves, valuable oil paintings, massive oak furniture of forest green leather, and parquet floors accented by exquisite Oriental rugs, was a creative lair for Craig when he was forced to spend time in Los Angeles attending affairs he now wanted to forget in a house he otherwise disliked.

He looked at a picture taken of Roz in England when they first met. He thought, *God, she was beautiful. And still can be.* Craig recalled how incredible she looked late that afternoon when she had shown up to tell him good-bye and deliver her last minute barrage of instructions. She was wearing a designer gown that hugged her body with intricate beading and elongated it with silver see-through netting. The chiffon wrap that floated loosely around her shoulders and hips shadowed any imperfections. Her blonde hair, expertly lengthened by weaving, softened her forty-five-year-old profile.

But her sweetness had disappeared.

She ordered, "Be sure and be sitting there in your dumpy chair at eight-thirty. That's when I'll show the Academy! And if anybody cares to ask, I'll tell them you're sick. *Not that you refused to attend my triumph!*"

Simia was equally striking as she left with Roz for the Oscars. Craig knew she was wearing some last minute loaner from Roz, who probably hoped the simple ensemble would play down Simia's beauty, but the dress did exactly the opposite; it made her more lovely. Simia had hidden the ugly scar at her throat with a scarf.

As she was leaving, Simia signed, "I'm troubled."

Craig took that to mean "nervous." He realized now that he too was nervous. He attributed it to watching too much television.

That thought of Simia triggered a need for Craig to again read the provisions he had made for her in his new will. He walked into his safe-room to get the legal documents he would take home to Encinitas after his upcoming Wednesday meeting with Packard. He scooped them up, returned to his chair, sat the papers on the oak table next to him, and glanced up at the Awards ceremony to see where it was in its laborious process. He knew Roz's chances were very good for her performance had been a strong one.

"And now footage from *Rain*, of Roz Marlowe's gripping portrayal as Miss Sadie Thompson, the strong-willed prostitute stranded on a South Sea island paradise with a confused and unforgiving minister and his stern, officious wife." The black and white cinematography was awash with shades of grays and the scene showed Roz in her infamous white boots and dirty and disheveled hair with the minister's doctor friend.

Roz rolled her swollen eyes, wiped her mouth with the sleeve of her dirty white dress, and smiled her dullest, sexiest smile and slurred, "Come on in. Have a shot of hooch. Got real good rye in that grip. Bring it along; will ya, Doc? You'll never know which shot does you in." Roz then laughed and slumped back onto an unmade mattress.

The awards presentation moved quickly to the next nominee. "And now footage from *The Broken Carousel*, of Marilyn Wilde's portrayal of a young woman working with handicapped children..."

Craig turned down the volume and was busy selecting the legal documents he wanted to check when he heard a shrill chime. Irritated, he stepped over to an electronic keypad on the wall and looked at it, but needed his glasses to be sure. According to the blinking red light, someone may have just opened or closed the door to the first floor exercise room.

"That's strange," he said to himself, but was distracted by the television. "And the winner is...Roz Marlowe."

There was much applause as a waving, smiling Roz ran to the podium. She wiped tears from her eyes and waited for the noise to subside so she could respond.

Craig said loudly. "Well, there you go, Roz. You can add this to your other trophies and maybe now you'll relax."

He sipped his scotch, picked up his glasses, and puzzled at the blinking red light. Craig wondered if it was a simple malfunction; he was sure he was the only one in the house. There had been no lights at the carriage house and Alan was in Encinitas attending an awards party. Anyway, Alan always called first on the private line, had his own key and would never come in by that door, and...

So what is this?

Craig returned to the safe-room to look at the bank of security monitors. All of them were functioning except the one covering the back of the house. On closer examination Craig found that it had been turned off. He flipped the switch on and it slowly focused, but showed nothing unusual.

A wave of uneasiness washed over him.

He returned to the massive oak table next to his chair, opened the heavy humidor, and removed his .38 mm handgun. He quietly left the sitting room for the dark of the upstairs hallway, eased himself behind a pillar on the balcony that connected his wing to Roz's, and studied the lower floor. It was darker than normal. The housekeeper must have forgotten to turn on the table lamp in the downstairs hall.

Strange. It was never off at night.

It was then he saw a figure stealthily ascend the long staircase. At the landing where the stairs split to serve the two separate wings of the second floor, the intruder didn't hesitate. He knew which way to go. From the light of the upstairs' sitting room Craig saw the glint of a gun in his hand.

Craig was queasy.

This was no accidental, electronic security system gaffe or movie set. It was real. Someone was in the house, with a gun, heading for his sitting room. And now Craig was nowhere near a panic keypad to call for help. He tried to stop breathing so loudly.

Without pause the figure passed underneath where Craig was standing, and Craig could vaguely make him out. He felt there was something oddly familiar about him and that he had seen the intruder somewhere before. Carefully, Craig raised his gun and watched the man stop at the doorway to the sitting room and look inside. Craig could now see the back of his head.

If it's him, why is he here?

As soon as the intruder entered the room, Craig quickly moved to its doorway. His hands were slick with sweat as he leveled his gun and pointed it directly at the back of the intruder's head.

"What do you think you're . . . ?"

The other man whirled.

The noise of gunshot shattered the sound of the television monologue and the stillness of the Bel Air mansion. A moment of uninvited death invaded the comfort of Craig Carlson's carefully orchestrated and well-mannered world.

Two

Monday Evening, Bel Air, California

Alan Gavin drove as fast as he dared to make Bel Air before the Best Actress award was announced. Why did Roz call to see if he would be watching with Craig? She never called him for anything. Pushy bitch. What if she didn't win?

He would have plenty of time with Craig. Roz wouldn't be home until four or five in the morning, and the driver would probably carry her dead weight to her room and lay her out like a comatose Cleopatra.

Alan grinned. He could see Roz's expensive gown twisted around her inert body; he wished her fans could see her that way. Lucky for her, the Oscar choices had been made before her slutty performance on the carousel horse. It was the last straw for Craig, at long last.

Nearing Bel Air, Alan tried to reach Craig on their private line, but no one answered. That had been a rule at any home they ever had. Call first. Alan was very protective of Craig's privacy, but even he couldn't do anything about the adoring fan or maniac who would pierce the most perfect protection.

Alan disliked Beverly Hills, Bel Air, and Brentwood. All the people were caught up in an obsession with the industry, eager to sell their souls to it. And the place was dangerous, a crossfire of drugs and drunken designated drivers. Many who wanted to escape Los Angeles moved to Santa Barbara, but in so many numbers that it had simply become "Movieland North."

That's why he and Craig had chosen to live in Encinitas. They owned a traditional, stucco bungalow with a Spanish tile roof high on the cliff overlooking the Pacific. There, people left them alone.

Alan pulled up in front of the Bel Air mansion and ran up the steps, eager to talk to Craig about the awards.

He opened the door with his key, stripped off his driving gloves, threw them all into the wooden bowl on the entry hall table, and entered the expansive interior. He noticed that the table lamp, always on in the lower hallway, was off. It made the dreary house seem even more glum. He snapped it on and bounded up the stairs towards Craig's lighted sitting room.

"Hey! I'm here!" he said as he rounded the doorway.

Alan couldn't breathe. It was as if someone had first sucked all the air out of his lungs and then sledge-hammered him with a blow so great and final that there was no recoil. The impact turned him to stone—cold, hard stone.

"Craig?"

Only the blaring television answered him.

"My God! What's happened?" Alan rushed to his lover and tried to pull him upright. He could barely move him.

"Craig? Talk to me! Move!" But he was scared by the chalky face and the stream of warm blood.

Alan pounded on Craig's chest. "Breathe, damn it! You're not dead. Breathe!"

Alan turned and shouted at the intruding television, "Shut up, goddamn it!"

Alan looked back hard at Craig. There was a bullet hole in his head, and the right side of his face was a mass of mutilated skin.

"Jesus Christ! What happened to your face?"

Alan was going to be sick. In his dash to the bathroom he jarred the table beside Craig's chair, knocking the phone and a stack of papers to the floor. He careened off the bathroom door, sank to his knees, and cut his cheek on the toilet paper holder. He vomited violently.

When Alan stood up, he had no strength. He was dazed. He knew he had to get help immediately. Surely someone could still do something.

He ran back into the room, picked up the phone, and dialed 911. He was numb.

"This is 911."

"I'm calling from the home of a friend and . . ." Alan couldn't continue.

"Is this an emergency?"

Alan took a deep breath and composed himself. "There's been an accident." He took another deep breath and continued, "I think a murder."

"May we have the address or phone number, please?"

"It's Bel Air. It's Craig Carlson's house. Roz Marlowe's house. Is that good enough?"

The 911 operator was looking at his screen with all of the information already on it. When the call had come in the phone number had activated the A.L.I. and the address, phone number, and who lived there had flashed on his screen. They had so many prank calls the operator simply needed some confirmation.

The voice changed. "Help will be there immediately. May I have your name?"

"Alan. Alan Gavin."

"Are you in danger?"

"My God, I don't know."

"Just stay on the line, Mr. Gavin. Please stay on the line until help comes."

"How long will that be?" Alan looked down at himself; he had blood all over him.

"Five or ten minutes, no more. Just stay on the line."

Alan had no strength, and knew the love of his life was dead. While clutching the phone with one hand, he reached for the control button on the television remote and turned it off. The sudden stillness was worse than the noise.

A second wave of nausea hit. He threw the phone onto the chair, rushed back into the bathroom, and threw up again and again. When he finished, his gut was sore and his head was pounding.

He didn't want to go back where Craig lay. He wanted to be the one on the floor. In a daze he sat down in Craig's chair and picked up the phone. "I'm still here," he said; mechanically as he bent over, picked up the spilled papers from the floor, and returned them to the heavy oak table.

The 911 operator used his Mobile Data Terminal to send an immediate E-1 message to the police that there was a possible homicide at name, address, and phone number. The 911 operator added that it is the home of two well-known celebrities. He knew the police would dispatch by priority, and hoped the media would not be alerted by the police radio traffic.

It was always embarrassing when the media got there before the police. The 911 crew had tried to solve that with a media relations office where the media could call to see if there was anything they should check into, but it didn't always work that way. Neighbors so often were the first to see the police and suddenly media were on the scene.

Alan held the phone tightly in his hand, stared at the clock, then at the body. Clock—body. Clock—body. The stillness was awful. He snapped the television back on just for noise and changed his routine. Clock—television—body. Clock—television—body. Finally, he dropped "body" out of the trio. He couldn't bear to look at Craig. He looked empty. No spark. No humor. No love. Just dead.

Alan tried hard to remain rational. The television news team were discharging their perceived obligation in their nightly news wrap-up from Los Angeles by reporting all of the horrible murders, rapes, and robberies that had just occurred. All Alan could think about was that if he had left Encinitas earlier, this might not have happened.

And Craig's face. Why did they have to brutalize his handsome face?

Where are you, emergency? What if this had been a medical matter? The patient would be dead! Alan slammed down the phone, snapped the television back off, and stared at his lover. It wasn't until then that Alan realized it hadn't been a stray robbery. It had been a personal attack on a celebrity. A cold, calculated act of violence to end the life of Craig Carlson. Alan shuddered with the possibility.

He tried to erase the thought. He left the chair and looked at pictures of he and Craig that had been taken all over the world. Pictures that recorded ten years of togetherness, ten years of struggle and reward, ten years of compassion and companionship, and, in most cases, ten years of secrecy.

Jesus. If only we had stayed in France.

*   *   *   *

Police were all over the mansion. There was no end to them and no end to the orders they gave. And to Alan, there appeared to be little consideration for the dead man on the floor. To the police, it was a corpse, a statistic. They took many pictures of it. Discussed its degree or lack of rigor mortis. Rolled it over. Marked where it was. Officially pronounced it dead. Zipped it into a bag and carted it down the stairs like a bag of mulch.

And in the middle of it all, Alan had been asked to step aside, sit in the adjoining bedroom, answer questions, stay handy, but stay out of the way.

"Why are your clothes bloody, Mr. Gavin? What time did you arrive? Were you the one who called? What was your relationship with the deceased? Why did you come here tonight?"

Simia arrived just in time to see them zip up the body bag. Her face turned stark white, and she swayed. A policeman caught her before she fell to the floor. When she came to, she looked at Alan, her eyes full of horror and grief.

Alan led her into Craig's bedroom away from the bloody scene. "Simia, Simia," he choked. He was holding up to some degree until he saw her. Then he no longer could control himself.

They held each other, sobbing—Simia for the loss of her best friend, Alan for the loss of his life's love.

Slowly they disengaged. They tried to get a grip on themselves.

Simia typed on the handheld computer she always carried, "Blood all over you."

"I know. It's Craig's."

Simia pointed to Alan's cheek and clearly signed, "What?"

Alan told her the whole story.

"Does Roz know?" she wrote.

"How could she?" Then Alan asked, "Should I call?"

Simia set her shoulders. "Let LAPD" was her message.

"Do you know where she went?"

Simia wrote, "Spagos."

Alan left the room, walked up to one of the many men in charge, and asked him if Mr. Carlson's wife had been called.

"That's taken care of. Please go back and sit down. *We don't want the crime scene walked into by you again.*"

That's a ridiculous request, Alan thought. He could count at least ten people milling around the room, touching everything, taking notes, taking pictures, looking through papers, talking into tape recorders. In despair, he returned to Simia.

Alan was unaware there was already a crowd outside.

The press had followed the police cars and the helicopters to the Bel Air mansion of Craig Carlson and Roz Marlowe. The television stations were jostling for position around the cordoned-off area. Smack in the middle of it all was Alan's car and someone had already made the plates and reported him as owner.

*   *   *   *

"I'm Homicide Inspector Roosevelt," said the heavyset man wearing civilian clothes. "I want to ask both of you questions. I'm sorry for all this. It appears it has been difficult for both of you."

He pointed to Alan. "You found the body?"

"Yes."

"Then I'll talk with you first. Miss, please stay here. I'll talk to you next."

Alan looked at Simia. She was very pale and was still clutching shoes that she rarely wore. He asked, "Can't she go up to her room and wait there? Or change her clothes, or do something other than just sit there?"

"She lives in the house?"

Simia nodded "yes" as Alan said it.

"Where?"

Simia pointed to the third floor.

"I'll see," said Roosevelt. He left them in the bedroom.

Alan asked, "Simia, are you afraid to be alone?"

Simia nodded "yes."

Roosevelt came back in. "They're looking at the third floor

now. As soon as they're done, she can go up if she wants. We haven't found any evidence that the intruder is still on the property. For now, Simia—is that how you say your name? Please stay here. Mr. Gavin, come with me."

The inspector took Alan into the sitting room where there was now nothing on the floor but a mark where Craig had lain.

"Who was that?" he asked.

"Craig Carlson," choked Alan.

"Are you positive?"

"I worked for him for ten years, I think I know—knew—him."

"Now, Mr. Gavin, please answer my questions as carefully as you can." Roosevelt asked him what time he arrived, what had been playing on the television, and the status of the room when he entered it.

Alan answered as best he could.

"Why is your face bloody?"

Alan told him what had happened.

"Why is there blood on these papers?"

Alan told him what had happened.

Then Inspector Roosevelt held up a .38 mm gun in a plastic bag and asked, "Do you know who this belongs to?"

"Where did you get the gun?" Alan asked.

Roosevelt didn't answer. He asked, "Did Carlson own a gun?"

"Yes. He kept it there in that humidor." There was no box where he pointed.

"We have it in plastic also," said Roosevelt.

"Can you describe your relationship with Carlson as normal, friendly, or not so? Did you ever have any special arguments about anything?"

"I was very close to Craig—Mr. Carlson. I am—I was his administrative assistant and financial secretary. I looked after almost everything that he owned or did."

Roosevelt looked up from his pad. "Please answer my question. Did you and Mr. Carlson ever argue?"

"Of course we did, but nothing that would result in this!"

Alan wondered why he was getting the third degree. He was the one who had called 911.

"Why did you come here tonight, Mr. Gavin?"

"Because I knew he would be alone, watching the Academy Awards." Alan suddenly realized how that sounded. "His wife, Roz Marlowe, asked me to be sure and be here when she was up for the Best Actress award. But I was late."

"Did you see anyone else in the house?"

"No."

"Anything unusual about the condition of the house?"

"No—yes. Actually, the light wasn't on."

Roosevelt skipped over it. "Is this Mr. Carlson's principal residence?"

"No—yes. I'm not sure what you mean. He also has homes elsewhere." Alan was thinking of their home.

"Such as?"

"Encinitas, Palm Beach, and Provence, France would all probably be considered major homes for Mr. Carlson."

"Do you know where he would keep his personal papers?"

Alan couldn't believe the determination of the questioning inspector. "A few here, most at his office in Encinitas."

"I see." Roosevelt paused for a moment. "Now, Mr. Gavin, can you think of anyone who would want to kill Mr. Carlson?"

The question surprised Alan. He stared blankly at the now blank television screen. For the first time, he could see in its dead reflection what a mess he was. His new suit was blood-stained, his face was bloodstained, and his normally well-groomed hair was disorderly.

Alan thought of one person, but tried to dismiss even the possibility of it. "No. No, I do not."

"What were you thinking, Mr. Gavin?"

"Nothing. I can hardly think at all."

And so it went for Alan. Dozens of questions. All being taped or noted. Photographs of himself taken. Instructions given for him to use some of Carlson's clothes so they could have his bloody ones.

Finally, Roosevelt said, "That's enough for here. You're free to go, but don't leave California. We'll talk to you later at the police station. Call me if you remember anything you didn't tell me. Here's my card."

"You need to talk to me more?"

"I'm sure I will, Mr. Gavin. I'll call you." Roosevelt turned away.

Alan knew it was a dismissal.

"Charlie, go get Miss Simia from the third floor."

Alan interrupted. "Do you want me to stay while you talk to Simia? It's going to be very difficult for her, she's mute."

"I already know that," was Roosevelt's curt reply.

Alan didn't know it was Inspector Roosevelt's third homicide that evening, and the fact that they were wealthy and of celebrity status made no difference to him. It was just a job.

"And Gavin, leave by the back door. Your car's there."

Alan was mad. "And how did you do that?"

"Simply found your keys in the wooden bowl and had a policeman drive it around back. There are hundreds of people out front. I don't think you want to deal with them."

"I'm sorry I snapped, Inspector. Thank you for doing that."

"No problem." The inspector held up another plastic bag. "Are these your gloves?"

"Yes." Alan reached out for them, and then stopped.

"Why are you keeping those?"

"Routine," said Inspector Roosevelt, and he turned away.

*   *   *   *

Alan walked out the back way. He could hear the carnival in front and saw the two helicopters that landed in the side yard. But once he hit the back street, the press was waiting there too.

"You're Craig Carlson's lover, aren't you?" someone shouted. The flash photo was bright as lightning.

"Craig Carlson's gay, isn't he?"

Alan kept silent. He tried not to look at anything. He tried not to cry. He was wearing Craig's clothes, which didn't quite fit. But they were Craig's, and they felt like Craig's protective arms.

Alan revved his car as he tried to put distance between him and the relentless media, which followed him until he was on southbound Interstate Five. Alan hadn't thought about where to go, other than home.

Thirty minutes later he had to pull off the interstate. It was all he could do to breathe, and his lean frame shook uncontrollably with his deep sobbing. He had been through the loss of a lover once before, and he had never wanted to do it again. With Craig, he was safe from AIDS, had financial security, and enjoyed an honest loving relationship. He had never thought about personal safety. His father had sternly warned him that his gay persuasion could ruin his life. It hardly mattered that it was happening now—his life was ruined anyway. His Craig was dead.

*   *   *   *

Roz saw the maître d' of the restaurant escorting two men toward their table who definitely were not celebrants. She had wondered when they would arrive. She looked at her watch. It was midnight. She took a deep breath and engaged Gregory Washburne, her selected and handsome escort of the evening, in a meaningless conversation. He had had a lot to drink and was laughing heartily. Some at the table asked her earlier why she seemed so forlorn and distracted.

Roz had told them, "I miss Craig."

She expected that some might find that difficult to believe.

Every so often, Roz would hold up her Oscar, look at it, and smile. Then she would put it back on the table and engage someone in conversation and then slowly drift away. Normally by now she would be flying high with drink.

"You should have won for *Salinas* as well," said Emily from her agent's firm.

"Now, Emily, we don't bring up that subject tonight, do we?" chortled the director of *Rain*. He hadn't won, but at least he had been nominated.

The maître d' bent over and said something to Roz.

Roz slowly stood up and held out her hand to the two men

one at a time. Smiling her practiced smile, she tilted her head in order to hear whatever they had to say above the noise in the room. Her manner was polite, not a constant behavior for Roz.

She had rehearsed her next scene as much as any that she had ever played. "My God. Oh, my God! My Craig?" Roz cried out with incredible wrenching agony.

"What's wrong, Roz?" Gregory asked, and stood next to her.

Roz clutched her throat with one hand and the tablecloth with the other. "He's dead! *Craig's dead!* He's been murdered!" With that, she fainted.

Most at the table gasped in shock. Many in the dining room had stopped talking and became attentive and still. They were all looking at Roz's table.

"What did you tell her?" asked a lady with the *Los Angeles Times.*

One of the men leaned over and said quietly to the table, "We have just informed Mrs. Marlowe that her husband, Craig Carlson, was found dead about two hours ago in their home in Bel Air." That's all he said. What he wondered was if he had used the word *murdered* when he told Roz. He was sure that he hadn't.

*   *   *   *

The word spread quickly through the room, along with disbelief. What a night. To win an Oscar and lose a husband at the same time.

Gregory scooped up Roz off the floor and helped ease her back into her chair. One of the inspectors popped an amyl nitrate capsule under her nose that snapped her back to reality. To catch her breath, Roz sat for a moment, but at the insistence of the police inspectors, it was only a matter of minutes before her entire entourage left. They formed a wedge around the devastated, distraught Roz, shielding her from the many watching the tragedy.

Roz Marlowe made a memorable exit from Spagos; it became known as the "tragic event of the night" and appeared in many magazines covering the super-hyped Oscar ceremony.

The camera crews were in the street, waiting for shots of the departing celebrities. As Roz's driver pulled up her limo, a private police car followed. The two police inspectors directed Gregory Washburne and Roz to get inside. The limo could deliver the others to their various destinations, but the police were going directly to Bel Air and wanted Roz at home for her protection and questioning. They thought that perhaps she might be next on someone's hit list, and they weren't taking any chances. The LAPD didn't need any more bad press.

*   *   *   *

Gregory had sobered substantially and suggested the police use the back driveway to avoid the clamor in front. Roz whispered, "I might as well face the music. I can do it." The senior inspector looked at her with disgust and directed the car to the back of the house.

Inside, the police had just finished interrogating Simia when Roz appeared.

Simia did not go to Roz or look at her. She was tired. Her eyes were puffy from crying, and it had taken a long time to communicate anything that she wanted them to know, let alone understand their questions.

Simia had gone through this once before, the night that Mikey Marlowe had died of an overdose. Roz was there, too. It had happened seventeen years ago in New York, and it had changed her life. Mikey always controlled Roz in one way or another, but after his death, Simia had been at Roz's whim and disposal.

"Simia! I can't believe Craig is gone." Roz choked out her words and cried distraughtly.

Simia turned away from Roz to Inspector Roosevelt, and typed on her handheld PC, "May I go now?"

"Yes, Simia, you may. And thank you very much."

Roz looked at Simia with disbelief and distaste. She had just taken her to the Academy Awards and now she wouldn't even look at her. Simia's reaction unnerved her. Until now, Roz had never really thought much about her mute intelligence. Hastily,

Roz decided to pass that insight off as needless information.

*   *   *   *

One of the last questions that Inspector Roosevelt asked Roz Marlowe was where Mr. Carlson kept his valuable papers.

Roz asked in a tight voice, "Why?"

"In case they were stolen. Nothing else seems to be."

Roz frowned. "I know where he keeps them. I'll go see and get them for you." She stepped into the safe-room, but came rushing back. "They're gone! I can't believe it. They were there earlier!"

"Are these what you're looking for?" Gregory asked. He pointed to a small stack of legal envelopes and a FedEx folder on the worktable next to Craig's chair.

"Yes. Yes. That has to be them. Let me check." Before Roosevelt could stop her, Roz picked up the stack and hurriedly looked through it.

For the first time that night, Roz was flushed, and Inspector Roosevelt didn't fail to notice either that or the unexpected importance Roz placed on the papers. Before then, she had seemed grief-stricken, yet abnormally controlled considering the situation.

"Mr. Washburne, you're an attorney?" Roosevelt asked.

"Yes. I work in the California law office of Victor Packard. I'm aware of some of Mr. Carlson's personal legal dealings, but not all. He reserved most of it for Packard."

"Will you sign for these documents as a vested party if we take them with us?" Roosevelt chose not to explain that there were spots of blood on some of them.

"Yes, I will." Gregory began to wonder about a couple of things that he had recently told Roz in the greatest of confidence and about some things she had him do—things that his boss, Victor Packard, would kill him for. He hadn't missed her sudden interest in Craig's papers. Now Gregory was beginning to think about the propriety of some of his actions. He had always done what Roz had asked because her requests always seemed so innocent—little things, like marking letters at the bottom, as if a blind copy had been sent. "After all," Roz would laugh, "what's a blind copy, anyway?" And great sex had always followed. But this was no longer laughable. This wasn't a dress rehearsal or an opening night or a simple blind copy. This was a murder.

Gregory said, "Roz, I think it's time to call Victor in Chicago and tell him what's happened."

Roz interjected, "Oh, Gregory, it's so late in Chicago. I would hate to wake him up. He's such a sweet man. Can't we tell him in the morning?"

Gregory said, "It is morning in Chicago—almost."

Roz gave Gregory a look that would have reversed the Nile. He got the message. He dutifully signed, and a woman in uniform promptly stepped forward, gave him a receipt, and took possession of the documents.

"Thank you, Mr. Washburne, for helping with Miss Marlowe." Roosevelt held out his hand. "You can go now, but please stay in town. We may have further questions."

"Roz, are you afraid? Do you want me to spend the night?"

"No!" She turned her back on Gregory Washburne.

"Inspector, do you mind if I pour myself a drink?" Roz walked to the bar, and, without anyone's permission, she served herself.

Gregory left by the back door.

*   *   *   *

It was nearly dawn when all the questions had been asked, and the last contingent of police had gone. Security personnel were left on duty, and Roz was told that she should get some rest.

Alone in her room, Roz lay back on her bed and looked at the ceiling. It had been quite a night, quite a week, and quite a scene. She had won her Oscar, secured her fortune, and gotten rid of her husband all in a few short hours.

"I need two Valiums, a sleeping pill, and, as old Sadie would say, 'a slug of straight hooch.'" Roz poured herself a full tumbler of scotch.

"Simia!" she shouted into her intercom.

But Simia didn't appear.

"Simia!" Roz rang her buzzer and shouted louder.

Simia still didn't answer.

"Where is the lazy bitch?" Roz gulped her drink.

Roz didn't have the strength or patience to go upstairs and see where her Polynesian maid was. She would worry about that tomorrow. Roz kicked off her shoes, topped off her drink, downed a handful of pills, and collapsed on her bed.

"My makeup can wait," she said, and plunged into her drugged and drunken world.

*   *   *   *

Simia was sound asleep in one of the more elegant guest suites in the front of the house, with the door locked and a special guard on duty outside. She had written him a note asking him not to bother her until she got up on her own. And if Roz Marlowe wanted her for anything, she simply was not available.

The kindly retired policeman understood completely, and felt the true grief of the stricken woman.

*   *   *   *

The captain said, "That Roz is one cold bitch."

Inspector Roosevelt said matter-of-factly, "We have either a contract murder or an inside job."

"And Carlson was gay, and his lover found the body," said the captain. "We know how many violent arguments gays have."

Roosevelt didn't respond. One of his nephews was gay.

With that, they lapsed into silence. They knew that tomorrow they would have to face the press and the prosecuting attorney's office.

"Do you want to bet, Roosevelt?"

"No," said Roosevelt. "I want to eat."

Three

Tuesday, Buttonwillow, California

The exhausted driver eased the rental car into an open spot in front of the immense all-night truck stop located at the Buttonwillow interchange on Interstate Five. It appeared from the map that he was about half-way to San Francisco and he knew he had to quit. He spent a few anxious moments looking for California State Patrol cars before getting out of the car. It was cold and he felt ill-at-ease wearing his expensive blazer at that hour at such an isolated location. Once inside, he purchased a warm windbreaker and an STP cap, put them on and found a booth insulated from the other customers. The restaurant was busy for three in the morning.

After ordering ham and eggs, he stared hypnotically at one of the intrusive televisions, until he had to tune it out. He had already heard enough on late night radio to terrify him.

"Craig Carlson was found murdered tonight in his Bel Air mansion while his wife, Roz Marlowe, won her first Academy Award. We'll be back with the morning edition for your full, updated report."

The truck stop offered sleeping rooms with private toilet and shower facilities—twelve hours for twenty-five dollars—and all he wanted to do was sleep safely and forget all he had been through. Considering everything, he was surprised at his appetite. He felt better after eating and now felt strong enough to lay out all of the confusing instructions he had accumulated in one safe place where he could understand for sure what they meant.

The cashier dutifully took his money for the food, his twenty-five dollars for a room and told him, "If you want a hell of a wake-up call, just set the alarm clock on the wall in your room. It'll get you up." She smiled knowingly at him and shoved a registration card across the counter. "Just give me the essentials."

He looked down at the card, picked up the pen and began to write—then stopped. Slowly he printed out the name Kurt Schmidt. Where it asked for a license number, he made one up and scrawled an unreadable signature hoping she wouldn't care.

She didn't.

She slid a key to number three across the counter and said, "Remember. Smack the red button on top of the clock or the clanging won't stop. It makes enough noise to raise the dead." She shoved the money in the cash register and turned away.

Once again he surveyed the parking lot and when satisfied there were no police, returned to his car, removed the thin briefcase from the front seat and the black bag from the trunk. He was happy to find room number three modern, clean, and well lit with neither phone nor television to intrude.

"God, but this will help," he groaned and plopped the bag on the bed and sat down beside it.

He didn't know whether to rest, take a shower, or dump the bag to see what he had put into it. He dumped the bag and the gun was the first thing to fall out to remind him he had just killed someone.

"Jesus!" he said. He thought, *I have to remember that Kurt Schmidt is going to have to use every skill he ever possessed to stay alive and that Craig Carlson is dead.*

A wave of fatigue and illness rolled over him and he lay back on the pillow trying to forget what he had been unable to forget since it had happened. As he moved deeper into the gray zone of exhaustion, it all started to replay one more time. The same sequence of events played over and over and his subconscious state was vivid, accurate, and terrifying.

*　　*　　*　　*

Craig Carlson fired one shot into the intruder's head and then collapsed against the door jam shaking violently. He had never known how to use a gun before filming *To Kill or to Die,* a hard-action film in which he had to play a perfect marksman, but he had insisted on learning how to hold a gun and shoot a bullseye.

Tonight, he was thankful.

With his gunsight still locked on the man's head, he waited for his shaking to subside until he could bring himself to approach the body.

Craig wasn't ready for his bizarre discovery.

"My God!"

The man Craig killed had done his stunts and stand-ins and even mock appearances for him for years. And he didn't have to touch him to be sure he was dead, he knew exactly where his bullet had gone. Straight into the middle of Kurt Schmidt's brain.

He watched the blood seep down Schmidt's face and onto the blue sweater underneath the gray sports coat. As he half-sat, half-fell into his chair, Craig's temples pounded with further discoveries.

"Jesus. That's my sweater!"

He recognized more. "My God. That's my blazer! Those are my clothes!"

His head spun with a stream of meaningless questions. *Why does he have my clothes on? Why did he try to kill me? He was here to murder me—wasn't he?*

Craig shook his head and closed his eyes. *What in God's name did I ever do to Kurt Schmidt? I was his ticket to a job!*

As the dead man's body molded into the floor, as if seeking a more comfortable position, Craig's churning mind hesitated, and then answered his troublesome question. Craig said quietly. "I've done nothing."

He stood up, walked around the body, and then slumped back into his chair as useless information flashed by in his mind. Roz and Kurt? Craig knew they had romped sexually on several sets together, but that wasn't new or meaningful. And that wasn't enough. He looked down and studied Kurt Schmidt.

Craig assessed their similarity. About one-hundred-seventy pounds, maybe Kurt not quite matching his six-foot height, same strong cheekbones, six or seven years younger, not quite as much gray hair . . .

Did something move?

As the body continued to settle, a white envelope began to show from Schmidt's inner coat pocket. Carefully, Craig reached down, picked it up, sat back in his chair and opened it.

Craig didn't understand. There were plane tickets to several destinations from LAX and a list of banks in six cities around the world where a million dollars had been randomly left in certified checks in each bank to names that all began and ended with letters similar to Kurt Schmidt. Well almost—he looked again. A Curtis Smith, a Charles Silvey, a Carl Stone . . .

He dropped the material on his lap and shook his head. *That was your payoff? That was what you asked to kill me? Six million dollars?* If it were true, the depth of the deception overwhelmed him, for this wasn't a frantic fan hounding him, this was a former friend.

Craig looked through it all again and then back at Schmidt. Slowly he began to realize that maybe now, maybe for the first time, he had the opportunity he had often dreamed of—anonymity. And he knew that if they, whoever they were, had missed him once, they would certainly try again.

"I'm dead. Someone wanted to kill me and they succeeded."

His mind raced. Not a haphazard prowler. My clothes. Simia out of the house. Lights off. Door unlocked. I'm dead. Kurt would be gone by now. Who would know that I wasn't the one dead? No one. Only me.

But someone wants me dead?

Craig shuddered. "But, there I am on the floor. Dead!"

Roz was on the big television screen, being interviewed by ABC. "Why isn't Craig Carlson with you at this moment of your triumph, Roz? Is it true that he's not well?"

Craig recalled Roz's cutting admonition as she left for the Awards. "You'll regret this." He watched hard as Roz faked a concerned look, "I feel so sorry for my Craig. He wanted to come tonight. But he's never fully recovered from the rigors of *The Corsican*. I hope he's alright. Nothing is ever going to happen to my Craig!"

Craig gripped the arms of his chair and hissed. "You went to the cabin at Big Bear Lake last week, *didn't you?* You planned this with your Las Vegas stud Beretta, *didn't you*? And the two of you hired Kurt Schmidt to carry out your dirty plan. *Didn't you!*"

In a wave of Greek fury, Craig swore, "You'll pay, Roz Marlowe. You can produce, stage, and direct my funeral. But it's my move!"

Craig's mind raced with possibilities. He had longed for escape for years. This was his chance to disappear from the celebrity limelight he hated. He was tired of the homophobic pressures of the industry and public. This was his chance to get away from the secrets that made his and Alan's life so confined. He was tired of the meddling IRS. This was Alan's chance to inherit millions from his will while he, Craig, was still secretly alive and could be at his side. He was finished with Roz Marlowe. This was his chance to get away from her for the rest of his life and she would never have another nerve of his to gnaw on. And there was even the bonus of possibly being able to pick up six million tax-free dollars. Wouldn't the goddamned IRS love that one!

Craig was jolted by the possibility. *Why not? I can do what I've always wanted to. Get the hell out. Disappear! I can call Alan after a funeral and tell him we are free to live anywhere in the world.*

The possibilities seemed endless.

When Craig heard, "And the best picture is..." he recklessly made his decision and knew he had to move quickly.

Craig took a towel from the bathroom and laid it on the floor next to the body. Then he picked up Schmidt's .38 mm revolver, removed Schmidt's gloves, and placed the items on the towel. Craig started to put his own gun in Schmidt's hand, then realized that was a mistake. After all, he had been surprised and killed. Why would he even have had a gun? He walked to his bureau, put another round in the chamber, wiped off his prints, and put the gun back into the antique humidor.

"I've got to remember that's me on the floor," he said.

Craig emptied Schmidt's pockets and checked Schmidt's wallet for credit cards and money. He found plenty. Then he dropped Schmidt's wallet and his other personal belongings on the towel and folded it. In Schmidt's jacket he found keys to a rental car and slipped those into his pants pocket. On his leather chair, he saw the envelope with Schmidt's curious instructions and plane tickets. He jammed those into his hip pocket, pleased that he had been able to keep blood off most of the items.

Satisfied, Craig walked into his safe room and removed from his safe ten thousand dollars, his alias passport of Craig Carlson and his legal passport of Constantine Papagos. From the closet shelf, he picked up his carefully documented Financial and Communications Control book that Alan always insisted he keep up-to-date with unlisted phone numbers, bank account information, credit card numbers, certain key addresses, and other such data.

He slipped a sports jacket from his rack on over the casual blue shirt and black jeans he was wearing, and shoved his stocking feet into a pair of beat-up Docksiders. Craig expected Schmidt would have clothes somewhere in the car to make his - escape trip to wherever.

He thought, *Why worry? I can always buy what I need.*

Craig thought of his own personal items. He picked up his wallet from the dresser, then suddenly realized even though he was now Kurt Schmidt, some security as Craig Carlson might be wise. He removed one American Express and one Visa card from many, but purposefully left his wallet behind.

Near giddy, Craig scurried back into his closet, picked up his quick-travel-pack that contained extra glasses, medications, and grooming aids and placed it and his Communications Control book into the bottom of a medium sized black bag.

Craig looked around, examined everything and tried to ignore how cold he was. Satisfied, he returned to the sitting room, placed the folded towel into the black bag and closed it. He sat down and thought, *What am I doing?*

It was only then that he noticed Schmidt's rugged boots. *My God. I don't even own anything like those.* Craig knew he had to get them off. It wasn't easy. Schmidt's feet were hard to manipulate and he had to pull and tug. Now sweating, from the raw adrenaline coursing through his veins, Craig knew he was running out of time. When he finally got them off, he was exhausted.

From the floor, Craig looked at the clotted blood on Schmidt's face. Only from there did he see something he had completely overlooked that would have been a disaster.

"Jesus!"

He saw the birthmark on Kurt Schmidt's face the studio makeup artists always had to cover up in order to make their facial features appear the same. "How stupid of me!"

Craig knew he didn't have time to change his chosen course, he had done too much to erase what had happened. And a claim of self-defense now would have some very interesting conditions to explain.

Roz's continued electronic presence spurred Craig to action. She was looking directly at him from four feet away, shoving the Oscar right into the television camera and his face. Driven by both hate and anger, Craig seized one of his Oscars from the mantelpiece and with all of his might smashed one side of Kurt's face until pulverized skin covered-up the birthmark. He knew he had erased the probability of anyone ever finding that flaw of his near-perfect clone, but the sight of his double's face now sickened him.

Without looking back, Craig picked up the boots and bag with one hand, while still holding the bloodied Oscar in the other. As he descended the stairs, he recalled a little boy carrying his shoes and one small bag the night he and his mother fled the Greek embassy in Rome. As quickly as the thought came, it disappeared.

Seconds later, Craig Carlson left his Bel Air home by the same door Schmidt had entered.

Outside, he slowed his pace, but kept dropping one of the boots. It was an awkward carry. The bag was easy, the boots slowed him down, and he didn't want to slip the Oscar under his arm with the blood all over it.

He dropped the other boot. "Damn!"

Craig heard Roz's dog, Bitsy, barking wildly from the staff quarters above the carriage house and realized Roz had even thought of getting her goddamned dog out of the house. "Well, Bitsy Bitch, you and Roz had better start looking for a less expensive place to live. I'm leaving."

He then wondered where Simia would live. "Simia!"

Craig knew there was no way Roz would take Simia to the Governor's Ball or any other special after-awards parties. She would ship Simia home by cab as soon as the ceremonies were over. He had to keep moving.

Craig remembered the special place in the rock wall where he and Simia had hidden secrets from each other for years. It had started with a birthday present. He had made a game of her finding it and they had used the cache for secret fun things ever since. Craig knew that for Simia, it was a break from the dull reality of her life. To his knowledge, not even the Japanese gardener had ever found their hole in the wall.

Craig changed course. He walked over to the niche, first tossed in the bothersome boots and then the Oscar. Less burdened, he hurried out the back gate.

He found the car, opened the trunk, threw in the black bag, and saw a brown suitcase. "Good. Extra clothes." As he slid behind the wheel, he noticed a thin briefcase on the passenger's seat. He flipped on the overhead light and found more instructions, passports and other documents relating to the material he had found in Schmidt's pocket.

He thought, *I'll examine this stuff later.*

Only then did Craig realize he hadn't even thought about his destination.

But Craig Carlson was now committed. To be dead. To be alive. To be free!

But to where?

* * * *

Soaked with sweat, Craig shot straight up off the pillow. He gripped the edge of the bed and forced himself to calm down. He looked around him—the clanging of something awful had woken him from a dead sleep. Roman candles of red light flashed around the room, he was on the run and the police were right behind him. Chasing him. He had to get away. Finally, he focused his mind, spotted the flashing light on top of a clock and smacked it with his fist. It stopped.

"Thank God," he said.

Craig had a crook in his neck, one arm was numb, and his back hurt. He had wound his body around a pile of things on his bed in a twisted position. When he saw the gun it brought him back. He sat up with a start and every muscle in his body screamed with pain. Either the room was warm or he had a fever, but Craig Carlson knew who he was, where he was, and what he had done.

He stripped off his wet clothes, stepped into the shower, and the hot water revived him. As he toweled off, he was sure his decision last night not to use any of the proffered escape tickets to Mexico City, Honolulu, Miami, or London had been a correct one. He examined his haggard reflection in the mirror and wearily decided his continued course.

His first stop would be the Wells Fargo Bank. He doubted if Roz or Beretta would have put that bank under surveillance this early from Schmidt's touch, and Craig needed to confirm that these certified checks actually existed. Maybe they had planned for his murder to cost them nothing!

Forty-five minutes later, a shaven Craig Carlson wearing his expensive blazer, emerged from Room Three. By nine o'clock, Craig was over the Bay Bridge and in downtown San Francisco. He found a parking garage near the appropriate branch of The Wells Fargo Bank as indicated on the information sheet and waited until a department store opened where he could find make up that he could use on his face to indicate a slight birthmark.

After Craig studied all of the American documentation for one Curtis Smith, he entered the bank and with great apprehension asked to see the manager. He told the officious secretary that it was a private matter and he could wait if necessary. He picked up the paper and tried not to read it.

Shortly, he was shown into the manager's office.

"My name is Curtis Smith." Craig handed Smith's fake passport, driver's license and a credit card over to the young man whose name plate read Aliotto. "I believe you're holding a certified check for me. I would like to pick it up, please."

"Of course," said Aliotto.

Craig watched Aliotto's reaction as he examined the identification material. Craig knew that all a bank needed was to authenticate this identity and then they would P.U.I.P. Pay upon proper identification. He hoped that with the sizable amount of the check some specific stipulations on the part of somebody as to how it was to be handled wasn't any different.

"Yes. Of course. Mr. Smith, the *Wall Street Journal* is there on the end table if you like. I'll be right back."

"Thank you, I've already read it," lied Craig.

With that the blue-suited young man left Craig alone in the room to wonder what was going to happen next.

Aliotto soon reappeared with an envelope. "I believe this is what you are looking for."

Inside the envelope Craig found a certified check for one million dollar made payable to Curtis E. Smith with the remitter shown as Wells Fargo Bank. No other information on the check gave him a clue as to where the money originally came from.

"Where do you want me to sign for this?"

Aliotto shoved a form across his desk and pointed to the signature line. Craig copied the signature of Curtis Smith as best he could. He realized in Room Three that someone had tried to make all of the signatures on the fake documents as close to Kurt Schmidt's scrawl as they could. Craig thought, *By the time this is over, I may not know who I am, but I'll certainly know how to forge a name.*

Aliotto was glancing at a memo on his desk. Whatever had just happened was either of little interest to him, or was common. Craig didn't detect for one moment that the bank manager was measuring him, would immediately call someone, or that what he had just done was unusual.

Craig thanked him and left. He thought, *The checks exist!*

He walked down the street into the headquarters of Bank of America, easily identified by the Black Heart sculpture, and once again introduced himself as Mr. Smith to a pleasant woman at her desk in the dark lobby. Craig outlined his request for a wire transfer of a certified check to an account of his in New York when he suddenly realized that his plan wouldn't work. He couldn't wire funds to an account of a dead man. Craig Carlson's accounts would soon be closed. Thank God he hadn't yet told her that name!

He cleared his throat. "Let's change those instructions."

The woman looked up over her glasses. Her gray hair was tied in a bun behind her head and she wore eight or nine strands of heavy beads that disappeared out-of-sight behind the top of the desk. She was ample and old.

Craig thought, *Probably a teller who stood on her legs until the bank took pity on her veins and finally gave her a desk.*

"There are changes?"

"Yes, please. I have to look up a different account number Just give me a moment."

Craig's mind was tumbling. He opened the officious-looking black leather book that he was carrying and turned pages slowly, trying desperately to think. *Now that I have the money, where do I send it?*

He had to make a decision, but his thinking was dulled by his exhaustion. There was only one person he could send it to, Alan. But how not to alert Alan as to the fact that something was really unbelievable. Monaco, of course! It would take Alan weeks to find out about activity in his private account there. Craig now knew what to look for.

"Ah. Yes. Here it is. Sorry for taking the time."

"Mr. Smith, take all the time you want," suddenly smiled the woman. "It's nice to rest my eyes on a face as handsome as yours. You remind me of somebody."

Craig was startled. Of course, his picture was on the front of the *Los Angeles Times* when he picked it up at the truck stop before he left and he was sure the *San Francisco Chronicle* would be displaying a similar spread. *God! I've forgotten. I'm a walking dead man whom everyone knows. I've got to get with this charade or I'll be out of commission one way or the other in a hurry.*

"Oh. Thank you. Here's the information you need. Please wire transfer this money today to a Mr. Alan Gavin in Monaco. Here is the number of the account, and I have the routing information right here. I'll try and be as helpful as I can."

By the time Gertrude in the gray bun had finished with him Craig was sweating profusely. She had raised her eyes when she saw the amount. And to Monaco of all places. She simply didn't understand. "Why didn't you just wire it from Wells Fargo? Why are you using the Bank of America to do it?"

Craig finally said, "It's a gambling debt I'm trying desperately to hide."

Gertrude seemingly had to have help from everyone in the bank, and all Craig could do was hold his hands up in front of his face, wishing Kurt's sunglasses weren't in the car. Finally, it was over. Alan Gavin would soon be a million dollars richer.

Craig all but ran out of the bank. He had hoped to rent a hotel room somewhere and rest, but it no longer fit his schedule. He had a lot to do before he had achieved step two of his plan: Get out of the country. But now there was another step. He had to alter his appearance so that he didn't look too much like either Schmidt or Carlson, yet still be able to fit the passport of whatever alias he used.

Craig had never played a part quite like this before. His freedom wasn't as easy as he had first thought it would be.

*   *   *   *

At a department store, Craig purchased a pair of large dark sunglasses, a hat he could pull down around his head, and a couple of silk scarfs he could throw around his neck. At a cosmetics counter he picked up various items he had used all his life which he knew could quickly add or remove age including a masque Craig knew drew so hard that if left on too long would wrinkle his skin. But, he was willing to use anything that would temporarily alter the appearance of the handsome Craig Carlson with the high cheekbones and smooth dark skin.

In the men's room at a busy restaurant, Craig doctored his face. At a travel agency, he paid three thousand dollars in cash for a one-way ticket for Hong Kong under the name of a British subject, Charles Silvey. He was careful not to leave any form of plastic trail under any name.

He glanced at Kurt's watch and was shocked to see how late it had become. Craig had selected Hong Kong for two reasons. Another certified check for a million dollars was waiting for Silvey at the Bank of China, and the one o'clock United flight was the earliest he could get out of the country to someplace where he didn't think they would recognize him quite as easily. He was sure whoever was responsible for the attempt on his life would still be looking for Kurt Schmidt in Los Angeles, and according to what Craig had read in Schmidt's documents, he believed that Beretta had cleverly tried to lead Schmidt into making Lloyds of London his first pick up. Only there was the money left in Schmidt's own name.

On the way to Fisherman's Wharf the rental car phone rang. Without thinking, Craig started to answer, but he stopped and thought, *What if someone is trying to locate this car? Kurt Schmidt should have left LAX for someplace by now.*

He shuddered at a possible near mistake. Craig was almost certain that Beretta was the money man behind Roz, and if so, could have easily set up tight webs at LAX and at London Heathrow to see exactly where Schmidt had gone. He was anything but relaxed and free. As he speculated more about

Beretta, his fears escalated. Maybe Beretta wanted to know where he was for another reason? Maybe Beretta and Roz had planned to double-cross Schmidt and terminate him from the beginning! That would certainly fit Roz's type of scheme.

Craig realized he wasn't just playing a part in a movie. He was a fugitive.

At the wharf, he mixed with the tourist crowds, then, while casually looking at the fishing boats, threw Schmidt's gun into the dark, polluted water under the pier with the rest of the trash. He was relieved to have that evidence out of his possession.

Craig drove to SFO and left the car in long-term parking, not with Hertz. At the terminal, he pitched the keys into a trash can and hurried to the international departure area just in time to clear customs with his black bag and Schmidt's brown one. Inside, he picked up a copy of the *San Francisco Chronicle* and *USA Today*. He would have plenty of time to read on the plane, it was a fifteen hour, non-stop flight that didn't get to Hong Kong until Wednesday evening at eight.

It wasn't until United 805 was off the ground that Craig Carlson began to relax. He decided he would read the newspapers later. He ordered a triple scotch, no rocks, and after killing the drink with one gulp he fell asleep. It had been the longest thirty hours in his life.

He tried not to think of where he was or what he had done and suddenly realized that he had been so busy he hadn't even thought of Alan. *My God! How does he feel about all this?*

But Craig's time was not inundated with other thoughts or memories. Fatigue won out. Carlson, Papagos, Schmidt, Smith, and Silvey were all asleep in the same seat as the big plane began its long journey over the Pacific.

Four

Tuesday, Los Angeles, California

Victor Packard was uneasy and unsure of what had happened. Washburne's garbled call at three in the morning had awakened him from a deep sleep. All he was sure of was that he had to finish packing and get his ass on an early flight to California. He had represented Craig Carlson through several very involved legal proceedings for over thirty years, and Packard, as Craig's sole executor, knew this one with Roz would be explosive.

Craig's death changed everything. Just what Craig didn't want to happen was about to. Except for his son, Andrew, Roz would inherit most of his large estate, and Alan and a few others, only an insignificant portion.

Victor Packard and Constantine Papagos first met on the football field during an intramural game between the Sigma Chis and the Betas. Papagos, a Sig, excelled because of his wiry, muscular frame and height. As he ran, he had an uncanny ability to twist, turn, and leap almost like a dancer, eluding even the most skilled defensive player.

Packard, who was a Beta, excelled because of his brute size. He was a force to be reckoned with. If he stuck out one arm or one leg, his opponent was stopped. If he accidentally collided with an unfortunate runner, his opponent was replaced with someone else. He was mean and big. Many misjudged his size to mean he wasn't bright. That was a mistake. He was in the top five percent of his class, and he looked forward to Chicago Law School as a challenge.

The Sigma Chis were ahead because of Constantine Papagos' running ability. The Betas decided to give Packard the job of permanently stopping Papagos. What followed was a series of near misses, complete misses, and finally one big hit. Even though the game was supposed to be the simple removal of two tags to stop the play, and nothing further, Packard's body block was planned and substantial. They carried Papagos off the field.

46

Packard felt it was his duty to call on Papagos in the University Hospital to see if he could apologize in any manner for his broken leg and four broken ribs. The propriety of the call soon changed from cool and polite to warm and attentive. It seemed that Packard's acute interest in the geopolitics of World War II and specifically in how Italy messed up Hitler's timetable because of their incompetence in the Mediterranean was of specific interest to Constantine. He particularly liked Packard's discussion of how the Greeks decisively defeated the Italians at the Battle of Koritza and threw them out before the Germans finally had to come to the Italians' rescue months later with their vicious invasion of the Greek archipelago and strategic capture of Crete by glider. They had a common World War II interest.

By the time the visit was over, it was Connie and Victor, and they found many other areas of interest, including theater. They agreed to see each other again, and a real friendship developed. Packard had been ignored because of his size and Papagos somewhat outcast because of his heritage. Even after Connie left Northwestern to study acting at Juilliard in New York and Victor moved on to Chicago Law, Packard made sure they kept in touch.

Washburne was waiting for Packard when his plane landed.

As soon as they were inside the limo, Packard ordered, "Tell me again what you told me last night and don't leave out any details." It had been a short night, and Packard had relied heavily on alcohol on the plane to keep him stimulated.

Gregory carefully described the evening up to the point where the police took possession of the documents. Then Gregory told Packard that Roz was the one who had not only approved but insisted that the few legal documents found on a table in Craig's sitting room be released. When he had suggested calling Packard for his approval, Roz had become quite agitated and insisted that Packard not be bothered. "So, I turned them over," he said cautiously.

Packard leaned forward with intensity. "And?"

"That's why I called you so early." Gregory rushed his words. "I called you as soon as I got home. Here's the police receipt for them."

Packard exploded. "The what?"

"I didn't think I had any choice; Roz was Craig's wife."

"You didn't think at all," Packard snarled. He grabbed the receipt out of Washburne's hand and gave it to the driver. "Go to this address at once."

The scene at the police station was quintessential Packard. The woman in the legal department in charge of impounded documents at that station was lucky she had had her coffee when she arrived at work that morning. She had a great deal of work stacked ahead of what had come in that night, but she knew that the Carlson murder would be top priority. She had already copied all of the documentation, and the property could be returned to whoever would sign for it as a vested party. She further explained that they had to hold on to several pages because there was blood on them, but copies of those pages were in the packet.

Once the documents were in Packard's hands, he and Washburne left for the office. Packard ceased all conversation, looking through the documents like a computer scanner.

Gregory was trying desperately to think of a defense for his actions. He didn't have a good one. He sounded too ridiculously stupid, and knew he had made one hell of a mistake.

Packard slammed the packet shut. "Jesus!"

The limousine driver was startled by the outburst.

"Craig Carlson has already executed his new will!"

"I thought that's what the two of you were going to discuss Wednesday before Craig did anything," Gregory said meekly.

"That's what I thought," growled Packard. He fixed Washburne with his dark, deep-set eyes. "We have one hell of a mess on our hands. How far are we from the office?"

"Ten minutes."

"Washburne, tell me how Roz knew that Craig was about to change his will. And after you finish that tall story, tell me why there are blind copies shown to Gavin on correspondence from me to you that I never sent to Gavin." Packard folded his arms across his ample chest and glared over his reading glasses. Packard knew his accusation was a gamble, but there had to be on hell of an extraneous force for Washburne to alter Packard's correspondence.

Gregory Washburne turned beet red. About ten days earlier, he had gotten very high with Roz and told her he knew a secret. After he told her of the upcoming change in Craig's will, she quit playing and threw him out. Later, Roz asked him to tell her all he could about it. It was after that she asked him to blind copy Packard's letters showing Alan as a recipient. Now he had to answer to Packard.

"I thought Roz should know," he said weakly.

"You thought?" Packard shouted. "Didn't they tell you about client privilege at Stanford?"

Gregory started to say something, but nothing came out.

"And to show copies to Gavin. Did you send him copies?"

"No, sir. I did not."

"Oh, great. What a relief. The police think I did!"

The limousine driver pulled into a parking lot as Packard snapped a paper into Washburne's lap.

"Those answers are so incredible and dumb. See if you can now tell me why Craig Carlson would ever send this kind of a fax to Alan Gavin!"

The car had come to a stop, and Packard could tell that the driver was trying to listen. "Get out of the car and wait for us outside," he ordered.

Gregory read the fax that Packard thrust into his hand. *"Alan, I signed a new will today, Friday. I hope this will make you happy and that you will now get off my back about money. You get so much, there will never be a need for palimony. I am faxing this to you so it's in writing and we don't get into a verbal argument about it. We can talk about details when I get home Thursday."* It was initialed CC.

Gregory read it again. He hadn't forgotten Roz's unusual interest in those papers on Monday night.

"How many times have you poked Roz Marlowe?"

Gregory's back stiffened.

"Is she that good a lay?"

"I like her." Gregory felt protective. "She's in a difficult position with Craig. She has to get her sex someplace."

"Oh! I see. Your dick becomes the great provider." Packard shuffled his substantial frame forward in the seat.

"So Roz thinks the will would have been signed tomorrow, Craig actually signed it on Saturday, and that fax indicates that Gavin supposedly received information from Carlson that a new will had been signed last Friday. Jesus!"

Packard slapped the files on his lap. "Gavin doesn't have a clue about being the heir to anything, and the police have the perfect motive for the man who found the body to be the one who murdered Carlson."

Gregory's breathing was now short and shallow.

"Great going, Washburne! Medal of Honor. A real hell of a case. You created the crap here. You tell Roz she's out of the will. You tell Gavin he's going to be the prime suspect. You tell the police Roz let you screw her then, in payment, talked you into this blind copy shit. Then just watch the California bar first explode and then throw you out. Your lack of judgment and legal acumen has answered all of my other questions. Just let me guess who the hell really authored that fax that was possibly never sent." Packard lunged out of the car.

Gregory helplessly followed Packard into their office suite. It had been one hell of a twenty-four hours. He was exhausted.

*   *   *   *

Roz awakened with a start. The morning light was blinding. Simia had opened the drapes and all of the windows while Roz was still sleeping.

"What the hell?" moaned Roz. She shielded her eyes and tried to make out who was there in the bright light.

Simia kept moving. She picked up a discarded pair of stockings and disappeared into the bathroom.

Roz tried to find the clock on her cluttered nightstand. Someone was knocking on her door, and it was only ten.

"Mrs. Marlowe?" Another knock. "I know it's early. But we must speak." It was Anne, Roz's personal secretary.

"Damn." Roz looked for a robe. She was amazed to see she still had on the expensive ensemble she had worn last night. "Shit!"

Roz groped her way out of bed, her head splitting. She stopped on her side of the door, told Anne it would be a couple of minutes, and wobbled into the bathroom. The shower was running, but Simia wasn't in sight. She looked at herself in the mirror. Her eyeliner, rouge, and powder were gone, but her mascara made her look as if she had two black eyes. "Jesus, I look worse than Sadie ever did. What a mess!"

Roz hurried into the shower and slowly the dullness disappeared, to be replaced by a frightened awareness. She knew she had to be smart. Alert, not confused. Hurt, not triumphant. She toweled off, wrapped a towel around her head, and put on a terry cloth robe; as she was returning to the bedroom, she saw a vase of beautiful white roses on her vanity.

Roz thought, *Oh, how nice. I bet they're from the Academy.*

She plucked the card off the spindle, squinted her eyes, and read the message: "You won, Roz. Congratulations. Craig."

"Oh, my God!" she cried. "Why these? Why now?" Roz was terrified. Simia appeared and handed her a note: "Came from florist this morning. Sure you would want to see them."

Roz was so shaken, she rushed out of the bathroom, then remembered Anne. It took Roz a few moments before she was composed enough to talk to anybody. But she knew she had to be tough. She put on a pair of big, dark glasses and stepped outside her safe haven.

"Yes," Roz said. She was still shaking.

Anne was waiting in the pleasant alcove at the end of the hall. A small table and two chairs were comfortably situated in front of a large window with a favorable view. Roz used it often to meet briefly with her staff, and then would disappear again behind the security provided by the door to her quarters.

Anne pointed to the tray with the fresh coffee and juice and waited for Roz to sit down.

"What is it?" Roz asked, drinking her juice and trying hard not to seem so hungover. "Oh, Anne, please sit down." Good.

She felt in control again.

"The police..." Anne looked down at her hands. "I'm so sorry about Mr. Carlson." She collected herself. "The police need you to identify—the—body—today."

Roz overcame the throbbing in her head and remembered her grief. She tried to cry but failed. "The police? Oh, Anne, it was so awful." She held out her hand for Anne to console her. "How could they ask so soon? They were just here."

"And there are hundreds of messages. The phones won't stop ringing. Some with congratulations, from those who know about the Oscar. Others with condolences, from those who know about Craig. And others who simply don't know what to say other than that they called to say they were thinking about you—and Craig. We are logging them all in and trying to give them as consistent a story as we can. But the police call is one you can't overlook. It's the third time."

Roz gulped her coffee. She realized she was tired and hungry. She wanted to go back to bed and cover up, and make it all go away—like she used to when she was a little girl in Lancaster, Ohio, after she had just been punished by her father. But later, in her way, Roz always got even with him.

This is a morning of victory, not defeat, Roz thought. Real tears ran down her cheeks. *What did I do and why did I do it?*

"Anne, let me dress in something presentable, and I'll come down for breakfast. I'll take the call in the breakfast room in about an hour." Roz turned to leave and then remembered the roses. "And Anne, call the florist and see when Mr. Carlson ordered a dozen white roses for me."

Roz returned to her room to prepare. Once inside, she tried to release some anxiety. "Okay, Roz, you planned this. Now you figure out how to play the day."

And there Simia stood at the foot of Roz's bed—as usual not making a sound, but evaluating all.

"Where the hell were you last night, Simia?"

Simia pointed to the front of the house and made the sleep signal for Roz.

Roz narrowed her eyes; without her contacts, she didn't see well, but it was impossible to miss Simia's swollen face, red eyes, and uncombed hair. Simia was defiantly wearing her native sarong, which long ago had been forbidden.

Roz turned to her closet. "Now, what should I wear?"

Simia started to cry and hurried out of the room.

*   *   *   *

In the breakfast room, Anne handed Roz the phone.

"I'm Inspector Roosevelt. Remember me, Mrs. Marlowe?"

"Yes, I do," Roz said absently. "What can I help you with?" Roz was in her bright breakfast room looking at the front page of the *Los Angeles Times*, devouring an English muffin, and washing it down with hot, black coffee. If she had ever wanted publicity, she had it this morning. Her Oscar and Craig's death had made the front page of the paper, with what she felt were appropriate pictures of each. The coverage of both looked extensive. She could hardly wait to read it all and hear it all on television.

"The morgue wants us to pick you up so you can identify the body immediately."

"Why? Didn't you all see it was Craig?" The request shocked her. It was something she didn't want to do. She hadn't seen Craig dead. She had left him alive.

"Didn't Alan Gavin identify him as Craig?"

"Yes, however, we need a spouse's identification before . . ." Roosevelt cleared his throat. "Before we do some work on him."

Roz covered the mouthpiece on the phone. "Anne."

Anne appeared from the side room.

"Are there many out front?"

"Everybody is there. All the media."

"Mr. Roosevelt, pick me up at the front entrance in thirty minutes." Roz hung up.

Anne said, "Mrs. Marlowe, everyone connected with the house has been using the back entrance. The police have it well controlled."

"Well, I'm going out the front." Roz left the dining room and started down the long marble hall. She knew Anne was horrified. Roz shouted back at her frightened secretary, "I want them to know my loss! And don't forget to find out when Craig ordered those damn white roses."

Roz stalked up the elegant mahogany staircase that was further accented with a rare Oriental runner, each tread fastened securely in place by small brass rods. At the landing, Roz hesitated, then forced herself to look up for the first time since last night at Craig's wing. A uniformed policeman was on duty and the door to his sitting room was closed.

The policeman looked down at her, but said nothing.

Roz wondered if he heard what she said to Anne. She sobbed dramatically, turned away, and continued up her stairs. She had just enough time to touch up her makeup and change her dress.

*   *   *   *

Simia was looking out the window when Roz entered her room.

"So, any messages?" challenged Roz.

Simia shook her head.

"Help me get dressed for the morgue, and while I'm gone, pitch those damn roses and take off that damn sarong!"

Roz had a private line, but she had always despised electronic devices. Hers rang only in the bedroom of her expansive suite, and the calls were stored by a simple recording machine. She had trained Simia to screen them for her. Simia would listen to the full message and then simply write for Roz the time, the caller, the phone number, and whether it was urgent or not. Nothing as to what they wanted. Roz would decide if she would return the call—and if so, at a time convenient to her, not the caller. Roz had become a master of playing the Hollywood power game.

What Roz didn't know was that Simia, after carefully taking down the entire message and editing it for Roz as requested, saved the entire message in a phone journal she kept upstairs in her room. Simia added that data on a daily basis to newspaper articles, about Roz or Craig, photos that Roz or Craig had discarded, a list of those who attended parties, a careful log of who came and who went and at what time, a log of where they went and with whom, and other matters of possible interest. Simia had also listed all those whom Roz had chosen to entertain in her bedroom.

Mikey Marlowe was the one who started her doing this for him. He wanted an archivist to capture all of his triumphs and disasters. He truly loved Simia. And she knew how to express love without words—by touch, by look, by romantic overtures, by flowers and fragrances. She was more than a mistress for him, she was a spirit and a confidant. He knew that she wasn't dumb because she couldn't talk. He recognized that she was smarter and more observant than most for that very reason. He felt she would be the perfect one to keep a record of his career.

And she was.

After he died, Simia simply transferred that function to Roz and then added Craig. Simia had never mentioned it to any of them, but saw nothing wrong. It had become a way for her to entertain herself and feel of value, night after night after she returned to her small quarters above to wait until Roz demanded her next service.

It was Simia's sole job to keep Roz's extensive chambers clean, fresh with flowers, and to supply whatever else Roz demanded. Simia knew that as far as Roz was concerned, she didn't exist. But as she grew to love and appreciate Craig and Alan, she persevered. Where else would a Polynesian mute find a full-time job? Now everthing was different, strange. Grief didn't explain it all. With Craig gone, something else had taken his place, and whatever that was terrified Simia.

*　　*　　*　　*

As Roz stepped out onto the front porch, she was disappointed to see that the police had cordoned off the front lawn and moved everyone back to the street. This didn't stop the press.

Once they caught a glimpse of her, they rushed the house.

She was now dressed in a conservative black suit, a pillbox hat with a black lace veil, gloves, and dark glasses.

Roz had memorized and was ready to deliver her first statement regarding Craig's death. "I'm not sure how my life can continue without Craig, but for my faithful public I will go on."

Inspector Roosevelt opened the door of the car for her and told her to get in. He was disgusted. On the way down the street the cameramen and television crews were struggling for footage, but Roosevelt told Roz to keep her window up.

This made her mad. No one got in the way of Roz Marlowe.

*　　*　　*　　*

The morgue took only a few moments.

Roz gasped in surprise when she saw Craig's mangled face. "He looks awful. Why would he do a thing like that?"

She turned her head aside.

"No one knows why anybody kills so easily," said the mortician.

Roosevelt asked, "Is this your husband, Craig Carlson?"

"Yes, it is." Roz looked again. "I'm sure."

"His service will have to be with a closed coffin, Mrs. Marlowe," intoned the mortician.

"I want him cremated as soon as possible," Roz responded.

"In California, that's tomorrow," said the mortician.

"Then do it," said Roz.

"It requires your signature," said the mortician.

"Then arrange it," said Roz. She walked out the door totally confused. She felt pain.

*　　*　　*　　*

Outside, Roosevelt asked, "When are the memorial services?"

"That's my business," Roz snapped. "I'll have them later in

the week. I haven't thought that far yet. But he can be cremated now."

She turned and glared at the inspector. "I hope you've enjoyed the morning. This has been hell for me."

Inspector Roosevelt said nothing. He noted that for someone seeing her husband dead for the first time, she hadn't called him by his first name, cried, or even needed a tissue. Roosevelt also noted that Roz referred to the murderer as "he."

They returned in complete silence to the Marlowe estate.

"Better start planning that service, Mrs. Marlowe. Lots of people are asking lots of questions."

The car they had taken used the back driveway. Without a word, Roz slammed the door and marched into her house. She didn't understand why Schmidt had to smash the hell out of Craig's face. It didn't make any sense to her at all. She wondered how far Schmidt had gotten. If Antonio Beretta hadn't called, she was going to have to call him. There were some questions that needed answering.

Anne was waiting for her with a clipboard and a long list of names of those who no longer could be ignored. They had to be called. Roz saw that Beretta wasn't on the list.

But Victor Packard was.

*   *   *   *

Alan had just finished talking to his mother in Monaco. She had heard the news and felt terrible for her son. She told him that she had made arrangements to fly to Paris on Wednesday morning and would continue to Los Angeles on Air France, and would hopefully arrive at about five Wednesday afternoon.

Alan had asked how his father had reacted. His mother told him she would discuss that with him in California. Alan very much appreciated her coming. Other than Craig, his parents were the only family he had. His sisters had little to do with him.

Alan was so depressed that he had trouble even getting out of bed. He had many phone calls from friends showing shock, concern, and support, but he had even more from people he didn't know, asking intimidating questions. And the calls from the media were endless and annoying. He was sure the press was responsible for giving out their unlisted number.

Even Chin Lee had irritated him by being oversolicitous one minute and crying like a baby the next.

Inspector Roosevelt had called, asking when it would be convenient to talk to him on Wednesday in Los Angeles. Alan figured he would drive up, meet with him, and then pick up his mother at the airport, and they could stay at—someplace nice. He set a mid-afternoon appointment with Roosevelt.

Alan now realized that with Craig dead, he would soon be without a job and without a residence. There was so much for him to understand. His life would be forever different.

The phone again interrupted his thoughts.

"Alan, I love you. I've just heard, and I know where you must be emotionally. You need a friend, and I'm it."

Alan puzzled only briefly about the voice. "Savannah?"

"Yes. I'm calling from London. I'm due for a curtain call, but I just saw it in the press. I'm devastated for both of you. What a loss. What a shame."

Alan smiled for the first time in hours. "Savannah, you have no idea what this means to me. Thank you."

"I have a damned good idea what it means. I remember lots of things you're not even aware of. When my father, Mikey Marlowe, died and Roz was there to reign, I was a nothing. As a twelve-year-old, I could do nothing. I was told to shut up and disappear. My father had died, and suddenly I was nothing. Only Simia remembered that I was his daughter. I buried myself in her bosom. We were like sisters. Mikey had just started us both taking lessons in signing, and we reveled in talking about Roz in front of her. It made her furious because she didn't know what we were saying. How is Simia? Is she still serving the Wicked Witch of the West?"

Alan didn't rise to Savannah's attempt at humor. "Savannah! If you only knew what it was like last night."

"But, my dear Alan, I do know. I'm the one who found my father. All strung out from drugs. Looking like a piece of dried meat. Then to hear nothing but unkind accusations about a gifted musician who, before he was dead, had been world-famous."

"Savannah, you never told me."

"No one ever wanted to listen." Savannah had to clear her throat. "Darling, I have to go. I'm due on stage in three—no, two—minutes. *Me and My Girl* is doing wonderfully well—so well that I'm leaving it tomorrow and flying to Los Angeles Thursday to hold you in my arms and watch Roz retch at my sight during the memorial service."

Alan finally laughed. It felt good. It helped.

"Alan, I love you. I'm thinking about you. You're young. Your life's not over. Remember that now. Remember that tomorrow. And also remember I'm now Lady Ashley. Ciao!"

As quickly as she was there, she was gone. Savannah Marlowe. Mikey's firstborn. She had survived the Roz/Mikey marriage, but four years of Roz without her father was enough. Juliette Savannah Marlowe just took off. She had hated her stepmother with a venomous passion for almost twenty years.

Alan knew he would survive. But how he missed Craig. Everything in the house seemed to await his return. Alan had to get his things together and get away from that memory.

But why? To go where?

Somehow he had to find out what the arrangements were going to be. He had no say in them. None. They weren't married. Craig was legally married to Roz. But Craig and Alan's life together had been wonderful. Much better than most marriages recognized by the courts in the world as "legitimate." Not deviant. Not wrong. Wonderful. So many special times together. So many laughs. So many warm and tender moments. So many achievements. A companionship of deep trust and love.

Alan shook his head, trying to clear it and shake his melancholy recall. He wondered who could tell him about the memorial service. His mother and Savannah would need to know. *He needed to know.*

He was glad they were both coming to be with him.

Five

Wednesday, Bel Air, California

Roz tried twice on late Tuesday to get through to Antonio Beretta at the Trojan Horse Casino in Las Vegas. He was not in or, more likely, not taking her calls. Her last message to his secretary was "Tell him if he wants to stay out of real trouble, give Roz Marlowe a call."

Now it was ten Wednesday morning, and still no call. She had already checked twice with Simia to see if the machine had any messages. It didn't. Tired of waiting, Roz dialed Beretta on her private line. This time, his secretary found him in.

"Tony, why haven't you called? I thought an Oscar would have deserved some congratulations," pouted Roz.

"Congrats. What about your dead husband?"

"Oh. That was terrible. Did you read about it?"

"In Vegas? Yeah, we read." Tony lowered his voice slightly. "How bad off was he? It said his face got messed."

"That wasn't sup—" Roz stopped. "That wasn't a nice thing to see." Roz shuddered. She meant it.

"I'm sure the whole thing must have torn you apart," he said sarcastically.

"It's been over a week since Big Bear Lake. I miss you. Why didn't you call?"

"Remember—we were going to cool it."

Roz lost it. "Bullshit! Our meetings and phone calls have gone on for years. Who would give a damn about another call?"

"You'd be surprised. You have my deepest congratulations and condolences. Later, baby."

Roz slammed down the phone; he had already hung up. "You can't treat me like that, you bastard!"

There was a knock on the door. "Yes!" Roz shouted.

"It's Anne. I have some things for you to go over."

Roz looked around the room, everything was in order. She could hear Simia cleaning up in the bathroom. Roz was pleased Simia was back to wearing her white, starched uniform.

"Come in, Anne." Roz tried to look bereaved.

"These are the arrangements for the memorial services on Friday morning. See if there's anything else you want."

Roz scanned the paper. "Do you know yet which of my three children are coming?"

Anne uneasily cleared her throat. "Jebb Marlowe will arrive from Washington National at four today. We have a room at the Bel Air Hotel for him. Is that satisfactory?"

Roz thought of her only child with Mikey. Simia had raised him before Roz had sent him off to boarding schools. His contacts with Roz had been distant and polite. Hers with him had been bothersome and monetary. He had excelled at each school he attended and graduated early from Columbia. She tried to think where he was working now. Her best guess was an insurance company, but she wasn't sure. She was sure it was in D.C.

"Yes. Have my driver pick him up. Leave a note giving him the details, and tell him we'll have lunch here on Thursday."

"Andrew Carlson and his attorney will be arriving from Palm Beach at six."

"I haven't seen Andrew for a year. That was the last time he was out here to visit us." Roz thought how she, Craig, and Craig's mother, Ellen Traver Papagos, all had such a fight over the young boy. A settlement was agreed upon, and Andrew had gone to live with his grandma in Florida. Craig saw their son, Andrew, most of the time in Palm Beach.

His visits to his son also allowed Craig to check in on how his crippled but mentally alert mother was doing. Roz knew that Mrs. Papagos could no longer travel. And if she had come, there would have been a fight. Anne was the one to tell Mrs. Papagos of Craig's death and that he would be cremated.

Roz and Craig's mother hated each other.

"Why with an attorney?"

"Andrew is only twelve. He should travel with someone, and I'm sure that Mrs. Papagos felt an attorney was appropriate.

Won't Andrew receive something from his father's estate?"

"Sure, stock." Roz's answer was short of any sentiment.

"I have them at the Bel Air as well," said Anne.

"Who's paying for all these rooms?"

"I gave them your name, Mrs. Marlowe. Shall I send the car for them as well?"

"Sure. Go ahead. Who's next? My daughter, Dorothy Field, who never contacts me?" Roz ignored the look on Anne's face.

Roz thought about the Ohio University jock who got her pregnant while she was still in her senior year at Dennison. Roz's father didn't know she had bedded most of the athletic teams at Lancaster High School. To him, she was simply Patti Ann Warren, his lovely, talented daughter who was so popular and impossible for him to manage.

I've come a long way since I married Field, Roz thought.

The divorce was Roz's idea. Three years after they had moved to Indianapolis, which Roz unkindly called "India No Place," her husband had fallen in love with the insurance business and handball. Often he said he was too tired for sex, so Patti Warren Field branched out. The Junior League and the many activities of the performing arts kept her active, but not sexually satisfied. It didn't take her long to show her raw talent not only in the theater, but also to the older and wealthier donors who appreciated her abilities. Visiting directors of traveling shows and especially attractive leads also received the same considerations.

Roz remembered vividly the fight that had taken place after Don Field had returned from an extended insurance convention and found out that she had sneaked off to New York and had surgery done on her nose, cheeks, chin, and butt. He was livid. She was ready to move on. After a particularly violent argument, Roz left him and dragged Dorothy back to her parents in Lancaster. She then left Dorothy with them and headed for New York City to find her acting career. It didn't take her long to get involved with X-rated, off-Broadway productions.

When her father found her parading around the set of *Oh Calcutta!* completely naked, he decided that he no longer had a daughter. He severed any support, and Patti Ann found out how expensive it was to live in New York without help from home.

But Patti Ann Warren Field was never short on plans. Soon after that, she met Mikey Marlowe at a bash in the Village and quickly became part of his entourage.

Roz never reclaimed Dorothy and neither did Don Field. She became a grandparents' child. Roz hadn't heard from her for fifteen years, and all Roz knew was that Dorothy worked somewhere in the Midwest. It always bothered her to send money on Christmas to a Lancaster address and never receive a thank you or an acknowledgment. If it weren't for legal advice, she wouldn't send that. Roz felt her daughter was most unappreciative.

Roz's recall was broken by Anne.

"You have a couple of calls you should be aware of. Alan Gavin and Inspector Roosevelt. And please remember your twelve-thirty luncheon meeting with Victor Packard and Gregory Washburne at the Polo Lounge at the Beverly Hills Hotel."

Roz cringed. *Oh, why couldn't Anne say simple things like, Have a good day, here's a bottle of Dom—go get drunk, Beretta is at the front door with flowers, or the* Today *show called? Why was it always, The reporter is here, the police want you, the gardener has a question.*

"Oh, thank you, Anne. Your help means so much during this difficult time. These arrangements look fine. Just be sure the police have arranged lots of security. Even though we're calling it a private service, I'm sure there will be plenty of people along the way. There always are."

Roz heard a glass or something break in the bathroom and thought, *Simia's getting clumsy.*

As soon as Anne left, Roz returned Alan's call.

"This is Alan."

"Roz Marlowe. What do you want?"

"I'm going to be in Los Angeles this afternoon for other matters. Do you mind if I stop by and pick up some of the private pictures of Craig and me that are in his sitting room?"

Roz had to think fast. He had never had to ask permission before. Should she say, "No; don't ever show your face in this house again," or be nice? This was the day Craig would have changed his will in Alan's behalf. She thought for a moment of the glorious meeting she would soon have with Packard on that very subject, and quickly returned to Alan.

Roz said, "They're of interest to you, not to me. And Alan," Roz paused, thinking of how gracious she could now afford to be, "that most expensive painting of the little peasant girl by William Bouguereau that you and Craig purchased in London . . ." Roz felt this was the icing. She liked the idea.

"Yes?" There was hesitancy in Alan's response.

"You can have that, too. I know it means so much to you."

She knew he would be surprised. She wanted his thanks.

"I appreciate that, Roz. Very much." Alan's voice began to waver. "That was our last time in London together."

"I have to go now. I may not be here when you stop by. But of course, you still have your key." Roz laughed. She liked the way she handled Alan. She went to her closet to pick out what to wear for the Polo Lounge. A navy suit or a red dress? Roz sneaked a cigarette out of the silver case she had hidden in her bureau. She inhaled deeply and looked out the window. She liked the idea of light in the room. Roz could see her estate as it spread forth beneath her.

Simia quietly placed an ashtray and a note next to Roz, and left. She had overheard everything the entire morning. She knew Roz wouldn't need her for anything for a while. She went upstairs and started writing before she forgot any of the details.

Roz read Simia's note: *"Why not have your two sons stay in the two front suites? I'll see they don't bother you."*

Roz crumpled it into a wad. "You're too old to play nurse-maid." She pitched the note and stubbed out her cigarette.

*   *   *   *

Packard was wearing a conservative suit with a splashy tie. He had thought a lot about Washburne's unnerving revelations. He wasn't sure whether to tell Roz about the will change today or to wait until it was read after the memorial services on Friday. It was a tough call. If he didn't tell her, he was withholding. If he did, the state of affairs for all arriving to honor the memory of a fine man would be overshadowed by a Roz Marlowe hate scene that he had seen so many times.

If he played coy, he could find out all she had really found out from Washburne, and whether or not she was the likely author of the fax that was so incriminating for Gavin. Packard had considered canceling Washburne out of the meeting, but decided he would like to watch their interplay.

Packard made his decision. He would offer no real information regarding the will. He would let Roz's conversation take its course and react, inform, and stall as needed. "Breast your cards, Victor," he said.

He saw Roz, with one bodyguard, moving dramatically toward him as he waited in the lobby. She was wearing an appropriate dress for one in mourning, but showed no signs of grief. *That's the way she lived*, he thought. *For the moment and for the press.*

"Victor," Roz let him kiss her on the cheek, "you look dashing. Love your tie!" She looked around. "Where's Gregory?"

"He's at the table. I'm very sorry about Craig. It's an ugly tragedy. He was one of my best friends. I see, by the paper they still don't have any leads."

"I know," Roz answered with some shortness. "I'm famished. Shall we go in, or is there something you wanted to tell me without Gregory?" She looked at him inquisitively.

"No. There's little I have to tell you of which he's not already pretty much aware. Let's go on in."

They entered the dark, intimate Polo Lounge. Roz looked at each table to see who might notice her. Packard had chosen the restaurant for just that reason. He knew Roz would enjoy it.

Small talk was not something Packard was good at, but he curbed his usual impatience. He could tell from their body language that things between Roz and Washburne were strained. He saw from Roz's demeanor and her discussion that she believed she was still the major beneficiary. He decided he would let their mini-drama continue until after coffee, and then he would do some probing of his own.

Gregory asked Roz, "Have you had to see the police again?"

"I have a meeting with that Roosevelt after this. Has he asked you any more questions?" She raised her eyebrows.

"No. Not since Monday. Why would he want to talk to me?"

"I just wondered," she said.

Packard knew it was time. He cleared his throat, sat back, placed a thin briefcase on the table, and looked at Roz. "There are some things we need to discuss."

Packard could sense Washburne's immediate unease.

"Craig did not want me to read his will to anyone until after any memorial service for him. As a friend of long standing, I'm going to honor that request." Packard looked directly at Roz. "However, do you have any small questions you might want to ask about it now?" He noticed her sudden anxiousness.

"No. I don't think so. It's probably the same old legal Mickey Mouse it always was. I know that Craig from time to time wanted to change things, but I don't think the poor dear really got around to it," she said, without evident concern or remorse.

Packard saw the shock of disbelief on Washburne's face.

"Do you have a copy of his current will?" Packard asked.

"If it's about four years old, I do. If not, I don't."

Packard cleared his throat again, and became more formal. "Mrs. Marlowe, Craig changed things in his will constantly for tax purposes and, once in a while, for other reasons. It's a normal thing for a man worth millions to do. I doubt if you have the current copy." He unzipped the briefcase.

"Oh, I see." Roz frowned.

"Craig had me do some major redrafting." He peered over his reading glasses. "But that's moot now, isn't it?"

Roz said, "Yes. I guess it is." She smiled as she played with her cutlery.

"Roz, what do you know about his life-insurance program? Did he ever mention a multimillion-dollar insurance trust to you?" As he asked the question he watched Washburne. He saw the surprise on his face and guessed Washburne had never heard of that from Roz. *God*, he thought, *Washburne would make a ter-*

rible poker player or negotiator. What did they teach him in law school?

"I have a slight recall," shrugged Roz. "But he never discussed all his insurance and trust matters with me. He just discussed his personal property and real estate, and his stocks, and his royalties, and other little things like bank accounts."

Packard knew much of Roz's response was clever acting.

She continued, "I don't remember much about any singular big insurance trust that you're talking about. I do know he had lots of trusts, charities, and such. Craig gave a lot of his money away, too. While living. Does that answer your question?"

Packard had heard what he wanted. "Yes, I think it does. If he had made a pledge someplace, and he hadn't paid it off, then his estate would. That type of thing."

Packard believed that Roz Marlowe knew nothing of her husband's newly signed will. He zipped his briefcase closed and decided to cut to the chase.

"Do you have your own attorney, Mrs. Marlowe?"

"Yes. Many. But aren't you my attorney on this matter?"

"No. I'm not, Mrs. Marlowe. I'm Craig's attorney and the executor of his estate. I think that on Friday afternoon you should have an attorney with you at the reading of the will, so that he has a perspective of what is contained in it."

Roz looked confused. Then she looked at Gregory. "Do you understand all this? Couldn't you be my attorney?"

"No, Roz, I have a conflict of interest." He ran his hand through his curly hair. "I work for Mr. Packard's firm. You need to get Bernie Orwitz or John Solomon there for you. You know, attorneys whom you always use when you fight with the studios over royalties and with directors over contracts." Gregory suddenly stopped talking.

Packard was staring at him. *He couldn't believe that Washburne had used the word "fight." "Fight" meant adversarial positions.* Packard knew that would happen soon enough. That inference didn't have to be brought up at the table two days early. He believed Roz was sitting pretty and dumb until then.

"But they don't know a damn thing about wills, do they?"

Roz asked of Gregory. There was no smile, Roz was troubled.

Packard answered for him. "No. Not as much as an estate-planning attorney. But maybe one of those men Washburne mentioned practiced estate law before they became so specialized. May I suggest that one of them attend to represent your interests." Packard kept on going while he still had the guts. "But, Roz, I can't wear two hats. I represent Craig Carlson's document." He tapped his briefcase.

"I see." Roz scowled. "Gregory, sometime this evening, give me a call. We need to talk." She pushed her coffee cup away from her and precisely placed her napkin on the table.

"Sure, Roz." Gregory appeared ill at ease as he made a note.

Roz fidgeted in her chair, then looked around the room.

Packard knew that this was not the meeting she had expected. And now she didn't know what to expect.

Roz looked at her watch. "I'm so sorry, I must leave. I have to be at police headquarters." Her voice quivered slightly.

Roz stood up. "Thank you, gentlemen, for such an informative lunch. I did enjoy it so." Now she was mad.

Both Packard and Washburne stood.

She then focused her eyes sharply on Victor Packard. "And, Mr. Packard." Now she was seething, "Never call me Roz again. You seem to prefer Mrs. Marlowe when you have something official to say. So from now on, see that you use it!"

Packard had seen Roz Marlowe in action before when she was mad. He was thankful she left without hitting someone or something.

"You're an asshole, Washburne!"

"And you're a liar, Packard."

With that, the two attorneys left the room separately.

Neither one had paid. Packard disappeared into the bar, but the waiter caught Washburne in the lobby. "It's his bill," he fumed. "He's staying here. You'll just have to find Mr. Victor Fucking Packard to pay your tab."

*　　*　　*　　*

Inspector Roosevelt had had a bad enough day before Roz Marlowe arrived for their meeting. Then it got worse. After the first few minutes of questions he didn't know whether it was worth continuing or not. His early attempt at warm-up sympathy was useless. Her barrage of smartass answers, furious answers, and incomplete answers, with one or two fuck yous thrown in, had thrown him off course. He didn't know she had just stomped out of the Polo Lounge to be beset by a barrage of media pushing and shoving for a shot of the famous widow. She wasn't in the mood.

He thought, *She's mad as hell, anyway, so why not get a couple of real reactions.*

He held his breath and said, "You know, Mrs. Marlowe, you seem upset about everything, but not about your husband's death."

Roz looked caught off guard. She choked and said, "You don't think I'm upset because crying buckets of tears isn't my style. Of course I'm upset. Craig hasn't been my bed partner for years, but his perverted love for Alan Gavin never changed my love for him. I hope you find the man who killed him. Whoever that is ended my Craig's wonderful career."

Roosevelt got his reaction. Roz was furious that Craig was gay, and she once again had referred to the murderer as a man.

"Mrs. Marlowe, do you have any idea who might have wanted your husband dead?"

"No," she said, and placed her head in her hands.

"Did he fight with anybody?"

"Besides with me, yes. With Alan Gavin. They were constantly at each other's throats. Two men trying to live together behaving like two women. They fought over money. Money, money, money." Roz caught her breath. "I'm glad they didn't live under my roof. Being on the periphery of their fighting was enough!"

Inspector Roosevelt thought, *One more. All I need is one more, and it will be hardball.* "Who inherits the bulk of Mr. Carlson's money? I'm sure it's a big estate."

Blood rushed into her face. "I'm sure whatever Craig did was fair. I'm sure it wasn't all to his *significant other*. And anyway, I'm protected by California law." Roz didn't realize she had clenched her fists.

"Oh, there was that possibility?"

The color drained back out. Roz looked trapped; suddenly she stood. "I can't answer any more of these questions. I'm too upset," she said sarcastically. Roz picked up her purse, and, abandoning her act, left Inspector Roosevelt sitting alone.

Roosevelt had learned a lot in twenty minutes. And Gavin wouldn't be there until three-fifteen. That gave him time to think about what she had really revealed and what he was going to ask Craig Carlson's *significant other*. Roosevelt hated that term. He was not anti-gay. How could he be? He felt people had the right to live as they chose as long as they obeyed the law.

One thing he did know, the murder of Craig Carlson was turning out to be a very complicated matter.

*   *   *   *

Alan Gavin arrived early and Inspector Roosevelt was ready.

"Good afternoon, Mr. Gavin. I hope this is a better day for you." Inspector Roosevelt was bound and determined to be civil.

"Better, but not good," Alan answered.

"I know. I guess from what we've discovered, you and Mr. Carlson were not only business associates, but also lovers. It must have been a great shock for you to be the one to find him."

"It was. I didn't realize how quickly my life could change."

"I know. We see it all the time. Tragedy knows no financial, racial, or social boundaries."

"I've always risen above any negative occasion and, with a dash of extra humor and extra physical exertion have been able to overcome most obstacles. But this time I'm faced with a broken life. I guess my only choice is to return to Monaco, where I used to work, and try and put myself back together again. But there are such limited opportunities there."

Alan took a deep breath and rolled his shoulders back. "My

mother gets in this afternoon at five after leaving France at ten this morning. But there's a nine-hour time difference. That's a long flight for a woman of her age, or for anybody. Inspector, I hope you appreciate what her coming means to me."

Roosevelt nodded his head affirmatively and made a note.

"I've thought some about what to do, but I have no idea."

Inspector Roosevelt sat back in his chair. Alan Gavin was such a relief from Roz Marlowe. But he knew he had a job to do. He looked down at his ever-present pad and started his questions.

"I know we've been through all of this once, but let's go through it again." And with that, Roosevelt's endless stream of questions from Monday night were repeated, with new ones added.

"How did you say again you had cut your head?" Roosevelt could tell Gavin was embarrassed.

"On the toilet-paper holder. Pretty awkward, eh?"

"And you jarred the table out of place on the way?"

"Yes. It may seem clumsy now, but I was out of it."

"We've looked at the blood on your clothes. It matches Craig Carlson's, but I guess we knew that, didn't we." Roosevelt could tell Gavin was surprised by the question.

"Whose blood would it have been?" Alan asked with concern.

Roosevelt looked down at his pad, made a note, and continued with his questions. "What exactly did you do for Mr. Carlson?"

"At first I just performed the tasks of an administrative assistant and secretary. But as he grew to trust me, and as things developed between us, Craig turned over almost all of his personal affairs and financial responsibilities."

"So you would have had access to his will, trusts, and other such legal documents?" Roosevelt tapped his chin with his pen.

Roosevelt watched as a look of concern clouded Alan Gavin's earlier open face. For a long time, Alan said nothing.

Finally, Alan sat taller in his chair and spoke with more authority. "Just a minute, Inspector. I don't think I need to answer some of these questions you just asked without counsel.

In fact, I'll only talk about what I saw, and what I found on Monday night and nothing more."

Roosevelt said, "That's your call."

Alan's voice sharpened. "All of a sudden, I don't know where you're coming from. Your questions have changed. I found a dead man. I found my lover.

"What I did for Craig Carlson, or how I met him, or what we did, or what I did today, or yesterday, or the week before have nothing to do with finding him dead. I know you want to gather information to solve a murder. I appreciate that. But I'm not the one you're looking for. And I'm not going to just sit here and say something to you that someone later will twist around my neck and hang a noose over it, just so the LAPD has a suspect."

Inspector Roosevelt looked at Gavin with respect and understanding. "Okay. You do as you please. But we will get more information from you either with an attorney present, or by subpoena. We will get it. Unfortunately, we have an ugly crime to solve."

Inspector Roosevelt stood, respecting Gavin's wishes that the meeting was over. "Thank you for your cooperation." He extended his hand. "We will meet again. You should have plenty to of time to get to the airport."

Alan firmly shook his hand and left.

*　　*　　*　　*

From the car Alan called Gregory Washburne. After thanking him for the information regarding the memorial services he realized that he and Washburne really didn't know each other. Washburne was a Roz thing.

"You know, Greg, I'm a little concerned with the line of questioning the LAPD started to use on me this afternoon. Sooner or later, I'm going to need an attorney. And frankly, I don't really feel that your boss, Packard, likes me all that much."

Gregory Washburne interrupted Alan. "He doesn't like me all that much, either."

"What?"

"No. We had a hell of a fight after meeting with Roz this afternoon, and I wouldn't be surprised if I'm out of a job."

"Then maybe you could be my attorney," laughed Alan.

"Wouldn't that upset everyone's apple cart," said Washburne. "But, I'm too close to Packard. You'd never get a fair shake. There are some good attorneys I could recommend, once I think about it."

Gregory was thinking about several things he wished he had never done, and he rashly wanted to ask Alan if he had ever received a fax from Craig about his will. He knew he could be of real help to Alan Gavin, but he knew that by doing so, he would only incriminate himself.

*   *   *   *

Alan was shocked at his mother's appearance. She was sixty-five and had always moved at a fast pace to accomplish anything. She looked old and tired. When she saw him, she started to cry.

Alan embraced her and held her as tight as he could. "I know, Mother. It's been a long trip for both of us."

As they worked their way through the mobs of people at the International Terminal, they were only able to catch phrases from each other. The noise level didn't permit anything more.

He was glad that he had the limousine. Earlier in the day, he had wondered if he could afford it. With Craig, it would have been expected. But five o'clock was an awful time at LAX, and Alan knew that she would be exhausted and the traffic terrible.

On the way to the Beverly Hilton Hotel, Alan and his mother lapsed into an uncomfortable conversation. Neither was sure what the next few days had in store for either of them.

"How's Father?"

"In good health," his mother answered tactfully.

"And how does he feel about his son now? Does he have any feelings or concerns at all for what has happened?" Alan knew that his father, who was the minister of finance for Monaco, was considered by many, including himself, as a cold, unfeeling man.

His mother took his hand. "Your father has just gotten over your affair with Nicki and feels that was a quiet matter. He feels this will be an international public outrage."

Alan said nothing. His father was probably right about the current situation, but his affair with Nicki was twelve years ago. He had been with Craig ten years.

"We'll talk more about your father in the morning," she said.

As they fought the traffic, Alan thought back to Nicholas Patsiavos. In 1980, while on holiday in Greece, Alan had become sexually involved with him. After one wonderful week together, they set up a long-distance relationship. It became difficult, and Alan finally convinced Nicki to move to Monaco and live with him. To all concerned, they simply shared an apartment.

Nicki found employment as a florist, while Alan worked at his investment job for the royal family. Because Monaco lived off gambling and tourism and was the epicenter for famous play-boys and playgirls, the prince often required Alan do the social honors at night with many of their visiting dignitaries. Alan's good looks had earned him the reputation as one of the most desired. To keep Nicki with him, Alan involved him in escort work. It wasn't until Nicki came down with AIDS in 1983 that Alan found out that he was selling his services to visiting gay men. Nicki had become a hustler.

Alan took care of Nicki during a year of several exhausting battles with pulmonary pneumocystis. When they were no longer able to hide his illness or their relationship, his father was furious. After Nicki died in 1984, he and his family became paranoid that he would be next. To combat it, Alan fanatically began lifting weights, running, eating right, and resting as much as he could. He swore off alcohol and gay sex. Only on a rare occasion would he escort for the royal family. As time passed, his HIV tests stayed negative, he stayed healthy, and Alan relaxed a few of his self-imposed restrictions. Drinking and escorting were two of them. He enjoyed being around handsome men and pretty women.

Alan vividly recalled the night he was escorting a princess to a party onboard the Warner Brothers leased yacht at the 1986

Cannes Film Festival, when she insisted on meeting Craig Carlson. It was a night that . . .

"Alan, I think we're here," said his mother.

*   *   *   *

Later in their room at the hotel Alan asked his mother,
"What do you want to do about dinner?"

"I'm too tired. I just want to go to bed. I'm going to undress,
I'm sure they have a robe in the bath. Just have them leave my
luggage here." She looked around the small space.

Alan felt for his mother. What a trip she had taken to be at
his side. "You'll never know how much I appreciate this. I love
you very much."

"And I love you," she said.

Six

Wednesday, Hong Kong

The passport bearer Charles Silvey, also known as Craig Carlson, was tired. The fifteen-hour flight to Hong Kong was worse than ever. Even first class had been an endless endurance contest. After his complete collapse for the first four hours, Craig awoke to pulling pains in the corners of his eyes and mouth. The tight firming masque that he had used to add wrinkles to create aging was still in place and had to come off. Craig thought, *At this point of the flight, who cares what anyone looks like?* He was happy no one had recognized him.

He soaked his face as best he could in the small airplane sink, used the moisturizer from his perk-flight-kit, and returned to his seat. He jammed his hat back on, pulled it down over his head, and dragged the blanket back up to his face.

Eleven hours, two movies, three meals, and two naps later, the plane began its descent into the Hong Kong area. It was nearing eight o'clock at night. Craig observed that the emotional fuses of the passengers were either very short or very dead. A few looked out the windows at the twinkling lights, but most looked as if they were eternally glued to their seats.

During the flight, Craig had read more than once every column of the *Los Angeles Times* and the *San Francisco Chronicle*. The one item he couldn't stop reading was who found the body.

Alan Gavin.

He couldn't imagine the shock that he had caused his lover, and was glad to see that there weren't as many back-up columns on or photographs of Craig Carlson in the papers as there were of Roz Marlowe. But the papers had been waiting for a winning Best Actress and had the material ready to roll. One of the captions under a picture of Roz running down the aisle read, "And The Winner Is . . . "

Craig found it hard to believe that at that same moment she had most likely scheduled for Kurt Schmidt to murder him. But he was glad the papers weren't ready for him to become a homicide statistic the same night. He knew the extensive computerized data of his career was available to anyone who wanted it and that the next day's papers would have more than enough about his life.

Craig hoped there would be no more about Alan Gavin. He also hoped there would be nothing but a blip in the international issue of the *Herald Tribune,* which was widely circulated in Hong Kong.

As the plane made its final descent to Kai Tak, it began its normal sudden and erratic maneuvers to avoid the mountains and the skyscrapers, aiming to hit the runway and not the bay. The new safer and less convenient airport, Chep Lap Kok, wouldn't be open until 1998. It would certainly provide the passengers a calmer landing than the immediate drop, sharp bank, squealing wheels, hard reverse, and firm brake of Kai Tak.

Craig knew from his extensive travels that no other major airport in the world was as demanding. The mountainous terrain of the Kowloon Peninsula and the skyscrapers built right up to the tarmac of the landing strip were bad enough. But the long single runway that projected straight out into Victoria Harbor made it one hellish landing. Somewhere in the literature onboard, he had read that French engineers had built it in the fifties.

The weary passengers descended the tall, metal stairs to the waiting buses to be transported to the old, hot terminal. The greetings were first in English and then Chinese. Craig and Alan had been there once before, and he knew that he wouldn't have any difficulty communicating as far as language was concerned. That was another one of his several reasons for choosing Hong Kong as his second destination.

After customs, he was uncommitted. He had thought about where to stay. He was familiar with the Peninsula and the Regent, but for tonight Craig chose the Grand Hyatt, where he could get lost somewhere in their 572 rooms if they had one left.

He could always change tomorrow if he felt uncomfortable. With his meager possessions, his black bag, and Schmidt's brown one, he entered the lobby. Registering under the name of Charles Silvey, he was soon in a well-appointed room overlooking the vibrant lights of Hong Kong.

He stood in a hot shower for twenty minutes, left a wake-up call for ten, and collapsed on the comfortable bed.

*   *   *   *

Thursday, Hong Kong

"Good morning, Mr. Silvey. Welcome to Hong Kong. It is ten o'clock and ninety degrees," announced a pleasant voice.

Craig responded. "Wrong room." He hung up and rolled over. As he faded back into the gray, a tiny voice said, "Think again."

The telephone instantly rang a second time. "You left a wake-up call for ten, Mr. Silvey. I hate to disturb you, but I don't want you to miss getting up if you want to."

"Thank you. I was confused. I'm up." He rolled over and fought sleep, but exhaustion won.

When Craig did wake up, the clock showed twelve-thirty.

For the first time, he unpacked Kurt Schmidt's bag to see what his wardrobe would be like. Some of it would work; most of it wouldn't. The clothes were for a more northern climate than a city just a few degrees from the equator. Craig knew that he had to buy a wardrobe, and there was no better city in which to do it. But it would take cash, and he would have to arrange for more of that shortly; his original one-hundred-thousand dollars had dwindled.

At two in the afternoon, Charles Silvey, dressed in the finest he could piece together, stepped out of the Hyatt and headed for the Bank of China. Craig assumed the main office was at the ultramodern, soaring glass structure designed by I.M. Pei. At least that was the address on Schmidt's detailed instruction sheet. Craig hadn't let that priceless document get any farther away from him than his jacket pocket.

With two days' worth of stubble on his face, and a cosmetic birthmark on his right cheek, Craig believed he could pass again for his alias without difficulty.

Craig had been amazed when he and Alan visited the city five years ago at how bustling and modern, ancient and old, and Chinese and European it was. That same reaction hit him today as he sidestepped the unending flow of people. Hong Kong possessed an energy and a noise that not even New York had. Craig wondered how long it would take for all that to change, when mainland China made the changes they really had in mind.

After purchasing a cheap metallic briefcase with a locking device, Craig entered the Bank of China. He found the pickup just as easy as at Wells Fargo. The bankers were fast and efficient. The certified check was in dollars and could be converted into any currency Craig wanted. They seemed unconcerned with the transaction.

Craig chose the Hong Kong–Shanghai Banking Corporation as the institution for wiring eight-hundred-thousand dollars to Monaco. He took the two-hundred-thousand-dollar balance in cash. He knew that wherever he went, he would have difficulty renting an apartment, buying a car, or purchasing anything if he didn't have cash. Credit cards and checking accounts weren't available to a dead man who was on the run and trying to stay invisible.

The request for cash caused a few moments of excited conversation in Chinese, but the bank still fulfilled his request. Craig tried to act as if filling the briefcase with that amount of money was an everyday affair.

Craig knew ten thousand dollars was a most generous limit for most countries, and the greatest danger anywhere he went would be in smuggling the cash through customs. He would have to find a craftsman in the city who could make him a sturdy, oversized bag with hidden inner compartments in which to carry it.

Craig picked up a copy of the *Herald Tribune* and headed for a mid-afternoon lunch at Man Wah at the Mandarin Oriental Hotel. While sipping a Lillet, he read about himself. It was a shock to see he was to be cremated, and interesting to see how the paper played him as an international star. He had never really thought of himself that way, but Craig admitted he probably was.

Craig thought about Lloyd's of London in Sydney, the next nearest bank on the Schmidt list. But he concluded that maybe by the time he could get to Sydney, it wouldn't be safe. Surely, someone soon would be looking for Schmidt or his alias someplace other than Los Angeles. And the first thing he would do, if he were him, would be to check the banks to see if that couldn't tell him where Schmidt had gone. Craig knew that when that happened, it would become a more difficult game. In the States it was only midnight Wednesday; Craig believed that for now, it was too early for whoever that was to be sniffing too openly around the sting operation as far away as the Orient.

But Craig was damn near certain it was Beretta, and that he wanted him dead.

Craig was amazed at the timing of the contract murder; he wondered how Roz knew that his scheduled meeting with Packard was to change his major beneficiary to Alan. Someone, somehow, must have told her. But there was no way she could know he had executed it. Both Roz and Alan were in for a hell of a shock.

When the food came, Craig couldn't eat. Being alive while being dead wasn't easy. It was like a bad dream. Roz's grief was a cover for murder. He missed Alan. He missed Encinitas. He missed being able to speak to people. For the first time, he even admitted that he missed being recognized—which made him wonder about himself. In truth, did he, too, need public applause for his accomplishments? Someone to say, "You're an achiever?" Maybe he had something in common with Roz after all.

He paid the inflated bill and left.

Once on the street, he wondered if Charles Silvey shouldn't change hotels and names. Silvey didn't need to be at the Grand Hyatt anymore for the bank to check on, or call for some reason of verification.

His inner control told him, *Yes. Move on. It's safer.*

Craig decided his new wardrobe and custom luggage would have to wait until tomorrow. He took a small suite at the Island Shangri-La on Hong Kong Island under the name of Papagos.

Once in his room, he turned on the television to the internationally syndicated program, *Entertainment World*. It had a tiny segment of coverage on his death and on Roz Marlowe's win. But the slot was big enough for it to indicate that Roz Marlowe was holding up miraculously well, considering. Then the commentator cut to a brief picture of Alan Gavin at Los Angeles Airport, where he was seen getting into a limousine with an older woman. Craig was sure it was Alan's mother. *EW* left nothing to the imagination: "This is Alan Gavin, Craig Carlson's alleged gay lover."

Craig was stunned.

EW continued. "Tune in Thursday night when *Entertainment World* will air a special segment. It will cover Craig Carlson's career, his marriage to actress Roz Marlowe, and how he and Alan Gavin first met and then lived a life of secrecy."

Craig was furious. He turned off the television and picked up the phone. But there was no one he could call.

He was dead.

*   *   *   *

The Riviera had been nothing but nonstop entertainment by the film industry and Craig was exhausted by the constant blast of photo-ops and have-you-mets, and furious with the intrusive paparazzi. But, he couldn't take his eyes off the dashing young man who was escorting some special guest at the Warner Brothers party. His dark brown hair, tanned skin, expressive eyes, trim but muscular build, all were as vivid now as they were in Cannes. Craig was instantly attracted to Alan Gavin and immediately knew he was gay. They talked for nearly half-an-hour, until they had to separate to perform social duties. Craig was the one who initiated a later get-together. He suggested the bar at Loew's Casino at midnight.

Craig clearly recalled the plush crystal interior with hundreds of men dressed in tuxedos and women in expensive gowns. The elegant, the well known, the rich, the famous—all gambling, positioning, and talking about whose guest they were, which yacht they were on, and where it was moored amid the boundless number that bobbed gracefully in the picturesque harbor.

Alan showed up exactly at twelve. He had passed his escort duty to someone else. It didn't take long for them to establish several things. They were both lonely and both searching. They were intensely attracted to each other. The twenty years' difference in age didn't alter their extreme interest. They had both been cautious for years, but that night, they abandoned all caution. By two in the morning, Craig was at Alan's home and in his bed.

Craig remembered Alan's long discourse the next morning on his flower-covered veranda overlooking the Rock, or old-town Monaco. Alan was wearing faded shorts and a bright workout shirt, and Craig was relaxed in a borrowed robe. They were enjoying thick, rich coffee and everything was perfection.

Alan was the youngest, and the only son of six children. Being the only boy, he was pampered and adored by his mother. His father was much too involved with his five sisters to give him any attention. After a guarded childhood, he enrolled in Paris at the Sorbonne to study accounting and finance. In 1976, Alan graduated with highest honors. While a student in Paris, Alan had immersed himself in the gay life and was quite open about it with his parents. His father was a Monegasque, a member of a small, unique group who could trace their families for hundreds of years as having lived in the tiny principality of less than one square mile. He was the minister of finance. His mother was originally from Provence, where her family was still involved in growing flowers for the fragrance industry.

His father was dismayed by his son's sexual preference, but his mother accepted it without acrimonious concern. She loved her only son.

After Alan graduated, he took a job with the French government in Paris in their department of taxation. Two years later, when offered a position working for the royal family in their accounting and investment office, he accepted and moved back to the Riviera. Alan told Craig of his affair with Nicki, and that what he wanted in life was to love someone who was monogamous, physically safe, and emotionally independent.

Craig told Alan of his total disenchantment with Roz and his discomfort with his total lack of privacy. He told Alan that what he wanted was a man who really cared for him—*for himself*, not because he was a celebrity.

That one affair sealed their love.

During the next six weeks he and Alan were rarely apart. Craig's publicity agent was furious with Craig's lack of discretion and concern. He told him Alan would ruin his career. Only after the heads of two studios and a director ganged up on him did Craig agree to go underground with his relationship, but he was adamant about continuing his involvement.

Two months later, Craig employed Alan Gavin as his administrative assistant and secretary. Alan's father was furious when his son left the safe employment provided by the royal family for an older movie star, even though Craig Carlson was a *major* older movie star.

Craig stayed in France with Alan and began his massive study on the life of Napoleon Bonaparte for a movie that he was to star in and direct. The working title for the film was *The Corsican.*

Within a year, Alan had become Craig's right-hand man, involved in social obligations, production finance, accounting, investments, and materials research. He and Alan purchased a home in Provence and only went back to the States on business or to see his son and mother in Palm Beach. Only once Craig flew alone to California to see Roz when she told him she was dying from a hepatitis infection that was complicated by her anorexia.

The mere recall of that trip made Craig feel nauseous.

Suddenly, Craig's churning stomach superseded his churning mind with the need to dash to the bathroom. His personal Achilles' heel, his gut, had finally caught up with the stress he had been feeding it.

Craig doubled over with pain as he paid his tribute to trauma. He knew that he would have to find a chemist's shop or a Chinese tincturist somewhere soon, or he would be in real physical trouble. His quick-travel-pack had several medications, but not enough to handle this. Craig knew it took a liquid herbal potion that only the Chinese seemed able to concoct. But they had, and it was a potent remedy.

* * * *

Thursday, Bel Air

Roz was hosting a lunch for her two sons and Mr. Alltop, Andrew's attorney from Palm Beach. She had told her cook to prepare a light but creative menu. She was dressed in black and wore only a simple pair of pearls. No other jewelry.

"Jebb, how was your flight, dear? It's such a long way to come. And so good of you. You really didn't know Craig."

"I knew him better than you may have, Roz." Jebb Marlowe so far had refused to call her Mother.

"Oh. I didn't know that."

"Yes. He and Alan contacted me often when they were in New York, and we would do dinner and theater. I really liked him. I think the entertainment industry has lost one of its best talents, and I've lost a friend."

Roz smarted at that remark. Jebb hadn't even mentioned her Oscar for *Rain*.

Mr. Alltop sized up the situation and stepped in. "Mrs. Marlowe, I think your performance in *Rain* was wonderful. May I congratulate you? I saw Rita Hayworth in the fifties version. What a difference. Why they ever made a musical out of that plot, I'll never know. And Aldo Ray only distracted from the basic story, although he was excellent. As was Rita. It just wasn't the success that your Sadie Thompson was." He continued, "Whose idea was it to film it in black and white?"

Roz liked Mr. Alltop. She beamed. "Thank you. It was a difficult role. To be such a slut and then to pretend religious conversion in order to be the victor over a dirty, old, repressed clergyman. I loved the challenge!" Roz had fought the director constantly over his decision to film in black and white, so she simply chose to ignore his question.

Jebb and Andrew were silent. Alltop pressed on. "Wasn't the fifties version a real test of the Hays Code? The film was about as sexually explicit as any that had been made up to that time. Isn't that about right?"

Roz wondered if Alltop was a movie trivia buff. Very few people would have known that. She knew that the steamy movie was considered a daring test of the repressive Hays Code, Hollywood's self-censoring "anti-sin law," and that Rita Hayworth's erotically charged performance, with its legendary dance for appreciative Marines, was among the most explicit of its day. It had been a huge hit; it had encouraged later filmmakers to test the limits of the code and established Rita Hayworth, like Sadie Thompson herself, as a sexual force to be reckoned with.

But Roz knew viewers today were shown everything. No holds barred. And by today's standards, *Miss Sadie Thompson* would have probably been rated "Bring the Family."

"I dare say that Rita Hayworth's rape scene—where, with one grasping hand she simply tore down a drape—and mine— where I was shoved to the floor, stripped naked, and raped with a psychotic passion—were very different." Roz looked at her sons to see if they were even listening. Jebb was. Andrew wasn't.

She turned to Andrew. "How is Mrs. Papagos, darling?"

Andrew was old enough to know there was nothing good in their relationship. "She's okay, considering all she deals with."

The sarcastic little bastard, Roz thought. "And school? Tell your mother all about your school. Do you get good grades?"

"It's okay. I do allright. I miss my dad."

Roz thought, *He's been brainwashed and he'll probably inherit all of Craig's stock in Papagos Food Wholesalers, but who cares. Who wants to own stock in lettuce and tomatoes?*

Roz hoped she would do better with her older son. "Where do you work now, Jebb?"

"National Life Underwriters Association in Washington, D.C. They're big. They represent all of the thousands of underwriters in the country in their constant battles with the giant insurance companies. You'd be surprised to hear about all that goes on."

"I'm sure," Roz said. She could care less. If he didn't care about her Oscar, she didn't care about his job. But she decided to give it one more shot. "Is there a special girl in your life? Someone as handsome as you surely has that problem."

"Plenty. But no one special," Jebb answered.

Roz decided to give in to reality. Her sons were not overwhelmed to be in the presence of their mother.

After lunch, Jebb insisted on seeing Simia.

Roz said, "I think she's out."

Jebb said, "I know better. And I expect some privacy."

Roz was angry, but she called Simia on the intercom and asked her to come down. In front of Mr. Alltop, she had no choice.

While waiting for Jebb, Andrew asked if he could have one of his father's Oscars. Roz said, "Of course you can. I'll get it for you tomorrow."

A few moments later, Jebb informed Roz that he would be back at seven to pick up Simia. She was going to have dinner with him. With that announcement, he walked to his rental car and waited for Alltop and Andrew to catch up.

Roz was glad her time with her sons was over. With them gone, she could get back to what she needed to do for tomorrow—plan her wardrobe and her acting for Craig's memorial service and the reading of the will. Friday was a special day.

Roz was looking forward to *EW*'s hour special tonight on television about her, and of course Craig and Alan. Roz was delighted they had pegged Alan as Craig's alleged lover. She thought, *Alleged? Hell, when I get through with Alan Gavin they'll know all they ever wanted to know.*

*   *   *   *

Thursday Afternoon, Los Angeles

Lady Ashley, whose stage name was Savannah Marlowe,

had no difficulty clearing customs. With her connections to the British royal family, she was a VIP who sailed through most political barriers. No one touched her bags. Her British Air flight had left London at noon and had arrived on schedule at three.

Once outside of customs, she spotted Alan. Savannah was shaken by how pale and drawn the handsome young man was. She had only been with him when laughter and high-flying plans made them all happy. Or when a very serious but very interesting matter was being discussed. And she had learned so much from Craig Carlson about the entertainment field. And so much from Alan about life.

Savannah hugged him and gave him a big, full-mouthed kiss. Her brunette hair was iridescent, her clothing immaculate. She looked as if she had just stepped out of a storefront window.

"Alan! My sweet, Alan! How wonderful it is to see you."

"Savannah! You have no idea what your coming means."

"Oh, darling! I didn't come for you. I came to shake up my stepmother's life." Savannah's smile was real. Then Savannah became serious. "I'm so sorry. What a loss. What a miserable, painful loss."

She hugged and kissed him again, and then linked arms and asked, "Where's our brass band? I expected someone to know that the star of the British stage was on that damn plane."

"Don't worry, Savannah. At this very moment we are being filmed. So look your brightest."

"Oh, really?" Savannah looked around the area. Sure enough, television crews and freelance photographers were shooting away.

"Why us?" she asked.

"Because. Haven't you heard?. I'm Craig Carlson's lover."

"But, darling, we've all known that for years."

"Yes, but it's national news now. But I guess the BBC doesn't worry much about our scandals. You cause enough of your own. How is your husband?" Alan smiled.

"Hugh? God, he's absolutely resolved to remain dull. But he's fine. And I love Hugh with my life. He's a safe harbor for a shipwrecked sailor, and I can be that most of the time. The royals? Well they're in a bit of a snit, but they are always in a snit."

"Let's get out of here," said Alan.

"Ditto, darling." Savannah squeezed his arm and they moved as fast as they could for the exit. But not fast enough.

A reporter stepped right in front of them with a microphone in their face shouting the question, "Who's your female companion, Gavin?"

Savannah thought for a moment that Alan was going to hit the man, and he probably would have if she hadn't moved faster. She grabbed the microphone out of his hand and asked, "Me. Who am I? Alan Gavin's real lover and the star of one of London's biggest stage hits. You don't know me? Shame on you!"

The shocked reporter barely caught the microphone as Savannah tossed it back.

"Now bugger off, darling." Savannah gave him a huge smile, and pulled Alan off with her.

"You haven't changed, have you?"

"Why should I? Most people live a lie. That little snot needed something like that to make his miserable week."

After her extensive luggage was stowed away, the driver began the unending fight to get away from the airport.

"Where are you staying, Savannah?"

"I've rented a bungalow at the Beverly Hills Pink Palace," she laughed. It was a wonderful laugh, deep and uncomplicated.

"Are you kidding? That place was lavishly redone."

"I only have a very big suite—one that the press can't fail to notice. You see, I want Roz to know I'm here before she sees that I'm here. I'm sure she'll soon get the message."

"Yeah. We'll probably be on tonight's news."

"Good." Savannah stretched her long legs in the car. "You're not driving back and forth to Encinitas, are you?"

"No. That's too much. My mother is here from Monaco. She got in yesterday. We have a small suite at the Hilton."

"God, I wonder if they've spent money on that since I was here last; it's not what Mother is used to. Is it?"

"It's okay."

"And it's not what you're used to, either, is it, Alan?"

"No."

"Thanks for being honest." Savannah leaned forward in the seat and tapped on the driver's glass.

"Stop first at the Beverly Hilton. We'll only be there for a moment."

"What are you doing, Savannah?"

"You and Mother are staying with me. I have way too much room, and I would love the company. Just dash up, throw your things in your bag, pick up your mother, and we'll continue our adventure."

Alan laughed. "You're hard to stop, Savannah."

"Of course I am." Savannah looked out for a moment to see where they were. "I was here for so long and now I haven't been here for ages."

"I didn't know you ever spent any time here."

"Oh, Alan, I'm a graduate of UCLA Law. You didn't know? I passed the bar and was going to make that my career. You're surprised I had the brainpower, aren't you?"

Alan laughed. "No. Not your mind—your motivation. I'm amazed."

"Well, don't be. As soon as I found out all attorneys are crooks or creeps, I headed for New York and the stage. There was too much Mikey Marlowe in me to hide in a law library."

Alan returned to her offer. "We really can't impose."

"Oh, pooh! If you're not ready in fifteen minutes, I'll be up after you." Then Savannah became very serious. "This has been one hell of a blow for you, and I'm all you have. I loved Craig and I love you. I am here for you. Please. I'll be waiting in the bar, if it takes you all night to pack. *But you're staying with me.*"

Alan said nothing. Savannah could see he was trying hard not to break down. He finally broke their long silence. "Who killed Craig, Savannah? And what for?"

"I don't know. But I wouldn't count out anybody whom you already know." With that, she fell silent. She was thinking of her father, Mikey Marlowe, and his drug death.

One hour later, the three took possession of one of the Beverly Hills Hotel's finest accommodations.

Alan's mother, who had never met Savannah, was delighted to have female companionship, and delighted with the change of hotels. Savannah's last remark as she closed the door to her room was, "I had the concierge from the Dorchester in London call ahead and make reservations for dinner tonight at seven-thirty at the Eclipse. That should create some newsworthy material! Your mother will love it! My husband would hate it. Thanks for joining me here. I despise being alone."

She entered her bedroom only to reappear at the door.

"Alan, you're my date, so wear your finest. And do be a dear and call the restaurant and change the reservation to three. Be sure and use my name."

Seven

Thursday Evening, Beverly Hills, California

Justine Truther, the assistant manager at the Eclipse, prided herself on how well she managed the politics of reservations. But today, she was truly worried. She first received a request for a party of two from a very precise Englishman for seven-thirty for an S. Marlowe. Then she received another request for a party of two at seven-thirty from a J. Marlowe. Then she received a third request for a party of two from the secretary of Roz Marlowe, also for seven-thirty. She couldn't believe what had happened. The Marlowes? All of them at the Eclipse at the same time?

She carefully set up three tables of two under the name Marlowe and left the sheet for the maître d' to work. She made a side note that these were not all the same reservation. When Henri came on duty and took over the book, he began getting calls relative to the Marlowe reservations before he had a chance to understand all she had done.

A man called to change Roz Marlowe's reservation to three, and another man changed S. Marlowe's reservation to three. Henri, knowing the Marlowe history well, tried to interpret and prepare for any eventuality. He figured the minimum Marlowe table would be three and the maximum, eight. So he picked two excellent tables well separated and began his job of not seating whom next to whom for the satisfaction of his other patrons.

At seven-thirty, Jebb and Simia appeared and asked for their table.

"There are only two of you?"

"Should there be more?" Jebb asked.

"No. Of course not, Mr. Marlowe."

Henri sat them at the three top, and had the busperson remove the third place setting.

Jebb was happy to be alone with Simia. And he couldn't get

over how beautiful she was in her dress. She told him that Roz had let her wear it to the Oscars. He was amazed at that.

Jebb ordered a bottle of champagne and told Simia they were going to celebrate.

Savannah, Alan, and Mrs. Gavin arrived within minutes.

"Are you of a larger party?" Henri asked politely.

"Always," answered Savannah, who surveyed the room and spotted Simia and Jebb. She made a dramatic swoop toward them.

"Simia! Jebb! What a fantastically marvelous surprise! How wonderful to see you." She hugged and kissed them both. The few that were already in the restaurant couldn't help but see the warmth of the welcome.

By then, Alan and his mother had caught up. After Alan appropriately introduced his mother, Jebb said, "Let's make this a bigger party." He motioned Henri over.

"We'd like a larger table," Jebb said without concern.

Henri retreated to his drawing board and looked at it. He could put them at the eight top and still be okay.

It was a happy reunion as the group got resituated. Mrs. Gavin was the only one who didn't know all of the others. But Jebb, Simia, and Savannah went way back, and Alan was loved by each of them.

Then Henri made his fatal mistake. Before he had the busperson clear, he reapproached the table, leaned over Jebb, and asked, "Are you expecting Roz Marlowe to join you?"

"Oh, my God. No!" Jebb replied.

Savannah immediately knew what to do.

She firmly put her hand on Alan's, who was about to likewise object, and said, "Of course. They simply must join us."

"How many are there in her party?" asked Alan with concern.

"Two, maybe three, I'm not sure," said the uncomfortable maître d'.

Alan shot Savannah a glance of real anxiety. She saw it, but ignored it. This was one of the reasons she had flown all the way from England—for a face-to-face with Roz.

Drinks were ordered and delivered, and soon the group of friends relaxed.

Simia was having a wonderful time. She had only tasted champagne before, never really drank it. It had always been frowned on by Roz, and never offered.

Mrs. Gavin began to find the evening enjoyable.

Henri was managing other patrons when Roz Marlowe appeared with an escort. As soon as he could get back to them, he did.

"Is our table ready, Henri?" Roz was trying hard to impress anyone watching.

Henri said, "Yes, Mrs. Marlowe. Are there only two of you?"

Gregory Washburne stepped forward. "Yes. I called this afternoon, when I thought there would be an additional party."

"And who was that?" queried Roz sharply.

"I misunderstood you to say that Jebb would be with us."

Roz smiled her practiced public smile and remained silent.

"It makes no difference," said Henri defensively. "Your group is waiting for you." He scooped up menus and headed into the dining area.

Roz followed, not understanding, until it was too late.

Savannah spotted her stepmother before Roz spotted her.

Savannah left their table and met Roz halfway across the room. "Mother! How wonderful that you could come. You have no idea what this means to me!"

The other diners at Eclipse were now watching with interest.

Roz quit walking. She couldn't believe her eyes or her ears. Savannah Marlowe here in L.A.?

"Oh, shit!" Roz said, loud enough to be heard.

Savannah continued, "What a great idea of yours to get us all together. A family at last. It's just what Craig would have wanted. No more animosity. No more meanness. Just one big happy family."

Alan felt like crawling under the table.

Simia just sat there with a knowing smile on her face.

Now embarrassed by the scene, Gregory stepped in and

intentionally nudged Roz forward.

Simia squeezed Jebb's hand.

Roz had no choice. She sat down, surrounded by the enemy—her children, foremost.

"More champagne for all," ordered Savannah.

"Code Red" was spread by Henri to his wait staff, placing them all on notice that all hell could break loose at table thirty-seven and warning them to tiptoe with their service at that table.

Roz tried hard to find her footing. Alcohol helped, and Roz relied on a lot of it to do so.

After several drinks, Gregory Washburne became amused at the situation. It was the first comic relief he had had for a week.

Savannah asked, "Gregory, haven't I met you before?"

"I don't think so." He laughed, and chose to ignore the many ugly warning looks he got from Roz.

Savannah became reflective. "You look familiar. Oh, well, I'm probably thinking of one of my zillion classmates at UCLA Law." She then turned her attention back to Roz.

The nervous waiter survived the initial round of drinks and served the first course. There was a bet on in the kitchen that his job wouldn't last the night with the Marlowes.

There was a great deal of loud conversation and laughter, and Roz tried desperately to focus on her portabello mushrooms. But Savannah wouldn't let up. Her questions were neverending.

Roz tried to shift to the offense. "Savannah, tell us about your stage success. Just what role do you play?" She wanted to add something nasty but didn't.

Savannah rose to the occasion and started to sing heartily, *"Me. I'm on the top of the tree. Just you look up and you see . . . "*

The waiter was at her side with her main course.

The revelers quieted down and began eating. The waiter poured more wine, and the bottle almost slipped out of his proper bottom-of-the bottle grip. Henri, the maître d', abandoned his rule of not drinking while at the restaurant and had a double.

Simia, somewhat anesthetized, stopped eating and noticed how much Savannah and Jebb resembled each other. She hadn't seen them together since Jebb was four and Savannah the teenager who ran away from Roz. She thought of their father. She still had a special place in her heart for Mikey Marlowe.

"Would anyone care for dessert or an after-dinner drink?" quavered the waiter. He thought, *One more hour, if I can only hold it together one more hour.*

"Yes. A last round of champagne and the dessert cart," said Jebb. "I have a toast I want to make to Roz Marlowe."

The table became quiet.

"Yes. Thank you. I'll be back with both," said the waiter.

Henri poured the champagne in fresh, chilled glasses as the waiter trundled up the dessert cart.

Jebb couldn't resist. "Here's to Sadie Thompson. Roz, you played the part of a prostitute with perfection."

Henri didn't move. He didn't know where to go or what to do. But he knew "it" was about to happen. The waiter stood dumbfounded by the cart.

Roz stood before anyone could raise a glass. "Gregory, I think we need to leave. I don't want to miss the special on *Entertainment World.*" She was seething.

"Oh, I had forgotten," he laughed.

No one had held up their glass.

"Well, Gregory, let's go!"

Gregory was too drunk to recognize his mistake. He warmly kissed Savannah and Simia, and heartily shook hands with the rest.

Now cocked for action, Roz nodded to the table, then, with one mighty heave, shoved the dessert cart over. It splattered, gooey and sweet, covering anything near, particularly the waiter.

With her head held high, she said, "Henri, this is the last time Roz Marlowe steps foot into this stinking diner!"

Oh! Thank God! Henri thought.

Then, somewhat staggering, Roz walked across the dining room. The Eclipse had just experienced a Roz Marlowe Hate Scene.

Outside, Roz walked right into the crowd of photographers that her publicist had alerted. She had to find her driver. The whole world was on her shit list, and at the top of her list was Savannah Marlowe. Roz thought, *That ungrateful fucking bitch would bed anything, anytime, anywhere just for a line in the British press.* "Lady Ashley, my ass!" she shrieked. "She was dropping acid at ten!"

Once inside the safety of her limousine, Roz started to cry. Why couldn't she stay in control? Why did she always have to get even? She remembered the night her father had told her she couldn't have the car. She got up from the dinner table, picked up the keys, and intentionally drove his new car through their new closed overhead garage door. Her father never denied her that particular permission again.

But Roz knew why. Her father started the contest for control when she was a little girl, and she had never stopped playing the game. He sent her to psychologists and psychiatrists about it. As an adult, she had sought out therapists on her own, to contain it. But sooner or later, she always blew it. She did with Mikey, with Craig, and with each of her children.

"Damn it! Damn it!" Her tears didn't stop.

*   *   *   *

Roz left a table of five who were having one hell of a good time, most of it at her expense. And they were all brought together because of a tragedy that had happened to one they still loved. After Roz's exit, they fell quiet. Alan wanted to watch *EW* and Savannah knew she had probably overacted. Jebb knew his toast didn't come out exactly as he meant it to.

The group brokeup and said their goodbyes.

*   *   *   *

Early Afternoon, Friday, Hong Kong

Craig was fourteen hours away watching *Entertainment World*. He didn't expect the program to be kind to *anyone*, particularly not to Alan. But he had to know what so many people would hear. He was prepared for some of it to be true, but most of it to be a product of a writer's or producer's imagination.

Entertainment World first reported that there had been no progress made in finding Craig Carlson's murderer and that they would begin their three-part series with data on Carlson.

"Craig Carlson was born as Constantine Traver Papagos in Rome, Italy, in 1933 to George and Ellen Papagos. . . ."

Craig blanched. He was registered at the hotel under the name of Constantine Papagos. He was so upset, he turned off the television. Nervously, he paced back and forth. He looked out the window. This was not what he had expected. Was there nowhere he could be? He was lonely. He missed Alan, missed his home, missed his bed. He looked out at a city of millions, with one of the densest populations in the world, yet there was no one for him. Tears welled up in Craig's eyes.

He forced himself back to his chair and turned on the television.

"Carlson entered Northwestern University to study the performing arts, much to his father's objection. After his diplomatic service in World War II, George Papagos had founded Papagos Food Wholesalers and wanted his son to study business at Massachusetts Institute of Technology. Papagos Food Wholesalers today is a multimillion-dollar empire owned exclusively by the family." Photos of the corporate headquarters appeared on the screen.

Craig groaned, "Now my son Andrew is exposed to kidnapping. I'll kill them if that happens."

"Here are several pictures of Connie Papagos taken during his years at Northwestern. In perfect physical condition, and eligible for the draft, his influential father was able to keep his son out of the Korean War."

"That's a flat-faced lie!"

EW continued. "After the family became naturalized citizens, Ellen Papagos spent her winters in Palm Beach. And in 1954, Connie, having grown tired of the Midwest, moved to New York and enrolled in Juilliard. He upset his parents by living in a loft in Greenwich Village."

Again more pictures.

"A handsome Constantine Papagos graduated with a degree from Juilliard in theater in 1956, and his mother gifted him with a trip around the world. His attachment to his mother has affected his life, and her hold on him to the day of his death was sizable."

"Those bastards." Craig hoped his mother wasn't watching.

"Now in his middle twenties, Connie was known as one of New York's most eligible bachelors. He dated many beautiful women, but *EW* has learned that even then he had other agendas. He continued his individual instruction in theater in the city from private instructors, many of whom were gay.

"At age twenty-seven, in 1960, Papagos moved to California to pursue a career in the movies. Paramount changed his name to Craig Traver Carlson, and while there, he was discovered by an athletic trainer who taught him that there was an alternative life in Hollywood. *EW* has learned that it may have been Carlson's first gay affair of any length." *EW* showed a picture of Craig with a handsome, muscled trainer.

Craig wondered how much they paid Ernie for the information.

"In 1962, Paramount gave Carlson a minor part in a picture that allowed him to show off his body and talent for physical contact. His extreme good looks caught the attention of David Bright, the British filmmaker.

"Bright signed Carlson on to play a minor role in one of his epics. The movie won an Oscar for Best Picture and Bright, for Best Director in 1963. As a result, Craig Carlson's name became recognized in the film industry." *EW* showed footage from the movie *The Burma Road,* with several stills of Craig with Bright.

"David was my big break," Craig acknowledged.

"Carlson, now often found in pages of movie magazines, was recognized as an up-and-coming winner. This infuriated his father, but his mother stood by her son. *EW* has learned that even then Carlson took as active an interest in men as in women, until the studio told him to quit it. Carlson went underground with his sexuality. He wanted a career."

Craig knew their reporting so far was basically accurate, if terribly slanted. It didn't seem an epitaph to a dead man. But he admitted he loved sex with another man far more than with a woman. There was something about being with a man that he needed, but he was afraid of the homophobic industry, his homophobic church, and his homophobic father.

"In 1968, at thirty-five, Carlson won his first Oscar as Best Supporting Actor for his role in *Dangerous Passage.* Now firmly established in the industry, Carlson had ten years of successful box office hits, but not one that compared in artistic quality to *Dangerous Passage.*

"In 1978, Carlson moved to London. In a hard-action movie, *To Kill or To Die*, he became proficient in the use of handguns." *EW* showed footage from the film.

"Thank God for that," said Craig.

"In 1982, Carlson made a different type of film. As a result, he won an Oscar for Best Actor in *The Prince,* a movie of a middle-aged man whose wife leaves him with three children as well as both his and her parents to support and take care of. Now of superstar status, Carlson could name his price and determine which roles he cared to play."

EW showed some excellent footage from *The Prince.* Craig swallowed hard; it had been a sensitive and gripping role.

"In 1984, while shooting another David Bright epic in England, Craig Carlson, the star, met Roz Marlowe, the newcomer. Carlson was fifty and Roz, thirty-four. They met accidentally while waiting out a heavy rainstorm under a tree. Marlowe's rabid position of support of Margaret Thatcher's policies so astonished Carlson they extended their political dialogue to a date. Their continued dating soon became the talk of the film industry."

Craig wondered now if his studio had arranged that talk.

"After their marriage they fought openly and often. But the union did produce a son, Andrew, who lives today behind the walls of the big estate with Craig's mother, Ellen Papagos."

"Why did I ever marry her?" Craig asked, but he knew why. One night while both were very drunk and very high, Craig told

Roz of his interest in men. Roz told him to stop worrying. "You're not gay," she said, "just attracted to them. You've never had a real woman. I can cure you of that."

He was so relieved, he thought it was true, and that she had the power to do it. They had great sex, and Craig loved to be seen with her. She was extremely beautiful, and they never failed to catch the attention of the public.

"After Rock Hudson died of AIDS in 1985, *EW* knows that most studios warned all of their male stars in no uncertain terms that gay lifestyles would not be tolerated. But just one year later, while Roz Marlowe was on the New York stage performing nightly in *Searching*, Carlson was in Europe at the Cannes Film Festival. It was there he met Alan Gavin."

EW showed pictures of Craig and Alan on the Riviera.

"We have Carlson's former agent with us, who represented him at that time. Wally, what did you say to Carlson when you were aware of his relationship with Gavin?" *EW* cut to an interview taken in Palm Desert.

"You traitor!"

But Craig knew that Wally had nothing to lose. He was a dead man, and Wally needed the money to pay his mortgage.

Wally said to the commentator, "I told Craig that I knew he and Gavin were having an affair. And I told him that everyone in Cannes knew it, and that if he didn't stop it, everyone in the world would know it and that would be the end of his career. He told me at the time that Roz had become impossible to live with, and that he had to find some way to obtain his sexual gratification. He wouldn't cheat on her with another woman, but he sure as hell would do it with a man of the quality of Alan Gavin. 'I love him, Wally.' Those were his exact words."

Craig relaxed. Wally didn't really betray him after all. At this point, with their secret out, Craig wanted the world to know he loved Alan.

EW showed a picture of Alan escorting a young blond onto a big yacht. He was young and tanned, and his angular face was topped with dusty brown hair.

Craig wanted a drink. It was only one-twenty in the afternoon, but he needed it. He had a lot to do in a short period of time. *EW* had completely demolished his safety as Constantine Papagos.

"We'll be right back with our coverage with Roz Marlowe next."

Craig started to gather his things. He had hoped the Island Shangri-La could have been home for a couple of days.

*   *   *   *

"Roz Marlowe was born as Patti Ann Warren in Lancaster, Ohio, to a family who owned a successful glass business. An only child, she established herself early in life as special. Here is a picture of Patti Ann while a cheerleader for her high school." The picture was angled so that Roz's breasts were the most obvious part of her physique. Craig knew the picture, Roz still had it in her quarters. He also knew that it was in high school that Roz learned from the boys how to really swear. She seemed proud of her extensive foul vocabulary.

"In 1968 she pledged Theta at Dennison University, where she excelled in theater. . . ."

As *EW* continued, Craig became involved with other matters. He wasn't as concerned with Roz's background. He put his two suitcases on the bed and started to fold his clothes into them. Then he remembered the money. *Damn! I can't go anywhere until I get that custom luggage I ordered this morning.* Craig started looking for the card from the luggage shop.

EW was showing pictures of Juliette Savannah Marlowe when she was a most unattractive twelve and of Simia when she was an absolute beauty at twenty-seven. Craig had never seen that picture of Simia. He was sure that Roz had long since destroyed it. He wondered where *EW* got it.

"After Mikey Marlowe's death, Roz changed her name from Patti Ann Marlowe to Roselyn Marlowe, and began singing in nightclubs. Being Mikey's grieving widow had brought her so much attention that agents sought her out. His death seemed to be her discovery."

EW showed a picture taken at Mikey's funeral in New York. Roz was crying profusely and holding the hands of a little boy.

"Great act, Roz. I wonder how you're handling my death?"

"In 1982, Roselyn Marlowe landed the major role of Cassie in the continuing stage production of *A Chorus Line* and for Playbill purposes, shortened her name to Roz, as we all know her today. It was after a long run in *A Chorus Line* that Roz was tapped for a minor role in an important film being shot in England. As we have reported, that's where she met Craig Carlson."

Craig found the luggage man's card under the phone.

"On their honeymoon in the Greek Islands, Roz and Craig had already started to fight in public." *EW* showed a picture of them at a sidewalk café in Mykonos obviously yelling at each other.

"Do you remember that one, Roz? It was about jewelry." Craig slid back into his chair.

"In 1986, Roz landed the lead in the Broadway production of *Searching*, a dramatic musical about a woman who continues to lose husbands to natural causes. She won a Tony Award for her performance. The haunting ballad she sang in *Searching*, a 1989 film, became an international hit, and she won a Grammy Award.

"Her role as Amelia in that film brought Roz much well-earned respect as an actress, but her public temper tantrums had also earned her a negative reputation. In fact, when the question was asked of her as to how she landed so many different leads, Roz has been quoted as saying on more than one occasion, 'That's the Hollywood game. Either play it, or get off the couch!'"

Craig said, "You've got that part right."

"We have examined two people of the triangle. In just a moment, *EW* will explore the third person. The life of Alan Gavin is possibly the most interesting of all."

Suddenly, the local TV station cut back into its programming.

"I'm sorry, but we are going to have to discontinue *Entertainment World's*, Carlson story. We will air the final segments of this special either on Monday or Tuesday of next week. We now return you to local programming."

The Hong Kong staff immediately took over. "A tragedy has just occurred at Kai Tak. We take you there live."

Craig was troubled. He didn't know where he would be on Monday or Tuesday. And what had happened to Kai Tak? That was his only escape route out of Hong Kong.

Cameras from helicopter newsteams were showing live footage of a 727 that had just crashed at the end of the runway. There were flames shooting into the air, emergency vehicles were racing toward that end of the runway, and other planes were taxiing back to the terminal.

They reported, "Incoming flights have been diverted to Bangkok and Singapore, and we must advise all outgoing passengers scheduled to fly out of Hong Kong today or possibly tomorrow to please check with your airline before leaving for the airport. We doubt if the runway will be cleared for some period of time."

Craig could see from the crash that it might be a long period of time. He felt for those onboard. Some of the slides were shown open, and some lucky passengers were escaping the burning plane. The name of the airline was not readable or identified by the commentators.

He shuddered and thought, *There's too much death in the world that happens much too easily.*

He turned off the television and called the luggage man.

"Mr. Ling, is that you?"

"Yes. What can I do for you, please?"

"This is Mr. Papagos. Do you remember me from this morning?"

"Yes. Of course."

"Well, something has happened. I need that suitcase tomorrow or sooner. Have you started on it?" Craig knew they wouldn't have even thought about it yet.

"No, no, Mr. Papagos. We can't have it for you until the first of the week at the earliest."

"Well, I'll double the price you quoted me if you can have it ready by noon tomorrow."

There was a long pause on the other end of the line. Craig could hear Mr. Ling talking to someone rapidly in Chinese.

"We can have it ready for you by ten o'clock tonight."

Craig was amazed.

"Do you want us to deliver it to your hotel?"

"Yes. That will be . . . No. Let me think. I may change hotels; they may need this room. I'll call back and let you know where you can deliver it. Thanks, Mr. Ling." Craig hung up.

Craig was soaked with sweat.

He had no idea where to go for one or two nights.

He had no idea where he was going to go from Hong Kong.

He had no idea when Kai Tak would be open again.

He got out his map of Southeast Asia.

He knew the passports of Carlson and Papagos were shot. All he had left were alias passports of names that someone would be looking for—*that someone being the one who arranged his murder.*

Eight

Friday Morning, Bel Air

Inspector Roosevelt studied his notes in the quiet of his office. Under "Roz Marlowe" he had written: (1) At Spagos, she used the word *murder*; (2) At her Bel Air home, her responses were abnormally controlled. She never mentioned Craig by name and only appeared excited or confused when Roosevelt brought up the legal papers; (3) At the morgue, the first place where Roz had actually seen her husband dead, she was abnormally nonreactive. She never mentioned him by name or cried; (4) At the morgue, a possible slip with the use of the word *he.* "Why would *he* do a thing like that?" Did she know that the murderer was a man? (5) At the morgue, Roz looked away without saying anything about the bullethole—only about the torn face; (6) At the morgue, the instant order to cremate him. Had she recognized someone else? (7) At his office, her emotional explosion when he said, "You don't appear very upset"; (8) At his office, her reaction to his question about Craig's assets, and particularly when she said they'd better not be left to his significant other; and (9) Overall, her obvious dislike for her husband and raw hatred for Alan Gavin.

Roosevelt knew hatred.

He had seen a lot of it. A degree in law, another in social science, and twenty-five years in the L.A. police department didn't always prepare him for the brutal violence he encountered in his job. Children killing their parents, parents killing their children. Former lovers annihilating each other. Hatred, the flip side of love.

Roosevelt knew that social status, financial position, profession, or education had little to do with the impulse for violence and hatred. It was all about raw emotion and the seven deadly sins. Saints and sages had warned against them since history began, but Roosevelt wondered if anyone had ever learned.

Roosevelt shook his head, then focused again on the sheet in front of him.

Roz's Motive: He had written two words. (1) Money; and (2) Getting even. After Alibi, he had written: (1) Excellent.

Then he turned to Alan's sheet, upon which was written: (1) In the mansion, he found the body; (2) In the mansion, his reactions were normal for someone who found his loved one dead; and (3) In the mansion, the blood on his clothes was that of the deceased, also normal.

On Alan's pad after the word Motive, he had written the following:. (1) Money. After Alibi, he had written: (1) None.

Roosevelt's phone rang. A ballistics technician wanted to see him right away. He told him to come on up. Roosevelt pushed the pads aside and waited. A young Chinese girl came in. "We have a problem, Inspector."

Roosevelt nodded. "Go ahead."

"Craig Carlson's gun was recently fired and a new cartridge inserted in the chamber. The bullet taken out of his head was the one fired from his gun." She placed two plastic bags on his desk and stayed quiet.

Roosevelt was stunned. He looked down at the bag with the gun and the separate bag with the bullet.

"And fingerprints?"

"None. The gun was wiped clean."

"And on the humidor?"

"Only those of Mr. Carlson's and the cleaning lady. We still are examining it to see if we can find any others."

"But it wasn't also wiped clean of all prints?"

"No, sir."

Roosevelt turned in his chair and looked at the cluttered wall. He thought of Alan's pad: Motive, money. Alibi, none.

"Any chance of error? Are the lands and grooves matched up well enough to make these findings unchallengeable?"

"Yes, sir."

"Do you have the written report?"

She placed it on his desk and said, "There's no way anyone

could shoot himself in the head without leaving a bigger mess."

"And a dead man doesn't reload his gun, wipe it clean, and return it to where it's kept." Roosevelt sighed. "Thank you. Let me know if you find any other prints on the humidor."

As she left, Roosevelt looked at his watch. He wanted to be at Carlson's memorial services to watch faces and body language. Now, more than ever, he had to watch Alan as well as Roz.

As he prepared to leave, he looked at his desk to see if there were last-minute things he had to do. On the stacks of papers pushed aside, he noticed that the copies of the legal documents he took from Carlson's sitting room the night of the murder had been added to the pile.

"It's about time," Roosevelt said. He had requested them Wednesday. He thought, *I'll read them when I get back.*

Very troubled with the technician's findings, Roosevelt was struck with an idea. He picked up his phone and requested two video cameramen meet him outside in the parking lot. They should be equipped with telephoto capability.

*   *   *   *

Roz didn't concern herself with the memorial service at the Greek Orthodox Church or the service afterward where Craig's ashes would be buried in a memorial garden. She had Anne make all of the arrangements.

Roz knew that Craig wanted to be cremated without a fuss, and that he and Alan had made arrangements. But Roz didn't consult Alan about them. Legally, Alan had no say. He wasn't his wife or his son. A cremation took the signature of either the spouse, or, if divorced, of all of the children of the deceased granting permission. And this approval could only be obtained after the death. All Roz had done was sign her name to forms requested by Anne.

For Roz, it was only a morning to get through it was the afternoon she was more interested in.

Following the services, Anne had arranged a luncheon for family and special guests at the Bel Air Hotel. The reading of the will would be after that at Roz's estate. Roz asked Anne to find out who would be there. Packard told Anne he had notified those involved. Roz knew Packard didn't want to give her the satisfaction of knowing. Since their luncheon on Wednesday, Packard had limited his contact to Anne.

*   *   *   *

In the church, Inspector Roosevelt found a spot in a side balcony where he could watch. He deciphered who everyone was from information he had solicited earlier from Roz's secretary.

Roz, Anne, Andrew Papagos, and Mr. Alltop, the Papagos family attorney, were in the front pew on one side. In the front pew on the other side were Jebb, Simia, Savannah, Alan, and his mother. Gregory Washburne sat one row behind Roz, and Victor Packard sat one row behind the larger family group.

Roosevelt found that the seating itself revealed interesting internal family stress and tension.

The rest of the church was filled with a combination of Craig's friends, Alan's friends, Roz's studio colleagues, Roz's employees, and the media. Outside, the police were trying to contain a growing crowd.

Roosevelt had told his cameramen to go straight to the garden and get advantageous positions. He felt it was there that facial expressions of the truest feelings would be captured.

The Greek Orthodox service was relatively short. The eulogy of Craig Carlson was delivered by an industry friend of many years who had worked with Craig on over twenty pictures. Nothing occurred other than what Roosevelt expected.

Roz seemed detached, and looked at her watch at least four times. But when she did turn around to look at others at the service, her composure was that of mourning and grief. Roosevelt felt that action in itself was abominable.

Andrew cried, and Mr. Alltop was the one who consoled him, not Roz, his mother. Alan broke down, and his support team of Savannah on one side and his mother on the other assisted him.

Simia was completely unable to subdue her grief. Jebb put

his arm around her to comfort her.

It was over. The first two rows were ushered out the side exit. Roosevelt noted that the individuals on the two sides of the aisle never exchanged glances or comments, and that Roz and Washburne had not spoken to each other.

*   *   *   *

"Why can't we ever go out the front of anything anymore?" Roz asked Anne peevishly.

Anne chose not to respond.

There was no hearse. Craig's ashes would simply be handed to Roz at the memorial garden.

It was a beautiful day, and the garden was a place of peace and beauty. Because of the beds of profuse flowers of every color and variety, cut flower arrangements were discouraged. Individuals were told that single blooms or small personal arrangements were welcome. The lawn and garden care was faultless, the pathways and rock walls flawlessly placed. Shade trees and shrubs perfected the serenity. A high wall and banked earth helped kill the invasive street noise.

The entrance had become a feeding frenzy for the newspaper, magazine, and television cameramen, news teams, and reporters. Print headlines had been inflammatory—"No Clues in Carlson Murder." "LAPD, Where Are You?" "Which Celebrity Is Next?"

The scandal mags were worse—"Carlson Meets Death at Hands of Lover." "Roz Free at Last." "Who's Your Next Hubby, Roz?"

Inspector Roosevelt was able to pierce the police barriers before the limousines arrived. He was satisfied to see that his two men were well placed and their presence, difficult to notice.

Coming through the mob, Roz put her window down and waved with one hand while dabbing her eyes with the other.

Mr. Alltop was mortified.

Anne, who never said anything, said, "Roz, for goodness sake, put your window up."

"Shut up, Anne! Don't tell me what to do."

Andrew reached over and pushed the button, and the window closed. "He was my father. Show him some respect."

Roz slumped back in the seat. She had to remember that she was grieving. She said, "I'm sorry." She became very still, but her mind was racing. *Don't blow it, Roz; you're almost there.*

Inspector Roosevelt noted that when the first limousine arrived, Roz was the first out—almost as an escape. The others let distance build between them. She was only accompanied by the two bodyguards.

Roosevelt calculated that something must have happened.

Roz didn't know that her facial expression was being carefully recorded on videotape. If she did, she would have tried to change the mask of raw hatred that pulled at every corner of her mouth and eyes. Her black dress and black gloves didn't fool the camera.

Those in the second and third limousine got out slowly and, as a group, helped each other. They moved as a unit. All came together at the foot of a wall, where a small portion of loose earth had been moved to receive the ashes of Craig Carlson.

The Greek Orthodox bishop who had preached the sermon solemnly handed Roz a small, hard, plastic container that was five by eight by eleven inches. He said, "Let us pray."

Roz, completely alone, looked down at the box.

Alan turned his head away, and his mother stood very close.

Simia got down on her knees; Jebb knelt beside her.

Mr. Alltop put his arm around Andrew.

Savannah never took her eyes off Roz Marlowe. She made no effort to hide her dislike and disgust for her stepmother.

Gregory Washburne and Victor Packard stayed in the background, but not together.

Roosevelt observed that the wife was the least upset, and the rest were in pure grief or mad as hell at Roz Marlowe. He had been to many funerals, even to those where two families required two rooms and two ministers for the service because they wouldn't speak with each other. But for him, this was a first. It was the wife against all of the others. Very sad.

Roosevelt found it impossible to believe that Alan Gavin could have ever murdered Craig Carlson. And he knew he was going to have a difficult time convincing himself that his feelings weren't his job. His job was to find out if Alan Gavin did kill Craig Carlson. And if he didn't, who did? There were no other suspects other than the possibility of a contract killer. And if that were the case, he could damn well guess who arranged it.

The Orthodox bishop finished his prayer. The service was over. He looked at Roz and then motioned to the ground. She stepped forward and placed the humble box in the shallow earth. Next to it was a garden trowel. Roz didn't touch it. She stood up and walked rigidly back toward the car. Her bodyguards followed. It was obvious to Roosevelt that she hated them all

Simia got off her knees, reached inside her soft handbag, and withdrew a lei of beautiful orchids. She placed the lei around Alan's neck and kissed him on both cheeks. Then Simia went over to Craig's ashes, took one large orchid from her handbag, and laid it on the ground in front. Simia picked up the trowel and shoveled one scoop onto the box. Crying without shame, she walked off into the garden.

Following Simia's lead, all of the others added their scoop of earth to the burial of Craig's ashes and left the wall.

The last was Alan Gavin. Tears were blinding him as he took three small photos and two rosebuds from his side pocket and added them to the gravesite. Alan finished covering the ashes, then stumbled away.

Savannah and Alan's mother went to his support.

It was over.

*   *   *   *

Friday, Hong Kong

Friday afternoon, Craig Carlson booked a seat for a Mr. Carl Stone on a Qantas Airlines flight headed for Perth, Australia, a daily flight with a stop in Singapore. He was told he would need a visa to enter the country. Panicked, Craig contacted the Australian Consulate and was told that since it was an emergency, if he would come right around, maybe they could do something.

That evening, Mr. Ling delivered Craig's custom luggage and also made a gift to him of a new "special" briefcase. Craig was delighted. In the hidden compartment in the base, Craig placed several passports, Schmidt's financial instructions, and ten thousand dollars. In the familiar internal space, he placed his precious Financial and Communications Control Book, along with other items that a briefcase would normally contain.

He zipped the rest of the money into the clandestine linings of his new luggage. It's as safe as it will get, Craig thought. He knew that smuggling two-hundred-thousand dollars was not a light offense. Then he finished packing it with his newly purchased clothes.

He filled Schmidt's brown suitcase with all of the discarded clothing, not yet sure exactly what to do with it.

Craig realized it made little real sense to move. It was late, and the probability of anyone connecting an in-house guest of Papagos with a dead Carlson would be most unlikely. He decided to risk one more night at the Shangri-La.

The early Saturday morning news was that Kai Tak would be operating on that day's schedules commencing at ten in the morning. Craig was relaxed. He heard later news that after all the bodies were removed from the Nam Airlines 727, big earth-moving equipment simply pushed the wreckage into the harbor. *Nam Airlines can sue Hong Kong as much as they want*, Craig thought. Kai Tak was Hong Kong's lifeline to the world, and they needed it open.

With Schmidt's birthmark in place, with Schmidt's suitcase in tow, and with Stone's precious Australian visa in hand, Papagos checked out. He had altered his appearance as much as he dared, yet still looked like Carl Stone's passport photo. He had decided on a plan and was in a hurry to execute it.

*　　*　　*　　*

Craig was seated in the beautiful and open first floor lounge of the Peninsula Hotel enjoying a light snack and a drink before his long flight. He and Alan had spent several romantic times there, and that was one of the things that drew him there.

He desperately missed Alan. But Craig realized there were more people he left behind than just Alan. He missed his son. He hoped he had provided for Andrew adequately in his will. And his devoted mother—how was she, and how had she taken his death? And what about all the others who had helped him along the way in his life and in his industry whom he had deceived and abandoned?

Craig ordered his second Bloody Mary—this time, a double.

And what about his insurance fraud? That was not without its consequences. The extreme amount of it had been a matter of contention and discussion with Packard on many occasions. He wondered how stubborn and difficult the insurance company would now be in paying the new beneficiary.

And what about a new residence? Where in the world could he and Alan really live, yet not be recognized and reported? Craig had come to the stark realization that being completely free also meant being completely isolated and alone.

Craig needed that drink and was looking for his waiter when he saw that a Caucasian man was paying an unusual amount of attention to him from the bar.

Craig boldly decided he would confront him now rather than give him a chance to follow him later. He reminded himself his name was Stone, stood up, and headed directly for the man.

Without hesitation, the person in question left.

Craig asked the bartender,"Do you know the man who was sitting here?"

"No, sir. I don't. But whoever it was asked me who you were. I told him I didn't know. We never discuss our guests even if we know them. Before you noticed him, he took several pictures of you with a small camera."

Craig attempted to hide his reaction to the unwanted news.

The bartender smiled. "Are you someone important?"

"No. I was unnerved at his degree of attention."

"Just a moment. I'll ask the host if he knew who he was."

Craig waited anxiously. He had checked his luggage in the lobby transit check room before coming down to the lower level. He was used to checking valuable possessions, but a bag stuffed with money was not a possession he was used to leaving in someone else's care. Trying to act unconcerned, he fumbled with his briefcase, and realized he could flee with just that if he really had to. He hated the thought.

The host approached Craig. "Sir, I have no idea who he was, or who you are. However, after you arrived, he was the very next to arrive," he said pointedly. "Is that of any help?"

Craig thanked him, tipped him, and turned away.

"My God," he said aloud. "He followed me in here!"

He carried his briefcase with added caution as he sought out the hotel concierge. "Can I speak with you privately?"

"Of course." He led Craig to a small office off the lobby.

Craig said, "I have a bit of a problem. It's one that requires utmost discretion. I know you understand those things." He handed the concierge two hundred dollars. "I need to take care of something personal and private before my flight this afternoon, and I don't want to be burdened with my luggage while doing it. Could you arrange for someone to deliver my luggage to me most confidentially at the airport at one?"

Craig looked carefully at the man, trying to get a reading if he was trustworthy. Then he realized that he had no choice; he had to trust *someone*.

"Yes. I know how to do that." His face was unreadable.

"Can you make sure that the luggage itself isn't followed?"

"Yes. I can also do that. Where will you be at Kai Tak?"

Craig hated to tell him Qantas. He had no choice.

"Your luggage will be at Qantas at one," said the concierge "May I have your claim tags? And I'll need to know your name."

"Stone. My name is Carl Stone." Craig handed him all but one claim check, and pressed another two hundred dollars into his hand.

The concierge's professional impassive mask didn't change.

"There's more," Craig said. "I want you to register the name of the man on this credit card for three nights. I have a brown suitcase I want left in the room, and I want that room messed up every night and the articles in the bag unpacked and strewn about."

Craig took a deep breath and handed him one of Kurt Schmidt's credit cards. "Can you also arrange that?" He was pleased that a K.S. was engraved on the old-style bag.

"Of course," the concierge answered. He looked down at the credit card and then back at Craig. "I'll be right back, Mr. Stone-Schmidt."

Craig couldn't believe what he had just asked would be done without question at the Peninsula. He went over to the transit check room and claimed Schmidt's suitcase himself. He would give that to the concierge now. He couldn't afford any mistakes.

The concierge returned with a registration card and a credit card expense slip for Craig to sign, and handed him back Kurt Schmidt's card.

"Thank you very much," said Craig. "Here's the bag."

"You're welcome, Mr. Stone-Schmidt." The concierge smiled.

*   *   *   *

Outside the Peninsula, Craig plunged into the surge of humanity, and immediately moved into the first massive shopping building, where he came across rooms and corridors full with vendors selling everything imaginable. Inside, he stopped, moved, watched, walked, purchased, discarded, and then, once out the other side, hailed a cab.

He had the cabbie take him to Stanley's Market. The tour buses had already filled the small area with thousands of people. He repeated the process. Finally satisfied that he didn't notice anyone watching him, he took another cab.

At Qantas, he purchased the ticket they were holding for Carl Stone. At customs, he was sure he would be hauled off for smuggling. Craig was sweating; he jumped at every noise and choked on every question. But his new suitcase, shoved full of money, made it. He carried on his black bag and briefcase, thus ensuring his instant mobility.

Craig made it a point to be the first on the plane in order to watch from his first-class seat all of the others boarding. He had made up his mind that if he recognized anyone paying too much attention to him, he would get off. He didn't relax until the flight departed on the first leg of its journey to Perth.

*   *   *   *

Friday Afternoon, Bel Air

Packard was pleased with the arrangements at Roz's Bel Air home. The dining room was large enough and the table ample enough to take care of all he had requested to be there. He understood from Washburne that at the Bel Air Country Club, Roz hadn't socialized with any of them, and, in fact, had spent most of her time outside talking to the press. Washburne said that no one tried to stop her, for no one cared. Packard wondered what had happened to Washburne's protective feelings for Roz.

At two o'clock, Roz entered the dining room. Any pretense of grief was gone. She was wearing a blazing red dress and seated herself at one end of the table with a drink.

Packard took up his station at the other end and asked Washburne to please sit next to him. He precisely ticked off those in attendance: Alan Gavin, Chin Lee, Simia, Andrew Papagos, and Mr. Alltop.

Savannah Marlowe and Jebb Marlowe were not included. They were in their hotels packing for their return trips to their homes and responsibilities.

Just before Packard was ready to start, another man arrived. Roz introduced him as Melvin Stein, her attorney.

Washburne leaned over to Packard. "Never heard of him. I don't think he has ever been involved with Roz before now."

Packard sent Washburne down to introduce himself and get his card. When Packard read it, he didn't recognize the firm. But somewhere way back in his mind, the name Stein rang a bell. And for some reason, it wasn't a pleasant sound.

Victor Packard cleared his throat, leaned back in his chair

and officiously looked over his reading glasses. On both sides of him were neatly arranged stacks of paper. He knew there was going to be hell to pay today before this scenario was over.

He wondered if Roz was ready for it.

He wondered if Alan was ready for it.

He knew what this would do to the murder case—*blow it wide open!*

* * * *

Friday Afternoon, Las Vegas

Standing vertical to the Strip, the Trojan Horse Casino was the pride of Italian architects who had done extensive work for Disney World. Although five years old, in comparison with other grandiose establishments, it more than held its own.

The head of the Trojan Horse was twenty stories above the street and two hundred feet wide. The mammoth body of the Horse housed endless gambling casinos, huge convention facilities, and super-sized VIP suites. On one side of the Horse was the entrance. Wide escalators moved endless streams of visitors and guests in and out of its cavernous belly. On the other side, a soaring tower contained two thousand guest rooms. At the Horse's tail were the swimming pools, tennis courts, restaurants, specialty shops, and the entrance to the unending underground parking garage for guests and employees.

The logistics of the Horse were hard to fathom. There were four thousand employees, thirty-two bars, seventeen cabarets, three celebrity nightclubs, sixty elevators, twenty restaurants, twelve kitchens, and an underground traffic area large enough for semi-trailers to offload produce and take out trash. The Horse had its own security force of four hundred men and women, including bouncers, bodyguards, internal security, external security, and financial security. The Horse even had its own emergency medical facility and pharmacy. At any one time, there could be over twelve-thousand men and women in the building. Crowded people movers, busy rest rooms, lines at telephones, and lines at slot machines. People sober, people drunk. People happy, people mad. Vegas at its best. The Trojan Horse was only one of the wonders of the Strip.

And Antonio Beretta was not only the manager, but had a piece of the financial action. It was not a light responsibility.

*   *   *   *

Beretta was seated at his desk looking out the huge, heavily tinted, convex, triple-strength window that formed one eye of the Horse. His office was decorated in all blacks, whites, and grays. Splashes of red and orange accented it. His desk was metal and of Scandinavian design. His leather chairs and couches were by a famous German designer whose name he had forgotten. The art on his walls was expensive and contemporary. All of it large, and much of it difficult to understand.

This was Beretta's office, where half of the head of the Trojan Horse contained the corporate and administrative sections of the casino. The other half was taken up by ten thousand square feet of living space for Antonio Beretta. It encompassed a huge master bedroom, master bath, master dressing room, state-of-the-art exercise room with sauna and steam room, an adult playroom, a spacious living room, another office-study, a kitchen, and two complete guest suites.

One whole wall of his bedroom comprised the second convex eye of the Horse. Beretta enjoyed that view as often as he could, and he used his well-appointed study in his living quarters for his more careful, special interests.

A steel-reinforced, but grass paper-lined hall separated the two halves of the interior of the Horse's head. Beretta's own private elevator serviced that dividing zone. Beretta could take the elevator from either his corporate office or his living quarters to three destinations: the security mezzanine, the main casino floor, or his private underground garage. Only he had the access code. If he wanted to expand those options, he had to rely on in-house elevators.

For Beretta, this fortress of security was needed to manage

the Trojan Horse Casino and still have a personal area in which he could have a life and feel safe and secure.

Beretta was impatiently waiting for a call from the manager of a Wells Fargo bank in San Francisco. His phone rang and he listened as a George Aliotto told him that Curtis Smith had, in fact, picked up his certified check. Beretta thanked him for his information and slammed down his phone. He spun out of his chair and stood with clenched fists looking out the window—this time, at the horizon.

"That fucking son-of-a-bitch!"

Now he knew why they were never able to apprehend Schmidt in LAX, London, or at his small home in Topanga Canyon. He had never gone back to any of them. He had driven to San Francisco.

Still standing, Beretta dialed Roz's private line. He knew that for security reasons he should call her from his private office, but since she wouldn't answer anyway, he charged ahead.

His message was terse. "Roz, we have a deadly problem with Guess Who. Get back to me! My private line."

Boiling with rage, he opened his office door to the corporate area and burdened his well-worn secretary with his mood and the fact that he would be out for the rest of the fucking day. He slammed that door and hurried through the steel door in one wall of his office into the dividing vestibule. He locked that door from the hall side, crossed the twenty-foot hall in five raging steps, unlocked the steel door to his own quarters, and entered his world.

Beretta immediately felt a sense of relief. All could be disaster on one side of the Horse, but his real life was where he was now. He ripped off his shirt, pitched his loafers, tore off his pants, and headed for the bar.

Nine

Friday Afternoon, Bel Air

Victor Packard examined the gathering.

Roz was full of energy and expectation. She fidgeted with her pen and tried to look omnipotent and concerned, while Packard knew she really didn't give a damn about anyone but herself.

Alan was silent—actually grim. He appeared as if his thoughts were elsewhere. Packard expected that Alan's only wish was for the day to be over.

He had never met Henry Alltop, but he simply looked like another dreary trust attorney who worked for dozens of wealthy widows in Palm Beach. Packard scoffed at such a practice.

Packard was surprised to see that Simia was examining the others just as he was. He didn't know her that well, but was taken with her demeanor; she may well have been the most observant person in the room.

A quick glance at Washburne completed his perusal. Washburne's expression was dour. It was the first time Packard had worked with him since the fiasco at the Beverly Wilshire, and Packard assumed that Washburne was already frightened of what Roz was going to say when she found out about Craig's last hurrah.

It was time, further delay was impossible. Packard cleared his throat and said, "Let's have a moment of silence in memory of Craig Carlson."

Packard savored the silence, knowing fireworks followed.

"Each of you will receive a copy of the will in its entirety at the end of this meeting. I'm going to go through it in a random fashion for the benefit of each of you."

Packard watched as Stein made a note.

"In item eight, Mr. Carlson has gifted Chin Lee twenty-five

thousand dollars." Packard glanced at him, but couldn't tell whether that was satisfactory to Chin Lee or not. Packard didn't care; it was a minor matter.

Roz smiled and said, "Oh, Mr. Lee, how nice."

"In item nine, Mr. Carlson refers to an irrevocable trust he had established for Simia's retirement twelve years ago. Called the Simia Trust, it was unknown to the beneficiary." Packard looked at the mute woman. She was watching him with keen attention.

"To date, Carlson has funded the Simia Trust to three-hundred-thousand dollars. He was gifting it on a yearly basis to avoid the onerous gift tax. His will provides that if at his death the Simia Trust didn't have a minimum of five-hundred-thousand dollars, his estate would gift the trust any shortfall and pay the gift tax."

Tears welled up in Simia's eyes and flowed across her cheeks.

Roz started to say something, but grimaced instead.

Packard smiled. "Simia, this means that additional funds will be added to your trust by his estate." He took off his glasses.

"And Simia, there is one more matter in item nine."

Packard dropped his first bomb. "You have the right to live in this house for at least one year after Carlson's death." He kept right on reading. "And your quarters are to change from the third floor to whichever front suite you select, if you elect to remain here at all."

"She'll stay on the third floor where she belongs," Roz said coldly. Simia's reaction was inscrutable. Packard continued to ignore Roz and pushed two thick envelopes to Washburne. "Please give these to Chin Lee and Simia when the meeting is over."

He continued. "In item ten, Craig Carlson has willed all of his stock in Papagos Food Wholesalers to his son, Andrew Carlson. If Andrew was still a minor at the time of his death, he appointed the trust department of the First National Bank of Palm Beach as the administrators of that stock until Andrew comes of age."

Alltop beamed. To Packard, he said, "Thank you." To Andrew he said, "Now, you and your grandmother control Papagos Food."

Andrew nodded, old enough to understand.

Roz went to the elaborate sidebar, picked up a heavy crystal decanter, and poured herself a full tumbler of scotch. "Lettuce and tomatoes, anyone?" she asked sarcastically.

Packard refused to rise to her remark. He knew what he said next would take care of her derision.

"In item seven, Craig Carlson left all the rest of his real and personal property that was not defined in his prenuptial agreement with Roz Marlowe or already placed into several trusts that are outside the will to Alan Gavin."

Roz gasped, and her knees buckled. She turned white and dropped her glass. She reached out desperately for the sidebar.

"No! No! No!" she wailed.

Stein jumped up to catch his client.

"No! It can't be. It isn't. You're lying. Liar! Liar!"

Roz's knees gave way just as Stein reached her. Roz stammered, "Help me!"

Stein half carried, half dragged Roz back to her chair.

"You could have been a hell of a lot more considerate, Packard," snapped Stein. "You could have told her this in private."

Alan Gavin was the only one not watching Roz. His head was back, his eyes closed tight. He was trying to deal with the unwanted reality that with unwanted death come unwanted possessions.

Roz stared blankly in front of her. Her breathing was a series of spasms. She refused Stein's offer of water.

Packard elected to wait until Roz's reaction was over.

Color began to slowly return to Roz's face.

"Do you want a recess?" Stein asked his client.

Roz shook her head. She was deep in thought—almost a trance. She began shaking her head from side to side. "Nothing. It was all for nothing," she whispered to no one.

Slowly Roz raised her eyes and looked at Packard at the

other end of the table. "How long have you kept this from me?"

"Craig signed a new will the Saturday before his death," Packard said matter-of-factly.

Roz began to laugh, then suddenly screamed. "I've been cheated!" She gulped air as someone about to drown, then laughed derisively. "The bastard cheated me!" Roz then uttered a shrill, gut-rending cry of hate and rage.

Melvin Stein was at her side. "I think we better take a break, Roz."

"Isn't this funny?" she laughed. "I think it's funny!" Roz screamed again—a long, pitiful wail.

Simia helped Stein remove her from the room.

*　　*　　*　　*

Roz appeared under control when Packard continued the meeting. His first guess was that the old Roz was back and he prepared for the worst.

"Are we all ready to continue?" he asked.

"Please do," said Melvin Stein.

"Wait a minute," interrupted Roz. "Let's go back to item whatever. The one that takes it all away and gives it to that— that scheming faggot."

Alan clenched his fists. "Watch it, Roz!"

"Watch it, my ass! You've been planning this great achievement for ten years. You got him to change his will for you, and then you murdered him!"

Melvin Stein put his hand over hers. "Mrs. Marlowe, I don't think you should—"

Roz jerked her hand away.

"Shut her up, Stein," ordered Alan.

"No one is going to shut me up! Just wait." Like a hurricane feeding itself, Roz's tantrum gathered strength. "I'll tell it like it is." Suddenly Roz directed her fury to Packard's end of the table. "And don't think you're not involved, Gregory Washburne. You are. And you're a lousy lay and a worm of an attorney. All I ever did with you was a waste."

Gregory Washburne didn't respond. He couldn't.

Roz continued her attack. "Let's cut to the chase, Packard. For years I was beneficiary of a multimillion-dollar insurance trust. Has that been changed too?"

Packard flushed and didn't immediately reply. Packard realized now he had underestimated Roz's acting ability.

"Well? Answer me, goddamn it!"

Packard summoned his strength, "That insurance trust is outside the will, and Carlson made Gavin the primary beneficiary about a month ago." He swallowed hard and continued, "For sound tax purposes, a charitable institution or institutions are secondary beneficiaries. It's moot to discuss it here."

Roz gasped, her face instantly pale again.

Stein was writing vigorously, no longer monitoring Roz.

Roz pulled the pins out of her severe Eva Perón hairstyle and shook her golden mane free. She looked vicious, "You don't think for one minute I'm going to take this crap, do you? The last I knew, Packard, I was that beneficiary. *Me!* You're not going to get away with cutting me out of what's mine. Nobody is!"

"It's all legal, Roz."

"Then what about my house? Are you going to tell me that's not mine, either?"

Packard was glad she was the one who brought it up. "It's not in the will, either. It's also in an individual trust. Gavin is the recipient of this real estate."

"That's not so!" Roz took a deep breath and then threw the diamond-studded hairpins down the table. "Here. Here's some of my jewelry. If you can afford the time, I'll go up and get the rest." She made no effort to rise.

Packard was undaunted. "Yes, it's so, Mrs. Marlowe. And don't give me that 'I was his wife' crap. Craig owned this home four years before he married you and before you all but gutted it. Unless you paid for the remodeling and reconstruction, you have no marital interest, and I know you didn't spend a dime."

Roz looked as if someone had struck her.

Packard looked at Alan Gavin. His face was filled with disbelief. Craig had basically left him everything that the government wouldn't take.

Stein said, "Mr. Packard, all of these documents will have to be examined for authenticity, considering the immensity of Mrs. Marlowe's losses and the most unusual timing surrounding their changes. California law is quite specific on separate and community property, and I'm sure these documents violate those laws."

Packard ignored Stein. He could see the real Roz was now interfacing with Roz the actress, and to continue would be useless. "Here are Roz's documents, Stein. Read them at your convenience." Packard pushed a pile of papers to Washburne and said, "Give these to Stein. There's no value in prolonging this meeting."

Packard jammed the remaining envelopes into his briefcase.

Roz's tone was sinister. "What about the meeting you were going to hold with Craig on Wednesday? What was that about?"

Packard was exasperated. "Mrs. Marlowe, your husband was murdered. He executed this will on Saturday, unknown even to me. Can't you get that into your head?" Packard shoved his chair back. "All that Craig Carlson left you was the right to live here for twelve months. Nothing else."

Roz again started to break. Her blazing face matched her blazing dress. "But what about his investment accounts? What about his film royalties, what about . . . "

Packard didn't let her finish. "All left in trusts outside the will, my dear. And his bank accounts are closed." Packard stood. "I've had enough of you and your temper tantrums for the rest of my life. I happily bequeath them all to Melvin Stein."

Stein said, "Packard, this is most irregular behavior. You are overly aggressive toward your deceased client's widow."

"Yes, but Stein, you haven't lived through one of the infamous Roz Marlowe egomaniacal, self-aggrandizing love feasts. Today has only been an appetizer. But, more important, this will is completely legal and binding!"

Roz picked up the envelope Washburne had just given Stein and threw it at Packard, but instead just barely missed Henry Alltop.

Alltop's face tightened as he stood. "Marlowe!" he said

sharply, "I've watched you in action for two days. If I were you, I would watch what I said, what I did, and to whom I did it." His knuckles were white.

"And Stein, I've seen Carlson's wills for at least ten years. His mother always got a copy, and therefore so did I. I'm also an attorney and I know who you are. I am amazed to find you here. You're only known because of your court challenges to wills. It won't wash this time. Victor Packard has consistently drawn complicated documents of strong legal value, and the trail goes back as far as Timbuktu."

Alltop paused for a breath then plunged on, "You know, it would be interesting for all of us to know just how long you've known your client Roz Marlowe. Has it been days or hours?"

Alltop dropped his voice. It was cold and uncompromising. "If I were you, Stein, I'd tell your loudmouthed client in the splashy dress you have a plane to catch!"

Victor Packard was floored—not only at Alltop, the quiet, unimpressive Alltop, but also because he now knew why the name Melvin Stein rang such an unkind bell. He felt like hugging Alltop and slugging Stein.

Roz was speechless. She had just been shut out and told off.

Stein set his jaw and looked directly at Alltop. "I take offense at your remarks. Mrs. Marlowe, I suggest we leave."

Packard canvassed the other beneficiaries. Gavin was upset, Simia watched Roz intently, Andrew appeared confused, and Chin Lee, lost. He was surprised how calm and in control he felt.

"Stein, Craig Carlson knew exactly what he was doing. I just wish he were here to tell you himself how many years I talked him out of divorcing Roz and how many years I talked him out of changing his beneficiary to Alan Gavin. He finally forced the issue. And I, for one, am damn glad that he did."

Packard fumbled his glasses back into his jacket. "And Mrs. Marlowe, for your information, divorce was next on his agenda."

Jesus! Packard thought. *With Stein in the mix, blind copies, and fake faxes, this could become a nightmare.*

"Wait until I talk to the press," warned Roz. "I'll tell them all how the man whose reputation I've protected all these years gave every penny to that, that" she pointed ferociously at Alan, "French male whore! He cheated me out of my fortune and the world is going to know it!"

Alan lunged across the table. "Shut your trashy mouth! There's no one in town you haven't slept with to get a job!"

Stein tried to restrain Roz and Simia reached out for Alan.

"Get off of me!" Roz shouted. "You're here to do a job. So do it, goddamn it!"

Stein removed his hand, completely bewildered.

Packard could tell Stein was overwhelmed by his client.

Stein looked at Alan. "Please relax, Mr. Gavin. This meeting is," he fumbled for words, "unfortunate."

"Then shut her up."

Slowly Alan settled back in his chair and said, "You know, Roz, I can't equate all of this material wealth with the value of Craig's life. I'd give it all to you if you could give Craig back to me."

Roz looked as if she had been slapped.

The room became very still.

A small voice finally broke the silence. "Can I still have one of my dad's Oscars?"

Packard said, "I'll see that you get one, Andrew."

"Aren't those mine?" choked Roz.

"No, Roz. They're not. Craig's personal property, which those are, now belongs to Alan Gavin."

Roz started to cry. She began to shake. "This isn't fair. Not fair. It could have all been different." Roz turned ashen. "I tried so hard to make it different. Nobody cares." She closed her eyes and shook her head from side to side. "Nobody cares."

Packard picked up his briefcase. "Simia, Alan, Andrew, Mr. Alltop, Chin Lee, thank you for coming. And don't any of you worry about anything." He nodded at Roz and Stein. "I'm far from finished."

Packard continued, "Washburne, please arrange a meeting with each beneficiary with me in our office tomorrow at a time that is convenient with them. Except for Mrs. Marlowe. She seems to be in informed legal company."

*　　*　　*　　*

"But why, in God's name, Simia, would you want to continue to live here and work for her, when you can come and live with me and Chin Lee in Encinitas?" Alan couldn't understand.

Simia wrote on her PC, "Must stay. What's yet to happen will open past to me." Simia looked at Alan to see if he understood.

Alan understood perfectly, but hated the idea.

"Do you even think she'll keep you?"

"Yes. Spoiled rotten. Hate at first, then forget me. As always."

"Simia, do you know where the Oscar is for *Dangerous Passage?*"

Simia shook her head and wrote, "Should be on mantel."

Alan said, "I gave Andrew the Oscar for *The Prince* and took the two he won for *The Corsican* for myself. But that one is missing."

"Here someplace," Simia typed.

"I don't trust Roz not to have thrown it out just so I wouldn't have it. Craig's life means so much to me." Alan stopped talking.

Simia took his hand, then made the sign for "I love you."

"And I love you, Simia."

*　　*　　*　　*

Alan arrived at the hotel to find Savannah sitting on the floor stretching in sweats. "I thought you'd be at the door with suitcase in hand," he said as breezily as possible.

"No. Not yet. I have a surprise. Your mother and I are taking Air France tonight for Paris. That will help her on her trip back to Nice."

"But I thought you were going to London."

"I was, but if I went with her as far as Paris, she can connect tomorrow afternoon for Nice. Isn't that wonderful?" Savannah supported the back of her neck with a towel and smiled.

"Savannah, you're the one who's wonderful. I know she

wasn't looking forward to the return. But what about the theater?"

"Oh, darling, my mad admirers can do without me for one more night." She flipped the towel and sang, "When I'm young and healthy, I'll find someone wealthy . . ."

"But Lady Ashley, I thought you had," Alan laughed.

"And I have. Hugh has zillions." Savannah stood up and hugged Alan. "As soon as he gets back from God knows where in Down Under, I'm going home to him. But tonight, we are going to enjoy a leisurely dinner. Nothing hurried and no command performances. Just the lovely three of us."

"I'll miss you, Savannah." Alan was sorry to see them both leave, but glad Savannah would be with his mother.

"So, who got what at the séance?"

Alan told her about the will. "It's so unbelievable. Craig was so generous to all of us."

Savannah said, "And my dearest stepmother gets what the bitch deserves. Nothing! Marvelous!"

"We're going to have a fight, Savannah."

"And, darling, you're going to win!"

*   *   *   *

Inspector Roosevelt read the copies of Craig Carlson's will, the separate immense insurance trust, and the fax from Carlson to Gavin that was damaging as hell. It wasn't quite clear as to which day the FedEx package reached Carlson, but he knew he could get that information from FedEx without difficulty. With a one-hundred-million-dollar motive, Gavin had much to gain by murdering Craig Carlson. And so far, he was the only one they could find anywhere near the Bel Air mansion that night.

Roosevelt could see it. An emotional argument, a light scuffle, Gavin knowing where Carlson kept his gun, a shot fired from fifteen feet, a new cartridge put in the gun, the gun wiped clean then put back, a call to 911. Pretty cut and dried. Easy.

Except, why did Gavin wipe the gun clean, and not the humidor? Why were there other prints on the humidor, but not his? The gun didn't jump back into the box. Why did he pick the toilet paper holder on which to injure himself? Why not some thing else in the scuffle? Those things didn't make sense. And Gavin's behavior throughout had been that of the greatest loss, and Roz's that of the greatest hatred.

But the biggest question for Roosevelt was: Why smash the hell out of his lover's face? That wasn't emotional, that was hatred, an intentional disfigurement he felt Gavin incapable of.

Inspector Roosevelt knew once again it was going to be difficult. The prosecuting attorney wouldn't care the least about Roosevelt's vague intuitions. He would only care about motive, alibi, and evidence.

Roosevelt watched the six o'clock news: "Carlson's French Lover Gets All." "Roz to Challenge Will." "Roz and her attorney, the famous Melvin Stein, will hold a press conference Saturday morning at her Bel Air estate."

Roosevelt felt like going home and weeding his garden.

*   *   *   *

After Simia drew her bath, Roz coldly told her to leave her alone. Maybe forever. As Simia retreated up the inside stairs to her quarters, she could hear Roz slam her own door to the hall. When Roz had remodeled the house after her marriage to Craig, she had a narrow stairway built from Simia's third-floor quarters down to her dressing room. It gave Roz easy access to her private slave.

Simia knew Roz was going to call Beretta. She had never intentionally eavesdropped before. Today, she returned down the inside stairs, cracked open the door, and listened. The fact that she never wore shoes and could walk as quietly as a cat had been one of Roz's complaints. Simia was often there when Roz didn't realize it.

Simia didn't catch the beginning of her conversation, but as Roz continued, she got louder and completely audible.

"What? He's gone? You let him get out of the country?"

Simia wished she could hear both ends of the conversation.

"You fool! You should have known he would do that. I never said he was dumb. Just strong. So where the hell is he?"

Simia was typing rapidly into her PC.

"Hong Kong or Sydney?" Another pause, a longer one.

"Well, my life is shot to hell, Beretta. Your Melvin Stein is no great catch. I hope he's as good as you say he is. And on our runaway, I'll do all I can to fix my end. You damn well better find his ass and fix yours."

When Simia heard the phone crash into its cradle she silently returned to her room.

*   *   *   *

Friday Afternoon, Las Vegas

Antonio Beretta had some serious work to do. He thought about Roz's conversation. So all their wheeling and dealing had been in vain. She didn't get the money and Gavin did.

"Shit!"

His handless desk clock told him it was four. He canceled his arranged harem for that night, touched a button, and left his office by the disguised bookcase door. He crossed the secure steel-lined vestibule and with his thumbprint, unlocked the door to his luxurious living quarters. Once inside his fortress, he stripped naked.

Beretta jerked on a tight pair of exercise shorts and tank top, and entered his extensive workout room. He was very upset. He had to get his contacts moving, and he knew Schmidt. He wouldn't be staying in some fleabag hotel. He would be staying at the finest. His grubby lifestyle in Topanga Canyon had always been a front. Kurt Schmidt liked the high life. And he kept it high with drugs, girls, and cars, and by spending others' money.

Beretta wondered where Schmidt was depositing his easily found fortune. He would have called some of his banking contacts in Switzerland, but it was already the weekend there.

"I'll hang that motherfucker by his balls when we find him."

Beretta began a heavy one-hour workout that he knew

would keep his forty-year-old body still looking like thirty-five. His muscles rippled under his dark Sicilian skin. Sweat turned his black hair to shining silk. He consumed water by the liter and tried hard to remove the gnawing problem from his mind.

Beretta needed sexual release. Maybe he would double his pleasure and have two massage therapists join him later for a much-needed frolic. He thought of Roz and how she could be a tigress when she was turned on. He had never known anyone like her. He could have any woman he wanted, but she excited him more than most. Once he had command of her, he could make her either a wild, raging animal or turn her into the softest, pliable flesh.

Beretta remembered the night he met Roz. His entertainment manager had gone all out on booking big-name celebrities for the opening of the Trojan Horse. Roz Marlowe was the featured star. She captured the crowd and finished her performance singing *I Dared to Love.*

Beretta went backstage afterward with two dozen roses. Simia let him in the dressing room. Roz was at her mirror.

"Mrs. Marlowe, these are for you. You were fantastic."

"Just give them to her; I'm busy." Roz didn't look up.

Beretta threw the roses into the wastebasket and said, "No one talks to me that way."

This got Roz's attention. First she looked at the unmistakable bulge in his pants and then at his face. Their eyes locked.

"Simia, leave us alone. I'll call you when I need you."

And that was it. He had been screwing Roz Marlowe ever since.

But he had other things to think about. He had extended his already overextended credit line an additional six million dollars based on a bonus payback of twenty million from the immense insurance trust Roz would have received. He needed it badly. He had debts to pay. And he had always intended to simply pick up the six million dollars in hit money himself.

Now he hoped that Melvin Stein could do for him what he had sent him to do—destroy Packard's credibility and implicate Gavin so completely that a judge and jury would send him to prison for the murder of Craig Carlson.

But his conversation with Roz bothered him. She was capable of tricks. Schmidt had to be eliminated.

He finished his workout with sit-ups and threw his soaked clothes into a hamper for Maria to take care of. Maria was his housekeeper, the only other person who had access to his domain.

Beretta stalked naked through his home like a sleek, heavily muscled panther through his private jungle. He had a timing, a presence, that was only his. It set him apart from other men.

He rarely misjudged an individual's capabilities. But he had missed on Kurt Schmidt. He looked at the clock—five o'clock. He still had to wait before he made his calls. He stepped into his combination shower–steam room, and after thirty minutes, turned the hot water to cold. As the icy water drilled his body, Beretta could feel his heavy testicles shrink with pain. He enjoyed that moment as much as any. It was pain at its finest, its most erotic.

A vigorous towel-off followed by a hefty line of the finest cocaine, and Antonio Beretta was ready to make his calls. He put on a silk kimono, lay spread-eagle on his bed, and looked at the sky through the second convex eye of the horse. He hoped his operatives in Hong Kong and Sydney were clever.

He knew it would take brains to bring Schmidt down.

Ten

Friday Evening, Las Vegas

Antonio Beretta was seated behind his chrome-and-leather desk in his private office. He touched a button on a small transmitter, and all of the drawers of his custom-built desk unlocked with an inaudible click.

The top right-hand drawer was lined in green velvet, providing special padding for his .45 Glock automatic pistol. The gun was made in Austria, and each clip held fourteen rounds of Teflon-coated bullets. It was Beretta's favorite weapon, sleek and quick, lightweight and deadly. It was adapted for a silencer that never left the gun; extra cartridges were in the drawer.

In the larger, top left-hand drawer was a thick black book that had names, phone numbers, security codes, and pictures with short biographies of top operatives, politicians, and financial executives all over the world. He referred to it when he needed information. He also had another book that Beretta called his Adjutant General, or AG. More correctly translated, the AG was his assassin's guide.

In the bottom left-hand drawer lay an assortment of other necessary items for his trade, a blackjack, brass knuckles, a billy club, assorted drugs, ether, a variety of cameras, tape recorders, and various paralyzing sprays.

In the bottom right-hand drawer in a false bottom, he kept a stockpile of thirty or forty thousand dollars in cash, and, above that, a supply of condoms and Kleenex.

Beretta's most constant battle was allergies.

Beretta's most constant entertainment was women.

He withdrew his AG and found the Communications Commands. On one page were listed the numbers for twenty pay phones located throughout the public areas of the Trojan Horse Casino, phones that were constantly in use by the thousands of visitors who poured through the casino night and day. Beside each number, Beretta found the control code that he needed.

Beretta randomly dialed one of the pay phones. It was busy. He chose another. It was also busy. But the third rang freely. As it continued ringing, he dialed in its control code and waited. Within ten seconds, a small red light came on at the bottom of the special phone he was using.

The solid red light told him that pay phone's line had been seized and was exclusively his. If anyone picked up the receiver of the phone in the casino, it would be dead. He could call anywhere in the world, and phone company records would show the call had been made from the pay phone downstairs.

Beretta waited thirty seconds to be sure the red light was not interrupted. Satisfied, he dialed an operative's number in Hong Kong.

A deep male voice came on the line. "Yes?"

"Is this Ian?" Beretta inquired.

"It is."

"Where and when were you born?"

"Parknisilla, Ireland, in 1960. Fourteenth of April."

"Thank you. I have an urgent request."

"Of course. Please tell me who my mother's father was."

Beretta looked at Ian's bio. "He was Timothy O'Donnel."

"Thank you. Your favorite movie was what?"

"*The Guns of Navarone*," replied Beretta.

"What is your request?"

"I must locate a man by the name of Kurt Schmidt. He's believed to be in Hong Kong and could also be using the aliases of Curtis Smith or Charles Silvey. I have your fax number. Let me send you his picture before we finish our conversation."

"I'll wait," said Ian.

Beretta transmitted Schmidt's picture, which had just been taken a week earlier when Schmidt had been in his corporate casino office. For anyone to gain access to that area, all were photographed for security reasons and possible later reference.

"It's on its way," said Beretta.

"Thank you. I'll let you know its quality."

"Here's information you'll need." Beretta told Ian that Schmidt lived high, not low, and to start at the five top hotels in Hong Kong. If not registered, he should go to each hotel and use "persuasion and observation," which meant cash and camera. Ian was to report back no later than 10:00 P.M. or sooner if he had something.

Beretta gave Ian the pay phone number that would ring in his quarters and also would be answered by a machine. The pay phone downstairs would be out of order a long time.

"His picture is clear enough," said Ian.

"Any other questions?"

"No."

"Ian, this assignment is urgent. And payment will be proportionate with performance. Understand?" Beretta hung up.

Beretta duplicated the same exercise with a man in Sydney, using a different casino pay phone. He marked one phone *H.K.* and the other *S.A.*, spun around in his chair, and looked at the clock. Six-thirty. Now all he had to do was wait. He didn't want to get a recorded message. He wanted a personal report so he could ask instant questions and give instant orders.

He slid out from behind his desk, picked up a copy of a current fitness magazine, and lay down on his firm leather couch. Beretta's silk kimono fell open loosely around him. He wasn't able to concentrate on the magazine. The cold, hard leather made him think of Roz. He recalled their meeting at Big Bear Lake, where they had planned their little fiasco. He would love her services now.

"God," he said, "that was ten days ago!"

He got hard just thinking of what she did to him. He knew she was a screaming, tantrum-throwing bitch about almost everything. But what a turn-on! They had sexual escapades that had gone for six and eight hours without a break. He always wondered who put the cabin or whatever they had used back into order after they had finished. It certainly wasn't either one of them.

Then he thought of Kurt Schmidt and the day the deal was struck in his corporate casino office. When they had finished, Schmidt was escorted back through security and disappeared.

Beretta recalled how crafty Schmidt had been with his arrangements. Still, he thought he had the upper hand and was sure Schmidt would have been eliminated within hours of Craig Carlson's murder.

*   *   *   *

Friday Evening, Beverly Hills

Victor Packard had sought out the darkest corner of Trader Vic's at the Beverly Hilton. He was concerned. Things weren't going well. He was afraid of Stein, concerned with what Roz would say in the morning, and worried about Gavin's freedom.

It was time for him to do some strategic thinking on his own about who murdered Craig Carlson and why, and who was going to prove what, to whom, about the will.

After his second double rye whiskey, he pulled out a yellow legal tablet and began listing names, drawing boxes, making notes, and drawing arrows. He quickly eliminated all but Gavin, Roz, and Washburne.

He didn't believe that Gavin did anything but be the wrong person to discover the deceased. He wasn't overfond of Gavin, but that still didn't establish him as the murderer.

He moved on to the next box: Roz Marlowe.

He was sure that she was quite capable of arranging a contract killing. Her alibi was perfect: Roz was shielded by the Oscars. And Roz was also quite capable of setting up Gavin with the perfect motive—money. But why would she risk it? Or with whom would she compromise to plan it? She certainly had used Washburne.

Packard was so angry with Roz, that he moved on to the last box: Gregory Washburne.

He knew that under oath, Washburne would admit to falsifying blind copies. And if Roz had arranged a contract murder that would make Washburne an accomplice.

"Dumb shit," he muttered.

Packard had his third double rye on the rocks.

Or was Washburne involved with Roz from the beginning? He sipped his drink and his analytical mind went to work. Packard started a column about his California colleague.

1. What do I know about his background? Nothing.
2. Who do I know in his family? Nobody.
3. What do I know about him at all? Very little.

Packard's writing was becoming more arduous as the alcohol began to limit his physical capabilities.

He wrote: (1) He graduated from Stanford; (2) He's thirty years old; (3) He's very attractive to women; (4) He's brought me at least eight good clients; (5) He's spent a lot of time in Roz's bed; (6) He lives alone. . . . Packard shoved the pad away. He realized he didn't know one damn thing about Washburne and that his associate's ass could be hanging out to dry if Roz were found to be the instigator of the murder. And his own credibility would be heavily damaged if that happened.

What can I do to protect him?

Or should I protect him at all?

What should I do to protect myself?

Packard's thinking dropped deeper into fuzziness and doubt. Couldn't Washburne have been in cahoots all the time with Roz, and simply covered things up with his answers to me? What if Washburne had his own agenda maybe to marry Roz? Or blackmail her?

Packard pulled the pad back and scrawled a big note: *Get information on Washburne!*

He said to his empty glass, "You hired him, idiot."

Packard needed to get busy.

He ordered his fourth double rye and began to think about how much he hated Melvin Stein.

*   *   *   *

Friday Night, Las Vegas

The phone rang at nine-thirty. Beretta looked at his watch—thirty minutes early. He tried to control his excitement.

"Beretta here."

"This is Ian."

"I recognize your voice. What do you have for me?" Beretta rapidly computed. It would be one-thirty Saturday afternoon in Hong Kong.

"I think I found your man."

"Great. Where?"

"I went to the Peninsula first. No one by any of the three names was registered, so I went down to the courtyard bar to observe for a moment before going on to the Mandarin Oriental."

"Yes." Beretta forced patience.

"The man who fit the picture you faxed was having a drink in the lounge. I took several pictures and was watching him, when all of a sudden I realized that he was watching me."

"Shit!" said Beretta.

"His next move surprised me. Instead of running, he headed right for me. So I hit the street and doubled back. When I got back, he was gone."

"You lost him?" Beretta tried hard to control himself. He knew that had to be Schmidt. That would be his mode of operation. There was a silence and heavy breathing on the other end.

"Wait for the rest of the information, whoever you are."

Beretta realized he had made a mistake. The man could have hung up. "Sorry. It's damn important we silence him. Go on."

"He evidently wasn't too bothered by my attention, because your Kurt Schmidt is now registered at the Peninsula in Hong Kong. He must have just stopped in to have a drink before hitting the front desk."

"Great!" Beretta was ecstatic.

"What do you want me to do?"

"Call me back and tell me he's not breathing."

"Is that an order?"

"It is."

"May I have the code that directs that sanction?"

Beretta referred to Ian's dossier and found the code. He asked, "Have you ever visited the graveyard at Land's End on a Thursday night?"

"Thank you. I'll not call you back until I visit Land's End."
Ian hung up.

Beretta shouted, "Yes!"

*   *   *   *

Late Friday Night, Las Vegas

Beretta called Roz on her private line. He knew it was late,
but he was sure she would relax some when she had the good
news. She didn't answer. He asked her to call—urgent.

Beretta didn't know that Roz was so depressed over the loss
of her home and fortune that she had taken one Valium and two
sleeping pills, and washed them down with a large dose of John-
nie Walker.

Needing distraction, Beretta arranged midnight entertainment, telling his in-house pimp he wanted them wild, young, and
strong enough to last until he collapsed.

Beretta would be celebrating Schmidt's demise.

*   *   *   *

Saturday Morning, Bel Air

Melvin Stein was busy. He gave all of his attention to the
details for the press conference. He had addressed the scene, the
star, the audience, and the script.

He decided to use the overlarge formal living room of Roz's
Bel Air home for the scene. The furniture, paintings, and the
other expensive trappings would represent the many irreplace-
able possessions that she was going to lose. If the will stood, they
would no longer be hers, they would belong to Gavin.

How cruel!

Stein had a twelve-inch platform brought in and set a table
on it. He had a lighting specialist focus amber light on it. He
knew that would give Roz viewable height and the right light
while seated. Stein then insisted that all of the cables and wires

necessary for the press conference be installed as intrusively as possible.

Satisfied with the scene, he turned his attention to the star. Stein had a makeup artist carefully create the facial mood on Roz he wanted to achieve. Then he insisted, over her most strident objections, that her clothing and hair be less stylish than was normally Roz. He wanted her to look burdened, used, exhausted, grieving, yet determined to set a travesty and dishonesty right. He knew she could play those roles.

Another woman misused by a powerful man!

For the audience, Stein limited the media coverage for the "press conference" to national television networks or strong California stations. He did the same with the print media. Only the *Los Angeles Times*, the *Washington Post*, the *New York Times*, the *International Herald, USA Today, Time, Newsweek, People,* and *Insight* were invited to cover the event.

He secretly allowed the *National Enquirer* to photograph Roz in mourning and gave them a full copy of the script.

Through off-duty police, he arranged tight security, and only those Stein approved got as far as the property. Packard and Washburne were not included. He allowed Roz's personal secretary, Anne, to attend, but forgot about Simia. Simia hid herself in a doorway where she could observe it all.

Stein felt the quality of the media audience was a ten out of ten.

At precisely eleven o'clock, with Roz sitting forlorn at the table and Stein standing supportively beside her, he gave his signal to the full room.

"Ladies and gentlemen, we have asked you to come into Roz Marlowe's home to hear the unfair, unheard of, and possibly, even illegal actions of those she thought were close to her." His delivery was firm.

Stein put his hand on Roz's shoulder. She didn't flinch. She looked up at him as her savior, there was hope and trust in her eyes. "The murder of her husband has been compounded with a legal travesty. A new will that has surfaced most irregularly at the last minute yesterday leaves all of Roz Marlowe's possessions to Alan Gavin, Craig Carlson's gay lover." Stein knew this was a lie. All of Roz's earnings from her own efforts had been placed in separate bank accounts at Craig's insistence.

There was immediate unrest among the reporters and cameramen in the room. Stein thought he had obtained the reaction that he wanted. Confirmation of what some of the press had already reported, but Stein knew it was more graphic when delivered live.

"Roz didn't even get the house that she and her deceased husband cherished—only the right to live here for one year, hardly enough time to pack one's personal belongings." He spread his hands to include the elaborate furnishings. "This is filled with treasures that she and Craig have collected over the years, and many of them were hers alone before they were married."

Stein knew it was another lie. Her personal property was still hers. But he didn't care. Who would take the time to prove him wrong? He knew under California law he had some grounds to challenge parts of the will, but he had his own code: Slander first, then let the burden of proving him wrong fall on the other party.

Roz started to weep. She looked more stricken than she did when playing her role as Sadie Thompson. Stein comforted her.

"We intend to challenge the legality of the entire will."

There was audible reaction.

"Not just the portions that give everything away to Gavin, but all of it." Stein knew it was safer to challenge the entire will rather than just bits and pieces.

"Later we will provide you with information about Gavin that will help you see how he intentionally planned an inheritance from the first day he met Craig Carlson in Cannes ten years ago. Most young playboys his age have but one objective— to strike it rich. He certainly accomplished that through this will." Stein ignored the loud rumblings of disapproval in the room.

"And we will further prove this will is a fake, and the attorney, Victor Packard, who just surfaced it yesterday, was working closely with Gavin on individual items in it."

If Simia could, she would have screamed, "Liar!"

Anne squirmed in her chair. She knew better.

"We will prove that Craig's mother, Mrs. Ellen Traver Papagos, also schemed with Victor Packard to exclude Roz Marlowe from any portion of his most valuable asset, his stock in Papagos Food Wholesalers, which is worth millions. It is a known fact that Mrs. Papagos has hated Roz Marlowe from the day that Craig married her." He looked down at Roz. "Mrs. Papagos has even alienated Roz's own son from his mother."

The reporter from the *New York Times* stopped writing. He knew Melvin Stein's reputation well, and he knew that he was hearing a pile of shit. He had a responsibility to be there, but he had his editorial freedom to write what he wanted, and he knew there was no need to continue to note slander.

Some of the television networks wished they weren't providing live coverage to this ridiculous circus. The O.J. Simpson trial should have taught some of their bosses more sense. It was sensationalism at its worst, and Melvin Stein at his sleazy best.

Roz had now gone from weeping to appearing resolute.

Stein continued, "There is still another matter, and that is the curiosity of the timing of the mysterious death of Craig Carlson at the same time as the surfacing of a new will." He didn't bother to reverse it and say that if Carlson had not died, the will would have been in place for years.

"We wonder what the prosecuting attorney is doing and why the most obvious has been so overlooked." Stein looked around the room; he knew he had probably pushed them over the edge.

"Bullshit!" said one magazine reporter. She slammed her pad shut and stalked out.

"That's all I have to say. I asked Mrs. Marlowe if she wanted to address this travesty, and she has declined." He looked down at Roz. "Do you still feel that way, Mrs. Marlowe?"

Roz shook her head. "No. I must say something."

Stein said, "Please do. This is your press conference."

"Like hell it's been," said the reporter for *Time* to the reporter from *Newsweek*.

Assisted by Stein, Roz slowly pushed herself up from the table. It appeared to take a great amount of effort.

"I just want to thank all of you for coming to my home. . . ." Roz had to stop for a moment, "and for supporting me at this most dreadful time of my life. To win an Oscar, and then lose a husband and then lose my life's possessions all at the same time is too much for me to cope with." Roz stopped for a moment to pretend to stay in control.

The reporter from the *Los Angeles Times* leaned over and said to the person on her left, "You should have seen her leave the Eclipse Thursday night. The bitch wasn't so frail then. I saw Roz demolish the pastry cart as she left."

Three television cameramen shut down.

Roz continued, "I have had to deal with Craig's affair with Alan Gavin for years." She stared down at the table in shame. "It was most difficult for me. I hated to hear them argue all the time about everything. Mostly money. There just wasn't any peace for me. I often wondered why they stayed together. But now I know." Roz then looked over at Stein. "I can't go on, or say anything more."

"She's better here than in *Rain*," said a leaving reporter.

"I just want justice," Roz said, looking at Stein. Then she looked straight into the room. "I demand justice!" Roz sank into her chair and reached for the tissues.

Stein put both of his hands on her shoulders. "That's all there is to say." We thank you all for coming."

"How about questions?" CNN demanded.

"Yes. How about some honest stuff," requested ABC.

Stein looked at Roz for her permission. Roz shook her head, "no." Stein withdrew his hands and gave the cutoff sign. A roar of questions and disapproval emitted from the room. Stein ignored them. He tuned out "What a joke!" and "We came here for *this* crap?" He hurried Roz Marlowe from the room.

*   *   *   *

Anne thought of resigning. She didn't know where to go that

would pay what Roz did, but she knew she couldn't continue to be any part of this.

Alan Gavin threw a heavy brass clock straight into his television, and the screen exploded.

Victor Packard taped the entire show. He said, "Fuck you Stein!" with every lie Stein told.

Gregory Washburne wondered about getting his own attorney.

Antonio Beretta laughed as he left his message to Roz, "This is Stud, baby. You cut Gavin's balls off!"

*　　*　　*　　*

Saturday Afternoon, Palm Beach

Mrs. Ellen Traver Papagos sat back in her chair and smiled. Earlier she had called two of the best attorneys she had ever known and had alerted them to the nationally promoted press interview. She had asked Mr. Henry Alltop to be with her.

"Henry," she asked, "do you realize what Stein just did?"

"Yes. I think so." Alltop was puzzled.

"I think we can put Stein behind bars."

Henry Alltop wasn't as sure. "I hope so, Ellen."

"Don't hope." Ellen Papagos smacked him on his leg with her cane. "Start on it!"

"Yes. I'll start immediately." He sighed.

"And there's one more thing." She leveled her blue eyes at her friend of many years.

"Yes."

"I know without a doubt who killed my son."

"You do?" asked Alltop with a degree of astonishment.

"Roz Marlowe put out a contract on him."

"How do you know that?"

"I know. She wants 'justice.' I'll see that she gets it. I'll see that she goes to prison for it."

Henry said nothing. He was amazed at the elderly woman.

"And Henry," she sighed, "I have one other request."

"Yes."

"Will you please push me outside. I need lots of fresh air right now."

*　　*　　*　　*

Early Sunday Morning, Perth, Australia

Craig Carlson was ill with exhaustion. He hadn't stopped since Monday night. His stomach was cramping and his beard, scratching. He hadn't had a decent meal for a week. He hadn't slept in the same bed for more than two nights. It seemed he had been on an airplane for eight hundred hours.

He dragged himself through Australian customs and found a room at the Sheraton overlooking the park that bordered the Swan River. He registered under the same name he had flown as—Carl Stone. He couldn't think beyond that at the moment. In fact, he could hardly think at all.

He just wanted to go home and be Craig Carlson again.

Eleven

Sunday Morning, Bel Air

Inspector Roosevelt had a premonition that his Sunday morning would be disturbed. The call from the prosecuting attorney came just as he was leaving for church with his family. "Meet me in my office in thirty minutes."

His wife said she understood.

Roosevelt had read enough and heard enough over the weekend to know what the prosecuting attorney wanted to talk about, but he wondered why he couldn't wait until Monday.

"Good morning, Inspector. I hope this wasn't too inconvenient," said Samuel Goldman, who indicated a chair across from his paperless desk.

"No. Of course not," Roosevelt lied. This was the only time he could spend with his family all week.

"I'm sure you can guess why I asked you here."

Roosevelt nodded. "The Carlson murder."

"Tell me about it. And don't leave anything out."

Inspector Roosevelt told Goldman all that he knew and all that he didn't know and couldn't explain. He tried hard not to reveal his bias about Alan Gavin to the prosecuting attorney. He knew that if he revealed it too soon, and made it an issue, Goldman would discount the relevancy of Roosevelt's opinions.

Goldman didn't take any notes. He just listened.

"Is that it?"

Roosevelt nodded affirmatively. "That's it."

Goldman turned around and looked out his window.

Roosevelt knew that was simply window dressing. He knew what he was going to be ordered to do.

"Interesting. Puzzling. And it seems fairly simple." Goldman looked at his watch. "I think you should pick up Alan Gavin tomorrow morning and bring him in as the prime suspect for the

147

murder of Craig Carlson. At least bring him in and find out what he has had for breakfast for the last thirty days."

Roosevelt knew that meant "bring him in and tear him apart."

"Do you have a problem with that?"

"No, sir." But Roosevelt couldn't hide his full concern.

"Anything else?"

"Yes, sir. Shouldn't we do the same with Roz Marlowe and Gregory Washburne?"

Goldman failed to hide his surprise. "Why? They were both at the Academy Awards."

"This could be a contract killing," said Roosevelt.

"With Carlson's own gun? Explain that one."

"I can't—yet," said Roosevelt.

"And what about the fax from Carlson to Gavin, and copies of the correspondence from Packard that Gavin was privy to?"

"I can't explain those items, either. But I think that Mrs. Marlowe and Washburne can answer some of those questions."

Goldman said, "Inspector, with all the media hoopla from yesterday's press conference and with the slam they gave our department, we could use some press of our own."

Roosevelt tried to broaden his base. "I think Packard could also shed some light on the matter. We've never questioned Carlson's attorney about anything."

"You know I think Stein is a creep, don't you, Roosevelt?"

"I concur, sir. I think it's whiplash at its worst."

Goldman folded his hands.

Roosevelt knew the sign, the meeting was over.

"Bring Gavin in. That for sure. And question Packard and Washburne. Don't bring in Marlowe. What we find out from others may possibly lead us back to her. But for the sake of LAPD, don't bring her in now. It's too early to start *Star Wars*."

Roosevelt stood. "Thank you, sir. I'll do as you direct." He was pleased that Goldman had dropped the words *prime suspect* from his last order.

Roosevelt already had an expert examining the fax from Carlson to Gavin. He didn't have the original copy, but knew by now that fingerprints would be meaningless. The examination of the fax as to who may have authored it would now depend on the phraseology and the machine with which it was written before it was faxed—if it ever was.

Roosevelt got back home in time to see his family finish Sunday dinner.

*   *   *   *

Sunday, Early Afternoon, Bel Air

Simia needed access to phone-company records.

She found Anne in her small, well-appointed office in the carriage house. Anne looked up when Simia politely knocked.

"Yes? Simia? Come in. What is it?"

Simia noticed Anne's puffy red eyes. She smiled at Anne.

"Please sit down. It's nice to have a break."

Simia handed Anne a note.

Anne read it, then reread it, then looked up with concern. The note said: "I know this is overstepping my place. But I question some things that have gone on. I can only do so much because of my limitations. You know I log all of Roz's personal phone messages. I need to see the bills. I don't know how much I can talk to you without seeming crazy. How do you feel about Craig's death? And how do you feel about Roz? I know you do everything she asks of you, and I know you can't tell her of this note. Please talk to me."

Simia knew her note was traitorous.

Anne handed Simia a draft of her letter of resignation and shook her head. "I don't know what's going on, but I simply can't continue." Anne faltered, then started to break down.

Simia stepped behind Anne and massaged her neck.

Anne sobbed. "I have noplace to go to make this kind of money. I have to take care of my two children. My father died eight years ago of alcoholism, and my husband divorced me because I spent so much time with my father. Now it's all I can do to keep my head above water."

Simia had never known anything about the efficient Anne. She had always seemed so together no matter what Roz threw at her. She was always dressed neatly and properly, and was always so professional. Sometimes Simia thought she was as hard as a rock and cold as steel. Now she knew why.

Anne regained her composure, "I don't know what came over me. I don't tell anybody that story. It's my problem, forgive me." They evaluated each other in silence. "How do you do it, Simia? She treats you much worse than she treats me. And that's awful."

Simia typed her answer: "No place to work. Friday Craig opened freedom for me. Not going until know that Alan not made guilty falsely."

After Anne read that message, Simia typed another one: "Sorry about father and divorce. Maybe I can help."

Anne was unable to conceal surprise at Simia's remark.

Simia wrote again: "You think Alan killer?"

Anne shook her head, but said nothing.

Simia pointed to Anne and then back to herself and wrote. "Maybe only ones prove not. Stein challenge legal papers. Soon have Alan in prison. I know."

Anne became quiet and looked at the latest draft of her resignation. Slowly she tore it up. She then went to her files and got out the U.S. West phone bills.

"Please give these back to me as soon as you can." She handed the bills to Simia. "If she finds out, all she can do is fire me." Anne walked around the desk and hugged Simia. "I'll stay. Now I have a good reason."

Simia smiled. She had an ally—a badly needed ally. She made the sign for "thank you," then left with her precious information.

*   *   *   *

Sunday Afternoon, Santa Monica

Roz and Stein were having a private, high-profile brunch in Beverly Hills at the Ivy on Robertson, near Sunset Boulevard. It was the former home of Douglas Fairbanks, and had been sought out by celebrities for years as the place to be seen.

Roz was resplendent in yellow—canary yellow with dark-brown piping—and she had accented it all with dark brown crocodile shoes, a wide dark brown crocodile belt, and a large crocodile purse. Even her dark glasses had crocodile frames.

They were both delighted with the attention they were receiving. They chose to ignore the bad press their performance had received yesterday. They discussed only the good press.

Roz had failed to call Beretta back. After Stein was through with her on Saturday, she had drunk so much and drugged herself so much that by evening, she was incoherent. And the number of messages that Simia and Anne had for her were so overwhelming that she ignored them all. Even Beretta. She was furious with him. He had let Schmidt escape, and Schmidt could ruin her life.

While downing Bloody Marys and listening to Melvin Stein run on, she decided she needed a good screwing from somebody. And she needed it tonight.

She thought of Gregory. She missed him, but he had messed up. No. Washburne was not a candidate for sex. At least not tonight. And her bodyguards were all beef and no imagination.

Stein was talking as Roz was thinking.

"Beretta!" she said.

"Pardon me?" wondered Stein.

"I just remembered. I have to make an important call." Roz's mind was racing. "Excuse me, Melvin." Roz hurried to the manager and asked him if she could use a phone someplace that would grant her privacy.

"Of course. My office, Mrs. Marlowe. It's not very nice, but at least it will be quiet and no one can overhear you."

He showed her into a small, cramped space overflowing with open liquor boxes half full, single bottles of expensive wines sitting in disarray where a case had just been opened, decorations from some forgotten party piled in one corner, adding machine tape that ran from his calculator to the floor, and counted or uncounted money lying on his desk with dozens of sales slips, along with many coins carefully stacked to be rolled—in short, a working office for a busy restaurant.

"Excuse the mess. Just make yourself at home."

Roz poked into everything on his desk while waiting for Beretta to answer his private line. She was surprised how quickly he picked up and how anxious he sounded.

"Beretta here."

"I miss you. Where can we meet?" Roz asked seductively.

Beretta said, "I can't leave Las Vegas today."

"Of course you can, Tony," she purred.

"I'm expecting a phone call about someone you know."

Roz ignored his message. "I need you, Tony."

Beretta said, "I left you several messages to call me. Where the hell have you been?"

Roz could feel herself getting mad, but she wanted to stay in control, she wanted Beretta to take her to bed. "Then I'll come there," she announced. "Send your plane down for me."

"Bad idea."

"Stop refusing me! Are you so screwed up and screwed out you can't perform?" Roz knew she was losing it and tried to repair any damage. "Please, Tony, I need to see you."

There was silence on the other end.

"Tony?" Roz heard nothing. "Please come get me." Roz found herself begging to a dead line.

When the manager returned to his desk he found his already counted money, ready for the deposit bag, all over the room.

*   *   *   *

Sunday Evening, Encinitas

Alan was adding columns of figures and checking balances, trying to figure out how to keep everything he already owned, or was to receive, financially afloat.

He needed information from Packard. Was the will really going to be challenged? Would the estate pay the bills during a long, drawn-out court challenge or during the period of probate? How quickly would the insurance trust money be available to him?

He had called Packard on Saturday after Roz's press conference, and twice again today. He had left a message each time, and Alan had confirmed that Packard was still registered in his hotel. But Packard hadn't returned any of his calls.

Alan knew he needed to find an attorney. Roosevelt had made that clear by the tone of his questions at their last meeting. Now it was compounded by the will. He wished Craig had used someone other than Packard. The only message he had received about the will since Friday was from Washburne: "Packard prefers to talk to you next week."

Alan thought Craig had always trusted Packard well beyond a point of reasonable safety, but Craig never listened to Alan's reservations about his old college friend.

Alan pushed his chair back from the desk and thought of his mother's concern, of Savannah's support, of his father's irritation, and of Craig's unconditional love. He recalled that one of the few arguments they ever had was over whether or not they should leave France and move to the United States in order for Craig to film *An Honest Lie*.

Alan simply didn't want to leave the tranquillity of Provence for the insanity of Hollywood; he had told Craig that. "It wasn't the film, but the fake people, the photographers in your face day and night, and of being too near Roz's beck and call."

"We can handle it," Craig had said without conviction.

"Here, we are two equal people. There, I will be your cute kept trick that you hide from the public."

Alan knew that Craig understood completely. But instead of taking it objectively, he took it personally. Craig shoved both hands in his pockets and stalked out of the house for an extended walk. Two weeks later, they made arrangements to leave France and Alan had obtained from Craig the commitment that they wouldn't live in greater Los Angeles.

Alan was amazed that even after writing the screenplay for *An Honest Lie*, Craig still couldn't enter a confrontation with the understanding that it was all right to disagree. He still was in hiding after saying and writing that he would no longer hide from the truth.

Now Craig was gone, and Alan would return to Provence alone.

Alan believed that if he and Craig had been able to get married, much of this could have been avoided. They had tried Holland, Sweden, and several other countries. They had even considered Hawaii, but after Congress passed their bill to make the illegality of same-sex marriage into law, they realized it was useless.

Alan didn't want a ceremony; he wanted a legality. Being a realist, Alan knew he would have to fight for anything Craig left him, sort out a new life, and be willing to face the constant charge that he had schemed from the beginning.

Alan threw his pencil on his desk and stood up. Figures made him tired. He knew a good jog would clear his mind. He pulled on a pair of gray jogging sweats and a faded blue sweatshirt. The Pacific air was chilly and invigorating. After the first mile Alan was thinking of his future rather than his past.

* * * *

Sunday Afternoon, San Bernardino

Victor Packard was talking to a small, wrinkled woman on her front porch in San Bernardino. At first, she didn't want to talk about anything. Then he had used persuasion—cold cash. Even with that, she had made it very clear that his presence was most intrusive. But it was the only lead that he had found.

"So Gregory graduated from law school at UCLA, not Stanford?"

"I'm not sure where he graduated from," she said defensively. "We haven't heard from him since . . ." She stopped talking.

"Since what or when?" insisted Packard.

"I think you should go. I didn't ask you to come here." The

feisty woman started to retreat through her door to escape Packard's bulky presence.

"But you are his aunt. You confirmed that. Where are his parents? Where is your sister, his mother?"

"Good-bye, Mr. Packard."

Packard pulled out his wad of bills again.

She hesitated.

"If you won't tell me anything more, just give me one person I can talk to." He skimmed off five hundred dollars and handed it to her.

She hesitated again, then said, "It's worth twice that." Packard skimmed off another five hundred. *This is like feeding a geriatric piranha,* he thought.

"His mother lives in Van Nuys. Her last name is Warley. Mary Warley." She took the additional money. "Now git!" She shot inside and slammed the door.

"But what's his father's name?" asked Packard to a closed door. He hoped he had deciphered the name Warley right. He pounded for five minutes until he knew it was hopeless. *There has to be a better way*, he thought as he started back toward Beverly Hills.

"Think, Packard, you dumbass!"

* * * *

Sunday Evening, Las Vegas

The phone marked H.K. rang. Beretta calculated it was Monday noon in Hong Kong. About time. He was exhausted from hours of waiting, of worrying, of drinking, of exercising, and of screwing. He needed some answers.

"Yes?"

"This is Ian."

"Finally. I wondered when you would call."

"My news isn't good."

Beretta could feel his stomach tighten. "Yes?"

"Our man, who stayed three nights at the Peninsula, was to

have checked out at noon today, but he never showed up at the desk to do so."

"You mean you waited for his move? You didn't make one of your own?" Beretta was furious.

"The first two nights he was able to come and go without our being able to understand how. During that time, I was inside his room twice. It would be a mess in the morning, the chamber maids would clean it, and he would sleep there again that night. His luggage had *K.S.* on it and the clothes there would fit a man of his size, but we never were able to catch him coming or going. So last night, I stayed in his room, waiting for him to come back, but he never returned."

"Unbelievable," shouted Beretta. "Fucking unbelievable!"

Ian said, "I know."

"Did he leave any messages with the front desk or concierge, or were you too involved in watching his door to ask?"

"I didn't just watch his door!" Ian said testily. "We watched the elevators and stairs and lobby areas. The Peninsula frowns on someone lurking in a hallway to stake out a room."

Beretta quelled his urge to scream into the phone, "Do you know what he's capable of and what he has cost me?" Instead, he asked, "So, do you have any idea where he went, this invisible Mr. Schmidt?"

"Yes. According to the concierge, a Kurt Schmidt asked a lot of questions about Sydney, Australia."

"Did he pay his bill or skip out?"

Ian paused. "It was prepaid," he said lamely.

"Shit!" Beretta slammed down the phone.

He immediately called his contact in Sydney.

* * * *

Monday Morning, Perth

Craig Carlson woke to sunlight streaming through his window. He had to think a long time before he realized where he was. He was hungry. He closed his eyes again, but hunger forced them open. He looked around the room. Slowly, it came to him.

"I'm in Australia," he said to the ceiling.

He had to call the desk to find out which day it was.

"It's Monday, Mr. Stone."

"Thank you," said Craig. *Mr. Stone. So that's who I am. I'll research that after I have something to eat.* He looked out the window and saw a beautiful park next to a wide river.

Craig's spirits lifted. *Perth! I made it. I hope I left that overly curious man behind in Hong Kong. Here maybe I can be myself again—an Anglo with a British heritage, and, if I want, with a British accent.*

Craig realized he had slept away a full day, but that rest was long overdue. He hoped that maybe today he could speak without his tongue tripping over his teeth from exhaustion.

Craig ordered a copy of the local paper and enough food to feed three. He decided he would look in the real estate section and find a flat to rent—a place he could call home for more than two nights. A place to pull himself together, and a place from which he could contact Alan and tell him the truth.

Craig knew that if it had been a long time for him, it could have been twice as long for Alan. He had been murdered and buried, and his will read. Craig just hoped that Alan would understand that he had put him through all of it in order to accomplish something of value by leaving Schmidt dead.

"Yes. It's time," he said.

*   *   *   *

Early Monday Morning, Las Vegas

Antonio Beretta had just talked to Herr Deitmueller at Le Credite Banque de Suisse in Zurich. He was satisfied that Deitmueller would find out from Bundersbank in Zurich and Lloyd's of London if Schmidt's money was still being held by those banks. Then he called his special contact in Sydney again.

His report wasn't satisfactory. There was still no evidence of any arrival of a man fitting Schmidt's description using any of the aliases supplied by Beretta. And they had a full-scale team of spotters and baby-sitters working on it. Beretta had been assured they were covering the airport with gate agents, washroom attendants, security exit personnel, personnel at car-rental agencies, along with dozens of well-planted tourists reeling from jet lag, strewn about the airport like pebbles on a beach.

Upset, Beretta left his private quarters and entered his corporate office through the bookcase-door. As it clicked shut, he was further angered to find His Peer sitting behind his desk with his feet propped up and smoking a cigar.

Beretta hated cigars.

"So, Antonio, when will we see some money from your latest scheme? Not soon enough, right?"

Beretta was enraged by the intrusion.

"So. We need collateral. The Horse is already loaned to the hilt. What about a little paydirt on your filly Roz Marlowe? I understand that since she won the Oscar for Miss Sadie, *Rain* is making a fortune." His Peer's smile flashed gold.

Beretta didn't try to hide his animosity; his face resembled a closed fist. "Do you know all that has happened?"

"Sure—you're down two million. Want to guess how much more you're going to lose?"

"No more," said Beretta. He wondered how the man knew.

"You wanna bet?"

"I don't gamble," said Beretta sharply.

"It's too bad Roz ever played the Horse. To have her here for the grand opening ends up such a tragic burden for you." His Peer flicked ashes on Beretta's spotless desk with impunity.

Beretta sat down across from him, sweat running down his face.

His Peer withdrew a contract from his pocket. "Here's a little document we think your filly should sign." He pitched it over to Beretta's side of the desk.

Beretta scanned it. It was a commitment for Roz Marlowe to assign all of her earnings from *Rain* to the Quaker Cancer Hospice in Philadelphia until seven million dollars had accumulated. At that time, her pledge would be considered paid in full.

Beretta threw the paper back across the desk. "This is too soon, too much, and unnecessary. I'm not finished with my project yet." He knew it was a strong response.

His Peer touched his cigar to the paper. "It's just an idea," he said, and dropped the paper.

Beretta slapped out the fire with his bare hands.

His Peer stood up. "You come up with either the money or something better by next Monday. Same time. Same place."

"How did you get in here?" seethed Beretta.

"Your secretary is such a doll. I'll send you another copy just in case you change your mind."

Shaking with fear and hatred, Antonio Beretta sat behind his desk. He had no choice. Now he had to call Roz after just making her furious by hanging up on her yesterday.

When he felt settled, Beretta picked up his phone to go through the old routine of leaving a message for Roz. He was amazed when she picked up the phone. She never did.

"What do you want, Beretta? You threw me away, remember?"

"I thought about our call. Let's meet at Malibu, or Palm Desert, or Big Bear. Your choice, baby."

Roz laughed harshly. "What's bothering my little stud? That was too quick of a change of pace, darling."

"No; you just don't understand my commitments sometimes. Now we can spend some fun time together. Say, noon tomorrow until Wednesday morning. Sound good to you?"

Beretta waited impatiently for a response. Maybe she would hang up on him. It hadn't been a good morning.

"Have you heard from your runaway?"

"I have news about him. That's all I'll say on the phone." It was the lightest and brightest he could fake.

"Will you send your plane for me?"

"Sure. Just name where. I'll be on it."

"Palm Desert. It was too cold at Big Bear Lake last time."

"Noon at the Santa Monica airport," said Beretta.

"I'll bring some toys," teased Roz.

* * * *

Monday Morning, Encinitas

Something woke Alan up from a deep sleep. When he realized it was the phone, he tried to clear his gravelly voice.

"Gavin? Is this Mr. Gavin?"

"Yes." Alan slowly recognized it was Inspector Roosevelt.

"We need to see you today; this morning, actually. I'm sorry it's such short notice."

"Great. My first day of peace and you want to see me. Where shall we meet? Halfway?"

"No, Mr. Gavin. In my office. And if you can't drive in, we'll have to send someone down to pick you up."

Alan felt a shiver. He could see the police car in his driveway being photographed by some stakeout photographer.

"Why?" asked Alan.

"We have lots of unanswered questions, remember?"

"I'm sure you do, but not from me."

"It's not my idea," admitted Roosevelt.

"Oh—I see. Either the prosecuting attorney or the district attorney listened to the Roz and Melvin Comedy Hour." Alan didn't feel as glib as he sounded.

Roosevelt didn't respond.

"Will I need an attorney?"

"Yes. I would advise it."

"I don't have one,"said Alan. "Every time I try to reach Packard, he isn't around."

"Then get someone else. But we have to talk." Roosevelt paused. "I must see you by Wednesday at the latest."

"I get two days to find someone who will defend me from the possible unwarranted charge of murder? Thanks heaps."

Roosevelt said, "I wouldn't go that far, Mr. Gavin."

Alan thought he just omitted the word *yet*. "If you can tell me how to find Packard, it will help me meet your request."

"Mr. Gavin, the California Bar will supply you with a list of attorneys from which you can choose, or we may be forced to appoint one for your benefit."

Alan's strength left him. This was serious. "You know damn well I didn't kill Craig!" Alan said earnestly.

Roosevelt said nothing.

Alan knew a gay attorney in Encinitas he would ask to represent him in a civil matter, but never a criminal one.

"If you don't give me an agreed upon-time, Mr. Gavin, I'll have the judge issue a writ or a warrant, and we'll pick you up in a police car. I don't want to do that."

Alan was cold. This wasn't a dream. "Wednesday at one. Is that soon enough?"

"It would be better earlier, but I'll accept that."

Alan asked, "Do you know how to get in touch with Packard?"

"Yes. I just talked with him at the Beverly Wilshire. He was in his room just ten minutes ago."

This made Alan feel better. "Why don't you see what kind of light he can shed on all this, Inspector?"

"I'm doing that," said Roosevelt.

Alan appreciated his frankness. "Is there anything else I should know?" he asked.

"No, except please bring in your passport when you come." Roosevelt might as well have said, "Run for the border."

"Bring my passport?"

"It's routine," lied Roosevelt. He hurried his closure, "I will see you Wednesday in my office at one."

Alan's mind was spinning. Roz had done something someplace, and his head was on the block. He called for Packard.

The operator told him that Mr. Packard had requested all calls be held.

"I know better. I just talked to him ten minutes ago and he's waiting for my call, so stop giving me the runaround."

She capitulated.

"Packard here."

"Packard, I've been trying to talk to you for three days, so don't put me off." Alan was angry.

Packard lied, "I just walked into my room from breakfast,

and you were first on my list."

Alan swallowed that one; he couldn't risk making Packard mad. "I need to talk to you about the will, about the police, and the insurance money. And I can't put them off. I have been summoned to bring my passport and an attorney with me by Roosevelt on Wednesday."

Packard said, "Interesting."

"We need to meet today, I need to know more about my future."

"I'm free for lunch," said Packard.

"How about driving this way some—say, Huntington Beach?"

"I'll meet you at the Ritz in Marina Del Rey at noon."

"Hell, that's as far north as you are now."

"That's all I can do. My schedule is very tight. Melvin Stein is headed for probate court with a will contest action. If he gets there before I do, we're looking at an easy six months of nothing but taxes."

Alan was listening now with interest.

"If I could get a declaratory judgment before he got there on some issues, it will help. But it looks like he's going, just as he said he would. But I can talk to you more about this at lunch. See you there."

Once again, Alan would have to wait.

Twelve

Monday Noon, Marina Del Rey

Packard heaved himself off the overstuffed sofa next to the large flower arrangement at the entrance. "Glad you're on time."

"Yeah. Traffic was easy," said Alan sarcastically.

Packard forced a smile. "I don't seem to have enough time right now." He wanted Gavin to like him today, because he knew he would hate him later. Packard had been thinking of his positioning with him all weekend.

After small talk and ordering lunch, Packard got down to business. "I haven't been back to you for several reasons and I did get all of your messages, along with dozens of others."

Alan was noncommittal.

"Stein is filing with the probate court to deny distribution to all beneficiaries of the Carlson will. It's a full-blown will contest action. And if the judge allows it, it will be difficult for even the minor recipients, such as Simia, to receive their share before it's ruled on. You, and Andrew Papagos for sure, will be put on the shelf until the trial is held."

"What kind of trial?"

"It's before a judge, with attorneys representing both sides, with witnesses, but there is no jury. The judge makes the decision. It's civil, not criminal, and whatever he says goes—unless it's appealed. And I think either side here will appeal any judgment. So we have a long, dry spell ahead of us with nothing but aggravation and expense. It's called a bench trial."

Packard watched Alan's reaction. He could tell it was going to be difficult for him financially.

"What are you going to do about it?" Alan asked.

"Get to the judge first and ask for a declaratory judgment. But if he smells a will contest coming, he will drag his feet on my

163

request. In fact, it will be moot. The best I will be able to do is get the minor issues exempted from the challenge."

"As Craig's former financial and investment advisor, will his estate pay me to continue to service his assets until the estate is settled? Bills and income will still be coming in that will have to be processed."

"Good question. I'm not sure," Packard dodged.

Alan furrowed his brow and said, "I need an attorney—a good one, and I need one now. I know they are going to try and make me the prime suspect. They don't have anyone else." He then told Packard all about the call from Inspector Roosevelt.

Packard added this information to his puzzle of facts he had been playing with all weekend.

"Don't feel too badly. Both Washburne and I have been summoned, and who knows about Roz? We're not the closest, you know." He faked joviality.

Packard could see Gavin relax slightly.

"But what about an attorney? Can you recommend one? Or could you represent me on Wednesday until I find someone?"

Packard was ready for him. "I can't be your attorney, not even on Wednesday. As the attorney for and executor of Carlson's will and estate, with you as the prime beneficiary, we have a conflict of interest that precludes me from representing you in a possible criminal matter tied directly to a civil one."

"What about Washburne?"

"Almost the same thing. He works for me, and was privy to information about the will." Packard wished he hadn't said that.

Alan looked across the room, apparently thinking about something else, Packard didn't think he caught his slip.

"What about the insurance that passes outside the will?"

Packard cleared his throat. "The insurance companies have, at this time, contested pay-out pursuant to their policy contract rights. And if you get involved in a criminal procedure, which you won't, they will bury the insurance policies and benefits until the outcome of that charge is determined. In short, the insurance companies always keep your money until they are hit over the head with twenty inches of notarized documents forcing them to release it."

Alan let out a long, deep sigh.

"A death certificate barely gets their attention." Packard failed to add that if Gavin were convicted of Carlson's murder, he would never see a dime.

"I guess I only have one question left. Do you know anyone whom you can suggest I contact?"

"I haven't been thinking about you needing anyone. Give me a couple of hours, and I'll give you two or three names you can check out. Since I practice principally in Chicago, I'll have to ask Washburne. Maybe one of his old buddies from Stanford would be just about right," Packard added sarcastically.

"Will you do it this afternoon?"

"Yes, I'm sure I can. Where can I get you at about four?"

"In Encinitas; I'm going to hole up there as long as I can."

"I'll call you. Give me your number again."

Lunch was over. Packard knew that most of his answers were unsatisfactory, but he rationalized that it wasn't his fault that Gavin found Carlson's body and was Carlson's lover.

* * * *

Monday Evening, Santa Monica

A troubled Gregory Washburne walked into his comfortable apartment over the garage of the stately mansion on Sunset Boulevard. The estate belonged to the landlords, but they were always traveling. One of the conditions of his being a tenant was to look after the security of their home while they were gone. Gregory had the run of the property.

That had proven quite useful to him. He not only had a Sunset Boulevard address, but had entertained select company in their home. When asked if it were his home, he had said yes.

Washburne sat down on his bed. He thought back on the tense dinner with his employer. Packard had accused him of everything that he knew was true, and he didn't know quite how to deal with Packard's truth, his anger, or his demand for a decision.

He really had very little latitude. He could take Packard's advice and direction, or end up on the street without a job and without anyone else who would ever employ him as an attorney again. He would certainly be disbarred. But the decision that he had to make would affect both Gavin and himself for the rest of their lives.

There were several issues. There was the matter of his background. There was the matter of his honesty and integrity—or lack of it. There was the matter of where he graduated from law school. He had always wanted to excel, to overcome the many obstacles that life had thrown in his path. Now this.

How to respond to Packard's edict? He either had to admit to manufacturing evidence, which would get him disbarred but might save Gavin's skin, or ask Packard to back him up in his fraud, which Packard said he would do in order to save his career.

Washburne knew if he asked Packard to support his falsification of documents, he would be enslaved to Packard for the rest of his life, and Gavin would stand a good chance of being convicted of murder.

He was scheduled to see Roosevelt in the morning. Gregory knew he had only hours to decide. Whose skin would he save? Gavin's or Washburne's?

*　　*　　*　　*

Tuesday Morning, Freemantle, Australia

Craig was happy. He had an apartment—a flat, according to the agent. He loved it. It was a permanent place. Craig unpacked and put his luggage away. He hid his suitcase with the money in his small kitchen in the dead space between the dropped ceiling and the floor above. Craig felt it was safe there until he could figure out how to deposit it into a bank account.

He rented under the name of Constantine Papagos. Now that he was finished crossing borders, he didn't think that name would mean anything in Freemantle, and was sure it was one Beretta wouldn't be looking for. Craig only had to use the name Stone to leave Australia, and six months from now, Beretta surely would have given up searching for Kurt Schmidt or one of his aliases.

Craig had chosen Freemantle at the mouth of the Swan River because of its quaintness. A short distance from downtown Perth, it was a little off the beaten path and still accessible to the city of two million people. Western Australia's capital was a bustling, modern port sitting on the Indian Ocean, exporting hundreds of millions in product to the booming countries of Indonesia, Malaysia, Singapore, and Thailand.

Craig also felt it was now safe to use a phone. As soon as it was a decent hour in California, he was going to call Alan. He had spent a lot of time on what he was going to say.

*   *   *   *

Tuesday Morning, Bel Air

Inspector Roosevelt was upset that Washburne had stood him up. He wanted to talk with him before Packard, not after. Phoning Washburne's apartment produced nothing. Finally at noon in desperation, he sent a squad car out to pick him up. Packard was due at two, and he wanted Washburne's answers before then.

The patrolman found Washburne dead in his garage, his sports car still running. A quick search did not surface a well-placed suicide note telling the world why.

Roosevelt was stunned with the unwanted news. He had liked Washburne. He sent a special team to see if they could find any paper trail as to why he killed himself.

*   *   *   *

Packard was punctual, and Roosevelt had decided to say nothing about Washburne. He knew it wasn't totally fair, but gathering information wasn't always about telling everything up front.

"I appreciate your promptness. There are a few questions I want to ask you, and then you're free to go."

Packard grunted his appreciation.

"What was your relationship with Gregory Washburne?" Roosevelt hated the fact that he used the word *was*.

Packard missed it. "He's my assistant here in California. You may not know that I'm based in Chicago."

"Yes, I do know. What all did Washburne do for you?"

"He checks out California law for me and helps me with a few clients. Just enough for me to maintain him as an associate. He isn't a partner or anything like that."

"When did you last see Washburne?"

"I had dinner with him last night. It was a meeting of sorts. Why?"

Roosevelt ignored his question. "Was it a quiet and normal dinner, or was something upsetting discussed?"

Packard became defensive. "You saw Washburne this morning. Why didn't you ask him that? It was a normal business meeting, as far as I was concerned. I'm sure you know that Craig Carlson's will is being challenged. That was our major discussion."

Roosevelt realized he couldn't withhold any longer. "Mr. Packard, do you know of any reason why Gregory Washburne would think of committing suicide?" He watched Packard's face.

"Of course not. Has he suggested such a thing?"

"No. He's done such a thing. Washburne is dead."

"Oh, my God!" Packard's head fell back and his mouth fell open.

Roosevelt waited for a moment before he said, "I'm going to make it my personal task to find out why."

Packard asked, "Did he leave a note?" He was unable to hide the tremble in his voice.

"I don't know, yet."

"This is very upsetting." Packard looked very upset.

"It's more of a terrible tragedy than upsetting, Mr. Packard. Are you sure you and Washburne didn't have some sort of disagreement about something last night? We believe you were the last one to have seen him alive."

Packard became quiet, then shook his head, "No."

"Well, that compounds this whole matter, doesn't it?"

"I don't see how," said Packard.

"I'm sorry, but Washburne was intimately involved with Roz Marlowe, involved with you, and involved with the will. He's involved. And people just don't go around killing themselves over nothing when they are considered normal and stable.—which Washburne appeared to be."

"I can't believe he's dead."

"Believe it." Roosevelt felt uncomfortable in his presence.

"What did you want to see me about?" Packard asked, trying to change the subject.

"Letters from you to Washburne about changes in Craig Carlson's will." Roosevelt notice Packard shift nervously.

"What about them?" Packard asked.

"Did you copy Alan Gavin on this correspondence?"

"Yes, I did," lied Packard.

"Why would you do that?" Roosevelt wanted a rational answer.

"To let him know what Craig was thinking," Packard responded without conviction.

"Is that normal, Mr. Packard?"

"It all depends. Craig Carlson and I go back forty years, and I knew how much Gavin meant to him, and I didn't want him left out of the loop on good news."

"Did Craig ask you to copy Gavin?" Roosevelt knew that Packard could now answer any way he wanted to.

"Yes, he did," lied Packard.

"Then why were they blind copies?"

Roosevelt knew that he had Packard squirming. He only wished he had been able to interrogate Washburne about the same thing. Roosevelt wondered if that was why Washburne was so reluctant the night of the murder to let those documents go.

"Washburne didn't leave any notes? Are you sure? That's unusual, isn't it?"

"You've skipped backward, Mr. Packard. Why are you so interested in that? Some do, some don't. What all do you know about your associate?"

"Actually, a lot that I just found out."

"Such as?"

"He wasn't what he pretended to be."

"When did you find that out?"

"This weekend. I began to feel funny about him at the reading of the will on Friday, and decided I didn't know enough about him. So I went to work." Sweat ran down Packard's face.

"Please tell me what you found out."

Packard sighed. "That he didn't graduate from Stanford. He only went there his freshman year. He was driving a natty sports car, spending money like water, entertaining all the young girls, and making excellent grades. He did quite well his freshman year at Stanford."

"And after that?"

"He didn't return to Stanford, and gave no explanation. But there is an explanation. His real name was Gregory Warbington. Do you recognize the last name?"

"No. Should I?"

"His father was Luther Warbington—the same Warbington who was the owner of the big savings and loan in Orange County that folded, taking down thousands of depositors as it did. Luther Warbington is presently doing time."

Roosevelt became quiet. "Go on." He felt sorry for the young man who had just ended his own life.

"So Gregory dropped out of Stanford, changed his name to Washburne, enrolled in UCLA at nights, and worked in the men's department at The Broadway during the day. He graduated from UCLA Law, not Stanford."

Roosevelt said, "That's pretty heavy. Did you confront him with all of this last night?"

"Yes, I did. But I had no idea that it would produce his suicide."

"Are you sure you didn't discuss the Carlson-Marlowe situation with him as well?"

"No. We never got around to it," lied Packard.

"Earlier, you said that was the topic of the meeting."

Packard's shirt was wet. "I'm sure we touched on both. Look, Roosevelt," he growled. "you've asked me a hell of a lot of questions without telling me first that my associate was dead. I believe that's a breach of something for damn sure."

Roosevelt made no comment. After a silence in which Packard grew visibly more uncomfortable, he asked, "Do you have any idea who killed Craig Carlson?"

Packard sighed, "I wish I did," he said honestly.

"Do you think Roz Marlowe could have initiated a contract killing?"

Packard's normal energy rose to the question. "Roz Marlowe is capable of eating a cannibal for lunch!"

Roosevelt looked down at his pad. It was useless. Carlson was dead, and now that Washburne was dead, Packard could say anything he wanted about almost anything to anybody regarding Craig Carlson, and no one would ever know the truth.

"You're free to go. Thank you for coming in. If I have any other questions, will you still be at the Beverly Wilshire?"

Packard nodded affirmatively.

"Oh, one last question. Do you have a secretary here as well as in Chicago?"

Packard nodded affirmatively.

The two men shook hands and Packard left.

Roosevelt picked up his phone. "Bill, get subpoenas immediately for the records of Craig Carlson at both of Packard's law offices. One is here on Wilshire Boulevard and the other is in Chicago near the Loop. Someone here will have the exact addresses. Get on it before he can get to them."

* * * *

Tuesday Afternoon, Palm Desert

Roz was sitting astride Beretta, sipping a margarita. They had just finished a joint and she was feeling giddy.

"Well, Stud, why did you bring me here? Certainly you didn't fly just to fuck." Roz laughed at her crude joke.

Beretta squirmed out from under her and got up on his knees.

"Why not? We've done it just for that reason many times before. Why does there have to be a reason?"

"Because there is one. You haven't told me anything further about Kurt Schmidt. Is that your surprise? Where and when did you finish his existence?"

Beretta stood up and threw a towel around his waist.

"We haven't," he said.

"What!" Roz was up. "You told me on the phone..."

Beretta interrupted, "I told you nothing. He's somewhere in the Far East and we can't bring him down. Your ex-boyfriend seems very well informed and very crafty. Or did you know that going into this?"

"Are you accusing me of being involved with Schmidt?"

"You're capable of being involved with the Devil."

Roz tried to slap him, but Beretta pinned her hands.

"Not so fast, baby! Remember who's in control here. I am, remember?" He let go of her hands and slapped her hard.

It hurt, but it was what Roz wanted. She calmed down.

"Tell me more about it." She walked naked to the dresser and picked up a cigarette. She had been smoking a lot lately. This hadn't been as easy as she had thought it would be. She looked at Beretta with contempt. "All the king's army and all the king's men can't find Humpty Dumpty?" She sat on the edge of the bed. "You're a shitty king."

Beretta stretched, his muscles rippled, and he was silent.

Roz knew he was deep in thought when he did that. She matched his silence and looked out the window at the dry desert.

"You're right. The king can't find Schmidt. Only the smell of where he's been. And I've had a visit from My Peer that I didn't want. He wants collateral on the money."

Roz said nothing. She wasn't going to let it be that easy for him. She pushed all the sex toys on the floor and curled up in bed, as provocatively as she knew how.

Beretta looked at her. He shrugged his shoulders and went to the bathroom.

"Well, what is it?" she called out to him.

No answer.

When Beretta came back, he lay down next to her, took the cigarette out of her hand, and pulled her next to him.

"You have a contract to sign," he said.

"Like hell I do!"

He held her tightly in a vise-like grip. "Like hell you don't. This entire affair wasn't my idea. You're the one who wanted Craig dead, not me. Remember? You came crawling to me at Big Bear Lake. You had panicked, you had to get rid of your husband before you lost it all. Remember? Before big bad Packard came to change his will. You don't remember, Roz? Well, I do. In fact, I taped it."

Roz fought to get free.

"And you were the one who suggested Kurt Schmidt. You said he had done satisfactory work for you before."

Roz was breathing heavily from being so restrained.

"I can send you up by just turning state's evidence," said Beretta. "That is, unless you sign a little document I have."

Roz managed to work her knee into his balls. Beretta only laughed and held on tighter.

"All right. I'll look at it. Let go of me!"

Beretta released all tension and sprang out of bed so she couldn't reach any part of him. "I think we should do a line and then see if I can pound your ass through the floor."

Roz liked the idea.

She loved being submissive to him as long as she could be master of the rest of her world. Roz smiled and laid her head back on the pillow, thinking.

*   *   *   *

Wednesday Afternoon, Freemantle

Craig was seated on a green bench in the park in Freemantle. It was in the middle of a small square surrounded by buildings that dated back to the end of the last century. The sun was warm and the air, cool. The mouth of the Swan River was wide, and oceangoing transports were loading and unloading their cargoes.

Craig had purchased a copy of Tuesday's *International Herald Tribune* and was leisurely reading its contents. He thought how wonderful it was to be so relaxed and to have time to read and watch the people as they strolled into the park, sat on the grass, had a bite to eat, or just did nothing but rest.

He had slept well in his flat and appreciated its quiet. He had tried several times to reach Alan, but he never answered. When Chin Lee answered, Craig had hung up.

He was involved in reading a report on affairs in the Balkans when he heard his name.

"Craig? Craig Carlson? I say, that is you, isn't it?"

Craig looked up in terror to find a short, heavyset man standing right in front of him, mopping his brow.

"You don't remember me, do you? I'm Hugh. Hugh Ashley. Savannah's husband. You know, the Lord Ashley bit."

Craig held his hand over his eyes to shade the sun and get a better look. That's exactly who it was. He seemed shorter and older.

Craig stood, not knowing what else to do. "Hugh, it's good to see you." Craig shook his hand.

"Oh, don't get up. Let me share the bench with you. I do say, you're the last person I thought I would see in this dreary little town."

Hugh edged himself onto the bench. "I didn't think anyone but me ever came to western Australia. What are you doing here? A film of sorts?"

Craig couldn't believe that Hugh Ashley didn't know he was dead. He sat back down beside him and smiled. "No. Actually I'm just visiting. Getting away from it all, so to speak."

"Oh. I can't blame you." Hugh continued to mop his brow. He was wearing a seersucker suit that looked as if he had worn it every day for four or five weeks.

"What brings you here, Hugh?"

"Sheep. See those tall, ugly, top-heavy boats out there at the end of that pier?" Hugh pointed into the sun.

Craig followed his finger. "Yes. I see them."

"Well, they're loaded with sheep. All headed for Indonesia and Thailand. Two hundred thousand of them on one boat. Can you imagine the smell? That's why I'm here. My family has been in the sheep business for over one hundred years one place or the other."

Craig was surprised that he began to relax. It was wonderful to talk to someone he knew, even though there was great risk involved. Craig wondered when Hugh would next talk to Savannah. She wouldn't be so out of touch with his demise.

"How's Savannah?"

"The First Lady of the theater. She's having a ball doing *Me and My Girl* at the Haymarket in London. I guess her fans love her. She has a year to go on her contract, and I have about six weeks to go on this damn trip."

Craig thought, *Hugh must not worry too much about news.*

"I was on a ship that took forever to get here, and as soon as I oversee this operation, I have to go on to Tasmania and then New Zealand. It's hell being rich, you know. Once in a while you have to look after your holdings." Hugh laughed. It was a nice, soft laugh.

Craig smiled. He really didn't know Lord Hugh Ashley. Savannah upstaged him at every affair where the two of them were together.

"Don't you ever fly?"

"Oh, my, no. I hate the thought. I'm scared out of my wits. But I don't travel on a sheep ship, I can tell you that." Hugh chuckled.

"When will you talk to Savannah again?"

"Oh, heavens, I don't know. She's so many hours away that when she's onstage I'm sleeping, and when I'm onstage she's sleeping, or something like that. We have a wonderful under-standing. We don't even try." Hugh looked at his watch.

Craig wondered what to say, if anything, to Hugh Ashley about his being dead. He would be hard to convince, considering the circumstances.

"I have to go back to the dock. We have two vessels leaving today, and one's about to go. Pictures and thanks and cheerios and all that you know." Hugh stood still, mopping his brow.

Craig held out his hand. "Give Savannah my love if you two ever communicate," he said.

"Oh, I will. Oh, yes, you're still with Alan, aren't you?"

Craig choked out the words, "Yes, I am."

"Good. Good. He's such a nice man. Well, cheerio, lad. I must check my rams and my ewes." Lord Hugh Ashley toddled off across the square and disappeared toward the docks.

Craig Carlson collapsed back on the bench. Ten minutes in public, and bam! "Hi Craig, how are you?"

He scooped up his paper and headed for his apartment.

Now he was in another quandary—whether to call Savannah, and if he did, what to say to her.

But Alan came first. He would try again.

Thirteen

Late Tuesday Evening, Bel Air

Simia had the day to herself. Roz was away with Beretta. As soon as she finished Roz's quarters, Simia returned to her room, lay on her bed, and closed her eyes. She needed to focus all of her attention on the project she was about to undertake. She wanted positive energy, even tenacious energy. Mikey Marlowe had taught her long ago how to summon those hidden resources from the furthest reaches of the mind.

Simia began her meditation and sidestepped the minefields she had to avoid, the minefields laid down by Roz Marlowe, before she could reach the positive place she wanted to find.

Soon, Simia was having a thought-and-response conversation with herself. Being mute, she did this even while awake. Simia would imagine what her voice would sound like. She could only barely remember what it was like before her accident.

She thought, *I had a such a wonderful love for Mikey Marlowe.* Then heard her young voice, "Roz, you destroyed the finest thing I ever had." She thought, *I was naive to believe the relaxed ways of Tahiti would transfer to America.* Then heard her young voice, "Roz, the first time I met you in Greenwich Village I hated you. She thought, *You never hesitated to use your position of power to abuse me.* Then heard her young voice, "I would have run away from you if I could have." She thought, *I will always believe you had something to do with Mikey's death.* Then heard her older voice, "And now you're involved in Craig's murder, and I'm going to find out how!"

Simia's eyes opened with a start. She felt feverish. She adjusted her position in bed, took a deep breath, and again closed her eyes. Simia imagined placing sandbags on them one at a time until the weight was so heavy she could no longer open them.

Simia thought, *I have Mikey to thank for teaching me how to keep archives.* And her angry voice said, "Now I'm going to make it pay off!"

Simia believed she had all the data she needed; she just needed guidance as to how to decipher it all to find out what it would reveal.

Simia dropped deep into a dark, cavernous void. There were no sides, no floor, no ceiling. Just space. At first, it was black and cold, but slowly it turned deep blue and a warm breeze rustled around her body. A pinpoint of light appeared on her horizon and a canary glow washed her being. Simia realized she was smiling. Her world was at peace, her power, unchallenged.

Simia awoke to find the sunlight that streamed though her windows dancing on the ceiling. It was being reflected by a glass ornament on her dresser. She felt wonderful. Her mind was clear and her body refreshed. She stretched and got up.

"I'm ready," she signed to the mirror.

Later, sitting on the floor among a deluge of photographs and papers, Simia wondered where to begin to organize her material. She decided to start at the 1992 Oscars and break it into three categories: (1) Roz and Beretta, (2) Roz and Washburne, and (3) Roz and others.

The information began to allow patterns. *It's here,* Simia thought triumphantly. *As I knew it would be. But how to follow it?*

She looked up at the white walls of her bedroom. *Of course!*

Simia gathered an ample supply of thumbtacks and moved her project up from the floor to the walls, where she could deal with it more easily. As the day and her work progressed, Simia discovered that Roz had spent a lot of time with Kurt Schmidt. She made "Roz and Schmidt" a separate category and dropped "Roz and others," because there were no "others" for Roz. Certainly no women friends. Only men. And the men weren't friends, either. Only lovers.

Simia placed Anne's telephone information next to the appropriate incoming messages. Slowly, a theme developed. Roz was more deeply involved with Beretta, Washburne, and Schmidt even more than Simia realized.

By late that night, Simia was tired, her eyes burned and her mind felt dead. She put the riddled scrapbooks back into her closet and tried to fall asleep, but the slips of paper kept rearranging themselves like fleecy sheep hugging the top of a hill. She tried to count the sheep. It didn't work. Suddenly, something ominous shadowed the pastoral scene. It was Roz Marlowe. She could enter Simia's room at any time and discover what she was doing!

Simia's eyes flew open. In the dim light, she saw the paper trail crawling up the wall. She was afraid. She had to take it down. The risk was too great.

*   *   *   *

Wednesday Afternoon, Bel Air

Alan Gavin, and George Wilson, Alan's last-minute attorney of choice, presented themselves to Inspector Roosevelt. Roosevelt then led them to a small, depressing conference room of gunmetal-gray chairs and a matching metal table.

Roosevelt inquired quietly, "Mr. Gavin, have you heard the news?"

Alan's guard was up. "About what?"

"About Gregory Washburne."

"No. Is there something I should know?"

"Yes. I'm sorry to be the one to tell you this, but he committed suicide Monday night at his apartment."

"No!" he gasped. "He couldn't! He didn't!"

"I'm sorry," said Roosevelt. "I thought you might have heard it from someone, but for now it's been kept from the media."

"Why did he do it? Why didn't Packard call me?" Then Alan looked hard at Roosevelt. "Why didn't you call me?"

"We didn't find him until yesterday, and I did call you, but you weren't home. I guessed you must have spent the night somewhere here in L.A."

"I did." Alan shuddered. He felt cold. "How did he do it?"

"Carbon monoxide suffocation."

"Does Roz know?"

"We don't know where Mrs. Marlowe is," answered Roosevelt.

"Jesus. Two good men. Dead!"

No one said anything in the room for a moment.

Roosevelt broke the silence. "Are you all right to begin?"

"Yes. Let's get at it."

Alan's attorney, George Wilson, asked, "Do you mind if I tape this?"

"No. Not at all. Many attorneys do," said Roosevelt.

Two hours later, Alan was exhausted. His worst fear had been confirmed: he was the prime and only suspect in Craig's murder.

"I only have one other matter," said Roosevelt.

"I hope so," said Wilson.

"Mr. Gavin, can you remember when you received your copies of these letters from Packard to Washburne about the will?"

Alan looked at the two letters, his mind blank. A rage rose within him. "I've never seen these!"

"So noted," Roosevelt responded.

George Wilson looked at the letters. "Do you know where the originals are, Inspector?"

"No. I wish we had them." Roosevelt didn't mention his subpoena for all of Packard's records relative to Carlson's will.

Alan was glad to have Wilson with him. He was calm, with a quiet professional power. But things weren't good. He noticed Roosevelt had one piece of paper he looked at often. But he put it back in his file. Alan thought, *I'll find out soon enough.*

The prosecuting attorney stepped into the room. "How is everybody getting along?"

Roosevelt tensed with the intrusion.

George Wilson stood and nodded to the prosecutor. "Just fine. Just fine." Then he looked at Roosevelt. "Well, Inspector Roosevelt, if there's nothing else, I think Mr. Gavin and I would like to leave."

The prosecuting attorney looked questioningly at Roosevelt.

"I believe you're free to go," said Roosevelt. "We have some serious questions that are unresolved that a grand jury might have to look into. But for today, I would say we are finished."

A look of concern covered the prosecuting attorney's face.

"Do you have your passport, Mr. Gavin?" Roosevelt asked.

"Yes, I do," he said.

Roosevelt paused and thought for a moment. "Keep it. Just don't leave California or the country and keep my office aware of where you can be reached by phone."

Alan was almost joyful. He wasn't sure he would have been allowed back out on the street. George Wilson practically pushed him out the door. "Move," he said under his breath. "Keep walking and don't hesitate or look back."

*   *   *   *

"The district attorney is going to be furious," said the prosecuting attorney to Roosevelt.

Roosevelt was angry. For the attorneys it was always all too simple. "That's his problem. We don't have enough to hold him without a grand jury investigation. We have nothing tying him to the murder weapon. We have only a drifting theory at best. We have a possible motive, but we have no real evidence. Zero. Zip." Roosevelt scooped up his papers.

"But the public is yelling for a suspect."

"The public isn't responsible for justice. His prints weren't on the gun or on the humidor it was in, yet the humidor was covered with the prints of others. Explain that one," said Roosevelt.

"But what about a suspect? We have to have one."

"If you feel so strongly about it, get someone else to do it. I can't. There simply isn't enough there to detain him."

"Roosevelt, why are you so upset? And why are you so defensive?" challenged the prosecuting attorney.

"I'm upset because another fine young man is dead. Gregory Washburne knew a hell of a lot about this case and now he's dead."

"I didn't know that."

"Of course you didn't."

Roosevelt left the conference room ahead of the prosecuting attorney. He was tired of the media and of elected officials who pandered to them. He was going to call in Mrs. Roz Marlowe for one hell of a questioning session just as soon as he could find her.

Later that evening, Inspector Roosevelt was further infuriated by the bungling work of one of the legal beagles who constantly second-guessed the police department. Someone in the district attorney's office had leaked a story. "Gavin Picked Up as Suspect." And even though most papers buried it, some chose to make the story page one because of the celebrity status of Craig and Roz. The Associated Press headline read, "Grand Jury to Look at Gavin."

*   *   *   *

Wednesday, Late Afternoon, Bel Air

When Roz returned home from Santa Monica Airport, Anne was waiting for her with her inevitable clipboard.

"I don't want any messages about anything or anybody," snapped Roz as she entered the house.

Anne didn't just disappear, as she normally would have. She stood her ground. "There are two you must respond to," she said with a new authority she had never used with Roz before.

Roz stopped in her tracks and was about to scream at her secretary when she saw the look in Anne's eyes.

"Oh, all right. Just two. But hurry up!"

"Gregory Washburne is dead. And the police want to see you today." With that, Anne walked away.

Roz sat down on the nearest chair. It was one of the first times in years she had been speechless. She hadn't planned it, so she couldn't comprehend it.

"Anne, wait. What happened?"

But Anne had gone. Roz looked at the dreary, empty hallway. She got up and snapped on the hall light, and slowly ascended the stairs to her suite. At the landing, she looked up at Craig's quarters. They were dark and silent. Roz quickly looked away.

"What have I done?" she whispered.

Simia was standing in Roz's bedroom with her arms folded over her chest, looking out the window at the meandering rock wall, when Roz entered her quarters.

"Hello, Simia," Roz said.

Simia nodded.

"Do you know about Gregory?"

Simia nodded again.

Roz sat down on her bed. She felt old and tired.

Simia handed her a note and left.

It said: "You have several messages, but Inspector Roosevelt has asked I give this to you when you got home. "'Mrs. Marlowe. Call me as soon as you get back. We need to see you immediately. If you don't call, I'll send someone to pick you up.'"

Roz collapsed backward onto her bed. A heavy crushing filled her chest. She wasn't prepared for this. She lay there a long time and no one came to her. She was exhausted and confused.

Beretta had never let up about signing her profits from *Rain* to his stupid hospice "front" in Philadelphia. Even after Roz promised Beretta she would sign before the day was over, he treated her roughly. And when she failed to do it at the airport, Beretta became nasty and abusive.

Her phone rang. Roz didn't want to move, but she wanted to talk to someone. Anyone would do. Roz Marlowe hadn't answered her own phone for months.

"Yes?" she spoke feebly.

"Roz? Roz, is that actually you?"

"Yes."

"I have good news."

She recognized the voice of Melvin Stein and wished she had never picked up the phone.

"What is it?" she asked listlessly.

"The probate court has accepted our petition. We'll have a full will contest before the court. The date hasn't been set yet. It will probably be in six weeks or so." Stein was upbeat.

"How nice," said Roz, with no interest or conviction.

"What's wrong with you?"

She wanted to say, "I'm tired, go away." Instead, Roz said, "The police want to see me today."

"I'll handle that," he said. "You sound awful."

"I'm not well," she said. "I must be coming down with something." Roz paused. "Yes. That's it. I'm coming down with the flu. You call them. I'm going to bed."

"Are you upset because Washburne killed himself?" Stein asked without emotion.

"Yes," said Roz. She added, "He was so young." But what she was thinking was that somehow she might have been responsible and there was no profit for her in Washburne being dead.

"His burial is tomorrow," Stein said.

"Good-bye, Melvin." Roz hung up the phone, returned to her bed, and sobbed uncontrollably.

She had never felt so alone in all of her life.

*   *   *   *

As Roz lay in bed, her father kept coming and going from her room. He wanted to know if Roz wanted to play another game of "Wanna Have—Canna Have," a game they had played often. He told her it was a father's version of "Mother May I." As the only child, Roz had been inundated with toys and gifts from her first memory, but when she was six, her father introduced her to his new game she had to play in order to obtain those trophies. He had made it up and constantly changed the rules to his advantage. Most of the time, Roz would think up things she wanted and get them, until her father said, "No. You can't have that." The objective for Roz was to get as much as she could as cleverly as she could until he said, "No; canna have."

By the time Roz was a teenager, she had learned his secret. As she used it to get what she wanted, he used it to control her. When he realized she understood his motivation, he quit playing. Except for one last time. When her father found her on the stage in *Oh Calcutta!*, he instigated the biggest "Can't Have" he could find. He disinherited her. Roz had vowed that would never happen to her again.

Roz awoke in a sweat. Craig was playing the game with her and once again a "Wanna Have" had become a "Canna Have."

*   *   *   *

Wednesday Evening, Santa Monica

Victor Packard was in Washburne's office. He had been there most of the day. It was difficult for him to forget the tragedy of Washburne's death. All he had to do was look at the police officer who was standing guard over the dead man's office to see that no additional files were permanently removed.

Packard felt responsible. He had given Washburne a lose—lose choice. But he consoled himself with the knowledge that he wasn't the one who had originally manufactured evidence. That is, until Tuesday afternoon, when he told Roosevelt that *he had blind-copied Gavin*, which he knew he hadn't. Now he had manufactured the evidence.

It was all so complicated that Packard's mind functioned like quicksand.

Wednesday had been a trying day. It started when he had approached the probate court with his request for a declaratory judgment that certain provisions be exempted from any challenge. It was denied. Stein had beaten him to it.

After he finished at court, Packard called his secretary in his Chicago office. She told him that just before lunch, she had been served with an injunction relative to the Carlson files. She told the police that most of them were with Packard in California. But she knew it was a lie; the office had backup copies of everything. It was a protective practice of his firm. Even if someone took the originals with him he had to leave a complete paper trail behind.

Packard told her to send everyone home and lock up for the

day and not to open the office again until he told her to do so.

On his arrival at the Santa Monica office, Packard found out that late Tuesday, Susan, Washburne's secretary, had received a similar injunction against the removal of any of the files pertaining to Craig Carlson's will. Packard didn't care, those files had already been sufficiently copied by the police. It was Chicago he was concerned about.

For part of the afternoon, Washburne's secretary was able to help him in trying to close down the files of his deceased associate. It was no easy task. There was more value there than Packard had realized and the police hovered over them to make sure that none of the files were destroyed or removed. But Susan was unable to last. She missed her handsome, gregarious boss who "had such a bright future." Packard got tired of her weeping and sent her home.

Now at seven in the evening, with files spread all over the desk, Packard realized he, too, had to quit.

He was wrung out.

Packard left the patrolman guarding nothing as far as he was concerned and headed for the dark security of Trader Vic's.

*   *   *   *

Thursday Noon, Freemantle

Craig felt so emancipated. He could use the phone. He hadn't been able to reach Alan, only Chin Lee's high-pitched voice. So he decided to get some other calls out of the way. The first was to the concierge desk at the Peninsula in Hong Kong.

After making sure he was talking to the right man, Craig said, "This is Mr. Stone-Schmidt. Do you remember me?"

"Yes, sir. I most certainly do."

"Did anyone inquire about me?"

"Yes, sir. They most certainly did."

"Can you give me any information that would be of value?"

"Certainly. I did more than you asked. Instead of my commuting all the way to where I live, I used your room for two of those nights myself. But there is more. Each night, I slept there and bathed there. And, Mr. Stone-Schmidt, I even had room service there. Thank you very much. I enjoyed our little charade."

Craig was pleased with his ingenuity, and thankful that the young concierge was still alive to recount his story. He had stretched Craig's request and compromised his own safety.

"But did anybody inquire?"

"Oh, yes. On Monday, a man asked me if a Mr. Schmidt had checked out. I wondered why he hadn't asked the front desk, but told him I would check. I told him yes, he had. He seemed very upset, and then asked me if Mr. Schmidt had talked to anyone about where he might have gone. I told him Schmidt had asked me a lot of questions about Sydney. I hope that isn't where you went."

"It wasn't," said Craig quietly. He realized it was a mistake to ask anyone else for help. What if he had gone to Sydney?

"Can I be of further service?"

"No, thank you. You have done more than enough," said Craig.

Craig thought, *I certainly got out of Hong Kong by the skin of my teeth. I don't think the one million dollars at Lloyd's of London in Sydney is worth my life, but maybe I can point my adversaries there.*

Craig considered calling Savannah, but didn't want to do it too soon. Surely Hugh wouldn't have yet talked to her, it didn't sound as if he would. Craig computed the time difference to London. He understood what Hugh was talking about. Perth and London were perfectly reversed. Day was night and vice versa.

"I'll call Savannah later," he said to no one.

* * * *

Wednesday Evening, Bel Air

Simia had to get fresh air. The big house was beginning to frighten her. Sorting her evidence had become a chore, and Roz had become more of a threat.

Simia had overheard Roz's phone discussion with Stein, and witnessed Roz's incredulous realization that she was not in full control of her world and that not everything in life was always going to go her way. Now, Roz was in a deep depression, but, Simia expected that she would recuperate with a vengeance. Just as quickly as mercury in a thermometer changes with heat, with the smallest incident, Roz Marlowe would climb back up and lash out.

Simia strolled through the yard, drawn to the secret cache that she and Craig had used so much and had such fun with. She reached down inside, hoping to find some forgotten memory.

Simia's hand touched something cold and hard.

Slowly, Simia worked her fingers around it and pulled it out into the fading light.

Simia found herself staring at the missing Oscar—the first one that Craig had ever received for Best Supporting Actor for his role in *Dangerous Passage.*

A shiver shook her to her soul. She couldn't move. Simia knew her find had tremendous meaning, but she wasn't sure what. She looked back up at the house and then at the carriage house to be sure that no one had seen her from a window. It didn't appear as such, and Roz's window was dark.

Back in the light of her room, Simia saw the dried blood on it, and she knew what she had found—evidence that proved without a shadow of a doubt that Alan Gavin hadn't killed Craig Carlson. Only she and Craig knew of their secret hiding place, no one else did. Not even Alan!

Simia felt triumphant.

But then she was staggered by another realization.

Fourteen

Thursday Noon, Bel Air

When Roz Marlowe exited the cemetery after Gregory Washburne's burial, two police cars were waiting at the gate.

Roosevelt's message to her was unequivocal: "Since you didn't return my phone calls, contrary to what Stein told me yesterday, you seem quite able to be up and about. You have a choice. Either have your driver fall in between our cars and we will escort you to the precinct station, or we will put you into one of our cars and drive you there."

The paparazzi were at the cemetery gate in force. They had followed Roz's limousine there. Roz slumped down in her limo as the driver followed option one. She hoped it would look like a police escort, not a police pickup.

She tried to call Stein from the car, but couldn't reach him. "Goddamn it! Goddamn it! Goddamn it!" Roz was frothing. "Why didn't Stein handle this?"

When she got out of her limousine at the station, she remembered just in time that she was returning from a funeral, so her smile to the cameras was sweet and sad.

"Follow me," said Roosevelt.

Sullenly Roz stomped behind him. "You could have at least said please."

"Please. Sit down!"

It was a command.

"This better be good. I won't answer a goddamn thing if you get nasty with me without my attorney."

"Why didn't you return my calls?"

"I was out of town."

"I thought it was because you were sick."

"Both." Roz was steaming.

"Why did Washburne kill himself?"

189

"How the hell do I know?"

"Unless I've forgotten, you and Washburne were very close. He was your chosen escort to the Oscars, not your husband, whom you left behind at home."

Roz exclaimed, "That was his choice, not mine."

"Whose? Carlson's staying home or Washburne's committing suicide?"

"Didn't he leave a note? Don't they always leave a note?" Roz's sarcasm was ugly.

"Didn't we just bury the man?" Roosevelt shot back.

"I'm leaving."

"Not this time. I only want you to look at one item. There will be a time when you'll need a very fine attorney. But not today." Roosevelt was adamant.

He reached into his file and pulled out the paper he had kept from Gavin. It was the fax from Craig Carlson to Alan Gavin about the change of will, with the expressed hope that there was now no need for a palimony suit.

Roosevelt shoved it across the table to Roz.

Roz watched him watching her.

She picked it up and pretended to read the note she had composed and typed on Anne's typewriter.

First Roz let her face cloud with doubt, then she reread it. Then she looked at Roosevelt. "My, my! Isn't this interesting?" Roz dropped it on the table. "I don't know anything about it."

"Look at the dates," he ordered.

Roz looked. The fax was dated on Friday, and it said the will was executed on Friday. But she now knew that Craig had executed it on Saturday.

"Yes. What about them?"

"Do you know when the will was executed, Mrs. Marlowe?"

Roz said, "It says here Friday."

"But it was Saturday."

"How do you know so damn much about the will?"

"You insisted we take the data with us the night of the murder, remember?" Roosevelt held her eyes steady with his.

"How do I know what was in Craig's mind when he wrote

this? Maybe he was going to do it Friday and didn't get it done." Roz pushed the paper away from her.

"Or maybe he didn't write it. We tracked the arrival of the will through FedEx. It didn't come until Saturday morning." Roosevelt shoved the paper back.

Roz said, "What Craig did or didn't do is not my concern. But he had no right to cut me out of anything. It was unfair, and unkind, and I won't sit here another minute without Stein."

Roosevelt slowly and deliberately took the fax back. "You don't have to sit here at all, Mrs. Marlowe. I'll keep this. You've answered my question perfectly well." Roosevelt stood.

Roz sat there without moving. "You tricked me here." Roz thought of her father.

"No. I didn't. You tricked yourself here," and he pointed to the fax. "You can sit here as long as you want. I have work to do." Roosevelt left Roz sitting at the table.

It was much harder for Roz to smile and wave sweetly at the cameramen when she left.

*   *   *   *

Thursday Afternoon, Palm Beach

Henry Alltop, Andrew Papagos' attorney, was talking to the senior managing partner of one of New York's most prestigious law firms. And the partner was dancing around Alltop's question.

"Why did your firm let Melvin Stein go? Or to put it more politely, why did your firm allow Melvin Stein to resign eighteen years ago?"

The senior managing partner told Alltop what he knew he would hear—that he didn't discuss other attorneys' private moves with unknown people for any reasons.

So then, Henry identified himself even further by attaching the name Ellen Papagos to his, and asked for an appointment in New York the following week.

There was silence on the other end. Papagos Food Wholesalers was one of their largest accounts. "I think that can be arranged."

"Good. How does Tuesday look for you? Mondays are always busy with weekend crises that really aren't," said Alltop.

"Tuesday noon for lunch? Can you be in our offices about eleven-thirty? We can go from there."

"Fine. I'll see you Tuesday." Henry Alltop hung up.

Ellen Papagos said, "Good job, Henry. They're worrying right now."

* * * *

Thursday Afternoon, Bel Air

Simia overheard every word of Roz's agitated conversation with Stein about Inspector Roosevelt, and she wasn't even trying to listen. Roz was in a full-throttle rage.

"Listen, Stein, I'm not used to fuckups working for me. And you just fucked up! Do it again and you won't work for me anymore."

As soon as Roz finished that conversation, she dialed Antonio Beretta. Simia lingered just inside the private stairs to her third-floor room.

"Beretta, it's me. Your well-abused whore!"

Simia was never beyond being shocked by Roz Marlowe.

"Where are you today on finding the trail of the invisible phantom? Is Sydney all that big and you, all that incompetent?"

There was an extended period of silence before Roz's violent outburst continued. "Goddamn it! Find him! Roosevelt is giving me a hard time, and I don't like it! Someone sure as hell is going to link the three of us together before you finally castrate him!"

Simia held her breath. She didn't dare miss any of the conversation. She wished she had her tape recorder.

"No! And I still won't sign your stinking paper! I thought I proved that to you in Palm Desert. Call me when you're civil."

Roz slammed the phone in the cradle so hard that Simia thought she had probably broken it.

Barefoot, as soundless as an animal stalking its kill, Simia padded upstairs.

"Simia!" shouted Roz.

Simia quickly began to type.

"Simia! Where the hell are you? Do I have to come up and get you?"

Simia stopped typing and raced downstairs. The last thing she wanted was Roz Marlowe in her room.

"Fix me a double double, draw me a bath, and get me some ice and fresh cucumbers from the kitchen!"

Simia nodded her understanding.

"You lazy Polynesian. What else did they breed down there besides mosquitoes? I don't know what Mikey ever saw in you." Roz was in her panties, standing on a two-thousand-dollar dress, and dropping ashes on it from her cigarette.

Simia quickly poured her a full tumbler of scotch, started the bath water and ran downstairs. *Something big must have happened with Roosevelt,* she thought.

She knew she had to talk to someone soon. There was too much for her to remember that needed to be processed by others. But she knew it wasn't tonight, Roz was on a rampage.

*   *   *   *

Early Friday Morning, Chicago

Packard took the red-eye from Los Angeles to O'Hare and arrived at 5:00 A.M. He slept briefly during the four-hour flight, but took a cab headed straight for the Loop.

Packard needed to get to his office before anyone else did. He had everything to lose if he didn't get a discrepancy smoothed out, and he had to do it himself; he couldn't risk asking his secretary.

Why Washburne had ever altered his letters was beyond him. It was a straight path. Two letters from Packard to Washburne about the changes of the will. Messages with internal legal language. Not even a copy shown, sent, or needed by Carlson. Yet Washburne, at Roz's insistence, had shown "bcc," or blind carbon copies, sent to Gavin.

Packard would never have sent copies to Gavin without copying Carlson. It just didn't make sense. Then Roz must have cleverly placed copies of those altered letters into Craig's other documents at the same time she slipped in the fax she had most likely authored.

It was a Roz thing. Nuts.

Now he had to unscramble it. His originals in Chicago showed no bccs, and the copies in California showed bccs.

Packard had a hell of a time pulling up the right file on his secretary's computer, but finally found it. He knew there would still be a disparity in the type style that Washburne had used in California on the letter, but prayed no one would ever see the difference or even make an issue of it.

Packard felt better when he was finished. Now all copies showed bccs and were similar—unless someone was astute enough to ask him why Carlson had copies of letters in his files that he wasn't shown as having been copied on at all. That was still a problem there was no way of correcting. It was a matter of police record.

By seven-thirty, Packard was finished. He was gone before anyone got to work and, with luck, he would be back at the Beverly Wilshire in time for lunch and no one would know he had left.

*   *   *   *

Friday Morning, Freemantle

From a pay phone, Craig called the toll-free number for the finest hotel in Sydney. To further confuse his adversaries, using the name of Kurt E. Schmidt, Craig made a reservation for four nights in one of their most expensive suites. Craig guaranteed it with Schmidt's American Express card and told them to be sure and hold the reservation, for it would be a late arrival that night. As Schmidt, Craig also requested two bottles of champagne be chilled and a dozen roses be delivered to the room. He said he wanted them waiting for him because he had been on a hell of a junket from Hong Kong that hadn't turned out to be as "incredibly overwhelming" as the travel agent had told him it would be.

Pleased with that diversion, Craig returned to his flat to see if he could reach Alan. En route, he picked up Friday's copy of the *International Herald Tribune*. On an inside page, he read the short, terse headline: "Grand Jury to Look at Alan Gavin." The four-line article further stated: "No other suspect other than Gavin was being considered in the Carlson murder case. Roz Marlowe was holding up well despite Carlson's recently changed will, which she was now legally challenging."

It was only noon, but Craig fixed himself a hefty scotch.

Things weren't going at all as he had planned. Nothing from the time he had walked out of the house in Bel Air had been as he had perceived it would be. Nothing! His feeling of freedom that he had just obtained in Freemantle was first shadowed by Hugh Ashley and now devastated by this news report.

He had tried many times to shove the guilt of what he had done to so many loved ones to the back of his mind, telling himself he could make everything right again. But he knew he couldn't. He had caused too much shock and grief, and he felt the burden of his absence had expanded in quantum leaps.

The man he loved was being accused of killing him.

The woman he hated was challenging the will he changed for the man he loved.

The young son he adored was being denied his rightful family inheritance because of his pretended death.

The mother who had nurtured him all of his life now needed nurture from him in her final years.

And his own life was in danger of being terminated at any moment by the smallest mistake he might make.

I didn't want any of these things to happen, Craig thought. *I'm miserable. And what can I do about it, other than to go back and say, "Look—here I am! I'm really alive! Aren't you all glad to see old Craig Carlson again?"*

Craig sat in the one easy chair and stared at the blank television. He couldn't turn it on. CNN was driving him nuts—not just about him, but CNN's continued presentation of world news in general from a narrow American perspective.

Now he didn't dare call Alan and glibly say, "Let's meet somewhere warm and wonderful."

But he did have to call Savannah. Maybe that was his threshold. Maybe she could help him find his way back. He computed the time in London, it would be one in the morning—probably a good time to get Savannah winding down at home from an evening performance.

* * * *

Friday Night, Encinitas

Alan Gavin was sorting through his personal belongings and making lists of what he wanted to take with him and what he would either leave behind or sell.

It wasn't an easy task.

The house had been lovingly put together a piece at a time by him and Craig. It wasn't as large as their home in Provence, but it was filled with their things. He wondered what it would cost to ship much of it back to France.

Earlier, Savannah had called him, asking about the bulletin in the Associated Press. She was stunned to hear about the grand jury and further shocked when Alan told her about Gregory Washburne. Savannah instantly saw a connection between his death and Craig's murder. They weren't able to talk long, for she had to get back onstage.

After Alan returned home from the cemetery, he took a long walk along the beach, thinking about Gregory. He realized his own near-suicidal depression was meaningless. After seeing the ugly result of such an emotional action, he knew he would put any thought of that away forever. He had much to live for. He was only forty-two.

"Why did Washburne do it?" he wondered aloud.

Savannah was very perceptive to suggest a *connection*.

There had to be something between Gregory Washburne and Roz Marlowe beyond a romp in bed. And copies of the letters that Roosevelt had shown him, which he was supposed to have received from Packard but never did, made no sense at all. If Craig had wanted him to know about the change in beneficiaries, he would have told him, not copied him to some other correspondence.

That was a *connection*.

And Roz's demand that he be at the Bel Air home specifically at the time of her potential Oscar win while she was with Washburne.

That was a *connection*.

Alan wondered if there was more. Could Washburne have left the Oscars, shot Craig, then returned without anyone missing him? Roz could easily have told Washburne where Craig kept his gun and at the award ceremonies, people were in and out of their seats all the time.

That was a *possibility*.

Alan thought, *I should have spent more time looking rather than reacting when I found Craig's body*. But he knew that was total hindsight, that night he had been devastated and scared.

But for Alan the most incriminating item was the life insurance trust. His just becoming the prime beneficiary of one hundred million dollars' worth of insurance was his biggest burden.

There even had to be a *connection* there someplace.

It just didn't add up.

Alan decided he would look for more *connections* tomorrow. As he got into bed, his last thought was of Roosevelt. Alan knew that Roosevelt must have felt his innocence, or he would be in Los Angeles tonight instead of Encinitas.

*   *   *   *

Early Saturday Morning, London

Savannah was in her robe, scanning the newest issue of *Elle* when her phone rang. She really didn't want to answer it. She was tired. She thought that *Me and My Girl* should be retitled *Me and My Exhaustion*. It was an energy-sapping role, and she still had nine months to cavort and dance all over the stage, laughing and singing at the top of her lungs. But whoever was calling had her private line, so it couldn't be all that bad.

"Savannah here."

"Are you alone?"

Her antennae went up—not only because of the request, but because of the voice.

"Yes. Who is this?" Savannah wasn't sure she wanted the answer.

"A man who isn't dead."

Savannah gasped.

"A man who didn't want to have to call you, but now doesn't have any choices left."

"Craig Carlson?"

"Yes."

"It can't be. If you're Craig, who's dead?"

"The man who tried to murder me and almost succeeded. My stuntman and double, Kurt Schmidt."

Savannah dropped her magazine and felt dizzy.

"It's a long story."

"I'm sure it must be." Savannah waited.

"I know I've caused a lot of hurt, but it can be explained."

"You can't even begin to know," Savannah said bitterly.

"I can still be killed at any time."

"I don't know how important that is," said Savannah coldly.

"Please, Savannah, believe me. I don't want to be where I am."

Craig's plea softened Savannah slightly. "Tell me, Craig, if that's your real name, why are you alive? Why is this other guy dead? Why isn't it the other way around? And why are you still in danger?"

"Can we talk?"

"My God! We have to talk. Do you have any idea of what all has happened because you're dead?"

"I can only guess about most. I've read whatever has been

reported wherever I've been. And I saw most of *Entertainment World's* presentation."

Savannah shook her head in disbelief.

"How's Alan? I've tried for three days to talk to him."

"I just did," said Savannah. "Why didn't you call him before now? You've been dead almost two weeks!"

"Savannah, I told you; it's a long story. And I'll tell it to you as best I can. But how is Alan? I miss him. I love him. And he's being accused of murdering me. I want to come home, but I can't. Not until this mess is cleared up. *Otherwise I will be dead!*"

Savannah's mind was not registering the scope of what he was saying. She wanted to slap herself, or scream. Instead, she took several deep breaths.

"My God, Craig. Is it really you? You're really not dead?"

"It's me. Ask me anything you want to prove it."

Savannah's voice lightened more. "Can you tell me where you and I last saw each other?"

"Of course. We had our picture taken together in one of those funny little booths at a mall. Alan was with us."

Savannah laughed. "And I still have it."

But then she became most serious. "Do you know how much trouble Alan is in?"

"No. Not in detail. I just saw in the paper today that he is headed for a grand jury investigation, and that Roz is contesting the will."

"There is so much more, Craig. So much. Things have been very bad since you died—or pretended to." Savannah wished she hadn't used that word, but it was the truth. It was pretense.

"I'm not going to ask for forgiveness yet. There is too much to explain. Are you willing to share information? It might take some time."

"If you think I could sleep after this, you're crazy. And maybe you are. But I never thought so. Sure, I can spend some time. I'm not due back onstage for twenty hours, and Hugh isn't here to bother me."

"I know."

"How do you know about Hugh?"

"I saw him here in Australia."

"My God! You're in Australia?"

"Where else do you think a criminal would run to? Remember, they were the ones that put it together in the first place."

Savannah was dumbstruck—not only to talk to a dead man, but to find out he's seen her husband, whom she hadn't heard from for three weeks.

"Well, start talking. You certainly have my interest."

"I hardly know where to begin. You won't believe most of it. I don't believe most of it."

"Craig, something you need to know. You have bestowed pain on so many that I love. What you have to tell me has to be damn good, or it will be difficult for me to ever forgive you for it."

Savannah continued to call it just as she felt it. "How would you like to be a mother who buries her son, or a husband or wife who buries a spouse, only to find out it was all a charade? It's not nice."

"I understand," said Craig softly. "Savannah, do you have any reason to believe your phone isn't secure?"

"Only if the royals have tapped it again." She laughed.

"Then let's trade stories. I guess I should start."

"I daresay that that would be the proper idea."

Fifteen

Friday Morning, Bel Air

Roz was sitting in her cozy breakfast room scanning *Hollywood Today*. She knew she had to get some positive publicity. There was too much negative, not-nice stuff out there.

Anne, with clipboard in hand, knocked on the open door and waited for Roz to acknowledge her presence.

"Anne," Roz said brightly, "it's so nice to see you this morning. Got something for me?"

Roz could see surprise register on Anne's face. She knew she had treated everyone pretty roughly lately. She vowed to change.

"You have several calls, as always, but one you should probably handle right away."

Roz stiffened immediately. "If it's Roosevelt, no!"

Anne didn't react. "No, it's the producer of your new film. He wants to meet you for lunch to discuss it. I believe they plan to begin Monday."

Roz beamed. That's just what she wanted. A fresh start. Something new and exciting. It was nearly time to begin filming and she had always liked the producer.

"Get Stewart for me."

Anne dutifully did as told, and handed a cordless phone to Roz. "He's on the line."

"Stewart, how lovely of you to call. I had almost forgotten about *The Empress*. I am looking forward to working with you closely through the entire project," Roz said suggestively, then remembered she hadn't read the script for weeks.

Anne placed Roz's other messages on the table and left.

"Of course I can meet you for lunch. I would love it! Let's go someplace bright and upbeat."

Roz was thinking ahead of Stewart. Where would she get the best press, not the worst? "Wouldn't Morton's work?"

She glanced at her other messages. Nothing of interest.

"Two is fine. Yes. I'll bring the overview of the screenplay. *Ciao.*"

Roz gulped her coffee. It was after ten. She wanted a facial, if possible, and would have to decide what to wear. It had to be special. Just to have lunch with one of the most powerful producers in Hollywood was worth mega-media.

"Anne," Roz called out.

"Yes, Mrs. Marlowe?"

"Get Heidi over here by eleven. Tell her to cancel anybody else, and I'll make it worth her while." Roz left the breakfast room in a flurry and moved rapidly up the wide staircase.

Simia was changing the bed. "Oh, Simia! I'd forgotten all about my new film. I've been so distracted with all these other dreadful matters." Roz started undressing.

"Run me a very hot bath. And add lavender. I want to be sweating when Heidi gets here. I haven't felt this way for weeks."

Roz stood naked in front of the mirror, checking herself out. "Not bad for my age," she said to Simia, as if she had always been a part of everything.

"Stewart called and we're having lunch," she continued breezily. "Can't you imagine how incredible I'll be as Catherine the Great?"

And then Roz noticed a tiny section of loose skin under her right jawline. "Jesus," she said, and rushed into her bathroom for a larger makeup mirror.

Simia left the terrified Roz alone as she examined her face.

*   *   *   *

Early Friday Afternoon, Bel Air

While Roz was out, Simia walked to the carriage house to see if Anne was in her office.

Anne looked up and smiled. "I'm glad you came to see me. I wish we could really talk. But whatever we do is good for me."

Simia held out her PC so Anne could read, "How are your children?"

"Pretty good right now." Anne crossed her fingers.

Simia smiled, put her hands together, and gripped them in the American manner that said, "Good job."

"What can I do for you?"

Simia took a note from her pocket and handed it to Anne: "I've been working several days on a project that I can only show you when Roz is out of the house. It's in my room and I can't move it anyplace else."

Anne looked up in surprise. "Simia? What on earth do you have in your room that you can't take out of it?"

Simia smiled. Then she beckoned Anne to come with her.

*   *   *   *

Saturday Morning, Freemantle

Craig thought about his talk with Savannah. He had thought about nothing else since then.

When he had told Savannah he was going to call Packard to help Alan, Savannah had advised him to wait, that it was too soon to conclude that Alan would actually be indicted.

But Craig was too worried to wait. He was filled with guilt about Alan. He had to do something now.

Fortified with a scotch and water, Craig called Packard.

The operator seemed to know Mr. Victor Packard well. "I'll connect you at once," she said.

Craig waited forever for someone to answer. Finally, a hoarse voice he hardly recognized responded.

"Is this a good time to call?" Craig asked.

There was an abyss of silence.

"Who are you calling? You must have the wrong room."

"I'm calling for you, Victor." Craig felt ill.

"Who the hell is this?" demanded an awakening Packard.

"Are you alone?"

"Jesus Christ! Who is this?"

Craig recognized raw fear.

"Do you remember a scrimmage game at Northwestern years ago when you sent me to the hospital?"

Craig could hear Packard's disbelief. It sounded like a pressurized coffee can when you first punctured the seal.

"If I didn't have to talk to you, believe me, I never would have called," said Craig.

"You're dead, Carlson. This isn't you!"

"I'm afraid it is, Victor. There isn't any will that any court can either probate or delay. I'm not dead."

"If you are, Carlson, do you have any idea what you've done?"

Craig could tell from Packard's voice that he was both shocked and furious.

"I know that Alan Gavin isn't going to prison because of murdering me."

Packard spewed, "Do you know how many crimes you've committed?"

"I'm not sure of them all. But I did kill a man in self-defense. You can worry about my crimes after you get Alan's neck out of the noose."

"Where are you? How can you be alive? You were identified as dead."

"Why hasn't anybody back there thought of looking up Kurt Schmidt to see if he was still around? I bet he's been gone exactly two weeks." Craig didn't feel as flip as he sounded.

"Schmidt? Your stand-in?"

"That's right. Didn't even just one person think of the possibility?"

"Why should they? Your lover found the body and your wife identified it at the morgue. No one ever thought it wasn't you."

"Then that part worked," said Craig. "But it's not working now. That's why I've called you." Craig decided he wouldn't mention Savannah's knowing anything about him to Packard.

"But why did you disappear? We're all involved in a great big game out here, and it's costing precious time, tons of money, and awful stress."

Craig wondered, *Where's the sympathy after all these years?*

Why isn't he glad I'm alive, even a little? He continued more cautiously, "Packard, for me it appeared to be close to a lose-lose situation, but you wouldn't know anything about being in that kind of place. I was. And others surely have been."

Craig thought he heard Packard choke.

"I had to call you. I want you to represent Alan. Get him through the grand jury investigation."

Only continued silence.

"Packard? My God, man, didn't you hear me?"

A strained voice answered. "I can't represent Alan. You don't understand. He is both the principal beneficiary and the prime suspect. I am your attorney, not his."

"You won't do it for me?"

"I can't do it with you dead!"

It was Craig's turn to be quiet. He had never had a conversation with Packard that was as strained or unusual. *But*, he reasoned, *it's not every day a dead client calls to tell you he's been alive all along.*

"Then I have to come home," said Craig.

"You can't do that, either," contested Packard.

Craig was sure he heard fear and tried hard to understand. He tried to think of both sides of the situation, but he still had no choice. If there were criminals, they were Schmidt and Marlowe, not Gavin. *But why would Packard be afraid? Why do I think he's not the least bit pleased that I'm alive?*

"I'll get back to you," said Craig.

"Wait! Don't go! How do I get in touch with you? Where are you? What if I need to find you?"

This time, Craig heard desperation.

"I'll call you again in a day or so. What we both need is time to think and have some answers. I would like to know exactly what all I'm guilty of. I'm sure of attempted insurance fraud, but I'm also sure they haven't paid out a dime yet."

"Craig—wait!"

"Goodbye, Victor."

Craig, deeply troubled, even suspicious, hung up.

He thought, *Savannah may have been right.*

It was only then that Craig finally gave some credence to Alan's constant admonitions about his placing far too much trust in Victor Packard.

* * * *

Friday Evening, Las Vegas

Beretta seized a pay phone in the casino and dialed his contact in Sydney.

"Worthy here."

"Do you have anything yet on Schmidt?"

"Yes. He's due in at the Four Seasons Hotel tonight after a cruise from Hong Kong. We will be waiting for him. Do you have any additional orders?"

"Just kill him," said Beretta.

"As I understood it, that was a standing order," said Worthy.

"Let me know where to send flowers." Beretta hung up.

* * * *

Monday Afternoon, Perth Airport

Craig Carlson gave the alias he had used to enter Australia, and cleared immigration and customs. With boarding pass in hand, he waited for Singapore Airlines Flight 224 to leave at four. He would get to Singapore at 9:20 Monday night and connect with Singapore Flight 326 for Frankfurt. A Mr. Carl Stone would arrive in Germany at 6:55 Tuesday morning.

Craig wasn't looking forward to another exhausting flight, but he felt that at least he was headed in the right direction—home!

Sunday morning, as agreed, he had called Savannah after her Saturday night performance to see if she had any new ideas or information. They formed a nebulous plan and Craig was pleased that Savannah would once again take leave of the stage to play a real role in his return to Hollywood. He told her he would work out the final details on his long flight, and would call her when they were both on the same time zone.

His follow-up call to Packard was even more distressing than the first. Packard adamantly would not represent Alan, and Packard would continue as if Craig were dead until proven otherwise. Packard further told him he would disclaim both phone calls from Craig, and that if the shit hit the fan, Craig Carlson would pay dearly for it.

The most curious reaction Craig got out of Packard occurred when he told him that if money was his problem, he had plenty to pay him with. Packard had asked, "And where the hell did you get that from? Your bank accounts have been closed for two weeks."

Tired of the confrontation, Craig had said, "The good money fairy," and hung up. He was pissed at Packard, and couldn't understand his obvious overwhelming discomfort that he was alive. He wondered what the hell was eating his former friend and confidant.

Craig decided to once again grow a beard. He was getting into familiar territory, where too many people knew him. And if Hugh Ashley could stumble upon him in Freemantle, God knows whom he would run into in Europe.

Without difficulty, Singapore Flight 224 lifted off into the bright blue sky and headed out over the Indian Ocean.

* * * *

Monday Morning, Beverly Hills

Victor Packard placed a call to Clarence Crawley, president, chief executive officer, and only shareholder of Midwestern Life Insurance Underwriters Corporation, better known to Packard as Mid Life.

Crawley's secretary recognized his voice. "Mr. Packard, how nice to hear from you. He's on the phone right now, but I'll put a note on his desk. I'm sure he'd prefer to talk with you."

Packard only had to wait a moment.

"Victor, where the hell are you today? I know you're not in your office. I just tried there."

"Still in Los Angeles on this Carlson thing. Are all of Carlson's insurance policies in order?"

Crawley hesitated. "I think so. Is there something specific you want me to check?"

"Yes. Be sure all one hundred million dollars is listed by which insurance company, when purchased, policy number, and all that garbage."

Crawley said, "I'll see that everything is up to date. I still have the copy of his death certificate you sent me here in my files, so I doubt if they even know a claimant named Carlson is dead. I don't believe anyone has inquired, and I'm aware of the status of the will contest by Stein and of the prime beneficiary also being considered the prime suspect. I'll just sit on all of it until something breaks one way or the other."

"Good," said Packard. "It sounds as if all is in order, but make damn sure. There's a lot of action on that matter right now," he emphasized.

"The insurance companies wouldn't begin to process or pay anything with the current status as it is, anyway," Crawley added.

"I understand," said Packard.

"Anything else?"

Packard asked, "Why were you calling me?"

"Oh, it was about another claimant—one of your clients' estates. But only small dollars, so I don't think I need to burden you with that today. We can talk about it next time I see you in person. You know, over a drink."

"I understand fully," said Packard. "But just who was it?"

Crawley cleared his throat, "That widow Talmadge who lived in Boston. She finally died in the nursing home. I think all is in order, but we can talk later."

"Sure. Fine. Good to talk to you."

Satisfied with the Mid Life situation for the moment, Victor Packard thought about his next move. Of course. Kurt Schmidt.

With great difficulty, Packard finally found Schmidt's phone number and dialed it. No one answered and there was no machine. He called the phone company back, and pleading an emergency, got the address. Schmidt lived in Topanga Canyon. Packard decided he better drive out and see what he could find.

*   *   *   *

Monday Morning, Las Vegas

Beretta was at his corporate desk before nine, sure that his unwanted "family guardian," his Peer, would keep good on his threat to be there same time, same place.

While waiting, he thought about Schmidt. Why was he having so much difficulty tracking him down and putting him out of circulation? He hadn't appeared that wily the night they had met, and Beretta had been both cautious and observant.

Roz had made the initial arrangements. She had instructed Schmidt to fly to Las Vegas, check into a specified motel, and wait for a 10:00 P.M. contact. It was the Thursday before the Academy Awards ceremony.

Beretta's bodyguard had picked up Schmidt, taken his picture, searched him for weapons, blindfolded him, and then drove him to Beretta's private underground garage. Then by Beretta's private elevator, he delivered Schmidt to his private office.

Beretta was the one who removed Schmidt's blindfold.

Beretta thought again of Schmidt's appearance. Except for his birthmark, he certainly looked like Craig Carlson. He was about the same size, yet more wiry—more muscular. But the way Schmidt dressed was not Carlson's style.

He wore rugged clothes, almost those of a rock climber— bulky pants with many pockets, heavy-duty shoes, and a bold plaid shirt. It was Roz's idea to have him wear Craig's clothes; she knew how Schmidt normally dressed. Now Beretta understood why she had been so fussy about that detail. If Schmidt had been seen by anyone dressed as he normally did, he might have questioned whether or not it was Carlson.

But Schmidt was thorough. He wanted a lot of guarantees and knew exactly how he wanted the money. He took his time, he examined the passports and plane tickets carefully, and he studied the biographies of the aliases in detail. He made Beretta add driver's licenses for the aliases and even insisted on one fake CIA identification card. When Beretta asked him in what name, Schmidt laughed and said, "Cameron Stanfield. That sounds important enough." Beretta told him that would really take some extra time; Schmidt said he would wait at the hotel until all was ready.

When they finished talking, Beretta photographed Schmidt for passport purposes, blindfolded him and had him returned to his motel by a different route.

*   *   *   *

The secretary interrupted Beretta's recollection. "You have a visitor."

Before Beretta could reply, the door opened and his "family guardian" walked into his office smoking a smelly cigar.

"Good morning, Antonio. You look well. The receipts at The Horse must be good."

This time Beretta was behind his desk in his territory.

"You haven't caught him yet, have you? Well? What do you have to say for yourself?"

"Sit down, Al. You don't have to stand in my presence."

"No. Can't stay." Al propped one foot up on an expensive chair. "I understand you've been screwing Roz Marlowe in the desert. Did you get a signed contract from her for her proceeds from *Rain?*"

"No." Beretta wondered, *How does the bastard know everything?*

"Did you even try to get it signed?"

"I did all but strangle her for it."

His Peer became silent and blew a big cloud of smoke directly at Beretta. He smiled. "Don't you know by now that Marlowe and Schmidt are working you?"

Beretta's face knotted. "Yeah—sure."

"Believe what you want. You'll see."

Beretta said nothing.

"Do you have Lloyd's of London in Sydney well covered? Another million won't be tolerated."

"How do you know he's in Sydney?"

"I'm surprised at you, Antonio. You give me so little credit, while I give you so much." Al laughed at his poor joke.

"If you're finished, I have work to do."

Al only stared at Beretta for a moment before he walked behind him and looked out the concave, mirrored eye of The Horse. "Better think of something as collateral, big boy, or you may not enjoy this view much longer. You know, I never realized the Strip was so far down from way up here."

His Peer flipped a photo on Beretta's desk and left.

Beretta looked at the picture. It was of Roz and Schmidt. Their arms were around each other, and they were smiling broadly, it had been taken in front of the MGM Grand. Beretta turned it over. Instead of a date, there were two words. "Guess When."

"Goddamn him! He's so good at it."

He hated the position Roz had put him in. Now he wondered if she did have anything to do with Schmidt's being so able to avoid him. But how could she? Beretta answered his own question; he told Roz damn near all that was going on. And when he was high or drunk he knew he would fill in anything and everything she asked without hesitation.

Anything and everything!

"Shit!" If Roz could arrange Craig's death in an attempt to collect one hundred million, she could surely arrange Beretta's fall from grace while Schmidt collected six million. Then Roz, loaded with money, could have Schmidt as her lover of choice back in her bed.

Beretta knew damn well Roz was capable of doing all of that without losing ten minutes of sleep over it. He wished he had inflicted greater pain on her in Palm Desert. But the problem was, that's exactly what she wanted.

Very angry, Beretta picked up the phone to confront Roz. He then realized that's exactly what he had just told himself kept her so well informed.

"Damn bitch!" he seethed.

Beretta told his secretary he'd be out the rest of the day. He decided to look into Schmidt's background to see if there wasn't something that could help him bring the bastard down.

* * * *

Monday Morning, Bel Air

A typed envelope attracted Inspector Roosevelt's attention. Roosevelt always looked at the return address and the postmark first before opening any outside mail that his secretary hadn't. It was a self-imposed investigative and security precaution. The envelope was postmarked Friday, but there was no return address. Roosevelt slit it open and removed a typewritten note and three snapshots. He looked at the color photos.

One was of Roz Marlowe and Craig Carlson. Another was of Roz Marlowe, Craig Carlson, and another man who looked like his twin brother. The third snapshot was a close-up of Roz Marlowe and the other man, who could have been Craig except for the way he was dressed, his hairstyle, and a mark on his right cheek.

Roosevelt was stunned at the picture. Fascinated, he read the note that was dated last Friday. "Inspector Roosevelt. Thought you should see these. The man's name with Craig Carlson and Roz Marlowe is Kurt Schmidt and he used to live in the Topanga area. At one time Roz had a heavy affair with Schmidt. Don't contact me in writing or by phone. We can only communicate in person when Mrs. Marlowe isn't home. I hope this may be of some help or lead somewhere. Thank you, Simia."

Roosevelt felt a million pinpricks. Astonished at the revelation of a clone, Roosevelt stared at the photos, then again looked at the typed envelope. Something about it was equally riveting, but he couldn't put his finger on it.

Why didn't I ever think of talking further with Simia? he thought. *She's there to see it all and hear it all. She just can't tell it all.*

Sixteen

Monday Morning, Hollywood

Roz Marlowe was ecstatic.

She was unable to sleep past five but didn't care; today was a new day for her. She had stayed off alcohol since Saturday and tried hard last night not to take a sleeping pill. But at midnight, she gave up and took two Seconal. Roz was afraid if she didn't, she would arrive at the studio with nothing but a dull brain, a thick tongue, and bags under her eyes.

The meeting with the producer began at nine. Roz was early. She was wearing designer jeans that fit just right and a white blouse that accented her figure. It was a greet-and-meet of the core group for Roz's new movie: the director, the screenwriter, the main cameraman, the art director, the costume designer, the composer who would create the musical score, and a few others were in attendance. Filming would start in ten days.

Roz was charming and warm to everyone she met. Her leading man, Forrest Williams, was new to her, but he had had much acclaim in Europe in several Merchant-Ivory productions, and was not unfamiliar with Hollywood. He was going to play the role of Grigory Potemkin, the most important of Empress Catherine's lovers.

The supporting actors and actresses were fairly well known to Roz, and she felt very good about the mix of personalities. She thought that Stewart had brought together a real team for a big-budget film. Almost all had shared with her their concern over the loss of her husband, and Roz had accepted their sympathy.

Roz was glad Stewart didn't get too specific about the script. She was going to have to crash program that assignment but certainly knew how. *Even Simia won't know me.* Roz thought. *I've been such a bitch to everyone, now I'll be so nice, so occupied. Not everyone has gone through what I have.*

The Hollywood group became silent as Stewart formally opened his meeting. "The film begins when Catherine is thirty-three and leads a coup against her husband Peter II in order to become the ruler of Russia. Catherine can no longer stand his personal and administrative incompetency. Peter was neurotic, nearly an alcoholic, and possibly impotent. Catherine's three children were all by other lovers."

As Stewart talked on about *The Empress* Roz found herself thinking about her own coup against her husband, about herself now playing a starring role, and about how hard her mother pushed her as a little girl to be different.

She had taken ballet when she couldn't dance, she had taken singing when she couldn't sing, and she had taken piano when she couldn't play. But her mother wouldn't give up.

Every night as Patti Ann Warren was put to bed, Mom would whisper in her ear, "You're different. You're not the same as other little girls. You'll grow up to hear everyone else say, 'She's special.'"

*　*　*　*

Roz suddenly grasped that the room had become quiet and all were watching her. She absently tugged on her neck, where she felt she needed immediate surgery.

Roz gambled, "Yes, Stewart. Will you repeat that please?"

"I said, if it suits you, for the sake of raw sexual passion, we will include Catherine's obsession for young boys after her love for Potemkin was over. Do you mind that?"

"Not at all," said Roz. "However, I prefer older men."

Stewart understood her inference. "I know. But Catherine was a little different. She would choose the boys entirely on their looks and move from one to the next. They were called 'kept girls.' I think we need to include this in order to keep sexual interest in the film as Catherine gets older."

"I can handle anything," said Roz, "as long as you don't make me look as old and chalky white as Bette Davis did when she played Queen Elizabeth in *Elizabeth and Essex*."

Roz appreciated the laughter. God, it felt so good to be alive again!

*　　*　　*　　*

Tuesday Morning, Frankfurt

Still using the alias of Carl Stone, Craig Carlson passed through German customs with his horde of cash zipped into the sides of his heavy luggage. He wasn't worried about his disguise; before they landed he had examined himself in the mirror. He thought, *I look and feel the same—a hundred years old.*

Craig had plotted and planned during the entire trip; now he wished he had slept. Outside customs he cynically said to himself, "Shazam! Now you're Curtis Silvey!" Using that name, he rented a car and headed for the Swiss border. In Zurich, Craig avoided the Dolder Grand, which he and Alan thoroughly enjoyed, and found a small hotel out of the tourist circuit.

Originally he had planned on going straight to Bundesbank to collect Schmidt's fee and keep moving. But Craig recognized that he was too fuzzy to do that. By four in the afternoon he was sound asleep.

*　　*　　*　　*

Tuesday Noon, New York

Henry Alltop was ushered into Paul T. Cabot III's office. It was a first. Never in his career had he seen big-game trophies in an attorney's office. Alltop felt as if he had just landed in Nairobi instead of New York, and Cabot certainly didn't seem to fit his chosen environment. He was short, round-faced, and had bushy eyebrows. Cabot's black leather-rimmed glasses completed his close resemblance to an owl. Alltop guessed he was in his late sixties.

After they exchanged pleasantries, they left for lunch at the Barrister's Club, of which Cabot's grandfather was a founding member. Henry Alltop then remembered having heard some attorneys at previous American Bar Association conventions refer to Adams, Balfour, Cabot, and Forbes unkindly as the Big Game Hunters.

"What service can I be for you regarding Melvin Stein?" Cabot asked after they had ordered.

"Why did you let Stein go?" asked Henry Alltop.

"How confidential will you be?"

"As confidential as you want me to be."

Paul Cabot fumbled for another cigarette. "Because we caught him manufacturing evidence in a will contest case."

"Why didn't you get him disbarred?"

"Because it would have come down very heavy for our firm, and we admonished him that if he was ever caught again, we would surface the case and get him disbarred. It was impossible to undo what he had done."

"Which was?"

After Paul Cabot recounted the nasty story of how Stein's uncontrolled maneuvering caused the total ruin of a good family and their privately held company, Alltop understood why the firm didn't pursue the disbarment. They simply didn't want to talk about Melvin Stein ever being part of the prestigious firm of Adams, Balfour, Cabot, and Forbes.

"Have you tracked him since then?" asked Alltop.

"Not really. He was a young associate with us at the time. We tried hard to forget he was ever here."

"I see. Well, he's resurfaced long enough to cause Mrs. Ellen Papagos a great amount of concern. He has challenged a will where her son left all of his stock in Papagos Food Wholesalers to his son, Andrew Papagos, her only grandson—a minor. She wants her son's last will recognized as legal so she can function as the controlling interest of the corporation."

Paul Cabot disappeared behind a new cloud of smoke.

"Do you have any evidence that he has manufactured or will manufacture evidence?" asked the shrouded Cabot.

"Not at this point, Paul. But you must be well aware of his current reputation. All Stein does is will contests all over the country. And if he doesn't win them, he collects a big fee."

"But in your case, has he manufactured evidence?"

"That I don't know, but I now know from you that he once did. He's obviously capable of it. All we want is for him to withdraw his will contest and get out of our lives. He's going to cost my client a lot of money and wasted time because of his greedy little scheme."

Paul Cabot's raspy cough was his only response.

"Well?" Alltop was irritated at Cabot's dance around the issue.

"I'll write you a confidential unsigned memo. What I put in it should send him to Brazil," Cabot said in his gravelly voice.

Alltop felt a wave of relief wash over him. He had been in knots since the confrontation in Roz's dining room, where he had let his mouth get ahead of his normally controlled demeanor.

Cabot changed the subject. "Have you ever hunted big game?"

One hour later, the two blue-suited men left the stodgy club. Alltop had Cabot's assurance he would have his memo before the end of the week and Cabot's best wishes for Ellen Papagos.

*   *   *   *

Tuesday Noon, Encinitas

Alan threw the keys of his new car on the hall table. A friend who had once said, "If you ever plan to sell your roadster, call me first" had really meant it. Alan thought the offer would have translated, like so many others, to "If you're ever in our territory, please stop by and be our guest." He was pleased to be wrong.

He had already put his friend's check in the bank and leased a new car for one year. Alan thought it was a wise thing to do. He couldn't even carry a large suitcase in his expensive roadster and certainly could use the money.

Alan was in the kitchen when the doorbell rang. He looked at the wall clock and thought the realtor was early for his appointment. When he opened the door, he was unable to hide his shock.

"May I come in?" Marcel Gavin said to his astounded son.

"Yes. Of course. Come in." Alan looked at the car in the driveway, further amazed that his father had driven there. He rarely drove in Monaco.

Alan didn't attempt to embrace his father, who had always rejected any such show of emotion from his gay son. In a state of disbelief, Alan walked into the living room and asked his father to sit down.

"When did you arrive?"

"Four hours ago. It took a long time to get the car."

"Did you come from France?"

"Paris."

Alan looked at his father. Something was eating him alive.

"May I get you some coffee or tea or a drink?"

"You can get me nothing!"

Alan had never seen his father so angry. He sat down across from him and asked, "How's Mother? I really appreciated her coming for Craig's funeral."

"That's not why I'm here," snapped his father.

"Why are you here? Do you believe the press and think I killed Craig? If that's why you're here, you've never been so wrong." Alan thought, *Why make up today? I've never gotten along with my father, not even as a child.*

The senior Gavin pulled an envelope from his pocket and thrust it at Alan. "Explain this."

Alan saw it was from the bank in Monaco where he had his personal account. He was angry. How domineering it was of his father to even look at his personal account. That was none of his goddamn business, and being finance minister didn't give him that right.

Alan opened the statement and looked at it. "I don't understand. There has to be a mistake."

"I knew that's what you would say," said his father.

"But . . ."

"It's not that easy," interrupted his father. "I've checked it and rechecked it. There are no clerical errors. Explain it!"

Alan was puzzled by his father's anger and his inference. He stared at the statement again. There were two entries he knew nothing about—a deposit of one million dollars and, two days later another deposit for eight hundred thousand dollars. Without those, his balance would have been sixty thousand francs.

"I know nothing of these. I've never had this kind of money, and these are not mine. They belong in someone else's account. The bank has made a mistake."

Alan handed the statement back to his father.

"They were wire transferred to your account immediately after Carlson's death." Marcel Gavin didn't take his eyes off his son. "The million is from Bank of America in San Francisco, and the eight hundred thousand from the Hong Kong–Shanghai Bank in Hong Kong. Now I would like to have a real explanation about both." He handed the statement back.

Alan threw it on the side table. His father had accused him all of his life of being wrong, being guilty, being inferior, being stupid, and not even being correct with his financial investments of millions for the royal family of Monaco. Alan was tired—tired of everyone being on his ass about everything.

"I don't know. I can't account for this money! What do you think? They're a payoff? Is that what you think? You're disgusting to fly all the way here and call me a paid anything. You used to think I was a paid gigolo. Now do you think I'm a paid killer? Or just a liar?"

Marcel Gavin remained stone cold and Alan could hear his labored breathing.

"Do you expect me to believe that two disparate banks in two disparate countries both made errors and both picked out your account number in Monaco? That's ridiculous and improbable!"

Alan became quiet. He suddenly understood his father's anger and his right to question. It didn't make any sense and it was beyond a clerical error.

"How did you come across this? It isn't routine or even proper for the bank to contact anyone but me. In fact, why didn't they contact me?"

"I don't know why. But they did contact me. You are my son, and you are a suspect in a murder case. I think they thought they were helping you." His father was breathing more normally.

Alan turned and looked at the Pacific Ocean. It was all so strange. The whole thing was strange. He looked back at his father, shook his head, and shrugged his shoulders. "I don't know what this means, Dad. I don't know anything anymore."

*   *   *   *

Wednesday Morning, Zurich

When Craig awoke Wednesday morning, he made still another predetermined name change. He became Herr Karl Steiff, the heir designate on Schmidt's information sheet to one million dollars waiting for him at the Bundesbank.

Craig checked out of his hotel, found a parking garage, and armed with his special black briefcase and a newly purchased gym bag, entered the bank's grand, old-fashioned lobby.

Unlike his behavior in San Francisco and Hong Kong, Craig first studied the bank and those in it before ramming forward to a secretary and saying, "I'm so and so and where's my money?"

Craig noted the cameras and thought he could pick out some of the security personnel. He could read German better than he could speak it, and was able to determine where he needed to go. Craig had always recognized a definite body characteristic about the Germans that set them apart from others; now he tried to adopt it as he made his approach.

In halting German, he said to the man behind the desk, "I am Herr Steiff, and I want to see someone about a cashier's check that has been left here for me. I need direction. *Danke.*"

"*Ja, mein Herr.*" The male secretary picked up his phone but spoke so quietly that Craig couldn't hear anything he said.

The man hung up, studied Craig, and told him to wait there. Craig didn't like that.

Craig watched his initial contact talk to an older man, who also made a call. He looked around to see if anyone was watching him. If anyone was, he couldn't tell.

Finally, his initial contact returned. "Come with me."

He led Craig deep into the endless compartments and corridors of the first floor. He opened the door to a stuffy conference room, and curtly told him to wait and that someone would be with him shortly. As he left, he closed the door.

Craig didn't feel quite right about his situation. He had often wondered why he was so hell-bent on picking up Kurt Schmidt's payoff money. But now he recognized he needed that as seed money to start a new life with Alan—a very private life that they could only dream of before.

The government bureaus, the IRS; the fundamentalist Christians; the conservative politicians and the hard-line, far-right rednecks were intrusive enough. But layered on top of that were the insidious media—the news reporters; the paparazzi; the constant television and print media requests for interviews about his life, with their constant misrepresentation of everything he did or said in public.

It was too much.

The final insult to his privacy was his loving fans, with their intense stares and incessant demands for autographs and their boundless need to share with him their feelings about one of his films.

Suddenly, Craig realized he had to get out of the bank. He had to move. His responsibility was to Alan, his lover, not to some setup that Roz, Beretta, and Schmidt had concocted over money. Craig realized he couldn't afford to just sit there and wonder what was going to happen to him next. He had to be the one calling the shots. His goal was home, but his challenge was to get there. He didn't need any further detours, and an inner voice was telling Craig Carlson that something was very wrong.

Craig quietly tried the door. It was locked. A cold chill ran down his back. *Don't panic, Carlson*, he told himself. *They do that for normal security.*

But why am I back here? Why not out front? The room had a window, but it also had a decorative iron grille on the outside.

Standing there with briefcase in hand, he noticed, for the

first time, the overlarge mirror over the credenza at one end of the room. That was enough.

Mirror, my ass! Craig thought.

Without warning, the door opened and a heavy-set woman with a heavy knit wool dress entered. She was Germanic and severe looking.

"You were leaving, Herr Steiff?"

Craig wasn't sure what to do. He didn't respond.

"I have some questions to ask of you, Herr Steiff, in order to get your cashier's check. Please sit down."

Craig recognized it as an order.

"Do you have a problem with my request?" Craig asked in halting German.

"*Nein.* I just have to get some reference information and identification that we need to make sure you are who you say you are. A million dollars is a lot of money."

Craig tried to read her, but couldn't. "I need to use the water closet before we start, *Fräulein*. Do you mind telling me where the nearest one is?"

"This will only take me a minute, and then I'll show you."

It was the answer Craig didn't want to hear.

"But I must use it—now. I have this chronic problem—a colostomy, in fact—and I need to attend to it."

She stared at him, concern showing on her face. "It's down the hall on your right. Leave your things here."

Craig left the gym bag but held on to his briefcase. It contained all of his identities and backup cash. He was dead without it.

"I have something in here I'll need," he said lamely.

She looked at the gym bag as if that weren't the likely place for something he might need.

"I'll be waiting here," she said, and reached for the phone.

Craig entered the hallway, and as calmly as he could, began to retrace his steps through the labyrinth that he had followed to get to the conference room. At one point he made a wrong turn, but at the end of that corridor he saw a door to the outside with a metal arm across it. He could tell from the sign above that it was an emergency exit.

He didn't hesitate.

He went straight through it as the alarm sounded with all its fury.

Out on the street, Craig let out a deep breath and hurried for Zurich's main bahnhof, which was just across the street from the Bundesbank. Craig ducked into the mass of people taking trains to all parts of Zurich and the nearby towns. Once so hidden, he turned around and looked back at the bank. Two men ran out the front door and immediately began examining the crowds of pedestrians. Instantly they were joined by two more, who were pointed toward the bahnhof and immediately headed his way.

"Jesus!" Craig exclaimed. "They know I'm here!"

Craig pushed his way onto a train that was boarding. He would worry about his ticket and how to reclaim his car with his luggage later.

When asked for his ticket, he found out from the irate Swiss conductor the train was headed for Rapperswill.

Seventeen

Wednesday Morning, Bel Air

Simia was gleeful over Roz's situation. The actress was in pain after cosmetic surgery on her neck, but she didn't dare shout, scream, or throw things as she usually did when unhappy. Tantrums were out; the surgeon forbade her to even talk. She could only write notes.

Simia spent the first night at the beck and call of Roz's tinkling bell and silly hand-made orders of: "More ice," "Prop me up," "Need a pain pill," and "Don't let me fall over again."

Simia knew the precious silence would last only a few days, but it was so peaceful. At least Simia felt safe in leaving things up on her wall so she could study them for longer periods of time and reflect on their meanings without fear of an invasion by the indisposed Roz.

Simia had discovered a great deal about Roz's many boyfriends. Kurt Schmidt was a heavy back in the early nineties. Then Roz switched to Beretta after she had played in Las Vegas, and much more recently to Washburne. But she kept going back to Beretta seemingly whenever she could. Compared to him, Washburne was a mere fling.

But it was Schmidt who interested her the most. Simia had forgotten how closely he resembled Craig. There was something there, and that's why she had sent the pictures to Inspector Roosevelt. Maybe he could detect it. Simia kept hoping she would find the missing piece of the puzzle before he came to see her work, but so far she hadn't. The Oscar for *Dangerous Passage* only confused Simia. Only Craig knew of that space, or so she thought. There was an answer, but Simia couldn't understand how that made any sense. If, for some reason Craig had survived that night, why would he still be missing?

* * * *

Wednesday Morning, Topanga Canyon

After ringing the doorbell and knocking hard on the door several times, Inspector Roosevelt walked around the small house looking through the windows. He was sure no one was home. Kurt Schmidt's house was ill-kept, surrounded by old trees and shaggy shrubs. An old Ford truck was parked in the driveway. There was no garage. Roosevelt could tell that the trash around the yard was old, not new, but it was difficult to tell from the outside whether anyone had recently been inside the house.

Roosevelt decided to look in on the neighbors.

At the first trailer, no one was home. At the next small house, there were two large dogs he didn't care to challenge. As he approached the neighbor farther up the hill, he saw he was being watched. Roosevelt realized the man must have been watching him the entire time he investigated Schmidt's house.

"I'm with the police department," said Roosevelt, pulling out his badge. "Do you know a Kurt Schmidt?"

The man nodded.

"Has he been around here lately?"

The man shook his head.

"Can you tell me anything about him?"

"You're like all the rest that've been here. What, why, and where? Don't any of you have anything better to do?"

That got Roosevelt's attention. "There have been others?"

The man nodded again.

"It looks like he's been gone awhile."

The man held up two fingers. "Two weeks," he said.

Roosevelt took notes. Carlson was murdered fifteen days ago. He had to find out all he could. "Where are your other neighbors?" he asked. The policeman was adept at this game.

"Not here."

Roosevelt thought for a moment and said, "Thank you." He turned to leave.

"Don't you want to know anything?"

Roosevelt shrugged. "Possibly."

The man rubbed his thumb with his first two fingers.

"I don't do that," Roosevelt said.

"Sure. You've never worked with an informant in your life," he said sarcastically.

Roosevelt often had, but his department didn't advocate the use of money. "Kurt Schmidt is a suspect in a murder case," he lied. "And if I were you, I'd hate to be the one who withheld information from the police."

Roosevelt watched his attitude change. The man hiked up his belt and looked down at Schmidt's house.

"There was a big guy. Bossy type. Not very nice, but he paid good money."

"Do you remember his name?" asked Roosevelt.

"Yeah. Packwood, or something like that."

Roosevelt hid his astonishment. Something big was happening with Kurt Schmidt to get Victor Packard's attention. "He's also directly involved," winged Roosevelt.

The man took his foot down from where he was resting it on the tree and shoved his hands in his pockets.

"And the next party?" asked Roosevelt, not knowing if there were any.

"Even meaner than the big guy. Got his card inside." The man made no move to get it.

Roosevelt had no extra money on him. "Have you ever heard of the silent witness program? You can collect money at a bank for your information if it's valid."

The man was interested. He looked back at the mess he called home and smiled. "I can always use money."

Roosevelt dangled the bait even closer. "I don't know why I couldn't apply that here and now. You give me something of value, and I'll call you back with a number that you can take to a bank."

"I like that," said the man.

"Now, may I see that man's card?"

"Why not?" He shuffled back into the house.

Thirty minutes later, after finding out all he could about Kurt Schmidt, the hard-hitting, hard-living stuntman, Roosevelt handed him back the card. He told him he would be calling him, thanked him and left. Roosevelt had never heard of Antonio Beretta, manager of the Trojan Horse Casino, in his life. Thanks to Simia, Roosevelt now had two men who were somehow involved in the Carlson murder.

As he entered his office, he was met by his secretary. "You're not going to like this," she said.

"So what's new?"remarked Roosevelt.

"The prosecuting attorney has gone around you. A grand jury has issued a true bill on Alan Gavin. He's indicted for the murder of Craig Carlson. His arraignment will be next week."

"Shit!" said Roosevelt, who never swore. The prosecuting attorney obviously felt that he was prejudiced for Gavin, or he would have called Roosevelt as a witness before the grand jury.

Most upset at the unwanted news, he asked his secretary to work up complete rap sheets on Kurt Schmidt, Victor Packard, and Antonio Beretta, including what their mothers read to them at bedtime. Once she did that, he just might pull in some favors owed him by a friend of his at the FBI.

*   *   *   *

Wednesday Evening, Zurich

Craig tried to calm his shattered nerves at a coffee house in Rapperswill. He had to retrieve his suitcase with his cash and get the hell out of Switzerland. As he watched the shuttle boats and tourist boats ply Lake Zurich, he formulated his plan.

Afterward, waiting for time to pass, he called Savannah and left a message on her machine, saying that Mr. Papagos would call her from Milan Thursday morning and to think about Jebb Marlowe possibly using his position in the insurance industry to find out all he could about the status of Craig's hefty insurance policies relative to the beneficiary, Alan Gavin.

Four hours later, a heavyset tourist wearing a flowered shirt and plaid pants with two cameras hanging from his neck arrived at the dock in Zurich at the height of the evening rush hour. Onshore, he hailed a taxi that took him to the garage where Curtis Silvey had parked his rental car. The taxi stopped behind Silvey's car, interrupting the flow of exiting cars. The tourist popped out of the cab, opened the trunk, removed one large suitcase, and got back in the cab. In thirty seconds the cab moved forward again in the stream of cars leaving the garage. The only attention they received seemed to be two horn blasts from an irate driver.

Craig was sweating with nervous energy, every car behind them an enemy. Back on the street, he directed the taxi driver to take him to Zurich International Airport. On arrival, Craig hurried into the terminal with his luggage and stepped into the nearest rest room. Minutes later a much thinner man in a blue denim shirt and blue denim jeans emerged, dropped a bulky package in a waste container, walked out of the terminal, and hailed a cab for the Dolder Grand.

In the Dolder lobby, Craig asked the concierge, "Have any drivers contacted you about a charter for a Papagos?"

"Yes, sir. Are you Mr. Papagos, sir?"

"I represent him. May I speak with the driver?"

"Immediately, sir."

The concierge made a call, and a young man wearing a chauffeur's uniform appeared and curtly introduced himself as Ludwig Gerhardt.

Craig drew him aside. "May I see some identification, please?" He waited as the driver reached inside his jacket pocket and produced his chauffeur's license.

"How long have you worked for Charlemagne Charter?"

"Two years," clipped Gerhardt.

"What did they tell you about this charter?" Craig asked.

"It was for twenty-four hours and could be to anywhere."

"Then let's go," said Craig.

"Yes, sir. Let me take your luggage."

At Craig's direction, they left the Dolder in the driver's big Mercedes for one of Zurich's more quiet residential areas. After slowly touring the area, Craig began to relax.

Craig saw no evidence of anyone following them, and his careful follow-up questions of the driver put him at ease.

Craig asked his driver, "How long does it take to drive to Milan by less-traveled roads? I would like to stay off the auto-bahn if possible."

*   *   *   *

Wednesday Morning, Las Vegas

Antonio Beretta was exasperated. Nothing was going right. Nothing! His attempt to find out anything about Kurt Schmidt in Topanga had been fruitless. His calls to Roz had once again gone unanswered. And Beretta had just hung up from talking with his banker-confidant in Zurich, who had called to tell him about Schmidt's thwarted attempt to withdraw his cashier's check from the Bundesbank. That information was devastating. And of course, Schmidt had somehow smelled a rat and gotten away, while all the time Beretta's contacts were blindly waiting for him in Sydney.

Beretta was finished with the failing services provided by his contacts in his assassins guide. He must directly intercede, but at the moment, he didn't know how. He simply couldn't understand how Schmidt could have outmaneuvered them in California, Hong Kong, Australia and now Switzerland. At best, London was a ripe target for his continued cleverness. The fact that Schmidt failed to pick up a million dollars in both Sydney and Zurich didn't for one minute put Beretta at peace. He felt Schmidt could double back at any time and pick off Sydney. He seemed to be capable of crossing continents and borders with impunity, without detection and without using any credit cards other than the one used in Hong Kong at the Peninsula, which had been a sham.

Beretta couldn't forget what His Peer had said: "Don't you know that Roz and Schmidt are together on this?" To date, there was nothing to indicate that might not be true. He decided to call

Roz on her house line and see if he couldn't get some information about her from someone on her staff.

"Anne Barnett speaking."

"This is Antonio Beretta, the manager of the Trojan Horse Casino in Las Vegas. I was wondering if there was any way I could get in touch with Roz Marlowe relative to a follow-up engagement at the casino. I can guarantee you I would make it worth her while." He knew Anne Barnett damn well knew him.

"Yes, I see. I'll give the message to Mrs. Marlowe."

"Is she in the city?"

"I'm not at liberty to tell you, Mr. Beretta," lied Anne.

Beretta didn't respond, he was mad. Roz was shielded when she wanted to be and available when she wanted to be. It was that goddamn control thing she practiced on everyone.

But not on him!

"Well, tell the bitch that her stud is in need, and would like her services!" He crashed the phone on his desk, ripped off his clothes, and strode naked to his steamroom-sauna-shower. He had work to do. Beretta began thinking of some of his few carefully cultivated contacts in southern Europe.

*   *   *   *

Wednesday Midnight, The Alps

The traffic was light, and Craig finally stopped studying those on the highway with them. With the exception of an old van driven by an elderly woman who passed them a couple of times and eventually fell behind, the trip was uneventful.

Craig rested fitfully during the first leg of the long drive. His driver seemed excellent, very polite, and steady, he took no careless chances and did not travel at excessive speeds. Before they challenged the more difficult terrain of the Swiss Alps, they stopped for fuel about halfway to the Italian border.

Craig used that opportunity to freshen himself in the rest room, while his driver asked permission to use his car phone to call his agency and update them on his destination.

Back on the highway, the driver told Craig that if he would get his passport handy, he would only have to bother him a moment when they reached the border, if Craig happened to be asleep. Craig sorted through his multiple-identity briefcase and placed Papagos' passport on the seat beside him.

Now quite relaxed, he entered his own twilight zone. Craig removed his all-important, bulky Communications Guide from his briefcase and used it as a pillow. He fell asleep holding his briefcase on his chest to ward off the blowing air. Craig knew it kept the driver awake, and it was the least of his concerns.

*   *   *   *

The young driver continued his speed toward the crest of a pass, his backseat passenger quiet. At the higher elevation, a late spring squall added a fresh coat of white to the shrinking snow that remained from Switzerland's long winter. The visibility was poor, and he could barely see the road signs as he passed them, but at that hour of the night, the highway was deserted.

As the driver rounded a sharp curve, he was startled by a blinding caution light and roadblock in front of him. He slammed on the brakes abruptly, pitching his passenger hard to the floor. A workman with an orange safety vest desperately waved his flag, but the speed of the car and the icy road made it impossible for him to stop.

The car was headed directly for a "Rockslide Ahead" sign, when the workman frantically pointed his flag in the direction in which the driver thought he should veer the car. The Mercedes crossed the narrow berm, left the highway, and plunged into the black void. Halfway down, the driver heard the two back doors pop open. He failed to see his passenger's body pitch into the blackness before his Mercedes came to a crashing stop on the floor of a shallow mountain ravine. On impact, the Mercedes exploded in a blinding flash.

The man above worked quickly. He stashed the "Rockslide Ahead" sign and the makeshift roadblock gear into the truck safely parked in the overlook pulloff on the opposite side of the road. He had chosen the spot carefully, looking for a small incline that would stop the car from plunging hundreds of feet farther down the mountain.

Using his flashlight, he carefully made his way down the ravine to examine the burning car. There was no sign of life. The trunk and all doors were open, and he could make out the body of the driver at the wheel. But the flames were so intense that he couldn't get a closer look. Fearing an additional explosion, and quite satisfied with his work, he hurried back up the mountainside.

The woman driving the old van was waiting at his truck.

"Nice job, Georgio," she said.

"Yeah. I saw this done in a film once."

"My little transponder is still beeping away. Do you think we ought to try and find it?" she asked.

"Hell no." Georgio laughed. "Not in that inferno. And who's going to be looking in charred luggage for an electronic device?"

The woman lit a cigarette and looked down at the burning wreckage. "This Steiff-Silvey-Schmidt fellow thought he was so damn clever. As soon as he picked up his suitcase at the garage in Zurich, he was dead meat."

"Yeah," Georgio said. "I feel sorry for the poor driver. He should never have reported his destination on his cellular. It's not everybody who takes this road at night for fun."

The woman ground out her cigarette on the highway and added, "If you hadn't been able to set up an intercept, we would have used our own resources. But it wouldn't have been as clever as this."

"Yeah. As subtle as a dozen well-placed bullet holes."

"But, who's Papagos?" asked the woman.

"How the hell do I know? And who cares. It was obviously just another one of Schmidt's clever aliases to keep moving. Your van's a little communications jewel, isn't it?"

"You'd be surprised at the jobs I get from corporations wanting data on competitors. It makes my eavesdropping profession legitimate."

A man appeared at the door of the van wearing earphones.

"Traffic two miles out," he said.

"Happy hunting," said Georgio.

"*Ciao*," said the woman.

As dawn broke, Georgio entered the outskirts of Milan and reported from a pay phone to Beretta that Kurt Schmidt was what Beretta had demanded: very dead!

*   *   *   *

Thursday Noon, Milan

Savannah called the Palazzo delle Stelline, one of Milan's finer hotels. The operator told her that, yes, a Mr. Papagos did have a reservation, but he had not checked in yet.

Concerned, Savannah decided she would call again in the late afternoon. Among other things, there was one part of Craig's message she wanted him to clarify before she called her step-brother Jebb in Washington. Craig had asked her to consider contacting Jebb regarding his extensive insurance policies. But Craig had also said, "Savannah, you may have been right. I probably shouldn't have contacted Packard. Something is very wrong with him, and the only thing I can think of is his concern about the insurance companies regarding the enormous amount of insurance payable to Alan at my death and the fact that I'm not dead."

Savannah thought Jebb Marlowe should be in an excellent position to find out plenty from his job at the National Life Underwriters Association in Washington. But she wondered if Jebb wouldn't speculate as to why in the hell she cared. She wanted to ask Craig if she dare tell Jebb that he was alive. Jebb certainly was going to know it soon enough.

By the time Savannah went onstage, she was more than concerned about Craig. She was worried. Savannah puzzled: *How am I ever going to locate a dead man traveling the world using aliases?*

*   *   *   *

Friday Afternoon, Bel Air

Alan Gavin had never felt as intimidated in his life as he had all day long by the probing questions of the prosecuting attorney. Nothing was sacred. The fact that traces of his blood were on Craig's clothes, on Craig's papers and on the heavy oak table in Craig's library, was most damaging, even though Alan's story of what happened was a complete explanation of it all. And the questions about his driving gloves were unending. When did he wear them? When did he get them? Why did he wear them? Did he wear them that night? Where did he take them off?

He was questioned about the fax regarding Craig's will and the palimony suit, and the letters where he was shown as having received copies about the will change from Packard. The fact that he said he had never received any of them seemed to be taken as a lie, not as the truth. But there was no one to prove he did or didn't. It was all his word against that of the prosecuting attorney, and it was all circumstantial.

But the fact that he was twenty years younger than Carlson, was on Carlson's payroll for everything he did, had been an admitted homosexual for years, and had escorted many men and women on the French Riviera appeared to be only of negative value to the tight-jawed jury.

The only time Alan was allowed to talk with his attorney was in the hall during recess. Alan told Wilson he had answered all of the jury's questions as fully as he could. Wilson sternly advised him not to overanswer, that all it would do was give them information they didn't need, would misuse, or would misunderstand.

The prosecuting attorney left until last that the bullet found in Carlson's head had been fired from Carlson's own gun. Alan knew that that evidence could bury him. As he forcefully restated his innocence, he knew the jury recognized that Craig couldn't have shot himself with his own gun without leaving a much bigger mess.

By the end of the day, Alan felt he had been lynched by the prosecuting attorney whom his attorney, Wilson, had so glibly told him to walk out on ten days earlier.

*   *   *   *

Saturday Morning, Zurich

The security on room 304 at the Universitatssptal in Zurich was tight. Only cleared medical and intelligence personnel with special badges had access. The man in the coma had been admitted as John Doe by the Swiss authorities Thursday afternoon after he was flown there by helicopter. Swiss security had called together agents with Interpol, British intelligence, German intelligence, and the CIA to help them with the problem. They were meeting in a small hospital conference room on the same floor as John Doe's room.

John Doe's medical condition was grim. When found just above St. Gotthard's Pass, he was barely alive. Considering the unusual circumstances around the accident, the local medical authorities had him airlifted to Zurich. Now John Doe's broken bones had been set and his open wounds stitched, and he was alive only thanks to life support.

His body had been found about halfway from the road to the crash site, all but buried in a snowdrift. The car was spotted first and the body discovered later by a truck driver who then contacted the nearby town of Altermann, who sent out their medical response team. The medics said the snowdrift had saved John Doe's life. It helped break his fall and kept his temperature subnormal without his freezing to death.

The medical opinion of the hospital's excellent staff was that John Doe had one chance in three of surviving his ordeal, but the doctors were far ahead of the intelligence community in their analysis.

The intelligence experts had no idea who he really was, where he originally came from, where he was ultimately going, or what he was doing—except there were thousands of one-hundred-dollar bills found around a piece of luggage that had evidently been thrown from the Mercedes and lay exposed due to a rip in the leather covering of the case. A briefcase also found near John Doe revealed he was carrying multiple passports, driver's licenses, and credit cards, as well as identification that he worked for the CIA. But from all the materials in the briefcase, no single identity was evident.

Swiss security said the dead driver was most likely Ludwig Gerhardt, a driver for the Zurich-based Charlemagne Charter Company, who had supplied the transportation for a client by the name of Papagos. Strangely, none of the multiple identification materials found in the briefcase were in the name of the man who made the charter, Papagos.

The identification question was further compounded for the agents on finding that all but two of the numerous identities were deceased. The CIA reported that a Kurt Schmidt was a resident of the state of California, still living, but couldn't be located. British intelligence reported that a Curtis Silvey was last reported to be a resident of London, but officially he had been missing for years. Curtis Silvey's picture was the only one they were unable to obtain.

There was absolutely no explanation for the CIA identification badge of Cameron Stanfield. The CIA had no record of a Stanfield as ever having worked for the agency.

If John Doe could answer questions, they might have had some clue as to what was going on. Maybe he would explain why all of the passports had his picture on them, why they all looked so much like Kurt Schmidt, why the large suitcase had a transponder implanted in it still emitting strong signals, and why that luggage had held so much hidden money. Or maybe John Doe would deny the most obvious conclusion—that he was involved in drug trafficking—or explain why there was no identification for the man he claimed to be, Papagos.

But at the moment, whether he was Kurt Schmidt, Curtis Silvey, or someone else made little difference. He was in a coma, and it was a miracle that he escaped almost certain death.

Interpol and the German authorities left the identification

and monetary puzzle for the Swiss, the CIA, and British intelligence to piece together. But all of them had concluded that they probably wouldn't know a damn thing until John Doe talked.

If he died, it would simply be another unsolved incident with intriguing international implications.

Eighteen

Thirty Days Later: Monday Morning, Bel Air

Roz adapted to the role of Catherine the Great as if she were Catherine the Great. Her queenly attitude affected everyone in her domain. Simia was her vassal; Stewart, the producer, her consort; Forrest, the leading man, her court jester. Roz had relegated all the others on the set, from the gaffer to the screenwriter, to her obligated subjects. She was omnipotent, and her suggestions, no matter how demanding, were given more weight than most—because if they weren't, there was Roz to answer to.

As a result, the filming of *The Empress* was already off schedule and overbudget.

Roz arose every weekday morning at four-thirty, and with Simia's attentive help, she plunged into a routine that would make an eighty-year-old nun look good. Ice, cucumbers, tea bags, and a facial preceded her departure to the studio at six-thirty, wrapped softly in silks and printed fabrics. Even Roz's driver was in a new role. Her car was her carriage, and he was the entrusted scout who prepared the way for her. Fresh flowers adorned her passenger area every morning, only to be thrown out for new ones in the afternoon. Roz convinced everyone that she must be pampered to properly play her role. The studio picked up the tab for extras they had never dreamed of in the budget. But her acting was superb, and only a few retakes were necessary because of her diligence. The producers of the film felt that with Roz Marlowe, they had a winner in the making. Roz didn't allow anything to interfere with the job or break her concentration.

She had Anne and Simia block her correspondence and calls. When she returned home in the middle of the afternoon, she was exhausted, and the gentle massage and hot bath that preceded her light supper and early bedtime were rarely interrupted by anything. She insisted that all messages of any kind be in writing and presented to her silently, in keeping with a royal presence. In the evening, as Roz read over her lines for the next day's shoot, candles were substituted for electricity and heavy Russian chants mournfully sounded throughout her quarters.

Roz Marlowe surrendered herself to the role and forgot about Kurt Schmidt. She hadn't talked with Beretta for four weeks. She had even repressed the secret relief she had experienced when Alan Gavin was arraigned for the murder of her husband. Free on bond, Alan's trial was scheduled to start the beginning of next week. Roz, as Catherine, would coldly murder a husband and that was the only murder she thought about.

Simia seemed to be over her strange mood and was back to providing services that pleased Roz. When she got home every afternoon, Simia had her room as she wanted it, and only rarely gave her a note needing immediate attention.

But today was different.

As Roz entered her castle, Anne presented her with a message on a silver tray. As soon as Roz picked it up, Anne vanished. Roz read it as she was climbing the long royal staircase to her elegant royal quarters:

"Mrs. Marlowe. I will be unable to continue working with you on the contest of the will. Things have come up over which I have no control and I will be out of the country for an extended period. I'm sorry, but at this time I cannot even tell you where I can be reached. Good luck. Sincerely, Melvin Stein."

She stumbled at the top step. "Goddamn it!" she shrieked. "That little no-good bastard! I'll have him executed!"

Roz pushed open the door to her quarters violently and shouted at Simia, "I need a drink. Get it now!"

Roz had drunk very little in the past month, and she could see the question on Simia's face.

"Don't think about it. Move your lazy ass!"

Russian music was howling in the background. The room sounded like an orthodox monastery.

"And turn that dreadful music off. I'm sick to death of those fucking Russian chants!"

Simia rushed to do both at the same time.

Everything had been so perfect—the film, Alan, the will contest, not a sound from Beretta—and now this. Roz wanted to scream. She wanted to castrate Stein. She wanted Anne to take the note back and say it was a mistake. The Empress should not be bothered with such petty details!

*   *   *   *

Tuesday, Encinitas

Alan watched as the moving men loaded the last of his furniture and belongings into the van. He had closed on the sale of his house, and it was over; the new owners would take possession tomorrow. He no longer had to drive to Encinitas—there wasn't a reason to. The treasures he had opted to store would be placed in a warehouse, while he kept a few personal items to make the small rental on Wilshire Avenue seem like home—among them, the Bouguereau painting of the little French girl.

Alan fully understood his plight and had no illusions about justice. He was about as sure of his chances of a fair defense from attorney Wilson as he trusted the nightly weather report to be right. And the fact that Victor Packard had suddenly stepped forward for Craig's sake to be of support and help for Wilson was of no great salvation. He still didn't trust Packard.

One bright spot in all this had been his father. When Alan refused to use the large amount of money in his account in Monaco as bond money, because he said it wasn't his, his father posted the two hundred thousand dollars that had kept his son free until the trial.

But today, Alan's loneliness was as thick as the Pacific fog that shrouded sea and land. He wanted badly to leave his past. His phone rang one last time.

"Gavin here."

"Alan, it's Henry Alltop."

"Yes." Alan tried to place the name.

"Remember? I was with Andrew Papagos at the reading of the will."

Alan now well remembered Alltop's verbal attack of Stein and Roz. "Yes. What can I do for you? Is Andrew all right?"

"Yes. He's fine."

"And how is Mrs. Papagos' health? How is she holding up?"

"Very disturbed at your situation."

"So am I."

"She needs to speak with you."

Alan was surprised.

"Alan?"

"Yes, Mrs. Papagos. How nice to hear your voice. What can I do for you?"

"It's what I can do for you. Melvin Stein has left the country, and the will contest has been dropped." Mrs. Papagos paused to take a breath. "Now, I am trying to find a good attorney for you, better than your current legal talent."

Alan felt a surge of hope. Someone cared.

"That's wonderful news, Mrs. Papagos."

"Will you be at this number for the lawyer to reach you?"

"No. You just caught me. I'm moving into Beverly Hills because of—because of the trial." He felt a warm comfort blanket him. Just talking to Craig's mother seemed to bring him close to his beloved Craig.

"Well, give Henry the new number and where to reach you. And keep your chin up. This is just like an election. It's not over yet. Remember that."

*   *   *   *

Tuesday, Bel Air

Inspector Roosevelt's secretary informed him, "A strange man insists on talking to you, but he won't tell me who he is. He keeps saying you'll know him."

Roosevelt wondered who the call was from.

"Roosevelt here."

"Do you remember me? I'm from Topanga Canyon. You know, neighbor of Schmidt."

"Of course, I recognize your voice."

"I have some good dope. Do I get paid for it?"

"That will depend on what it is," said Roosevelt.

"It's worth real money."

"We'll see. What do you have to offer?"

"Someone from the CIA was here looking for Schmidt."

This surprised Roosevelt. "How do you know they were CIA?"

"His badge. He didn't give me any more than that to go on."

"When were they there and what did they want?"

"How much is it worth?"

Roosevelt sighed. "The same as last time."

"Not enough. Let's double my trouble."

"OK," said Roosevelt. He was tired.

"This CIA guy was here two weeks ago. He asked a bunch of questions and then finally showed me two pictures. One was Schmidt, the other one looked like him."

"What were the pictures?"

"One was kind of an identification photo. Just the face. That was definitely Schmidt. The other one was of a man whose face had been all beat up and was swollen. He was wearing kind of a hospital gown. That could have been Schmidt, or at least a very close relative."

Roosevelt's pulse quickened. His trip to Topanga may not have been wasted, after all. "What did they ask or tell you?"

"So many questions it's hard to remember. Except—did he deal in drugs? I said I didn't know, but I'm sure he uses them."

"You have a name or a phone number of the agent?"

"The name is Frederick Miles, and his phone number is three-oh-one-something."

Roosevelt recognized the area code as being that for Langley, Virginia. "Anything else? Any reason why they were looking for him?"

"Just whether I knew if he was dead or alive. Don't forget my money." Roosevelt's informant hung up.

His secretary left a written message on his desk: "Anne Barnett at Roz Marlowe's asked that you call her regarding a possible meeting with a Simia." Roosevelt's head was spinning. He expected he would be a witness for the prosecution. He wondered how the D.A. would like for him to be one hell of a witness for the defense. It wasn't his fault they didn't call him to the grand jury.

*   *   *   *

Tuesday, Las Vegas

Beretta had tried to forget Roz. He missed her, and it was more than sexual, but he had given up trying to reach her. Not one of his calls had been returned. He knew she was in a new film and probably in bed with a new lover, and that made him crazy.

After Georgio called him from Milano about Schmidt, Beretta arranged for the cashier's checks at Sydney, Zurich, New York, and London to be remitted to those who had originated the money. It took some doing, but it got done without his having to send someone in under false aliases to pick up the four million dollars. He felt more at ease with His Peer, who only bugged him now about two million instead of six. It was still a problem for Antonio Beretta, but he knew he could scam that amount off the Trojan Horse in a couple of months without difficulty.

*   *   *   *

Tuesday, Zurich

Exactly two weeks after he was discovered in the snowdrift, John Doe came out of his coma. At first the agents from British intelligence and the CIA were hopeful, but when they discovered that John Doe had amnesia and had no idea who he was, their hopes of solving his identity folded. They had narrowed their field and were looking for a breakthrough.

The only physical resemblance John Doe had was to Kurt Schmidt. Photos obtained of Steiff, Stone, and Smith didn't look at all like those on the alias passports. But Curtis Silvey, a British subject, still left open a possibility. They were unable to get an adult photo of Silvey. He had lived in Liverpool, last worked in London, and had disappeared after a small cruise ship on which he was thought to be a passenger caught fire and sank in the Baltic. Many bodies were never recovered or identified.

Silvey had no family, and British intelligence was unable to come up with any photos of him other than those showing Silvey as a young boy attending school in Liverpool. Not even the passport office had a duplicate picture on file. The government admitted it was an unusual situation for them not to have anything more concrete on one of their subjects.

But it was Curtis Silvey who had rented a car at the Frankfurt Airport, and it was Curtis Silvey's car that was later found in a parking garage in Zurich that placed him in Zurich just before the accident at Altermann.

The agents agreed that John Doe was most likely Kurt Schmidt, and less likely Curtis Silvey. But even in this determination, the fingerprints of John Doe hadn't helped. Neither Schmidt nor Silvey were in the AFIS data bank, they had never been fingerprinted. But ultraviolet photography proved that Schmidt's passport was real, not forged. And his use of words indicated he was either of American or English origin. He spoke with a light British accent. The psychologists agreed that John Doe wasn't faking amnesia, he really didn't know who he was or how he had gotten where he was. All he knew from the agents was that he was healing from wounds incurred from a crash in the Alps that might well have taken his life.

The agents didn't tell him about the money or the transponder or ask him why the car he was riding in suddenly skipped the highway for the mountainside, or that his driver was killed. They wanted that information to come from him without prompting it.

British intelligence suggested that once John Doe was well enough to travel, they first would like to question him in Liverpool, then London. If that didn't prove anything, the CIA could take him to California to see if Schmidt's home or his work wouldn't jog John Doe's memory.

The CIA agent, Frederick Miles, had made one trip to Cali-

246 | RANDOLPH H. DEER

fornia and indicated he was thinking about making a second. Miles was convinced that John Doe was Schmidt, that he dealt in drugs, and that all they were doing was wasting time. Schmidt's passport indicated an abnormal number of trips to Mexico. Miles was convinced that John Doe was faking amnesia, and warned his colleagues they were dealing with a Hollywood stuntman and they shouldn't be surprised at anything.

But one thing was sure. None of them knew what to finally do with John Doe. There was no crime in the area that he might have committed, yet transporting that much cash would have been a criminal offense if he had crossed the Italian border. But for all of their intelligence networks, they had failed to get a positive make on him. And since they had hospitalized him under "house arrest" conditions, they didn't feel they could just dump him on a Zurich street and say, "Have a good day."

D-Day could only be a couple of weeks away for the agents.

*　　*　　*　　*

"John, do you feel well enough to travel?" asked the round and balding British agent, Beckett.

John still had plenty of aches and pains, but the overall feeling of being a punching bag had subsided. Only his wrist was still in a cast. They had removed the tape from his four broken ribs two days earlier. The swelling in his face had gone down considerably, but the red scars from stitched facial wounds were still disfiguring.

"I guess," he said. John wondered where they were going. "You're the experts, not me. I don't know who I am."

"The medics say you can travel. We just want to help you find out who you are," Beckett said kindly.

"Why are you so interested in me if you don't know who I am?"

"We've been over that, John. There were some unusual circumstances around your crash. Your identity was compounded by materials you were carrying in a suitcase and a briefcase. We don't want to tell you more than that, for fear it will directly affect your capability to recall freely who you are and what you were doing," added a taller, more severe man named Miles.

John Doe didn't respond. He wasn't sure it was the truth.

"We'll leave in the morning for Liverpool," said Beckett.

"Liverpool?"

"Does that mean anything to you?" Miles asked.

"No."

"Get your things together and—"

"What things? I have nothing. All I have is a hospital gown."

John could sense Beckett felt stupid.

*   *   *   *

Wednesday, Liverpool, England

John Doe, chaperoned by Miles of the CIA and Beckett of British intelligence, flew to Liverpool directly from Zurich in a private jet. John felt a little better; they had given him a black briefcase they said was his, and a new small piece of luggage with toilet articles and a simple wardrobe. When he had asked them if he shouldn't have some money on him, they gave him a few British pounds.

They read from a single sheet of paper a brief outline about the life of a Curtis Silvey and asked him if he knew him. He said he didn't, and asked to see a picture of Silvey. They only showed him pictures of Silvey when he was a boy.

John Doe felt frustrated and lonely. He knew how to do things, say things, and reason, and he knew where he was, but he just didn't know who he was or how he got there. He reasoned he had a real life somewhere in the world.

That night, John could tell that Liverpool was a disappointment for them. It meant nothing to him. All the places they took him and showed him drew a blank. After a late dinner, Beckett and Miles took him to his room and said their good nights. For the first time that John Doe could recall, he was alone and he liked the feeling.

He had difficulty going to sleep. His wrist throbbed and he

was overly exhausted. Finally, he turned on the radio and listened to the BBC. As they started a program called *On a Deserted Island*, John Doe began his drift further into the unknown, and hopefully to sleep.

"And now that you're going to your own deserted island for your vacation, what is the first record you would take with you?"

"The Beatles' *Yellow Submarine*," answered a perky female voice.

"That's interesting. Tell us why, and then we'll play it for our audience."

"Because after watching them sing that song, I always wished I had one."

"I see. And how long have you known about *On a Deserted Island*?"

"Ever since I came to England. I understand it's been on the air without interruption since 1942. I think that's simply marvelous! What a wonderful idea of how to take London's mind off the German blitz. I think we need something like that now to take our minds off the royals. . . . "

John Doe rolled over, feeling ill at ease. He wasn't sure if he were asleep and dreaming about music, or actually hearing it. The melody was *Greensleeves* by Vaughn Williams. He knew the tune well. It had been a favorite of his.

"How much longer will you be playing at the Haymarket in *Me And My Girl*?"

"The way I've performed lately, give them a fortnight to find a replacement and they'll jolly well pitch me." A lazy, good-natured laugh followed.

"What do you mean?"

"I've not been up to par. One of my dearest friends has disappeared, and I want very much to find him again."

"Can you tell us who he is?"

"Oh, no!" laughed the celebrity who had been invited by the BBC to explore the wonders of their deserted island that evening. "I don't want to dampen the program for those that depend on it for a break in their dull routines of life."

"If you insist. What's your eighth and last requested record?"

"I would like to hear *Edelweiss* in honor of my friend. . . ."

John Doe became feverish and short of breath. He was tossing wildly in his bed. There was something he knew. He was in a car. He was cold. There was blowing air on his chest. His head hurt. He had hit it hard on something. Was it the floor? He couldn't remember what it was. It all had happened so quickly. He could hear the strings of *Edelweiss*. He loved that music—but he was so tired. Exhausted. Ill. Wrist broken.

"Well, that about wraps it up. You know what the last question always is, don't you, Savannah?"

"Yes. What luxury I would take to the island. I only get one, right?"

"That's correct. Our guests always come up with so many interesting luxuries. What will yours be?"

The familiar voice was as clear as if the speaker were in the room with John Doe.

"I would like to take an old friend with me who is no longer with us. I would like to take the famous actor Craig Carlson with me. He was so smart and so wonderful. His death was such a loss to the profession. If I had him with me, he could tell me so much that I need to know. I miss him. He is the luxury I would like to take with me."

John Doe sat bolt upright in bed and instantly shed his non-identity. He was Craig Carlson, and he remembered being pitched to the floor of the car he was in on its way to Milan! He looked wildly around him and tried to understand why he was in a hotel room. He tried to think.

"Well, that was an interesting evening with Savannah Marlowe, star of *Me and My Girl*, now playing at the Haymarket. Please, all of you, remember Savannah as she departs our Deserted Island again for real life."

Craig was soaked. The bed was soaked. He stood up and began shaking with cold, fear, and the awareness of something awful.

*　　*　　*　　*

Thursday Morning, Liverpool

Craig spent the rest of the night piecing together what he could about his situation. He learned he was in Liverpool from hotel literature in the room. He learned the date from a newspaper in his room. He learned from a note on his dresser that he was John Doe, and there was a Beckett and a Miles on each side of him. He was to contact them if he needed anything at all. He also discovered his door to the hall was locked, and he had a connecting door with either Beckett or Miles.

He didn't know which, because he didn't know how the rooms were numbered outside. He didn't recognize his clothes, but was happy he had his black briefcase. On inspection he found it was minus his all-important Financial and Communications Control Book and all of the alias passports and fake documents that he had become so used to. His custom-built suitcase with almost two-hundred-thousand dollars was not with him. In a different wallet, he found very little money and no identification. This discovery quickly led Craig back to his briefcase.

He remembered ten thousand dollars was hidden in its secret compartment. He was astounded to find that it was still there.

That discovery gave him hope of finding a way out.

Craig thought, *I have to be a prisoner of men connected with the fiasco in Zurich. But if so, why am I in Liverpool, and why am I alive?* He knew that group had wanted him dead. It was all very confusing—one minute to be on the road bound for Italy, and the next to be in England.

He could remember so little.

A book on his bedside table was his only possible clue as to why. It was titled *What You Should Know About Amnesia: A Guide for Caretaker and Patient*. Craig wondered how a victim could know much about his condition.

His broken wrist and cut-up face told him he had been in one hell of an accident, and the last thing he did remember was being violently thrown to the floor in the back of the Mercedes.

Craig painfully pieced his situation together.

From Milan till now, he had either been out of it or someone else. But somehow, dear Savannah had brought him out of amnesia. But why England, and why Beckett and Miles? He didn't have a clue. Craig decided that in the morning, he had to fake amnesia in order to discover the real answers.

Then Craig realized how difficult that would be. He didn't know what John Doe had been like, and didn't have any idea as to what either Beckett or Miles looked like!

With his head pounding, Craig Carlson lay back down on his bed to wait for morning.

Nineteen

Thursday Morning, Bel Air

Inspector Roosevelt was met at the back driveway by Anne Barnett. She escorted him to the stairway to Simia's floor and told him to go on up; Simia was waiting for him.

Anne said she would be at the table in the alcove on the second floor; she also stated that she had given the household staff duties that would keep them occupied for most of the morning, and that the alcove allowed her full view of the back driveway in case Mrs. Marlowe came home early from the set. She said that if Mrs. Marlowe kept to her normal schedule, he and Simia would have at least two hours together.

Inspector Roosevelt was astounded by Simia's research.

It was irrefutable evidence that a double for Craig Carlson did exist, which Roosevelt already knew from the photos that Simia had sent him. But Simia had a lot more to tell him.

Schmidt was a close confidant and lover of Roz Marlowe, and had known the layout of the Bel Air mansion. From phone records, Simia showed Roosevelt that Roz had called Schmidt three times the week before Craig was murdered, after a long dry spell of months of no communication to Schmidt. Simia also showed Roosevelt the log of two returned calls by Schmidt to Roz on her private line the Wednesday before Craig's death. The calls were lengthy.

Roosevelt added this material to his information about Schmidt. According to his neighbor, Schmidt had disappeared the day before Craig's murder. According to the studio, Schmidt was an expert in handling firearms. According to Frederick Miles of the CIA, Schmidt might be the man in their custody in Europe who was apprehended while traveling with a great deal of cash that could well have been payoff money.

If Roosevelt adopted the theory that Kurt Schmidt was the

trigger in Carlson's murder, his proof was still circumstantial. But his gut knew, and it was no less circumstantial than what the prosecuting attorney had on Alan Gavin. And Gavin's motive of money was matched by Schmidt's motive of money. They just came in different packages: one through a will, the other by cash payoff.

Roosevelt placed a lot of weight on Roz Marlowe's incentive to find her husband dead before his will was changed. He hadn't forgotten the many verbal mistakes she made with the police immediately after the crime, and now he knew Roz had access to large sums of cash from a questionable man named Antonio Beretta in Las Vegas. Roz's trail of telephone conversations and messages that Simia had so meticulously kept directly incriminated Beretta, and Simia told Inspector Roosevelt that Roz had gone to Big Bear Lake to meet Beretta on the Tuesday before Craig's murder.

The recorded messages after Craig's death between Roz and Beretta were also incriminating. Who was the man who "had to be terminated but got away?"

By the end of the first hour, Roosevelt concluded that three people could have planned and executed Craig's murder: Roz Marlowe, Antonio Beretta, and Kurt Schmidt. But once again, it was all circumstantial. He continued to rely on his instincts.

If Simia had stopped at that, Roosevelt could have clearly presented just as much evidence as the prosecution as to who killed Carlson—certainly enough to save Alan Gavin. But Simia had more evidence that confused him.

Simia had boots. Big boots. A shoe size that Roosevelt doubted Gavin or Carlson could comfortably wear. Something he could easily check out. And if he had enough time, Roosevelt could see if there were still prints made by those boots either in Craig's library or in the halls leading to his suite. Roosevelt recognized the difficulty of finding such evidence after six weeks had gone by, but if the boots proved to be Schmidt's, the inspector's scenario would begin to change from conjecture to reality.

Roosevelt was troubled; as the leading investigator on the case, he would be a witness for the prosecution. By court procedure, he would be cross-examined by the defense. If he was too effective as a defense witness, he could probably kiss his job good-bye.

Roosevelt was sure the defense would use him as their prime defense witness after the day with Simia. And, because the discovery period on evidence had passed, the prosecution would not have discovered the boots, pictures, or phone messages until they were put into play by the defense in the courtroom unless Roosevelt told them of their existence.

It was a real ace in the hole for the defense team, and a real problem for Inspector Roosevelt. How could he possibly withhold the evidence given to him in trust by Simia from the prosecution?

"Simia, you've supplied me with a lot that will help to bring out the truth. I don't believe Gavin killed Carlson. Do you mind if I ask why you waited so long to contact me?"

Simia typed: "It took me a long time to go through all I have on Roz. Not easy." Simia opened her closet door and showed Roosevelt stacks of photo albums and clippings.

"Now I understand. Thanks." Roosevelt looked at his watch and began to gather his things.

Simia held out her hand and stopped him, indicating there was something else.

"You mean there's more?" asked Roosevelt with surprise.

Simia nodded her head "yes."

Simia opened the bottom drawer of her bureau and removed a bulky object wrapped in a towel. Roosevelt was staggered. The Oscar had dried blood on it, and was obviously the weapon used to disfigure the dead man's face.

Roosevelt would submit it immediately to serology to find out the blood type of the bloodstains on the Oscar. But before he could ask any questions, Simia took him out back and showed him the cache in the stone wall where she had found the Oscar and the boots. Simia told him via her handheld PC that only she and Craig Carlson knew of its existence.

The hiding place unnerved Roosevelt; his theories about the murder began to unravel and he began to understand why

Simia hadn't contacted him earlier.

She had tried to find a reasonable explanation for the location of the boots and the Oscar but couldn't, unless a scenario that didn't make any real sense was applied—that Craig Carlson was alive and Kurt Schmidt was the one found dead.

In a daze, Roosevelt took Simia's findings, and left her with a stern warning that she should leave the premises. He said, "When Roz Marlowe finds out about this data, which she will from the court the first of the week, there will be hell to pay, and even your life could be in danger."

Simia nodded her head "yes."

"And I wouldn't like to be in Anne Barnett's shoes either," he added.

*   *   *   *

Friday Morning, London

It had been a nerve-racking morning. If the two agents hadn't addressed each other by their names, Craig wouldn't have had a clue which one was Beckett and which was Miles.

But slowly, particularly from the prattle of Beckett, Craig pieced together enough information about himself to realize how not to reveal he was no longer John Doe, and that he didn't know at all what he had done even yesterday.

Craig was very quiet. He thought Miles looked at him with suspicion on more than one occasion.

They flew from Liverpool to a British airbase near London and soon after registered at the Hyde Park Hotel in Knightsbridge. Beckett wanted to hurry Doe off to Harrods, where a Curtis Silvey used to work, to see if that triggered any recall.

Miles was not in such a hurry-up mood, but knew that London was Beckett's last crack at Doe, and then Doe would be all his. Miles didn't intend to be quite so considerate to the man whom he was convinced was a celebrity drug runner. He could just imagine who Schmidt's clients were in Hollywood—all paying top dollar for his clandestine services and guaranteed confidentiality.

Craig had been in Harrods dozens of times, but pretended it was his introduction to the huge store. He found if he acted dumb, it worked. He was thankful for his training and ability.

"You used to work here," said Beckett. They were in the Cartier store on the first floor at Harrods, but no one recognized him.

"I did?"

"Yes, for three years."

"I hope I was a good employee," said Craig wistfully. He noticed that Miles had distanced himself from the two of them.

"Do you remember Harrods at all? I think it's one of the most popular department stores in the world." Beckett was hopeful.

"No," said Craig. "But I would like to use their men's room. It's been a long time since Liverpool."

"Of course," said Beckett. "I'll show you where it is."

"If you don't mind, just tell me. I need to spend more than a passing moment there. I'm not going to run away, Beckett. You and Miles are the only connection I have to reality." Craig hoped he was convincing.

"All right," said Beckett. He then told Craig precisely where the nearest men's room was.

As Craig walked away, he noticed Miles watching him in a mirrored wall display, and believed he would probably follow him at a discreet distance, but Beckett was busily examining a piece of jewelry.

He had to risk it. Once around the corner, Craig took off at a quick pace through the mob of shoppers. If he went too fast, security would have stopped him cold. He was abnormally identifiable because of the cast on his wrist. He exited by the side doors, and found himself on a small street he knew well.

Craig would have loved to double back to the Hyde Park Hotel and pick up his briefcase, but knew he couldn't risk it. After they had checked in, he had removed as much money as he dared from its base and shoved it in his pockets and underwear. Craig didn't have identification in any name, but with the cash, he didn't feel quite as vulnerable and unable to operate on his own.

Craig jumped into a taxi. "Let's go. Avoid Knightsbridge Road. I need as much distance from Harrods as I can get as fast as you can drive."

The cabbie was curious. "What's the rush, laddie?"

Craig said, "My wife's following me."

"Aye. Been there myself." The cabbie smiled.

"I'll tell you our destination once we get out of here." With that, Craig slouched down in the backseat, watching the door he had just exited.

Sure enough, as they turned the corner Miles came running out.

Craig had formulated a simple plan. He didn't know when and if he would have any opportunity to make a dash for freedom. His chance occurred earlier in the day than anticipated.

The driver was aggressive.

Once Craig felt that Miles was unable to follow him, he directed the cabbie to Trafalgar Square. Not wanting to chance Miles having seen the taxi's license plate, Craig tipped the cabbie handsomely and dismissed him. Then he walked rapidly to a small shop he knew well that dealt in all kinds of theater costuming.

Satisfied with his choices, Craig left with a substantial amount of merchandise. He had a different cabbie take him to a small hotel in the West End. Craig would hole up there and rest until near the time of Savannah's final curtain call.

He had Savannah's unlisted phone number in his Communications Guide, but that had disappeared. Craig guessed that if Beckett and Miles had found it they would have known he was the deceased Craig Carlson.

*   *   *   *

Thursday Evening, London

Savannah felt terrible. Once again she had performed miserably. Her guest appearance last night on *On a Deserted Island* had taken a great deal out of her. She had been worried sick for a month about Craig's unexplained disappearance, and throughout the radio program it was her final desperate cry in the dark. A reach. An ending.

Savannah knew that her role as the peppery stitch who bounced around the stage had suffered. The director of the show had already asked her if there was something bothering her. Savannah lied and told him that Hugh's long, drawn-out business trip to the Far East had proven to be hard on her and that she missed him. But however much Savannah loved Hugh, it would be difficult for anyone to believe she missed him so much that it would affect her onstage performance. The actress was much too professional for that.

The show was almost over, and Savannah planned to go home and have a stiff drink, a hot bath, and a long cry. She knew last night that the radio show would solve nothing. It was her swan song to a man she loved. She would always wonder what tragic ending he had come to.

Savannah couldn't tell Craig's story to anyone. Most of her dearest friends thought she was loony already. The story of a dead man circling the globe, calling her from faraway places would push them over the edge.

Savannah tried to think positively. How could she use any of this to save Alan Gavin and punish that Bel Air bitch, Roz? She could kick herself for not using her insight before now. Alan's trial was scheduled to commence Monday. She thought, *The least I can do is call Jebb about Craig's insurance concerns.*

There was a knock on Savannah's door.

"It's open," she called.

"A note for you, Miss Savannah." The security man at the rear stage-door entrance handed her an envelope and left.

Savannah looked at the stationery. It was from a hotel in the West End. With interest, she opened it.

She began to read the note casually and then gasped, "Oh, my God!"

She reread it. It said: "Savannah. I heard you last night on *On a Deserted Island.* I have firsthand information about Craig Carlson's whereabouts. He is alive. Please meet me after the theater at the Café Romero near Picadilly. I know you, and will contact you there after you arrive. Please be there. It is very important." The note had been typed and was not signed.

"Yes!" exclaimed Savannah.

Tears flooded her eyes. "He's alive," she whispered. Her last hurrah had paid off! Someone was listening who cared and who could help. "Thank God!"

Savannah looked at her watch. Minutes from now she should know of Craig's whereabouts!

Savannah's last few moments on stage were electric. She all but stole everyone's final moments. The director wondered what had happened to her, but she didn't give anyone a chance to ask. Two minutes after the last curtain call with much of her makeup still on, Savannah was out of the Haymarket, headed for Picadilly.

*   *   *   *

Café Romero was dark and crowded. Savannah was thankful; here she wouldn't stand out.

"Do you have a reservation?" asked the maître d'.

"No," said Savannah. "Just me."

He studied her and decided she was a somebody. "Table or booth, madam . . . ?"

"Marlowe," she said hurriedly.

"Ah, yes, I thought it was you. I've seen your play. I enjoyed your performance."

Savannah followed him to a booth against the wall.

Nervously she ordered a drink and tried not to scan the restaurant. Her drink arrived, but no informant. She gulped it and became wary of a trick. "Oh, God, a prank," she moaned.

She paid little attention to an old man, overweight and stooped, until he got up and approached her table.

"May I sit down?" he asked.

"That depends," she said. "Are you the one who sent the note?"

"Please don't scream, Savannah. It's me."

"Jesus! God! Mother Mary!" A lump as large as a boulder filled her throat. Savannah wanted to scream. She recognized his voice.

"Oh, Craig. Yes. Yes. Sit down. Please sit down!"

Craig slid into the booth on the other side and locked her eyes with his. "It's been a long journey," he said quietly. He placed his good hand on the table for Savannah. She took it and held it tightly in both of hers.

Craig started to cry. They were the first tears he had shed since leaving his home, lover, and life.

"Oh, Craig, is it really you? I thought you were really dead this time."

Craig fought to regain emotional control. "I know, Savannah. It's going to be hard for anyone to forgive me—particularly you, Alan, Andrew, and Mother. But I pray you all will."

For a long time, neither of them was able to talk. Finally Craig said, "Can we go to your apartment, Savannah? I haven't been safe or in a private place in six weeks."

*   *   *   *

Craig and Savannah talked until almost dawn. Craig was physically tired and emotionally exhausted, near the breaking point.

Savannah was watching him. "Go to bed, Craig. That's an order. I'll get you up when Arthur gets here. All we need is a photo and your signature. You don't need to worry about anything other than that."

Craig had turned gray. His eyes were bloodshot and swollen, reflecting his misery and desperation. "Oh, Savannah. Why did I do what I did?"

Savannah remained silent.

"I thought I could be invisible, that I could escape the hatred of those who didn't understand the price of being a homosexual. I could escape those who always wanted to exploit me. I could escape the pushing, laughing crowd that adored me or hated me depending on the part I played. I was wrong. All I want is some peace and to be with those I love. Is that too much to ask?"

Savannah went to Craig and cradled his head in her bosom.

"Will anyone ever understand? Will you all ever forgive me?" Craig started to cry. The cry became a roar. His whole body shook with pain.

"I'm so tired I can't even walk without my knees telling me to quit. I'm so tired it's difficult to make sentences. I want to rest, but I can't. I have to make right what I made wrong."

"Craig, I think you should stop," said Savannah.

"No, Savannah. I can't. I've hurt everybody."

"I think you're a damn good man," she said quietly.

Savannah held him tighter.

Craig became quiet. "Savannah, I need to go to sleep. Do you mind? Can I just go into that wonderful room and lie down and get up when I need to, not when I have to?"

Savannah led him to the bedroom, tucked him in, then lay down beside him. When he was finally asleep, she left the room quietly and closed the door.

*   *   *   *

London, Saturday Morning

Craig was wrapped in one of Hugh's ample but short dressing gowns, sipping black coffee and dripping raspberry jam on a muffin as Savannah floated effortlessly around her Kensington apartment in a blue silk chiffon robe that flowed freely over everything it touched. Savannah was waiting for a good friend to arrive with his equipment.

"Now much will this cost?" asked Craig.

"I think he said four thousand."

"I think I have a little more than that," said Craig.

"Save it for the States, " said Savannah. "He'll take a check, and my dear Hugh will never miss it."

Craig wolfed down the rest of the muffin.

Savannah laughed, "If you look out this window, you usually can see a royal coming or going when they shouldn't."

Craig hadn't heard gossip or engaged in it for a long time.

"Are you still cavorting with the queen's son?" he asked.

"Me and a hundred others!" Craig felt at home in Savannah's apartment. "'You have a beautiful place, Savannah." It was warm. Rare antiques and fine paintings mixed with Asian and traditional pieces. A home of good taste and appointment, yet not some decorator's showcase.

"Hugh prefers the family country estate," Savannah smiled as she turned away from the window. "He can mount a hunting stallion and pretend he's riding with the hounds. You should see him in his boots and jodhpurs. He looks like Gunga Din in drag."

"You love him, don't you, Savannah."

"Ah, yes," she smiled. "He's a good man with a good heart. I love him terribly."

Craig knew Savannah had had an awful childhood. First, a druggie father, and then drugs herself as a teenager, and then a egomaniacal woman for a stepmother. If it hadn't been for Simia, Juliette Savannah Marlowe could well have followed her father with a drug overdose.

"We have to get to Los Angeles, Savannah. I can't let Alan be accused of murder."

"And we'll only get there if Beckett and Miles don't apprehend you fleeing the country in a cast. Our biggest problem is getting out of here. You have the perfect plan to get into the States and I have a damn good idea how to get out of here.

Craig couldn't have found a stronger ally than Savannah. She had talent, was creative, daring, and had spirit. She had obtained social position and knew the ropes in Britain.

Craig only wished Alan had the same support. He learned from Savannah that two attorneys named Wilson and Packard were representing Alan.

He had no idea why Victor Packard was suddenly helping and involved.

Twenty

Sunday, Vancouver, British Columbia

The British Airways flight over northern Greenland from London, which departed London at five in the evening, would arrive in Vancouver at six that same evening. It was the kind of travel that wreaked havoc with Craig's internal time clock. He doubted that it would affect his durable friend, Savannah.

Saturday afternoon as Craig rested in London, Savannah purchased a new wardrobe for him. Saturday night, as Craig composed fictitious phone messages to Roz and Beretta, Savannah stole the show at the Haymarket and then told them she was taking ten days off.

Sunday morning, as Craig repaired his scarred face, Savannah made numerous phone calls, including one to Jebb Marlowe. Sunday noon, as Craig packed, Savannah met an actor friend at the Dorchester to put into play parts of their clandestine program. Sunday afternoon, as Craig rested, Savannah packed enough clothes in her suitcases for a month and received Craig's false documents from Arthur. When the Rolls-Royce Savannah had ordered arrived at three, Savannah was ready and cheerful.

Just watching Savannah exhausted Craig.

He knew that Heathrow might be mined with Beckett's hired hands, but Craig knew none of them had been briefed on the tricks that Savannah Marlowe was capable of. Craig was in a wheelchair, his right arm in a sling, his left wrist in its cast, and a bandage covered half his face. He thought his own disguise would have been adequate, but Savannah said no, they would be looking for an old, overweight man with a cast. They wouldn't be looking for Lord and Lady Ashley pushing abroad so soon after Hugh had been thrown from his horse.

Their arrival at British Airways was impossible to ignore.

Savannah was issuing orders to everyone around her while waving a dozen red roses as imperiously as a matador's cape summons a bull.

Craig told her the roses were overkill; she drew everyone's attention anyway.

Savannah laughed and said, "Of course they are. I work hard to maintain my notoriety."

With Lady Ashley at the helm, immigration and customs waved them through without question. Lady Ashley had also arranged for assistance for her broken husband inside the international departure area. It was a continued parade and performance all the way to the VIP lounge.

Craig felt his big risk, other than his fake passport, was that he didn't look a thing like Hugh Ashley. But according to Savannah, Hugh was so reclusive that he could be at a party with her and the guests wouldn't know for sure what he looked like or if he was even there. Savannah had quieted Craig's fears by saying, "Hugh's the only one who knows who he is and where he is, and right now he's in New Zealand. So worry not, darling."

Once over the green fields of the pastoral countryside, Craig felt they were safely out of England. He had chosen Vancouver to avoid all East Coast international entry cities. Craig didn't want to be picked up by the CIA.

Savannah had chosen Vancouver because she knew Canadian customs would choose not to hassle the Ashleys.

* * * *

Monday Noon, Port Angeles, Washington

After a much needed night's rest in Vancouver and a quick flight to Victoria's airport, Craig and Savannah boarded an Alaska Airlines commuter plane for Seattle. It was scheduled to land at Port Angeles, clear U.S. customs, and then proceed to Seattle. It was an easy way for locals to avoid the hassle of customs at the Seattle airport.

Now minus the wheelchair, the face bandage, and the sling, a very subdued Lord and Lady Ashley quietly entered the United States.

Craig remembered from his trip to the San Juan Islands with Alan that at the Port Angeles airport, while one person handled both immigration and customs, another ran security and the reboarding of the plane. The procedure was cursory, and processing a plane took only minutes.

Craig recalled Alan saying that if Hannibal could have reached Canada, he could have made it into the United States with his elephants unnoticed by way of Port Angeles.

Craig was anxious to get home.

Alan's trial would have begun, and they wouldn't arrive in Los Angeles until noon. Their arrival in the domestic rather than international terminals eased Craig's concern about the CIA looking for him. Craig appeared older and overweight, and had altered his facial countenance as much as he could. He no longer had borders to cross or customs to clear, but he still didn't want anyone to report that the deceased Craig Carlson was seen wandering nonchalantly around Los Angeles airport.

*　　*　　*　　*

Monday Evening, Brentwood

Craig and Savannah were entrenched in the home of a dear friend of Savannah, who was on a world tour. Savannah had located her in Istanbul on Sunday and arranged for her caretaker to pick them up, let them in, and then leave them alone. Over a long supper they polished their plans.

"Craig, you can't just barge into the trial and say, 'Look everyone—it's me. I'm not dead! Come on, Alan, let's go home.' Roz will get away with having committed a crime, free to get her face tucked and hair done whenever she feels like it. There are but a handful who know she is guilty of conspiracy to commit murder."

Craig was unnerved.

Savannah continued, "Remember, Schmidt can't talk. He

was cremated. All you have as evidence are fake documents you don't possess, a tale of troubled travel, and money you stashed away in Alan's bank account or shoved in your own pocket."

Craig now began to listen.

"It's our job to flush out those who are guilty and to free Alan. Just relax long enough until I figure out how. I'm an attorney, remember?"

Craig said, "I didn't know that."

"Oh, yes. A UCLA prima donna cum laude!" Savannah laughed.

Craig smiled. Being with Savannah made him feel the age difference. She was thirty-one and he was sixty-three.

"Let's watch one more news report about the trial. Maybe that will give me insight." Savannah punched the remote and settled in on *CNN Headline News.*

"The first day of the Carlson murder trial is over. The prosecuting attorney, Ari Melon, challenged the jury with their task. The lead defense attorney, Victor Packard, lectured the jury on both circumstantial evidence and premeditated murder. Judge Helen Bridges warned the media on four different occasions to control themselves, and at the end of the day told them sternly that if they repeated their performance tomorrow she would throw them all out."

Once again, Craig saw Alan on television. He looked tired, alone, and afraid. Seeing Packard and an attorney beside him was anything but reassuring. Roz looked as if she had been crying all month and was mad as hell about something.

*   *   *   *

Monday Night, Beverly Hills

"I appreciate you meeting me here," said Packard.

"I wasn't at ease doing this at the precinct station, but these surroundings are a little much," said Roosevelt. He was always put off by the stuffiness of the Beverly Wilshire Hotel. Packard had made quite an issue of Roosevelt meeting him at his hotel.

"Is this everything Simia gave you?"

"I think so."

Roosevelt hadn't told Packard about the Oscar that he had sent to an independent crime lab. There was something significant about it; even the name of the film Carlson won it for, *Dangerous Passage*, had meaning for Roosevelt. He decided he wouldn't reveal that piece of evidence to anybody until it was necessary. He knew the prosecution had to disclose any evidence they were going to use in the trial, but they didn't know of the Oscar's existence. The defense didn't have to reveal the evidence until the trial itself because of the time of its discovery. Roosevelt decided that he would wait for the independent crime lab's report on the blood types and on any fingerprints lifted from it.

He had sent it to an independent lab because the LAPD crime lab was so backed up that he had no assurance on how soon he would have the result. And if he didn't have the report on time, it wouldn't be the first lab work that followed a conviction rather than prevented it. The only hope Roosevelt had for timely performance was because of the public interest in the Carlson case. The O.J. Simpson trial was an abnormal example of quick lab performance. Roosevelt knew the nation's criminal labs were so overworked that most findings were often too late to be of value.

At least the independent lab gave Roosevelt a feeble excuse not to give the Oscar to Packard or reveal it to the prosecution. And he further rationalized that, after all, it was the murder weapon.

Packard looked up over his notes. "Has Simia left Roz Marlowe's residence? This stuff is dynamite."

"When I talked with Anne Barnett today, she told me that tomorrow would be the last day for both of them. I surmise Simia is going somewhere with Miss Barnett."

"Do you have Miss Barnett's address and phone number?"

"Yes." Packard failed to hide his impatience.

"Well, can I have it?"

Roosevelt didn't want to give it to him. "It's at my office," he lied.

Packard looked at him carefully. "I need it tonight. Can't you call someone and have them read it to you?"

"No," said Roosevelt, wondering about Packard's concern.

Packard didn't appear satisfied with his answer. "I think we should know how to get in touch with Simia to verify things."

Roosevelt chose to ignore his request. "If that's all, I'll be going. I've got a lot of work to catch up on."

Packard insisted, "Come with me to Trader Vic's, and we'll have a nightcap and a toast to the success of the trial. We're going to embarrass the hell out of them with this stuff."

"I have to go."

"Roosevelt, how often have you had the opportunity to be the real hero? This is your chance. Everyone thinks Gavin did it. You're going to stun the world with the fact that the famous Roz Marlowe had her husband executed. Think about it." There was a hint of desperation in his voice.

Roosevelt became quiet. There was something about Packard that bothered him. He was already sorry he turned over the material that Simia trusted him with. There was a little voice inside him that said, *Something's wrong with this man but maybe if I spend a few moments with him, I can put my finger on it.*

Roosevelt said, "Okay. Just one."

"Good. Where did you park?"

"On the street."

"Good. You can drive, and that way I won't have to get my car out for the night."

Roosevelt knew Packard often got so drunk he couldn't drive.

*   *   *   *

Monday Night, Bel Air

Roz was in turmoil. The phone message from Kurt Schmidt on Sunday had turned her self-centered life upside down. She called the Dorchester in London, and they confirmed he was there, just not in his room at the moment. When they asked if she would like to leave a message, Roz slammed the phone in their ear.

Simia was the one who handed her the message. Roz knew she had read it and hoped it meant nothing to her: "Roz. I've made money pickups all around the world and I'm in London. As soon as I polish off Lloyds, I'll head for the Chase Bank in New York and then Las Vegas. After I touch base with Beretta, I'll be back to you. I hope you're ready to see me. Love and kisses, Kurt Schmidt."

Roz told Stewart, her producer, late Sunday that she had to be at the trial for the rest of the week, and that they could shoot *The Empress* around her.

Stewart was mad and told her he had shot around her enough.

Roz then told him to just start over without her.

Roz's truce with Simia was also breaking down. She could tell something was eating at Simia. Since Friday, Simia had been preoccupied. Roz knew Simia was fond of Alan and concerned about him, but Roz made it clear to Simia that *she,* not Alan Gavin, was paying her salary and to shape up her lazy ass.

By Sunday night, Roz had consumed a fifth of scotch, and had called for Beretta four times without success. She was positive Beretta was responsible for Kurt's remaining alive. The whole story of not being able to catch up with Schmidt and kill him was pure bullshit!

Roz was ripe for blackmail and wanted to choke the life out of Beretta. Sunday night she gulped sleeping pills like candy and passed foggily into Monday morning.

Monday was continued disaster for Roz. Her appearance at the trial was grim, and she was visibly distressed. The media reported that Roz was grieving for her dead husband. But when Roz returned from the courthouse, Simia handed her another message. Roz thought, *God, Simia's going to wonder what's going on.* But the message surprised her, and Roz was jubilant. It fit right into her scheme of things.

*   *   *   *

Monday Night, Las Vegas

Roz Marlowe's pleading calls on Sunday meant nothing to Beretta. What meant something to him was Kurt Schmidt's message from London. Kurt Schmidt was dead according to Georgio, and Beretta had paid him handsomely for the service. When he tried to reach Georgio in Italy, there was no answer.

Beretta was furious, and felt the complete fool.

Once again, Beretta read Schmidt's message: "Beretta. All of your drops proved challenging. You beat me out of Sydney and almost caught me in Zurich, but I have you by the balls in London. It's too bad you didn't realize all this time that I had help from someone close to you. Let's see who takes New York. Schmidt."

Beretta confirmed Schmidt's presence at the Dorchester with a live contact in London. After Schmidt's successful ruses in Hong Kong and Sydney, he wanted to be sure. According to his contact, Schmidt occupied a penthouse suite and was living it up. Beretta's contact was able to take a photo of Schmidt. He enlarged the photo and faxed it to Beretta. This time Beretta was positive. It was Schmidt!

Monday noon, sure that Roz would be at the trial, Beretta left a message of his own on Roz's answering machine: "Roz, I miss you. After seeing you on television, I know you need more than a hug. Meet me at Big Bear Lake tomorrow. Call me and confirm. Much Love, Tony."

*   *   *   *

Monday Night, Beverly Hills

Alan was mad.

He was more than concerned about his defense team—he was terrified. Legal help from Mrs. Papagos had not yet arrived, though her lawyer Alltop assured him it was coming soon.

Monday night, it was attorney George Wilson who debriefed

Alan. Packard wasn't there. When Alan asked Wilson where Packard was, he never got a straight answer. Alan guessed that Wilson didn't know.

Wilson told him that Tuesday would be a parade of witnesses for the prosecution, and that other than cross-examinations, their turn wouldn't really come until Wednesday or Thursday. Alan wondered how they could overcome the circumstantial evidence against him. Washburne's death became much more significant when he realized that the mute Simia was his sole living ally.

Alan felt abandoned and alone. He thought of calling Inspector Roosevelt, but knew that was off base. He tried to reach Savannah in London on her private line for moral support, but was only able to talk to her answering machine.

Knowing it was useless to try and sleep, Alan devoured a half gallon of ice cream and watched a late-night movie.

His own testimony was the only protection he had between freedom and conviction of supposedly killing the man he loved.

*　　*　　*　　*

Trader Vic's wasn't as busy as usual. Packard had his own booth they kept open for him at this hour anyway. Roosevelt was seated across from him and they had ordered—Roosevelt a beer on tap; Packard, a double rye.

Just before the drinks arrived, Packard placed a thick envelope on the table, which contained some papers and fifty one-hundred-dollar bills. As the waiter approached the table, Packard shoved the envelope toward Roosevelt.

"Have you seen this lie detector report on Gavin?"

Roosevelt was not surprised. "No, I haven't. And take that money out of the envelope, or I'll arrest you for trying to bribe an officer."

Packard reached over and grabbed the envelope. "Sorry. My mistake. Let's have our drinks, and then you can look at it." Packard put the envelope in his pocket.

Roosevelt looked up with anger. "Don't treat me like one of

your paid informants, Packard. One slip and I'm gone."

A tall, heavyset man wearing blue jeans and a plaid shirt unexpectedly appeared at the end of the booth.

"Crawley!" exclaimed Packard. "What on earth are you doing in L.A.?"

"I'm on business," he said. "Can I join you?" Without waiting for a response, he pushed himself into the side of the booth that Roosevelt occupied and extended his hand. "Just call me Crawley. Everyone else does. I'm in the insurance business."

While Roosevelt was busy shaking Crawley's hand and making room for the two of them, Packard dropped a mickey into Roosevelt's beer. The bubbling brew was a perfect mixer to hide its presence.

"What will you have to drink?" Packard asked Crawley, waving the waiter over.

"The usual," he said.

Packard could see he was about to lose Roosevelt. "Okay, let's toast the trial; and then when you want to go, please do so. I'm sorry about the lie detector report, I'll just give it to you. Read it at your leisure." Packard withdrew the fake report from the envelope and raised his glass to Roosevelt.

"You're in good hands," said Crawley to Roosevelt. "I know the two of you will succeed."

"To truth," said Packard.

Roosevelt merely nodded and drank his beer.

"What brings you to Los Angeles?" asked Packard.

"A client of importance," said Crawley with a smile.

Roosevelt ignored the conversation. His beer was half gone when Crawley's drink arrived. "I'm leaving," said Roosevelt.

Roosevelt looked at Crawley. "May I get out, please?"

"Oh, come on. Stay for another."

"No. I don't . . . want . . . another . . ."

Crawley held on to Roosevelt so he didn't fall onto the table.

"Did you get all of the pictures?" asked Packard.

"Of course I did," said Crawley.

*   *   *   *

Monday Night, San Fernando Valley

Mrs. Roosevelt answered the phone, expecting it to be her husband telling her where in the world he was. He was late. They had planned a family night, and he hadn't called to tell her that he would be any later than eight. This wasn't normal.

"May I speak to Inspector Roosevelt, please?"

"May I ask who's calling?"

"Certainly. This is Miss Anne Barnett. I worked for Roz Marlowe, and I have messages for him from Simia, who also worked there."

"Yes. I know who you are. He isn't home yet, but I can ask him to call you when he comes in."

"Do you want me to give you the messages?" asked Anne.

"No. I'd rather not. I'd rather you talk to him so you can fill in anything that he needs that I don't know about. He should be home at any moment. I'll have him call."

"It's important," said Anne.

"I understand," Mrs. Roosevelt said. "He'll call you, he seems unusually worried about this case."

*   *   *   *

Tuesday Morning, Bel Air

Tuesday was an early day for Craig and Savannah. Savannah was going first to Roz's to see Simia, and then to the court to see Alan before the day's session began. She left Craig by the phone for her update from Simia. If she ran into Roz, Savannah would tell her stepmother she came to support Alan, if she told her anything at all. Savannah arrived just as Anne and Simia were pulling out of the back driveway.

"Simia! I'm so glad I caught you. I can't believe Roz has allowed you to go to the trial." Savannah hugged her dear friend and shook hands with Anne.

"We're not going straight to the trial, Miss Marlowe," said Anne. "We've both quit, and first have to get rid of this stuff."

Anne's car was loaded with clothes and boxes of files and other paperwork.

"Oh, how wonderful for both of you! It must have been pure hell working for Roz."

Savannah noted how peaceful Simia appeared and remembered her own incredible sense of freedom when she ran away to escape Roz's presence when she was a girl.

"We're going to the trial after that. Mr. Gavin needs someone's support," said Anne.

"That's also why I'm here," said Savannah. "Is Roz at court?"

Simia shook her head, and Anne told her Roz had left for Big Bear Lake to meet with Antonio Beretta.

"You're kidding. While Alan's up for murdering her husband?" But Savannah knew it was because they both received carefully contrived messages from England that pointed them toward each other with knives drawn. She was delighted it had worked.

"May I use your phone?"

"Yes. My office is right there. It's somewhat torn up, I I hope that won't bother you."

"Not at all, I love disarrangement! Before you leave, Simia, is there anything I need to know that would bring me up to date?"

Savannah couldn't believe all that Simia had uncovered and accomplished. "Does Roosevelt still have all that material?" She didn't tell Simia she knew why the Oscar was found in the wall.

Simia indicated that she didn't kow.

Savannah called Craig. "Well, Mastermind, Roz and Beretta took your bait. They're headed for Big Bear Lake as we speak."

"Savannah, that proves my theories about Beretta being the money man were right. If you hadn't told me what Simia had told you about Roz and Beretta when you were at my funeral," he hesitated. "I wouldn't have been so sure. This proves it."

"No one ever said you were dumb, Craig."

"Then I'm going too," said Craig.

"What? How can you? How can we afford the risk? What about Alan?" Savannah was perplexed.

Craig's response was instant. "You're the one who's made me realize that just getting Alan off isn't enough. Roz has to be brought down for this. Remember yesterday, Savannah, when you said I just couldn't walk into the trial and say, 'Hey—look at me'? I can't be there today, anyway. Do you know of a better chance of my catching them together?"

Savannah had to admit that was true, but she was very uneasy. "Who do you think you are, James Bond?"

"I'm going, Savannah."

"Do you hate Roz more than you love Alan?"

At first Craig didn't respond, then he said, "I don't know, Savannah. That's one hell of a question."

"Well, think about it. I'd hate to come all this way and have something else happen. You seem to be accident-prone."

"Savannah, I love Alan more," Craig said. "But that doesn't change what I must do. Give him a big hug for me when you see him. I'll call you as soon as I get back."

"Then happy hunting, darling. I'm off to the trial."

Twenty-one

Tuesday Noon, Big Bear Lake, California

Roz told Beretta she would be at the cabin by eleven and insisted that he drive, not fly. She told him she didn't want anyone knowing that on the day of the trial she had opted to meet her lover instead of seeing that her husband's murderer was being brought to justice.

Roz had driven across the desert, up into the scrub pines, and into the mountains. As many times as she had been there, it was still difficult for her to find the sharp and immediate turnoff at the curve. By ten o'clock, she was on the narrow dirt road that led to Craig's secluded cabin. Roz caught a glimpse of the sparkling blue water dancing in the bright sunlight. She was excited, it was a perfect day for Big Bear Lake.

Roz hurried inside the cabin to the utility closet, found the special flashlight, and placed it on the kitchenette counter. She unscrewed it, removed the top battery, and checked the contents in the bottom. Roz found three gram containers full of the finest celebrity cocaine. Satisfied, Roz screwed the top on as tightly as she could, put the flashlight back, returned to the Bronco, and carried in the few provisions. Pleased she had beaten Beretta, Roz sat out front on the waiting bench in the cool air and contemplated her conquest.

She hated the son of a bitch. No one betrayed Roz Marlowe the way he had. Nobody! He would never control her again! Roz felt sexy in her tight, blue, designer coveralls. When she heard Beretta's car on the road, Roz picked up a magazine and lit a cigarette. She wanted his first view of her to be of a relaxed woman of passion who didn't have a care in the world other than a tryst with her torrid lover.

She ran to his Range Rover, hugged him hard, and gave him a possessive kiss. "I'm so happy you're here."

"Yeah. Me, too. Why the hell couldn't I fly?"

"I told you. They know us at the airstrip."

"Sure. So what. We've met there a dozen times."

"I told you that, too. Not during the trial!" she snapped.

Realizing that wasn't what she wanted to project, Roz purred, "I like your soft safari jacket." As she ran her hands over him, she felt the bulge in his lower jacket pocket that told her he wasn't traveling alone. Beretta's face was tanned and his dark hair, slicked back. His strong cheekbones accented his incredibly handsome countenance.

God, she found him hot! The bastard!

Beretta's conversation seemed guarded to Roz, but on entering the cabin, he immediately began his normal ritual of laying a fire. Beretta had a mania about a wood fire that Roz figured had to do with being raised in Brooklyn, where they were probably rare or nonexistent.

With Beretta distracted, Roz approached him and ran her hands up and down his thigh. "You feel tense. Let's do a teensy little line to relax us. I want this to be a very special day."

Beretta grunted approval as he loaded the large, open stone fireplace with wood and kindling.

Roz walked to the closet, removed the flashlight, and took it to him. "Unscrew this damn thing. I can't budge it. And choose which container you want to use."

Beretta stopped, gave a short twist to the flashlight, and dumped all of its contents into his large hand. He deftly removed the three lids and checked the cocaine on his upper gum. "Use this one." Beretta turned back to his fire building.

Standing in the kitchenette in full view of Beretta, Roz made two small piles on a mirror she had removed from a drawer. Roz lit a cigarette with a cheap yellow plastic lighter, inhaled deeply, and placed the lighter on the counter next to the mirror.

"I'm so happy you called. I've missed you terribly."

Satisfied that Antonio was occupied, she turned her back on him, removed a half-gram container of white powder from the base of her lighter, and quickly added a significant dose to one of the piles. She put the container back into the base of the lighter and returned it to her pocket.

She again faced Beretta. "How's it going, Boy Scout?" Diligently Roz chopped her materials, smoked her cigarette, and watched him watching her. It was all natural. The ritual had been performed many times in the same way in the same place by the same people.

Finished, she returned to the living room, sat the mirror on the table, and smiled seductively at Beretta. "Pussycat, here's to a great day. There's a lot I need to get away from." With that, Roz picked up a plastic straw and inhaled one of the lines. She released a sigh of pleasure and presented him with the mirror.

"Not yet, baby. I'm still busy."

"Oh, come on. Or I'll be so far ahead of you, I'll find some thick stick of wood as a substitute for your dick." Roz pushed the mirror in his face.

Beretta wiped his hands on his trousers, picked up the straw, and inhaled the remaining line.

"Wow! That's good," he said, and returned to his labor. It wouldn't be long before he would light his masterpiece.

"I'll cut us a backup," Roz said. In the kitchen, she put the used straw in her pocket, cut two new lines out of the full gram bottle, and picked up a new straw.

"Do you want a drink? I need one."

"Sure, baby. I've just about got this fucking thing licked."

Roz poured two full scotches and returned to Beretta's side. "Here's to my stud," she said as Beretta clinked her glass, took a big gulp, and sat it down on the raised stone hearth.

Roz unzipped her coveralls, and her breasts bounced out provocatively. She took the matchbox from him. "I'm ready to play," she teased. "Undress me."

Roz saw Beretta look ruefully at his logs, but knew he had been away from her a long time. She could see the bulge extend down his pants leg.

And this will be the last time! Roz thought.

*   *   *   *

Antonio Beretta knew exactly what he was going to do to Roz Marlowe, the little tease from hell who had cheated him out of millions—fuck her all day, slap her till she bled, then blow her brains out.

Beretta could feel the cocaine.

He unzipped her coveralls and roughly pulled them off her shoulders. He explored her privates with his big hands to find Roz already wet. Beretta withdrew his hands and kissed her hardened nipples. Feeling his own rush, he pushed her against the cold, hard stone and scorned her. He knew she loved abuse.

"You worthless bitch! Get down on your knees and bring some real life into my cock."

Roz kicked off her shoes, slithered out of her coveralls, and, naked, sank to her knees in front of him. When she unzipped him his oversized penis exploded from his pants. Beretta found its release from confinement an added pleasure.

As Roz put his warm organ in her mouth, his hands felt hot and twitched, his neck stiffened. "Goddamn! You're good. Even my neck is getting stiff." Without disengaging, Roz shoved him hard back into the wall and slid his pants down around his boots, confining his movement.

Beretta could tell Roz was experiencing pure pleasure. The cocaine added abnormal burning sensations throughout his body, followed by waves of joyous numbness. *No one ever does for me what Roz does*, he thought.

"Goddamn. What a turn-on!" he groaned.

Roz looked up at him and smiled.

"Wait a minute!" Beretta tried to push Roz away from him. "My head hurts and I'm getting dizzy." Beretta's face shifted back and forth from pain to pleasure.

Roz didn't disengage; she only sucked harder. His penis was engorged with blood, and she yanked his balls down as hard as she could. Beretta found the pain incredibly erotic.

"I think I need another hit," Beretta said weakly.

Roz got up without delay. "Of course, I've prepared it."

Beretta sank down on the raised stone hearth and ran his hand over his face. It was an odd sensation, one or the other was numb. There was no feeling; they didn't seem to touch.

"Here," she said, and held out the mirror. "You choose."

It was all Beretta could do to inhale the line. He watched Roz inhale hers with ease and drink the rest of her scotch.

Without warning, Beretta's feet shot straight out in front of him and his back slammed against the wall. "What the hell's going on?" he shouted with fear.

He tried to get his hands on his .45 Glock automatic, but couldn't make them do what he wanted them to do. Slowly and painfully, Beretta understood. He looked at Roz with hatred. He writhed back and forth in agony and attempted to speak, but couldn't open his mouth, it was as if he had lockjaw. Beretta's face became a frozen mask of pain, and a fire of hate raged in his eyes.

Roz stood in front of him and taunted him. "You were going to kill me, weren't you, stud? First fuck me, and then kill me. Weren't you?" she screamed. "You think that Kurt Schmidt and I double-crossed you?" Roz's laugh was ugly. "Is this what you were going to kill me with? Your dick?" Roz squeezed his balls with all her might and then viciously bit his penis.

Beretta didn't scream. He couldn't.

Roz effortlessly untangled the gun from his safari pocket as Beretta watched in horror, unable to control his spasms.

"Well, we did double-cross you." She laughed.

"Schmidt's waiting for me now at the airport. He just flew in from New York after cashing in your millions. We're going to take a small vacation. How do you like that?"

Beretta's body bent backward until his head touched the hearth, while his feet were on the cabin floor. His safari jacket was wrapped around him like a rag, and he was naked down to his boots, which were bound together by his trousers. Beretta could see his huge cock flap uselessly back and forth—back and forth. He was no longer in control of anything except his mind.

Beretta knew Roz had poisoned him and he was about to die, and there wasn't one damn thing he could do to prevent it. The bitch had won their final contest. She had outmaneuvered him.

Beretta's blood pressure dropped precipitously, and he tried desperately to breathe.

Roz laughed. "Have you ever heard of dog button, or mole nots, or mole death? Well, of course you have. I'm sure you know what's happening."

Beretta was in one constant spasm, writhing on the floor one minute and jumping up into the air the next.

"You see, darling," she took the cigarette lighter from her pocket and showed him the half gram vial, "this contains strychnine, a colorless, crystalline powder. I laced your first line with it. You've used so much cocaine, you can probably snort pulverized bird shit and your membranes wouldn't know the difference."

Shut-up, Roz! Beretta thought. *Shut the fuck up!*

"And everyone thinks I poisoned Mikey Marlowe—you know, Beretta, everyone. But I didn't. I didn't get to do it! The dumb bastard overdosed before I could do it."

Beretta couldn't close his eyes. He just stared at Roz in an awful open manner, the pain excruciating.

"And I am going to kill Schmidt. Just for you, darling. He would blackmail both of us in a minute. I just might do the same thing to him I did to you. It's fun to watch. Or I might use this." She waved his gun in front of him. "You know, stud, I added a touch of arsenic just for the hell of it." Roz slapped him as hard as she could. "That's so you'd have a warm rush before you turn stone cold!"

Beretta could barely hear her.

"I think it's wonderful that you're right in front of your favorite fireplace. What an innocent position for someone who stupidly tries to start his wood with gasoline." Roz shrieked with laughter.

Beretta's final grimace set. Rigor mortis kindly stopped his spasms. Antonio Beretta was dead.

*   *   *   *

When Roz knew Beretta was dead, she kicked his body over

and over until her bare feet hurt. Then she sat down beside him and cried. When Roz stopped crying, she realized she had to move.

Still clutching Beretta's gun, Roz wiped her eyes on the back of her hands, picked up her baby-blue coveralls, and hurried outside. She laid the pistol on the bench and slipped into her coveralls. She hurried back to the cabin, picked up two lanterns, then ran to the tool shed. Roz filled them with kerosene and a five-gallon tractor can with gasoline. She put the two lanterns on the waiting bench and, back inside, splashed gasoline generously over Beretta's body and the main living area.

Back outside, Roz headed her Bronco away from the cabin and left it running. She then pulled Beretta's Range Rover right next to the cabin. Without any lingering farewells, Roz lit the kerosene lanterns and pitched one through the open door. She didn't need the second one; as soon as the glass on the lantern broke the roar was instant. Craig Carlson's secluded getaway ignited with a fury that knocked Roz to the ground.

In a panic, Roz jumped into the Bronco and drove down the lane. She knew the fire tower would spot the fire, and volunteers would be on their way. There was no doubt in her mind that by the time they arrived, Antonio Beretta would be nothing but a charred, unidentifiable remnant.

She reentered the main dirt road at high speed and headed for the paved highway. She could see the black smoke curling up behind her. She heard a blast and figured it was the gas tank on his car, or maybe even the shed that blew up.

Roz knew she had started a forest fire, but didn't give a damn about that. What she cared about was that Antonio Beretta could no longer be called to the witness stand to testify against her. And he sure as hell couldn't blackmail her. Beretta was out of her life, and if anyone asked, she hardly knew him.

As Roz pulled into Los Angeles at about five in the afternoon, she remembered the second kerosene lantern that she had left in front of the cabin. She told herself not to worry—surely the fire would have spread at least that far.

*   *   *   *

Tuesday Morning, Bel Air

Savannah caught Alan's eye as she entered the courtroom. A wave of relief spread over his face. Then Savannah pointed to her side, and Alan saw Simia and Anne. He smiled and waved bravely.

The first session was anything but normal.

The prosecution's main witness, Inspector Roosevelt, wasn't there, and neither was the wife of the murdered man, Roz Marlowe. When Judge Helen Bridges asked the prosecuting attorney, Ari Melon, if he wanted a delay, he said, "No. We have the same incriminating evidence from other witnesses, and really don't specifically need Roosevelt."

Seemingly unconcerned, the prosecutor presented his case. The lab technician, the mortician, the ballistics expert, the criminal photographer, and several assorted police personnel were called to the stand while the police searched for the missing Roosevelt.

But that wasn't all. Savannah was appalled at Packard's cross-examinations. They were all but nonexistent. In a couple of cases he simply said, "No questions, Your Honor."

It was a difficult morning for Simia. She wrote Savannah that she wasn't sure why, but she feared only the worst for her friend Roosevelt. Simia also messaged Savannah that if Packard didn't surface the evidence, all of her hard labor to save Alan was worthless, and that she should never have turned over the Oscar to anybody, not even to Roosevelt.

Savannah knew the wrong would be made right, and wanted to flatten Packard with her fists. No defense attorney performed as he had. None. It was disgraceful. It was blatant. Packard didn't care—and the worst part was that he didn't care that everyone knew it.

Savannah needed to call Jebb back. She began to believe there might be some hidden reason why Packard wanted Alan convicted, and the insurance was the only existing connecting element between Victor Packard and Alan Gavin that Savannah could think of. She knew of nothing else, and admitted that even that was a reach.

Savannah would call Jebb in Washington just as soon as the morning session was over, but first she wanted to hug Alan and try to convince him that everything would come out all right.

Savannah knew she could stop the insanity of the trial at any time by surfacing Craig, but she didn't want to do that unless she had to.

When Judge Bridges called the first recess and asked the attorneys to see her in chambers, Savannah took the opportunity to approach Alan.

"Alan, you're holding up well. What can I do to help?"

"For God's sake, Savannah, get someone to represent me. I'm going to lose this thing. There is nothing to stop the prosecuting attorney. Remember that he was strong enough to get an indictment on circumstantial evidence and a wild story about my killing Craig after a scuffle with his own gun."

Savannah asked, "Why is Packard so transparent with his nondefense? Do you know any reason why he's not doing his best?"

"None. Packard has been a roadblock for me from day one. He has never given me a straight answer to any of my questions, and Wilson deferred to him as soon as he entered the case. I thought he would be more effective than Wilson, but now I don't trust either of them. Savannah, I remember you telling me at the Eclipse that you're an attorney. Is there anything you can do?"

Savannah asked, "Do you want me to sit at the defense table with Packard and try to force him to perform?"

"Yes. Anything! I'm running out of time. Mrs. Papagos told me some outside attorney was going to help, but he never showed up. Packard keeps telling me he has surprise material, but I don't know what it is and I don't believe that, even if he does, he'll use it. I don't understand why he doesn't care about the outcome."

"What's the status of the insurance money, Alan?"

"According to Packard, it's buried until after the outcome of this trial. Why?"

"Just asking," said Savannah. "Alan, I'll be happy to represent you. Just let me scribble a note on a piece of paper and I'll take it to the judge right now while they're in her chambers."

Alan watched Savannah with appreciation as she wrote a short paragraph and had him sign it. As soon as he did, she was off and running.

*   *   *   *

Judge Bridges had all but concluded her meeting with the attorneys about the whereabouts of Inspector Roosevelt and whether or not the trial should continue without him, when the bailiff answered a knock on her door.

A striking blonde handed him a note for Judge Bridges. Upset with the interruption, she read the note: "I request that Miss Savannah Marlowe, who presented this note, and is a member of the California Bar in good standing, be allowed to sit in second chair in my defense. This assistance to begin immediately." It was signed Alan Gavin, defendant.

This irregularity only confirmed for Judge Bridges something was wrong that she couldn't quite get a handle on. Judge Bridges asked that the woman be brought into the room.

Packard's reaction to Savannah's presence and Gavin's request was adamant. "She knows nothing about this case, and has no reason or right to be involved."

Savannah said, "I know more about the case, than you might imagine, Mr. Packard, and I have been requested by the defendant. You can check my credentials by a phone call either to the Bar Association or to Bernie White at UCLA."

"You're nothing but an actress," Packard snorted.

Judge Bridges didn't like Packard's tone or implication. "You let me be the judge of whether or not she is seated with you at the table, Mr. Packard."

"Bailiff, I want to talk to Bernie at UCLA and to Mr. Gavin.

The rest of you are excused. Ms. Marlowe, stay close, I may have a question or two."

Judge Bridges talked with Bernie White at UCLA, who knew Juliette Savannah Marlowe well. Then she talked with Gavin until she was satisfied he knew the ramifications of a potential mistrial and really did want Ms. Marlowe. She dismissed Gavin and called the attorneys and Ms. Marlowe back into her chambers.

"Ms. Marlowe is in second chair of defense," she declared.

Attorney Wilson's reaction was one of dismay. He had no idea of what was going on.

*   *   *   *

Tuesday Noon, Big Bear Lake

Craig's charter flight from Santa Monica to Big Bear Lake was uneventful, and the minute he landed at the small airstrip, he rented one of the few cars they kept on hand and headed for his cabin. He was ready for anything. His adrenaline was pumping, and Craig believed he could cope with any kind of confrontation Roz and the unknown Beretta could throw at him. The two people he was sure had triggered his misery were just up the road, and it had taken one hell of a long trip to get to them.

He couldn't believe how accurate he and Savannah had been in London as they pieced together who in the vicious triangle of Roz Marlowe, Kurt Schmidt, and Antonio Beretta had done what to execute his murder.

As he neared their side of the lake, he could see smoke, and wondered what was burning. He didn't know whether the county had had a wet or dry spring, or how high the fire danger was. Craig tried to recall the last time he and Alan used the retreat, but gave up.

Just before the turnoff, Craig became much more concerned about the fire; it had to be near his cabin. Suddenly a Bronco driven at reckless speed all but knocked him off the road.

"Jesus!" Craig swerved to avoid a collision.

As he pulled off the paved highway for the gravel, Craig had a funny feeling and his stomach knotted up. Something was too familiar. He took a deep breath and tried to dislodge the thought, but Craig knew that a first reaction was usually a correct one. It was damn likely that that had been Roz Marlowe driving her Bronco. Almost positive now that it was his cabin on fire, Craig sped up the dirt road.

His quiet mountain retreat was an inferno—melting, exploding, and disappearing all at the same time. A four-wheel-drive vehicle parked near the front of the cabin was also in flames. Craig knew it wasn't one of theirs. He got out of the rental and tried to approach the cabin, but couldn't, the intense heat driving him back. He knew the driver of that vehicle most likely was still inside. Craig had to see the license plate. He pulled his shirt over his head and shoulders, and got as close to the back of the truck as he could. It had Nevada plates.

Craig felt the intensity of the fire would make it difficult to identify any body found inside. He didn't feel sorry for Antonio Beretta, but despite the heat, Craig shuddered. Another of Roz's passionate lovers was dead and wouldn't be driving anywhere.

He thought, *What was I married to for all those years?*

On the waiting bench he had built, Craig saw a lantern and a gun.

"So, Roz, that's how you did it," Craig said in horror. Slowly, he examined the gun then slipped it into his pocket. He left the lantern where it was.

Craig suddenly realized his burning cabin was the last place on earth he should be, and recalled Savannah's admonitions for him to be careful as hell, or else all of their plans would be for naught.

Craig ran to his rental car and made it back to the highway before anyone else appeared. If it had been in season, neighbors would have already arrived.

He surprised his pilot by telling him he was ready to go back to Santa Monica. The pilot asked no questions; it was none of his business. But on the way home, Craig realized how lucky he had been. If he had confronted Beretta and Roz, they would have killed him. He shuddered. Savannah had been right.

Craig also realized he was lucky to have paid cash and used Kurt Schmidt's name to charter the plane and rent the car. The implications of who had started the fire could easily point to none other than Kurt Schmidt.

*　　*　　*　　*

Tuesday, Late Afternoon, Bel Air

Roz left the Bronco in the driveway and rushed into the house. She had to shower, she had to have a drink, she had to have a hit, she had to have pampering, she had to have attention, she had to. . . . Roz was thirsty and hot. She had forgotten to take water in the Bronco, and dared not stop anywhere on the road in case she was recognized. She barely had enough gas to make the round trip.

Roz rushed upstairs. "Simia! Simia! I need you!" Roz opened the door to her quarters. The smell of perfume was overpowering. "Simia!"

Roz looked in disbelief at her room.

"No!" she screamed. "No!"

The floor was covered with hundreds of hangers, the bed was stripped, and her breakfast tray was still on the table, with soiled plates. Roz rushed into her closet. All of her clothes were on the floor. All of them!

"No! No! No! You bitch, you rotten-ass Tahitian whore!" Roz shrieked at the top of her lungs.

She charged into the bathroom. Her sink was full of perfume, and all of the expensive empty glass bottles were in the toilet.

"I'll kill you!" she screamed, and ran up the inside stairs to Simia's room.

It was empty. The bed was made. The room was neat and orderly. But there was nothing personal in it. Roz pulled open Simia's main closet and found it empty.

"No! . . . You can't! . . . You can't! . . . You can't leave me now! I need you. Simia, you bitch, I need you now!"

Roz ran down Simia's main stairs into the house. In the upstairs hall, she grabbed a phone and punched the intercom for Anne . . . "Anne, pick up, goddamn it. Anne!"

There was no response.

Roz ran down the long staircase and out the back door to the carriage house. "Anne! Where are you? I need your help!"

Roz entered Anne's office, to find it empty. She thought that maybe with her gone, Anne had finished everything and gone home. Anne's desk was totally disarranged, but Roz was so rarely in the office that she didn't know what it normally looked like.

She slammed the office door and ran to the kitchen. "Where the hell is everybody?" she yelled at the Hispanic cook.

The cook shrugged her shoulders, shook her head and said, *"No sabe donde."*

"Learn to speak our language, goddamn it! Where's the refrigerator?"

The cook pointed to the unit and stared at Roz.

"What the hell are you staring at? Do I look like a freak?" Roz opened it, removed a bottle of water, and stalked upstairs. Now she could smell the perfume clear out in the hall.

Roz stomped across the room toward her bar, intentionally breaking as many hangers as she could. Roz removed the scotch bottle and drank directly from it. Her throat burned, and she chased it with a gulp of water from the plastic bottle.

Holding a bottle in each hand, Roz looked at herself in the mirror. "My God!" She hadn't seen herself since she'd left Big Bear Lake. Her face had black smudges all over it, her hair was plastered to her head from sweat and heat, her blouse was stained with sweat, and her hands were filthy. She could smell gasoline. Roz didn't see the singed hair at the back of her head.

"Jesus! I need help."

Roz sat down on the side of her tub, took another long draw on the bottle, and absently looked at her shower. Slowly she set the bottles down, stripped off her filthy clothes, and got in the shower. "I'll feel better after this," she said.

When Roz reached for her towel, it wasn't there. She stepped out into the bathroom to get one, but there weren't any.

"I'll kill you, Simia. I swear to God I will!"

Roz saw a remnant of a towel sticking out of the clothes chute. When she pulled it out, she could see the chute was stuffed full of towels. Roz reached down and pulled out a couple more. As she stood up, she was dizzy. "I stood up too fast," she said, and started to dry herself off. But all of a sudden, Roz knew she had to lie down or she might faint.

Lying naked on her exposed mattress, clutching a wet towel, Roz Marlowe began to sob, then cry, then shake. Then she screamed, "Help me! Somebody help me! Please—somebody come to me. I need your help."

Roz counted. Her dad was dead, Mikey was dead, Craig was dead, Washburne was dead, and now Beretta was dead. And Simia and Anne were gone.

Roz Marlowe knew no one would come.

Twenty-two

Brentwood, Tuesday Evening

Craig and Savannah interrupted each other dozens of times before they finally settled down to tell their stories of all that had happened and all they had discovered during the day.

The prosecution had rested its case late in the afternoon, and Savannah knew the ball was now in her court. Packard had remained intransigent and sullen, and continued not to cross-examine. Savannah knew she had the perfect defense for Craig but still didn't want to jeopardize Simia's damning information from becoming admissible evidence because of its late discovery until after the court had convened for the day. Only then did she ask Packard if he knew anything about boots or phone bills. Savannah didn't refer to the Oscar, either Packard knew about all of Simia's material or none of it. If he professed to know about none of it, Roosevelt must have kept the evidence to himself, which wasn't what Simia understood he was going to do.

"I haven't the foggiest idea of what you're babbling about," was Packard's answer. "I just wished you had kept your unwanted inquisitive ass in London where it belongs. I'm going to lose this trial because of your meddling, Savannah. Just watch."

"You're going to lose this case because you *want* to," said Savannah. "I'll be back in the morning, and don't think I won't have my own agenda. I'll have plenty to say."

When Savannah had arrived home there was a phone message waiting for her from Jebb Marlowe: "I am en route LAX from Dulles International. Will call you as soon as I arrive for directions as to where you are. Findings explain Packard's behavior."

*   *   *   *

291

Craig was again describing the fire at the cabin when Jebb's call came in. Savannah's expressions of disbelief during her conversation added to Craig's fury at Packard's betrayal of Alan.

"Jebb will be here shortly. I don't think you'll be pleased."

"You haven't told Jebb I'm alive, have you?"

"No, I haven't. I think your presence is something we can hold until we damn well know who all has committed what crime, and then we'll plunk you down as the ace of spades. When Jebb arrives, you can hole up in a bedroom. He won't come in there."

"Has there been fraud?"

"Jebb was pretty grim. We'll soon know."

*　　*　　*　　*

"Savannah! It's wonderful to see you." Jebb Marlowe hugged and kissed his half-sister.

Savannah held his arms down to his side and looked at him. "My, but you're handsome. You look like you just stepped out of a modeling agency after a shoot."

Jebb flushed. "Come on, Savannah. You've been on the stage too long."

"Have not!" She laughed. "Come with me into my secret courtyard, and tell me what guarded messages you bring me." Savannah led Jebb into the living room.

"I can't believe how much Alan needs you right now," said Jebb. "I think it's incredible that you came to help him."

"My woman's intuition," said Savannah. She became serious. "You must have potent stuff to bring it in person."

"It is, and it's unbelievable," said Jebb.

Savannah became even more serious and leaned back in her chair.

Jebb opened his briefcase and removed several sheets of paper. "I'll try to make the story as short as I can, yet give you what you'll need."

"Do I need to take notes?"

"No. I have a copy for you after I cover the stuff."

Savannah settled in to listen.

"For the past fifteen years, Craig Carlson has paid to Mid-Life Insurance Company, an insurance underwriting firm located in Illinois, a lump sum for yearly premiums due to keep multiple policies now totaling one hundred million dollars of life insurance in effect. That premium cost last year amounted to roughly two and a quarter million dollars."

Savannah whistled.

"That's right, Savannah."

Jebb continued, "In the beginning, it would have been a lesser amount, but as policies were supposedly added, that premium cost soared to the two-million-dollar figure. Packard apparently supervised Mid Life to be sure the policies were in good condition by using the personal services of Clifford Crawley, the president and owner of Mid Life."

Savannah was listening intently.

"I know from overhearing mild disagreements between Craig and Alan when they discussed Craig's insurance program that Alan felt the amount of insurance excessive and the way it was handled, reckless. Craig always responded by telling Alan that Packard believed such a hefty amount was reasonable because Craig now commanded twenty million dollars a film and that his life was certainly worth more than that aggregate amount. Savannah, I think Alan only brought this subject up when a third party was there to diminish Craig's angry reaction from being questioned as to his wisdom of trusting Packard so completely. According to Alan, Craig hated paperwork, detail, and fine print. He depended on Packard to take care of all that for him, and he trusted Packard blindly."

"Would you like something to drink, Jebb?"

"I sure would."

"Good. Then I'll join you." Savannah busied herself while Jebb used the bathroom.

A few minutes later, Jebb continued, "Each year, Craig issued to Mid Life one lump-sum check and depended on Packard to be sure Mid Life's invoice was correct and all policies, current."

"My God, Jebb. I can see what's coming."

Jebb nodded. "I'm sure Packard has on file all the policies necessary with separate companies showing today that Craig Carlson has one hundred million dollars of life insurance."

"But . . ." said Savannah.

"But he doesn't. Craig only has in force two million dollars' worth. It's the original policy issued on his life fifteen years ago."

"My God!"

"That's putting it mildly. Craig has been scammed by his lifelong trusted attorney to the tune of roughly thirty million!"

"How did Packard do it?"

"It's easy if he's in cahoots with Crawley. I found out at my office that Crawley, who is synonymous with Mid Life, has been investigated by the Illinois State Insurance Examiners several times, but has always gotten off with only a slapped wrist. As long as Craig let Packard and Crawley handle it, they could run with it. You see, Savannah, nowhere do the issuing insurance companies keep an industry-wide compilation of the total amount of insurance that one person carries on themselves. Each company knows the amount they carry, but they have no idea how many other companies have issued policies on that individual and for what amount."

Savannah shook her head. "Don't you have that kind of information at your association?"

"No, we don't. And I didn't know that until I started looking into Craig's insurance after your call from London."

"Amazing."

"I also found out that Packard and Crawley have been buddies longer than anybody. They played football together at Kankakee High School and later married first cousins."

"How convenient," said Savannah. "But if no one keeps a total, how did you find out that only one policy has been issued? Couldn't Craig be carrying them with some companies you haven't checked?"

"No, and I'll tell you how I know. It's the tricky part. In the industry, there is a Medical Information Bureau, known as the MIB, located in Boston. Industry-wide, the medical information of any applicant for life insurance is reported to the MIB. They code it, log it in, and it's there forever. If an individual is taking out a second or third policy, the MIB will not only take the current medical information from the company considering issuing the insurance, but will report to that company all of the historic medical information they have on the applicant, whether it's good or bad."

Savannah shook her head, trying to keep up.

"If Craig applied for additional insurance every year for fifteen years, and on the sixteenth year he does it again, the interested insurance company would receive from the MIB historic medical information on Craig for fifteen years."

"And . . ."

"The MIB has only received medical information on Craig Carlson once, and that was sixteen years ago. There has been absolutely no traffic on Craig Carlson's life since then."

Savannah jumped up and began pacing.

"And, Savannah, that MIB information is closely guarded and very confidential. They only give it out to a requesting insurance company when new medical data is submitted for potential new coverage. The MIB doesn't know and couldn't care less what action the insurance company takes with the applicant."

"How did you get it, Jebb?"

"A girl I dated in college who works for them and was willing to look into Craig Carlson's file and give me the dope on the sly. She could lose her job over this if they found out."

"But why didn't Craig know this? Didn't he have his life insurance policies at least on file with Alan, his financial and administrative guru?"

"That was always a part of their argument. Alan thought the policies should be kept in their office, but Craig was willing for Packard to keep them. I'm sure that Packard has policies that show the coverage. It's an easy thing to fake a policy. It's done all the time with 'not-taken policies.' It's one of the things we have to mess with at the NALU. You'd be amazed at the insurance scams that go on in this country."

"So Packard *wants* Alan a convicted criminal so he *can't* collect. No wonder that bastard's railroading him to prison."

"That's not all, Savannah."

"There's more?" Savannah shook her head in dismay.

"Early in the game, at Packard's direction, Craig formed an insurance trust and made Packard the trustee. This was done supposedly so that Craig was spared the messy ongoing paperwork and could change beneficiaries of the trust with one quick swoop rather than by doing it policy by policy. And from day one, the trust named as a successor beneficiary the charities of the trustee's choice at the time of Craig's death."

Savannah pulled her legs up under her and shook her head.

"One of Packard's explanations to Craig as to the need for so much insurance was that at his death, the proceeds wouldn't be taxable, and therefore he would screw the IRS. Packard knew that Craig hated the IRS and would do anything to avoid taxes. With that pitch, the scam was even easier for Packard to maintain. I only know this because Alan told me in private about the touchy subject once in New York after one of those uncomfortable discussions with Craig about Packard."

Savannah couldn't believe a man with Craig's talent would be so stupid. And then she thought of how trusting her Hugh appeared to be of damn near everybody. But Hugh had people fooled into thinking he was a simpleton. Savannah knew he used the ruse well and had bettered many a man on many a deal.

"You see, if Alan were deceased, or unable to qualify because of criminal activity, Packard could say he distributed the millions to charity such and such, if anyone ever asked. But who would ask? There aren't any charities waiting to receive their money. And there aren't any insurance companies fretting about paying out funds. The policies don't exist. Well, one does."

"What if Roz had been the beneficiary at Craig's death? Or what if Alan were not involved in a murder trial? How do you think Packard planned to handle that?" Savannah asked.

"I guess by running to Brazil," said Jebb. He rattled the ice in his empty glass and continued, "I can only guess that if Packard and Crawley are working this on Craig, they are working it on other selected clients."

"That scheming son of a bitch! He's willing to convict a man of a murder he knows he didn't commit just to save his own thieving hide!" Savannah was furious.

"Can I have another drink? I'm parched."

"I'll make them both a double."

At the bar, in the quiet of the moment, Savannah was stunned with the realization that Roz Marlowe had planned to murder her husband for money that didn't exist. If she had succeeded, it would have all been for nothing!

Thirty minutes later, after thanking Jebb profusely, Savannah kissed her stepbrother good night, and he left for his hotel.

*　　*　　*　　*

Savannah knew the moment she walked into the bedroom that Craig had heard it all. He was in the process of picking up the phone.

"And who might you be calling? The *Los Angeles Times?*"

"No. That son-of-a-bitch, Victor Packard!"

"Craig, we just discussed that. Please don't."

"That's what you said this morning, Savannah, and look what I found. Someone dead. Do you think I want to find this Inspector Roosevelt the same way? If Packard can extort millions from me, he certainly can see that Roosevelt's been pitched into a four-wheel trash masher. He probably drugged his associate Washburne kicking and screaming to his garage and gassed him!"

Savannah became quiet, then said, "You're right. Two bodies in one day is bad karma." She wasn't joking.

"You told me Simia thought Roosevelt was going to turn her stuff over to Packard. So what has he done with it?"

"I don't know, but I'm glad Simia's away from Roz. At least she's safe," said Savannah.

"Victor Packard, please," said Craig.

"How do you know where he's staying?"

"You told me, Savannah. Are you sure you're an attorney?" Craig was irritable. Earlier when Savannah told him of Jebb's findings, he went into a complete rage.

Savannah became quiet and listened. She was thinking of how to proceed, but knew this would affect it dramatically.

"Then give me the manager on duty," shouted Craig. He covered the receiver and said, "The operator first says he's not accepting any calls, and then says she doesn't think he's registered there. Those two goddamn things don't go together!"

"Ummm. One lie at a time," said Savannah as Craig stretched his need to talk to Packard to crisis proportions to the manager.

Craig listened attentively. "Thanks much." He threw the phone in its cradle and looked around, preparing to leave.

"I know that movement. Where is the deceased actor going?"

"Trader Vic's at the Beverly Hilton. According to the manager, Packard calls the Beverly Wilshire every night and has a limo come pick him up at Trader Vic's about ten, so drunk they have to help him to his room."

"Interesting," said Savannah. "That explains his color and his breath." She didn't move to intercept. "I know you're mad, Craig, but are you going to try any sort of disguise, or do you think no one will read tonight's paper or watch the evening news?"

Craig calmed down, he looked at Savannah with appreciation and love. "I don't know what I would have done without you. I'd still be in London looking for my next meal, or being dragged around by Beckett and Miles, not knowing who I was. Thank you, Savannah. We all need to thank you."

Craig leaned over and kissed her on the forehead, and then went into the bedroom to fuss with his masquerade. Craig didn't bother to change his clothes—only his face. He slipped on the jean jacket he wore to Big Bear to ward off the evening chill and left Savannah to deal with the reality of tomorrow.

*　　*　　*　　*

Tuesday Evening, Trader Vic's, Beverly Hills

Craig was glad the bar was crowded.

Satisfied that no one looked at him twice, he asked the man at the door if he knew a Victor Packard. He told Craig exactly where he could find him.

"Hello, Victor."

"Jesus Christ!" Packard's face turned ashen.

As he eased himself into the booth, Craig saw the panic in Packard's eyes.

Packard tried to say something, but couldn't get it out.

"We have a few things to talk about, don't we?"

Packard looked wildly at the bar, seeking reinforcement.

"You don't seem happy to see me."

"How dare you come back!"

"Oh? That's an interesting greeting from a trusted friend. Tell me, why are you now representing Alan, when you told me you wouldn't and you really aren't? You're just letting all the prosecution's prejudicial questions and answers go straight to the jury without challenge." Craig's tone was cutting acid.

"How did you get here? How did you find me here?"

Craig recognized true terror in Packard's voice. "Packard, you're such a shit, I don't know where to begin."

"You're a murderer," charged Packard. His voice was ugly.

"Yes. I killed a man in self-defense," Craig answered.

"How dare you come here!" Packard repeated.

"You've already said that, Victor. Are you speechless? At least I don't think you were in on the plan with Roz to kill me— were you? She had lots of help."

Red color rushed back into Packard's face. He held up his hand and a waiter magically appeared. "Get me another!"

"And I'll have a double scotch on the rocks," said Craig.

"What do you want with me?"

"Information and satisfaction," said Craig.

"You son of a bitch! In about two minutes I'm calling the cops."

"Speaking of which, do you know what happened to Inspector Roosevelt?"

Packard flinched, and his eyes narrowed. "The rat's ass

skipped," he said. "We were counting on him as a hostile witness."

"Oh? Why?" asked Craig.

Packard glared at Craig.

"You know, Packard, I believe that as much as I believe you're carrying all of that insurance on my life."

Packard choked. He took several deep breaths, then all but whipered, "What are you talking about?"

The waiter brought their drinks. Craig watched warily as Packard gulped his down.

Without warning, Packard slammed his empty glass on the table and attacked. "I've kissed your ass for years, Carlson. You're a faggot! It's hard to get companies to insure a fairy."

Craig was shocked. "Shut your dirty mouth. You're drunk!" Packard had never used these kinds of words with him. He could hear Alan's constant warning about Packard: "He's no friend of gays."

"Bothers you—doesn't it?—To be called a faggot. Well that's what you are. My folks would have beaten the shit out of me if I ever was a sissy like you." Packard's eyes became mere slits, and he leaned back in the booth, his stomach pressing the table.

Craig tried hard to control the urge to fight him. But with his own wrist in a cast, and considering Packard's brute size and the public place, he decided it was a bad idea.

"Do you think I liked calling all those states and asking if it was okay for two queers to marry? Do you think I liked calling all those embassies with the same question? They all thought *I* was the one—me, Packard—who wanted to sleep with another man. You can take all the gays in the world and ship them to Germany. They used to know how to deal with them."

Craig was furious. He jammed his hands in his jacket pockets, only to find Beretta's .45 Glock automatic still where he put it at noon. It startled him.

"I'm going to see you do time for murdering Kurt Schmidt," slurred Packard.

"Oh! Roosevelt did give you Simia's information. You're not

clever enough to come up with Schmidt's name on your own."

Packard waved for another drink with one hand and pounded the table with the other. "I'm about to tell this whole goddamn bar who you are, and then let's see who's calling the shots."

"Where is Inspector Roosevelt, Packard? You know, don't you?" It was a longshot for Craig. He knew if Packard was capable of fraud, he probably considered kidnapping ethical.

As the waiter set another double rye on the table, Packard said, "Call Crawley for me."

"How interesting. The president of Mid Life is here the same time as you. I understand you men are inseparable."

Packard tried to neutralize Craig's knowledge by continuing his attack. "He doesn't like queers any more than I do. All these years you thought I liked Gavin. Bullshit! I can't stand the little freak. Why should I cross-examine anybody for his sake? He's worthy of conviction. He can go to prison, where they'll make good use of him all day long!"

Craig bit his lip and clutched Beretta's gun hard. He wondered what to say to the drunken homophobic attorney.

"You're a nasty bastard, Packard. Once I thought you were tough and no one understood you. I was wrong. You're a cheat who's vicious and unwanted. You're fired!"

Craig started to leave before he did something rash, then remembered Roosevelt and what Savannah said about two bodies one day. He decided to take another tack, Roosevelt's life was far more important than personal revenge.

"What did you do with all of Simia's stuff? Destroy it? Savannah told me Simia made Roosevelt give her a receipt for all of it, and he logged it into his case sheet as evidence."

Packard's brow knotted and his mouth dropped open, "She's a meddling bitch."

Craig knew he hit paydirt, and called the bartender back. "Get the manager for me."

Packard stopped playing with his rye and emptied the glass.

The manager was beside the booth. "Yes, sir. Anything wrong?"

"Mr. Packard here would like a Mr. Crawley to join him. Do you know where he might be?"

"I assume up in his room," said the manager. "Do you want me to check?"

"No. That's sufficient, thank you."

"You son of a bitch! I hate all you gays!"

"You hate gays, Packard, and you're afraid of them. And if I were you, I'd calm down and quit calling me a sissy, or you may regret it. Let's you and I go up and see Crawley rather than have him come here." Craig's fingers further tightened around the gun.

"No need," said a tall, heavyset man in jeans and a plaid shirt. "I'm Crawley." He started to get in on Craig's side.

Instinctively, Craig pulled the gun from his pocket and supporting it with the table, pointed it straight at Packard's heart. Without looking at Crawley, he said, "Don't bother to sit. We're all going back up to your room. I'm so pissed off at you, Packard, it wouldn't bother me a damn bit to pull this trigger. See the silencer? I'm sure if you slumped over, they would just think it's time to call the Beverly Wilshire for your nightly limousine."

Packard paled and stared at the gun.

Crawley didn't move.

Craig knew Crawley neither rcognized him nor knew what had transpired between him and Packard.

"I've suffered through hell to get back here, Packard. One word from either of you, and you're dead. You think I didn't enjoy killing Schmidt? I loved it. I'd do it again in a heartbeat," Craig lied. "Think about where that bullet entered his head, Packard. Center of the brain. I'm a marksman par excellence, so both of you move!"

*　　*　　*　　*

Late Tuesday Night, Brentwood

Craig, Roosevelt, and Savannah were awaiting the arrival of

Roosevelt's wife. Savannah had prepared hot soup for the dehy-
drated police officer, and had completely dropped her stage pretense of "everything's coming up roses" and "let's have a ball."
Craig knew Savannah's love and concern for him, his reported
death of Beretta by fire at the hands of Roz, and now Roosevelt's
shivering from a kidnap were all too sobering for her to pass
them off with *Me, I'm on the top of the tree.*

Craig had found Roosevelt in Crawley's suite, tied and
gagged to the bed. While Craig had busied himself with keeping
his adversaries at bay and freeing Roosevelt all at the same time,
Packard and Crawley ran out the door. They knew he wouldn't
shoot, and he didn't try to stop them. The police could deal with
them after he dealt with their victim.

As soon as Roosevelt was strong enough to walk, he took him
by the service elevator to the kitchen and out the back door. The
last thing Craig wanted was to be the one in possession of the
kidnapped inspector. It seemed to him that his near-crimes all
day long were too close for comfort.

He could have killed Beretta. He could have set the cabin on
fire. He could have kidnapped Roosevelt!

And who was he? None other than the deceased actor, Craig
Carlson, who did kill Kurt Schmidt. It was all too much, too
scary, and too close to home.

Craig had been through enough. Tomorrow had to be his
last day dead.

The amazing thing for Craig was that Roosevelt somehow
knew exactly who he was. *Only Simia could have prepared the
way*, Craig thought.

It was past midnight when Mrs. Roosevelt felt her husband
was strong enough to ride with her back to the San Fernando
Valley. Savannah extended an invitation for them to spend the
night, but understood when Roosevelt said he wanted to go
home, where the kids were waiting for him.

Craig and Savannah sat very close to each other after the
Roosevelts left.

"What kind of a life do we lead, Savannah?"

"Insanity," she answered. "Our profession is insane, our values distorted, and our actions meaningless. Don't get me started or I'll head for the pill bottle."

"Can you sleep?"

"I have to," she said.

"Me, too. Are we ready for tomorrow?"

"We have to be," she said.

Twenty-three

Wednesday Morning, Los Angeles

Judge Bridges knew when she called counsel to chambers that she was in for another day of surprises. Defense attorney Packard failed to appear, and attorney Wilson deferred entirely to Savannah Marlowe. Ari Melon was almost arrogant about his position. She advised them all she would put up with no shenanigans.

Savannah Marlowe told Judge Bridges there was some evidence uncovered late last night that would have to be ruled on as being admissible or not. Judge Bridges wondered what in the world could have been uncovered in the middle of the night, but stayed silent.

She also wanted to ask Savannah if it were true that she was Roz's stepdaughter.

*　　*　　*　　*

"Savannah, you're my lead defense attorney?" asked Alan.

"That's right. Your life is in better hands than yesterday."

"What happened to Packard?" asked Alan.

"He's disappeared," said Savannah. "And you better be damn glad that he has. He was putting you on a one-way bus."

"Do you really know enough about the case?"

"More than you could ever imagine," said Savannah. "You're not going to be convicted of anything. I guarantee it."

Savannah understood why Alan doubted her, but hoped before the court was in session she could convince him he was in safe hands.

Alan still had questions.

"Why is Wilson still here?" asked Alan.

"He can help me procedurally, I think," said Savannah.

"Have you ever been a trial attorney before?" asked Alan.

"Yes. I did three hundred and twenty-nine performances of *Who Killed the Magistrate?* on Broadway six years ago. I played the part of the prosecuting attorney. All I have to do is reverse the roles. I'm capable of that, Alan."

Promptly at nine-thirty, Judge Bridges gaveled her court into session. The galleries were full and the media in overabundance. Savannah was satisfied that all of her witnesses were in place, and that the witness list was complete as far as the court was concerned, except for the name Craig Carlson. He was in a limousine watching the proceedings on a small television, armed with a cellular telephone if Savannah needed him.

Savannah had ignored Roz's look of hatred when their eyes locked just before court began. Roz's hair was wrapped in a bandanna, and she was wearing a simple sheath dress. Her normal public aura of the untouchable actress was diminished.

Savannah knew why.

Savannah noticed the poisonous looks Roz traded with Simia and Anne. She thought, *Roz makes her enemies one at a time, and the fact that she now has to deal with them on a wholesale basis is of her own doing.*

Savannah turned her attention to the court. They were waiting for her.

"Your Honor, I would like to call my first witness, Alan Gavin."

Savannah could tell Alan was stunned. If she had told him he would be first, he would have tried to talk her out of being on the stand at all. Savannah ignored the audience's rumble of doubt of her legal competence. She had a job to do, she had to put her first witness at ease.

Savannah began by establishing Alan's independent credentials in the financial world, thus explaining his capability of managing Craig's business affairs. Then she openly explored his gay relationship with Craig. Following that, Savannah slowly led Alan through the awful night of his discovery of Craig's murder. She was very careful never to mention that it was Craig on the floor of the library; Savannah always referred to it as "the body." She brought up Alan's driving gloves, the blood on his face, and the fingerprints on the documents, and, from Alan's testimony, obtained a totally different point of view of what happened than what the prosecuting attorney had presented yesterday.

She tackled the motive issue aggressively by using Alan's unbending statement that he never received the damning documents the prosecuting attorney surfaced yesterday. Last night, Roosevelt had supplied Savannah with the dated FedEx information when Craig actually signed the will. Savannah made it crystal clear that Alan Gavin had no knowledge that he was the one to receive the immense insurance trust, and that Roz Marlowe was quite aware of its existence and quite aware that Craig was about to change his will to Alan's benefit.

Savannah's approach was aggressive. She didn't ignore negative issues. She raised them. She gave the worst-case scenarios and then showed how they were wrong.

Alan was an excellent witness in his own defense and Savannah was pleased with both his sincerity and his anger at having been accused of Craig's murder.

The most damning evidence was the bullet in Craig's head being from his own gun. That was a tough one to get around. Savannah began to develop the possibility that *someone else*, the real murderer, had had that scuffle with Craig and shot him with his own gun, *not* Alan Gavin.

Alan was on the stand for over an hour before the prosecuting attorney tried to punch holes in his story during his cross-examination. Savannah felt that at the end of the testimony given by her first witness, a credible doubt had been placed in the jury's mind as to Alan's guilt.

Judge Bridges called a recess before Savannah called her second witness.

It was at that point that the media swarmed around Roz and wanted to know why she hadn't been there Tuesday. Savannah heard the story Roz was telling was that she was home ill. When they asked her if she knew anything about the fire at Craig Carlson's cabin, Roz confessed she wasn't aware of it, and said how awful it was that it had burned!

Savannah's second witness was Simia, and a woman who could read Simia's sign language spoke fluently for her. It was at this point that Savannah pushed for the phone messages, the phone bills, the photographs, and the boots to become admissible evidence. Despite strident objections from the prosecution, she got all of them into the trial as exhibits.

When asked why she knew of them now and why they weren't known by the defense yesterday, Savannah said simply that Packard was less than industrious with information at his disposal, and that she just took possession of the data last night after Packard quit.

Judge Bridges had to gavel down the media at this juncture.

This information only heightened the ongoing question of "Where is Inspector Roosevelt, and why did he disappear?"

Savannah elected not to mention the Oscar. The independent crime lab still had it, and it wasn't physically available for her to submit as an exhibit. Roosevelt had given her a picture he had taken of it, but she didn't want questions about why someone went to the trouble of disfiguring Craig Carlson's face.

Savannah obtained from Simia's testimony specific details about the hateful and argumentative relationship between Roz and Craig. She also had Simia testify as to the harmony that existed between Craig Carlson and Alan Gavin. Savannah was glad that Roz had been absent yesterday. With the prosecution having rested their case, Roz's opinionated lies about Craig and Alan had not been heard by the jury.

Savannah spent a great deal of time with Simia on Kurt Schmidt—how he resembled Craig, the relationship he had had with Roz, and the phone traffic he had with Roz just days before Craig's murder.

Savannah felt that the precise detail of Simia's data would be difficult for the prosecution to puncture, and Simia's testimony, verbally presented by the woman who interpreted her signing, was effective.

After Simia's cross-examination by Ari Melon, Judge Bridges adjourned the trial for lunch.

Savannah was rushed by the press and was tempted to give

them the flashy Savannah Marlowe act, a defense mechanism that surfaced on call, but decided against it. She knew it wasn't the time or place.

"Are you really Lady Ashley?"

"Are you really Roz's stepdaughter?"

"How did Mikey Marlowe really die?"

"What was Simia's relationship with Mikey Marlowe?"

"Is this your way of getting even with Roz?"

"Where is Packard? How much did you pay him to leave?"

Savannah turned a deaf ear to all and forced her way out of the courtroom. Outside in the hall, there was the same pushing interrogation until she ducked into a woman's rest room for protection. She wondered, *How am I going to get to Craig?*

When she came out, two bodyguards were waiting. Savannah sensed the hidden hand of Inspector Roosevelt had come to her rescue. She thought, *Roosevelt knows he's my third witness, and probably wants me coherent.*

With the bodyguards' help, Savannah made it to the limousine. She and Craig returned to the house in Brentwood, where Inspector Roosevelt and his wife were waiting for them.

Craig wanted to know about Alan, and Savannah told him she had told Alan there were some loose ends she had to deal with, and left him in the good hands of Simia, Jebb, and Anne for lunch.

Savannah brought all parties up to speed on some inside problems that they had no way of knowing about, since they only watched the proceedings on television.

When lunch was over, Roosevelt handed Savannah a carefully edited list of questions he wanted her to ask him about Roz Marlowe's abnormal statements during his investigation of the murder.

Back at the courthouse, Savannah and Mrs. Roosevelt left the two men waiting inside the limousine behind the darkened glass until Savannah called for them.

*　　*　　*　　*

"I would like to call Inspector Roosevelt to the stand."

The room became an uproar. The prosecuting attorney screamed foul, and the judge asked the attorneys to approach the bench.

"Ms. Marlowe, I warned you this morning there would be no shenanigans. Are you responsible for Roosevelt not being here yesterday?"

"No, I am not. He was found last night tied and gagged at the Beverly Hilton. I saw him just long enough for him to give me the material that Simia had given him. After that, he returned to his home in the San Fernando Valley."

Judge Bridges believed Savannah, and was appalled at the peripheral developments that plagued the trial.

Ari Melon said, "That's hard to swallow, Ms. Marlowe. You have a reputation for high performance and clever maneuvers."

"Of course I do, in the theater. This is a court of law, and I respect it as such!" snapped Savannah.

"Then I object on the grounds that his name is not on the defense's witness list, Ms. Marlowe."

"Oh, yes, he is! Remember the last line of the defense's witness list? It says our list is inclusive of any witnesses the prosecution has listed. He was on your list, Mr. Melon, and you would have called him if he had been available."

"Seat your witness, Ms. Marlowe. Let's get on with this trial."

Roosevelt was pale and looked tired. It was obvious he had been through some unpleasant ordeal.

Savannah asked him to tell the court why he wasn't there on Tuesday. At the conclusion of his amazing story, which had some interesting gaps, she then asked him if he knew where Packard was at the moment. Roosevelt said he didn't know, and that there were warrants out for his arrest as well as for his accomplice, a man named Crawley.

Savannah built Roosevelt's credibility just as she had Alan's and Simia's. She hit dramatic paydirt when she asked Roosevelt questions about Simia's materials, and she used Roosevelt's own meaningful questions to surface his findings during his investigation of the case.

"Mr. Roosevelt, what were Roz Marlowe's words at Spagos when first told by the police officers that her husband was dead?"

"He's dead. Craig's dead. He's been *murdered*."

"Mr. Roosevelt, what were Roz Marlowe's words at the morgue then she first saw her deceased husband?"

"Why would *he* do a thing like that?"

"Mr. Roosevelt, what was Roz Marlowe's reaction at the home in Bel Air when you asked her about certain legal documents?"

"They're gone! I can't believe it. *They were there earlier.*"

In each case, Savannah pointed out the curious uses of the words or phrases that Roz made that didn't fit the normal reaction of some innocent bystander.

And so it went, the prosecuting attorney objecting at every turn, but Judge Bridges was riveted by the adroit actress, and found all of her questions admissible. The gnawing question throughout the day for the judge was, *How does this woman from London know all of this?* She thought, *I would love to put her on the witness stand myself and find out.*

The cameras began to pan Roz Marlowe. She was chalky, biting her nails, and staring at her lap, until she realized she was on camera. At that, she perked up and a look of defiance set in her face.

The fact that the lead case inspector had been kidnapped by the lead defense attorney made no sense at all if he was such an excellent witness for the defense. Those who could follow the conundrum were shaking their heads in disbelief. Writers for newsprint were having one hell of a time making any sense out of their own notes.

Savannah could see Roosevelt's exhaustion was beginning to work against her, and decided she'd better hurry up and give him to the prosecuting attorney.

"Mr. Roosevelt, do you think that Alan Gavin murdered Craig Carlson?"

"I found no evidence of any kind to indicate he did, and further do not think that he emotionally could have."

Judge Bridges had to gavel the courtroom to order.

"Just a few more questions. Please tell us what you know of a Kurt Schmidt."

Ari Melon objected violently, but was overruled.

Roosevelt answered Savannah's question in detail.

"Who do you think did allegedly murder Craig Carlson?" Savannah wondered if anyone caught her word, *allegedly*. Throughout the day she had never said that it was Craig Carlson who was dead.

"I believe it was a contract murder that was conceived by three people," answered Roosevelt with conviction.

There was chaos in the courtroom.

"Inspector Roosevelt, how many of those people, who planned his murder, do you believe are still living?"

"Just one," said Roosevelt.

Judge Bridges was having a very difficult time—not only with the chamber and with the prosecuting attorney, but with herself.

"Inspector Roosevelt, is that person in this room?"

"Yes, *she* is."

Savannah's statement that she had nothing further to ask couldn't be heard. Judge Bridges gave up trying to quiet the court. She called for a fifteen-minute recess, handed the gavel to the bailiff, and left for her chambers.

Savannah knew she had dropped enough bombs to flatten any possibility of Alan Gavin's being convicted of Craig's murder. That's all she had wanted to accomplish. Now it was all downhill at a bobsled pace for a mistrial the minute Craig appeared.

She rejoined Alan, who was sitting in a glow of happiness overshadowed by a stupor of disbelief. "What aren't you telling me, Savannah? Why do you know all of these things?"

"Just be happy I do, darling. We're not out of the woods yet. I'll fill you in when we have time."

"That's not good enough, Savannah."

"I know it isn't, but we have Ari Melon to deal with right now."

Savannah knew that the prosecution would have little to

ask Roosevelt. They had been sandbagged by their own man, and it would be political dynamite to stand in front of the television cameras and crucify your own kidnapped lead witness.

*   *   *   *

Melon was distraught. He didn't spend much time with Inspector Roosevelt. He knew his chance of obtaining a guilty verdict was finished. He wanted to go home and kick the dog, but instead, he excused Roosevelt from the stand and turned the trial back to the insufferable Savannah Marlowe. He hated all of the Marlowes.

Savannah addressed the judge, "Your Honor," then she turned to the courtroom and announced, "I would like to call Roz Marlowe as my next witness."

Roz said over the roar from the audience, "I'm not about to subject myself to your vicious slander. I'm leaving!" Before those in her row could stand, Roz stalked in front of them toward the aisle.

Judge Bridges interceded. "Mrs. Marlowe, this is my courtroom, not yours. I have jurisdiction over everybody in it, and that includes you. You will come forward to the witness stand."

Roz's demeanor changed. She looked around like a trapped animal. "I'm going to be sick. I need to go to the hospital."

"You can do that after you've testified. Now come forward, or I'll have the bailiff or one of the marshalls escort you."

The courtroom became very still.

The prosecutor said, "I object to this witness."

"Overruled, Mrs. Marlowe will testify," said Judge Bridges.

Roz again changed her bearing. She held her head up high, glared at Simia, Anne, and Jebb, then marched by Savannah without recognition.

The courtroom became silent as Roz Marlowe was sworn in.

"Mrs. Marlowe, I'm not going to burden you with a lot of questions, so you can relax," said Savannah.

Roz fixed her eyes on her stepdaughter, her face a mask.

"Are you the wife of the alleged deceased?"

"Of course I am," Roz answered tartly. Then she looked at the jury and then back to Savannah. "My poor Craig." Roz fumbled for a tissue.

Savannah was unimpressed. "Mrs. Marlowe, I want to ask you about your husband's will. Did you know that he was in the process of changing the major beneficiary from you to Alan Gavin?"

Roz made two fists. "No, I did not."

"I want that as a matter of record, Mrs. Marlowe. There is much evidence to the contrary. Do you want to reconsider your answer?"

"Are you calling me a liar?"

"I'm not calling you anything, Mrs. Marlowe, I am simply asking you a question. When did you find out that your husband was about to change his will?"

"Objection," shouted Ari Melon.

Judge Bridges was stern. "You rephrased your question, Ms. Marlowe. If you want to return to your earlier question, I will ask that she answer it."

"Thank you. Mrs. Marlowe, did you know your husband was changing his will, making Alan Gavin the prime beneficiary instead of you?"

Roz looked at Judge Bridges.

"Answer the question."

Roz touched her chin with her fingers, thinking. "Yes. Let me see . . . yes, I did. But I didn't think Craig was going to do it until Wednesday."

Savannah heard Ari Melon's groan. Roz couldn't have answered her question in a better way for the defense. Savannah wanted to ask Roz, "Which Wednesday?" She waited until the room settled down instead.

"*Did* you know a man by the name of Kurt Schmidt?" Savannah carefully used the past tense.

Roz projected great discomfort. "Yes. What does that have to do with anything?"

Savannah ignored her remark. "*Did* you know a man by the name of Antonio Beretta?"

"Objection," shouted Ari Melon. "The defense is dragging up names that have nothing to do with the case."

"Overruled. We don't know that," said Judge Bridges.

Roz remained silent. She folded and unfolded her hands with rapidity. She kept glancing at Judge Bridges.

"I repeat," said Savannah, "*did* you know a man by the name of Antonio Beretta?"

Roz played with the back of her bandanna.

"Answer the question, Mrs. Marlowe," directed the judge.

Roz looked at the judge and then at Savannah. She slowly nodded her head "yes."

"Say it so the court reporter can hear it, Mrs. Marlowe," directed the judge.

Savannah was glad the judge had no time for Roz's antics. "Yes," whispered Roz.

"When did you last see him?" queried Savannah.

Ari Melon was on his feet. "Objection. This is not relevant to Alan Gavin's trial."

"Please approach the bench," instructed Judge Bridges.

"Where are you going with this, Ms. Marlowe?"

"Antonio Beretta was one of the three who arranged to murder Craig Carlson," Savannah said bluntly.

Judge Bridges was amazed at the two-day defense attorney. She thought, *I will find out more about this Savannah Marlowe.* "I will allow the question," she said.

Savannah repeated, "When is the last time you saw Antonio Beretta?"

"Yesterday," said Roz angrily.

Judge Bridges had to pound the expectant courtroom into order. When she did, it returned to expectant silence.

"*Was he in Craig Carlson's cabin yesterday when it burned down at Big Bear Lake?*"

"Objection," screamed Ari Melon.

"Sustained. Ms. Marlowe, I think you should get back to the reason we are here."

"I only have one more question, Your Honor."

"I'll hold you to that," said Judge Bridges.

Savannah could see the judge brace herself. She took a deep breath and asked, "Did you mastermind the plan to murder your husband in order to collect one hundred million dollars in insurance and before he signed a new will?"

Judge Bridges' courtroom erupted into chaos. Some media rushing to get out of the room were stopped at the doors; some in the audience were shouting; and Ari Melon was screaming, "Objection! Objection!"

Judge Bridges pounded her gavel until she finally just sat back and let the bailiff try to obtain control for her.

There was no order in her court.

Roz sat in the witness box as unconcerned as if she were at home watching an old movie of herself.

At first, Savannah didn't care if Roz answered the question or not. She was finished. Alan Gavin would go free without Craig Carlson's appearance on the witness stand. She knew Roz Marlowe would never be convicted of planning his murder, no one could prove it. It was all circumstantial. The two men who could say she did were dead. Savannah knew that Roz could be found guilty of murdering Antonio Beretta, though. Craig had told her about the second kerosene lantern that Savannah was sure had Roz's fingerprints all over it, and he had shownd her the pistol that had *STUD* engraved on the handle—obviously Beretta's. Savannah thought, *Isn't the punishment for one murder the same as for two?*

But then Savannah saw the looks of hatred on Simia's and Alan's faces, and changed her mind.

The bailiff had accomplished his task. He had Judge Bridges' courtroom silent.

Judge Bridges said, "You may proceed, Ms. Marlowe, and I think you should restate your question."

Savannah knew the judge had her on a very short leash. "Yes, Your Honor. Mrs. Marlowe, did you conspire to murder your husband in order to benefit from his will and insurance trust before they were changed?" Savannah thought that might pass.

"Objection," Ari Melon again shouted.

"Overruled," said Judge Bridges.

Savannah was pleased with the judge. "Will the witness please answer my question?" asked Savannah.

The judge firmly instructed the witness, "You are required to do so, Mrs. Marlowe, unless you take the fifth amendment."

"Oh, I don't need that," said Roz. "I didn't plan to kill poor Craig. Really I didn't. I was winning my Oscar, remember? I was at the Dorothy Chandler Pavilion. How could I have had anything to do with his death? I knew he would be home alone watching me on television. He didn't tell me he wasn't going to my Oscar ceremony until a week before. I watched him win his Oscars. Don't you think he'd watch me win mine?"

Roz busied herself tucking her hair back under her bandanna. "And Kurt Schmidt isn't dead. He just called me Sunday." She smiled and looked out at the lights, the cameras, and her fans.

"I have no further questions of this witness." Savannah sat down next to Alan.

"Jesus H. Christ!" said Alan.

The courtroom became remarkably quiet, all eyes were riveted on Roz Marlowe.

Roz made no effort to leave the witness stand. Instead, she fumbled in her purse, found a pair of reading glasses, and put them on. Then she looked over them at Judge Bridges. "Judge Bridges, you're in control here, aren't you?" She smiled compassionately. "I've always liked being in control. Do you like it?"

Judge Bridges looked away from Roz. "Mr. Melon," said the judge to the prosecuting attorney, "do you care to cross-examine?"

"I'll defer any cross-examination at this time, thank you." Ari Melon was terrified of what else Roz might say.

"You may step down now, Mrs. Marlowe," said the judge.

"Oh, thank you. I'd like that."

Roz stood up very straight, smoothed out her dress, then addressed the judge. "Please take any phone messages for me. I'm on my way to St. Petersburg."

Judge Bridges scrutinized Roz carefully. She knew Roz Marlowe was a powerful actress, and chose not to respond. She ignored the gasps of disbelief from the audience.

Roz walked proudly down the aisle and out the back door of the courtroom.

"Does the defense rest, Ms. Marlowe?" asked Judge Bridges.

Savannah could feel the eyes. She had to make a decision. "May I speak with my client for a few moments in private, Your Honor?"

"Yes. We will have a fifteen-minute recess." Judge Bridges let Savannah and Alan Gavin use a small conference room off her own quarters. She was ready to go home. She knew the trial would be over shortly.

The trampling exit of the media from the courtroom was similar to a soccer-fan riot.

Twenty-four

Wednesday Afternoon, Santa Monica

"Incredible job, Savannah. But you've avoided answering any of my questions. I'm grateful as hell for what you just did, but I'm also curious as hell. I feel like the left-out kid of the family. Simia knows this and Roosevelt knows that. And Savannah from England knows it all, but Alan doesn't know a damn thing, and he's been the target all along!"

Savannah looked at him lovingly and really didn't know what to say. She certainly knew where he was coming from, and it wasn't like her to be indecisive, but she knew his future life was on the line now in a very different way.

"Alan, I can bring in one more witness and send Roz to prison for this crime, or someone else can send her to prison for killing Antonio Beretta. Whether I do or not will depend on how you respond to what I'm about to tell you."

"Just tell me why you didn't tell me this big secret this morning before you put me on the stand." Alan shook his head.

"Alan, I couldn't. You wouldn't have been the witness you were and I wasn't sure of everything this morning." Savannah knew he had no idea what she was talking about.

"So tell me, Savannah," Alan said sarcastically. "There's nothing that would surprise me now. Nothing. You could tell me that your next witness was the Queen of England, and I would think, 'Of course.' Seat her at once."

Savannah wanted to slap some sense into Alan, but tried to stay positive. She was surprised at the depth of his animosity. "Okay. We have only ten minutes before we're back inside. You have to tell me in that time frame whether or not I call this last witness. Either way, it will affect your life forever. But my guess is that if I leave the witness undisclosed, your life will be much easier."

319

Alan took a deep breath. "Okay, Savannah. Let me have it."

"Craig Carlson is alive. He's outside at a safe place, ready to appear at my request."

Alan started to shake. He covered his face with his hands and made no effort to hold back his emotions. "No! No! It can't be. *It can't be!*"

Savannah held him and let him cry.

Suddenly, he pulled away. "Why did he do this to me? How could he put me through this? Does he have any idea how I've felt, what I've gone through?" Alan's words were mixed with choking sobs.

Savannah said, "Stop sniveling and pay attention to me! Then maybe you'll be able to understand my reasoning."

Alan dropped the protection of his hands and looked at Savannah. "I'm sorry, Savannah. I'll try."

"If possible, Craig's been through even more hell than you have. He's been a hunted man, running from killers all over the world from that first moment he escaped death by killing the man Marlowe sent to kill him. He looks old, Alan. He's very, very tired, and has pushed mountains to get back to you to save you from Roz and Victor Packard."

Alan struggled for air. "Who was found dead if it wasn't Craig? I identified Craig."

"You heard today and may have even begun to think, *What if it was Kurt Schmidt I identified as Craig?*"

Alan looked hard at Savannah.

Savannah knew he probably felt cheap and used. After Craig Carlson had called her, at first she hated him.

"So he tricked me! He didn't call and say, 'I'm not dead.' He let me bury him!"

Savannah stayed silent.

"How long have you known all this, Savannah?"

"I've only been with Craig since last Friday night."

"And what are my wonderful choices?" Alan asked bitterly.

"If I call Craig, without a doubt in a different trial Roz will be found guilty of orchestrating a murder, and Craig will have to defend himself from the charge of killing a man in self-defense and then running away. Your trial will be dismissed, and Roz will probably be held in custody as of today."

Alan moved away from Savannah.

"Alan, Roz is the only one left. Despite what you heard her say, Schmidt is very dead and she murdered Beretta just yesterday."

Alan wiped his eyes with his hands and listened.

"If Craig appears here and now, your life with him will always be one of dishonor and being on the run. That is, Alan, if you decide to stay with him." Savannah hoped Alan was following her. It was a lot to take: a corpse, a funeral, a will, a trial, and now a dead man returned to life.

"If I don't call Craig to the witness stand, this trial will still be over—not a mistrial, just over. The prosecuting attorney will probably dismiss the case. Roz will most likely be tried for the death of Antonio Beretta, and most likely found guilty. Roz may even be tried for the conspiracy to murder Craig Carlson. That's up to the authorities. I don't know. Craig will not have surfaced, though. You two will have a much better chance at making it in the world someplace else. It's what Craig was trying to accomplish. Everything from the beginning was first for you and second for him." Savannah knew she was reaching.

"Sure, Savannah. I feel so good about what he's done."

"Alan, I think that Craig believed it was his opportunity to disappear from the vicious, intrusive life that he hated and find peace with you, until he found out that it wasn't possible because of the dangerous springboard he used to begin his adventure. Craig can explain all that to you. It's very complicated, deep, and extremely involved. But one thing I know. He loves you more than anything else and was willing to risk his life a second time to get back to you."

There was a knock on the door. "Two minutes, please."

Savannah felt it was a curtain call. Alan's eyes were bloodshot, his nose was running, and he was still in shock. "I just don't understand."

"I don't think I can go over it again; there's so much more.

There's immense insurance fraud, there's millions in payoff money, there's even amnesia from a deadly car accident that Craig was lucky to have survived. He's made it all the way back for a reason, Alan. It didn't have to happen."

Alan took a deep breath, sat up straight in the chair, and leaned forward to Savannah, silently, once again seeking her protection.

"Then don't call him to the stand, Savannah. Let him stay dead. As long as I can see him as soon as this session is over." There was no joy in Alan's voice.

Savannah took the cell phone out of her purse and dialed the limousine. "Craig, I won't be needing your services. You don't have to be my ace of spades. There's someone here who needs to speak with you. But sister Savannah thinks it better that you and Alan meet each other anyplace but a limousine with cameras flashing everywhere. If you agree, have the driver take you to Brentwood. Be sure he's not followed by the press, and then dismiss him. I'll bring Alan to you the minute this crazy day has been declared over by Judge Bridges."

Savannah listened for a few seconds, and then snapped the phone shut. "It will only be a matter of minutes, Alan—not a matter of days."

"Why didn't you let me speak to him?"

"No way! Not in the mood you're in. You two need to work out your difficult reunion in person."

Savannah knew she had more than stretched some of what she had told Alan about Roz's being found guilty of both murders. But it didn't matter, Roz's borderline personality could make her violent one minute and passive the next, without her caring or even knowing which she was.

Savannah knew Roz was already living her own prison sentence. But Savannah seriously doubted if Roz was as nutty as she pretended on the witness stand. She believed that Roz was simply acting her ass off for the sake of her own defense, and could probably get off with a temporary insanity defense concerning Beretta's death. But Savannah knew there was probably enough circumstantial evidence in the planned death of Craig

Carlson to make that one a close call for her. It certainly was premeditated.

Savannah also knew that Alan had made the only choice he could make if he ever wanted to stay with Craig Carlson. On their return to the courtroom, Savannah rested the defense's case, and Judge Bridges didn't hesitate a minute. She adjourned the court for the day.

* * * *

Wednesday, Late Afternoon, Brentwood

Craig Carlson was waiting in the comfortable family room that overlooked a lap pool and exercise area. He heard the door open and close, followed by Savannah's cheerful voice. "We're home!"

"Down here," he said, with as much discipline as he could muster.

"Good. I'll see you later, Craig. I have some errands to run. We're having a party later! *Ciao!*"

Craig heard the door close again, and then all was quiet. Suddenly he didn't know whether to seek out Alan or continue to look outside. Instinctively, he half-stumbled toward the doorway, wanting to be in some form of action when he first saw him.

Alan entered the room with his hands in his pockets. He thought, *I don't know how to act. I don't know what to say.*

Craig walked to him and hugged him tightly. "I'm back."

Alan didn't remove his hands, nor look directly at Craig, nor try to escape the embrace. Alan said, "I know," He thought, *I've missed you terribly. You've been gone seventy-two days.*

Craig released his hold and tried to make eye contact with Alan. "Forgive me, Alan. You have no idea what I've been through." He thought, *Look at me! I've just gone through hell.*

Alan stepped back and looked intently at Craig. First he noticed Craig's cast, then the red scars on his wan face, and then he noticed that his salt-and-pepper hair had gone solid gray.

"My God, you look terrible!" Alan bit his lip, trying hard to keep his feelings in check. He thought, *I love this man. Why am I so bitter?*

"I love you, Alan. I thought I was doing all of this for us." Craig thought, *Why am I miserable instead of happy?*

Pulled by some unseen force, Alan's hands left the protection offered by his pockets and encircled his lover. He began to shake all over.

Craig crushed Alan with his own embrace.

"I'm glad you're home," said Alan.

"Me, too. And you don't look so damn rested yourself."

As the two men moved into a fragile posture of reconciliation, their thoughts became their actions, and it soon became evident that it was Alan who had the stumbling blocks to overcome. One was that Craig had never lost anybody to death, he always knew they were both still alive. Alan thought that Craig was gone. He was dead. He would never return. The pain was immense. And he stood trial for that death.

A surprise stumbling block was Alan's feelings for his family. His father and sisters had finally warmed to him for the first time in their lives, and Alan knew that Craig's reappearance would end that thaw completely—something he didn't want.

It was only after Craig told Alan his entire story that he began to soften his attitude of being betrayed. Two hours later, the two men went upstairs to join the others who had come to celebrate Craig's homecoming and Alan's freedom.

*   *   *   *

Savannah never believed it could have ended quite like this. She was hosting a party—well, almost hosting. They were using up liberal quantities of food and booze at the home of Savannah's friend who was somewhere now in the Greek Islands, according to the itinerary thumbtacked to the board in the pantry for the benefit of the household staff, who had been told to remain absent until the caretaker called them back.

Inspector Roosevelt and his wife had stopped by only for a few moments before they returned to the Valley to be with their children. Roosevelt was exhausted, but he felt his job was secure. The prosecuting attorney had received so many wounds Wednesday, that Roosevelt knew Melon couldn't politically afford to threaten his position on the police force.

After dinner, Anne left to go home to her children after thanking Simia profusely for liberating her from Roz, and Craig for the retirement fund he told her he would set up through Savannah.

Simia fluctuated between hugging her family of loved ones and sitting on the couch in tears, which flowed from her well of happiness. She was wearing a Polynesian sarong that she had removed from her bottomless handbag.

Savannah was ecstatic, enjoying the rakish and carefree lifestyle she had perfected as a shield.

Savannah waved her champagne glass. "I'm even with the Wicked Bitch of the West! In fact, I feel sorry for her. If Roz never goes to prison, my reward has been simply divine."

Savannah sat on the back of a couch, crossed her long legs and laughed. "Darlings, how many of us get to put our mothers on the witness stand for all the nasty things they've done to us as children?"

Craig knew that Savannah had had a lot to drink, but she had a lot to celebrate. Without her, this party would never have taken place. He tried several times to become happy-go-lucky himself, but Alan's reserve made it impossible.

Alan vacillated between his normal entertaining self and sitting on the couch with Simia, holding her hand, totally withdrawn.

Jebb Marlowe tried to mediate the uneasiness between Craig and Alan by shoring up each one as needed. Finally, he gave up and suggested they get an update, and flipped on the nightly news. It was filled with how actress Savannah Marlowe wrought devastation on the prosecution in the Carlson murder trial. After resting the defense's case, it was the reporter's opinion that the prosecuting attorney would be best off if he dismissed the case against Alan Gavin.

The nightly news also reported that Roz Marlowe had been

admitted by Roly Stewart, the producer of her new film, *The Empress*, to a private local hospital for mental exhaustion.

There was a bulletin that Victor Packard and Clarence Crawley, implicated in Inspector Roosevelt's kidnapping, were apprehended in the international departure lounge at Los Angeles International. They had purchased tickets for flights to Costa Rica, but the ticket agent had recognized them and tipped off the police.

After saying their goodnights, Jebb left for his hotel, and Savannah found Simia a suitable room. Craig and Alan were left alone to continue to patch together two lives that should never have never been separated.

*   *   *   *

Thursday Morning, Los Angeles

When the court convened, prosecuting attorney, Ari Melon, dismissed the case against Alan Gavin.

Afterward, Judge Bridges asked Savannah if she would see her in her chambers for a few moments. Savannah asked Alan, Simia, Jebb, and Anne to wait for her outside.

"You know, in my career, I've never presided over a trial quite like this one," said Judge Bridges.

"I know," said Savannah. "I appreciate your generosity. You could have thrown me out."

"No. Not really. A couple times I wanted to, but that was more for my judicial sanity rather than for legal reasons. How did you do it, Ms. Marlowe? To me, that's the unanswered question. How did you know all that you did, having just arrived in the States three days ago?"

Savannah smiled, but said nothing.

"I did some checking, and you entered through Port Angeles in Washington and were traveling with your husband, Lord Ashley. Ms. Marlowe, very few people, if any that I know of, would fly to Los Angeles from London by way of British Columbia and Port Angeles in Washington. Where is Lord Ashley, Ms. Marlowe?

Why didn't he participate in your victory?"

Savannah said, "First, please call me Savannah, Your Honor. Everyone else does. Once in a while the British press gets stuffy and throws Lady Ashley at me, but not too often. You know, of course, that my main interest is acting. I love to act. Trial law is really no different. I tried to be a lawyer here in California, but was too restless and too young to stay with it. This was fun. But I'm glad this trial had the ending it did."

"You're evasive, Savannah."

Savannah laughed. "Ah, yes—your question about my husband. Off the record, my dear Hugh is on his way home from New Zealand, where he's been looking at sheep."

"And the Lord Ashley who entered the States with you?"

"He's alive and well."

"Thank you. I hoped you would be honest with me. Not even my curiosity-prone husband will ever know. In fact, he gave up asking me questions years ago."

"So did mine," smiled Savannah.

"May I ask one last question?" Judge Bridges inquired.

"Of course, I'm not on trial here." Savannah sobered instantly.

"No. You're not. You were brilliant. I was proud for you, and I'm not going to ask about Kurt Schmidt."

"Thank you," said Savannah, truly surprised and appreciative.

"Did Roz really plot to kill her husband?"

"She most certainly did. She's one of those egomaniacal types who are incapable of loving anyone but themselves. And this time, it came home to roost."

"And her exit from the stand—was she acting or was she really crazy?"

"It could be either. Roz Marlowe is not the sanest person in the world, but I think time will tell."

Judge Bridges stood up and gave Savannah a hug. "Good luck in whatever you do. I like you."

*   *   *   *

Friday, Beverly Hills

Friday noon, Savannah had lunch with the producer Roly Stewart at the Ivy on Robertson. After talking about many other things, Stewart told Savannah that Roz was still in the hospital and doing fairly well, but he didn't know what he'd do now about *The Empress*.

Savannah mockingly advised him to exercise the greatest restraint when dealing with Roz Marlowe: "She can be quite lethal."

Friday, Jebb returned to Washington, D.C.

The same day, Inspector Roosevelt presented Simia with the Oscar that he had received back from the crime lab. Roosevelt told Simia, "You found it. I asked Craig, and we both want you to have it. We certainly don't need it at police headquarters. It's too dangerous."

On Saturday, family and friends said their farewells. Savannah was scheduled to return to London via British Airways, and the others were headed for Palm Beach by private jet to gather up Craig's disbelieving mother and son. Savannah's limousine was waiting.

"Will you contact me from Montserrat?" asked Savannah.

"Yes, after your phone stops ringing with legal offers," said Craig.

"Aren't you afraid of being traced?"

"That's why I chartered in the name of Miles Beckett, used a British accent, gave a Perth address, and paid cash." Craig laughed.

"You're insufferable."

"No, I'm paranoid. I've faked my name so much it was easy. But the press might just be watching Alan right now. And if he and Simia boarded the same commercial airline with a disguised Craig Carlson lurking in the same compartment, it could be an open invitation for some unwanted publicity."

"Hmmm. So you're still on the run. What name will you use?"

"I don't have a clue," said Craig.

Savannah turned to Alan. "Have you forgiven me?"

"Absolutely!" Alan smiled.

"Thank goodness. I wouldn't want to go through all this again just so you could turn grouchy."

"No. I'll stop being the Grinch who stole anything. I love you, Savannah. I owe you everything."

"You only owe me laughter," said Savannah.

Craig became serious. "Savannah, what can I ever do to repay you for your love and support?"

Savannah threw her arms around him and said, "Write one of your winning screenplays for little old me. You certainly have enough original material lying around. I want to hear those magical words. 'And the Winner Is . . . Savannah Marlowe'!"

Savannah then kissed him and said, "I'm so pleased that you and Alan are finally beginning to act more like the two delightful men I used to know. Keep it up."

Simia hugged Savannah, then miraculously produced a floral lei from her magic handbag and placed it around Savannah's neck.

Alan's good-bye was emotional. "Savannah, you've taught me something very important. It's about a blessing. Sometimes you never know what a blessing is until you've lost it. And by then, Savannah, you can no longer count it."

Savannah hugged and kissed Alan. "Oh, I know, I know. I really do."

She hurriedly turned to the driver. "Let's go, darling. If I stay longer, I'll get mushy and ruin my makeup."

Savannah turned one last time to her small family. "Alan, I'll try hard to remember about the blessings."

*   *   *   *

Inside the privacy and protection of the darkened limousine Savannah Marlowe was at last able to relax. She felt as if she had been on stage forever, giving the performance of a lifetime. Exhausted but exhilarated, she wrapped herself in a warm glow of anticipation. She smiled. Her Hugh would be waiting for her at home.